CUE UP

Murder capital of Wyoming?

The calendar has flipped to March but a winter chill of murder still stirs Sherman, Wyoming.

The latest death involves an off-season dude ranch and its staff, ardent rivals in a quest for buried treasure, a wildlife whisperer who seemed to know no enemies, and legends and exploits of long dead outlaws. Elizabeth and her fellow investigators must fan out across Cottonwood County and time to find answers.

They balance that with plans for an upcoming wedding, while the KWMT-TV crew adjusts to new ownership. Everyone hopes spring hires will breathe much-needed life into the understaffed local station.

If only Sherman had a draw . . . besides puzzling murders.

Caught Dead in Wyoming series

Sign Off
Left Hanging
Shoot First
Last Ditch
Look Live
Back Story
Cold Open
Hot Roll
Reaction Shot
Body Brace
Cross Talk
Air Ready
Holiday Bullets
Cue Up
Head Room

More Patricia McLinn mystery

Secret Sleuth series

Death on the Diversion
Death on Torrid Avenue
Death on Beguiling Way
Death on Covert Circle
Death on Shady Bridge
Death on Carrion Lane
Death on ZigZag Trail
Death on Puzzle Place
Death on Riddle Road

The Innocence Trilogy

Proof of Innocence
Price of Innocence
Premise of Innocence

CUE UP

Caught Dead in Wyoming,
Book 14

Patricia McLinn

✧　✧　✧　✧

DAY ONE
TUESDAY

CHAPTER ONE

Spring had sprung in the newsroom of KWMT-TV in Sherman, Wyoming.

At least Wyoming's version of March had sprung.

Don't think of daffodils and azaleas. More like being grateful daylight eked out a bigger share of the twenty-four hours. Maybe some stirring awe as calving season began.

To me, March in Wyoming meant trying to minimize exposure to it. At the moment, that meant cutting the elapsed time from vehicle—the station's NewsMobile—to inside KWMT's double set of glass doors.

As usual, I beat Diana Stendahl in that sprint.

She had the disadvantage of being weighed down by tools of her trade as the best cameraperson I'd worked with in a TV news career from Dayton to St. Louis to Washington, D.C., to New York, before crash-landing here.

It was a testament to our friendship that I did not plunge into the warmth and desert her. I stopped and held the door—from inside. It was awkward, but got me out of the wind.

When Wyomingites say the wind's biting, think *Jaws*, not a puppy.

"Thanks . . . It's natural people want to know about the wedding," she continued our pre-sprint conversation.

"Then they should talk to Tamantha—" That's my stepdaughter-to-be, the only daughter of Thomas David Burrell. We will make our familyhood official at the end of June. "—or my mother."

I turned left from the entry hallway into the open bullpen with battered gray desks scattered like ectoplasm from an exploded gray blob. I might have watched a vintage sci-fi movie recently with Tamantha. She'd criticized the science. I gawked at the effects. Not believable, but entertaining.

Diana followed me to the third desk from the windows, the one with the E.M. Danniher nameplate, resting her equipment bag on it. "People asking about the wedding plans is their way of wishing you well."

"Urging me to add pigeons is—"

"Doves."

"—not wishing me well. It's inviting a bird to poop on the bride. On top of which, our esteemed school district trustee was trying to drum up business for her son, the recently minted dove wrangler. One of forty-seven jobs he's had in the two years I've been here. I can't even imagine how many trees would die to print his complete resume."

After unwinding my scarf, which had held the coat's hood in place and muffled my lower face, and stashing gloves fit for the Antarctic in the pockets, I slid off my coat. People who wore jackets must not have temperature sensors in their legs. Or they went numb at the end of September and haven't felt them since.

"That's an exaggeration," she said mildly.

"Not much. And—" I stopped and looked around. "Something's wrong."

Newsrooms have atmospheres and they're seldom subtle, certainly not to those of us who've spent a lot of time in them.

In these past months, there'd been a palpable feeling of spring-like hope in KWMT's newsroom. It being a much happier place was not me projecting my state of mind—or heart—now that Tom and I were together. Instead, it was the considered opinion of every member of the staff I talked with about the subject.

Granted that did not include a couple grumpy holdouts who, no doubt, missed now-forfeited benefits accrued from currying favor with the previous regime.

In fact, the newsroom mood registered downright jovial since Mike Paycik became majority owner in November. It had nothing to do with our surroundings—he was putting money into other parts of the operation than décor. And the mood endured despite everyone working extra hours because luring new hires to Wyoming in deepest winter proceeded at an appropriately glacial pace.

Mind you, jovial in a newsroom tends to consist of dark humor. At this moment, though, I didn't pick up a hint of even the darkest, driest humor.

I scanned two fellow workers in the bullpen, with their heads down and headsets on as they stared at their screens, their expressions far from ebullient. I'd get nothing out of them. With Diana right behind me, I made a beeline for staffers clustered where the entry hallway turned left, marking the end of the bullpen and carving out an awkward triangle of space that used to be the staff breakroom, but now housed the assignment desk and news aides' station.

Audrey Adams was at the assignment desk keyboard, which controlled three monitors, instead of the previous one. Other staffers ranged on either side of her.

"What's wrong, Audrey?" Her glum expression made that an obvious starter question.

"The latest listings of towns in Wyoming are out and Sherman didn't make it. Again."

I looked around at the other long faces. "They've delisted Sherman as a town? Can they do that? When it's the county seat?" With the courthouse in the center of town to prove it.

"What are you talking about? Of course it's still a town," Audrey said.

"You said—"

"I said the listing of Wyoming towns is out—you know, cutest towns in the state or most historic towns in the state or best towns to visit in the state or best hidden gems in the state. Sherman didn't make it on any of those lists."

"Has Sherman ever been on these lists?" I could see how dropping off such a list might lower spirits. Slightly. Momentarily.

"No, but that doesn't mean we don't belong," Leona D'Amato said dourly.

She's been with the station forever, officially as the part-time social and cultural life reporter. Unofficially, she's our into-the-breach anchor.

She hates hard news. Hates anchoring. Hates full-time. All that hate is wearing on her.

Something needed to change. Though I was not fond of the most obvious fix—my becoming the anchor.

"That's right. Sherman deserves to be on there *somewhere*," Audrey said. "And other towns hogged multiple spots. How is that fair? Especially since . . ."

"Especially since what?"

She gusted out a sigh. "Mike was counting on it. He said that if we could promote Sherman and the county, maybe we could get more applicants for the management jobs and anchor. But we need something newsy to peg it off of. You know, *Just named the town you'd most love to visit that you've never heard of,* something like that."

The faces grew longer. After months of improved morale, I hated seeing this.

"Why should we let someone else's list stop us? Who are these people making the lists, anyway? If Sherman's not on a list other people made up, then we make our own." My speech wasn't quite Mickey Rooney and Judy Garland saying, *Hey kids, let's put on a show!* But it was close.

In those old movies—yes, I've also watched some of them with Tamantha—the rest of the kids bounce up and follow their brave leaders with enthusiasm.

I got blank stares.

"Like what?" Audrey asked for all of them.

"A tour of Wyoming towns named after Civil War generals. Sheridan, Sherman . . ." It was the best I could do off the top of my head, but I ran out of generals.

"Rawlins," Diana offered.

"Buford," Walt, one of the reporters, said. "That's the town sold for almost a million dollars back around 2010. Advertised as the country's smallest town."

Audrey snorted. "Not even Wyoming's smallest town—at least not all the time. Hartville's gone down to a population of one, bounced back up to four or five, then back to one. And it has all sorts of historical claims, too. I know because it's all over these lists." She tapped her central screen. "Just look—Wyoming's first town, longest operating bar, and that gets it the most historic town overall title, too. It's hogging all those categories."

My suggestion had not noticeably lifted anyone's spirits. "It doesn't need to be Civil War generals."

"Wilson was named after one of the first Pony Express riders," offered Jerry, who ran the studio cameras.

"Wasn't the Pony Express route in southern Wyoming, largely along the same route as the railroad—generally where I-80 is now?" I was not without some knowledge of the state and its history after nearly two years here.

More importantly, after nearly two years of acquaintance with and tutelage by Emmaline Parens. Now officially retired from a long career as a teacher and principal, she hadn't slowed down any in disseminating knowledge, whether the recipients liked it or not.

"Right," Jerry confirmed.

"So, how does that help Sherman?" Leona asked.

"It doesn't." His deflated admission dropped the mood another notch.

"At least it's not Laramie," Walt said.

"What's the matter with Laramie?" I asked. As the location for the University of Wyoming, it usually got good reviews.

"Named for a French-Canadian fur trapper who went into the mountains and never came back," Diana said. "Jacques La Ramée or LaRamie. They named the mountains and river and then the town after him. So they're all named after an explorer who you could say failed to explore."

"I read he was killed by jealous fellow fur traders," Jerry said.

"See," I said brightly, "at least Sherman didn't die. Well, until he did die, of course. But he survived the war and he's not famous *because* he died."

My failed attempt at cheer had everyone—including me—looking eagerly toward the sound of someone approaching from beyond the hallway's right hand turn at the door to the news director's office door. From there, the hallway led to the new break room, editing bays, studio, and deeper into the building.

Dale, a news aide, came into view around the corner, clearly more absorbed in what came through his earbuds than where he was.

He's a good kid. But seeing him makes me miss Jennifer Lawton even more.

Once our news aide extraordinaire, computer whiz, and major part of a group of us solving murders, Jennifer was now living just north of Chicago, immersed in a special program at Northwestern University. A major coup for her. A major loss for KWMT . . . and me.

Dale said good-bye, apparently ending a call, and focused on us. "Did you hear? Someone died out at Elk Rock Ranch. Shot. I heard it on radio traffic—"

Before anyone else reacted, Leona exclaimed with spurious excitement. "I've got it! How we make Sherman stand out. We claim it as the murder capital of Wyoming."

"Sherman, Wyoming. Small town living, lots of dying," Walt immediately suggested.

"Great place to live—if it doesn't kill you," Jerry said.

"Live and die in W-Y," contributed Diana.

"Only the last one works in this case," Dale said solemnly. He does tend to be literal. "This one's out of town. Like I said Elk Rock Ranch."

"Where is this ranch?" I hadn't heard of it before. Not that I knew all the ranches in the county or anywhere close. But I'd learned some from working for KWMT-TV and more from my connection with Tom. He owned the Circle B, north and west of town, nestled partly into the mountains, where the vegetation was lusher than the eastern part of the county, which required irrigation to wrest a living out of the Big Horn Basin's semi-arid plateau.

"Way down in the southwest corner of the county, closer to Cody than Sherman, so it gets most of its business from that direction, closer to Yellowstone."

"Why does that location give them business?" Last I heard, cattle didn't care how close to Yellowstone they were. Except for being closer to Yellowstone's wolf packs. *That* the cattle might care about, since the wolves didn't recognize park boundaries.

"It's a dude ranch," Diana said. "Draws tourists."

Ah. A different kind of livestock entirely.

Audrey cursed under her breath as a light on her console flashed. "That's Mike. Hoping for good news."

Mike had bought KWMT-TV largely from saving and investing his earnings during an NFL career with the Chicago Bears. Wisely, he continued his job as a sports reporter/part-time anchor at a network affiliate in Chicago.

He's deservedly on the rise in his career. No reason he should give that up.

Besides, his visibility there helped get our first new hire here—Nala Choi, a December graduate from Northwestern. We had two more in line for later this year.

We had exciting changes cued up . . . if only we could fill the anchor, news director, and general manager jobs.

"Hey, there—good to see a crowd," he said cheerfully from the screen. He immediately caught the mood. "What's up?"

Audrey flicked a look toward me. I looked back steadily.

She'd wanted—and deserved—a position of authority in the newsroom. That included delivering bad news.

She drew in a breath. "Sherman's not on any of the town lists."

Mike's turn to mutter a curse.

As Audrey started to cover the same ground of other towns hogging spots on the lists, Walt melted away with a few words about a verdict watch at the courthouse, Jerry didn't bother with an excuse when he headed toward the studio, and Leona pointed at Mike on the screen and said, "No excuses. Get somebody," before marching off.

"I can't stay on long," Mike said after Audrey finished. "Elizabeth, if we can set up a call soon—"

"Sure." His tone didn't promise leads on those other hires.

But I couldn't be too pessimistic because, at that moment, Nala Choi came in the outside doors, reminding us all that Mike's first hire was smart, hard-working, and learning fast.

We waved her over to say hi to Mike.

After a few sentences, he started the classic meeting wrap-up. "If that's it . . ."

Audrey interrupted. "One more thing. I'll let Dale tell you."

She gave the news aide a look that I suspected resembled the one I'd given her—the *yes, I could do this for you, but I'm not going to, because you don't really need me to* look.

His Adam's apple dropped and rose, but he didn't hesitate.

"There's some other news." Speaking up was a big step for Dale, though he still flushed red into the roots of his hair. "Keif Doobie from Elk Rock Ranch died."

Keif Doobie was how it sounded to me, anyway.

"Keith?" I asked. I didn't recall Dale using "f" instead of "th" before, but maybe I'd missed it.

"*No,*" Mike said emphatically—clearly in response to the news, not my question. "That's a shame. A real shame. Dale's right on the first name—Keefe, not Keith. Short for Keefer. Last name's D-o-b-e-y. It's pronounced DUE-bay."

"Of course it is," I grumbled.

When I'd first encountered the fact of Dubois, Wyoming, being DUE-boys to locals, I'd balked. Though considering LAIR-ah-me came from La Ramée, I shouldn't be surprised.

Besides, learning the pronunciation of Dubois was a rebellion made me much fonder of it. At least according to legend, locals of the time disliked it being named after a senator—not even one from Wyoming—and rejected the French pronunciation.

I liked that story so much I didn't care if it was true.

"You know him?" I asked Mike.

"Everybody knew him."

As I started to roll my eyes, my gaze connected with Nala's and we exchanged a look of commiseration as Cottonwood County *nobodies* who hadn't known Keefer Dobey.

"He owns this ranch?"

Mike clicked his tongue. "Nah. He's worked there pretty much his whole life, though. Year-round, too, while most of the staff are college kids in for the summer."

"*Staff?*" I'd heard ranch workers referred to as hands, help, a rider, or—most often—their familial relationship to the speaker. Never *staff*.

"It's a dude ranch," Mike said. "Has been longer than I've been around. And Keefe's been there as long as I can remember, too. He's good on a horse, decent with a rope. Mostly quiet. Real knowledgeable about wildlife. Spends a lot of time alone in the outdoors. But he did love Cottonwood County High's football teams." He slid to fond sorrow in those final words.

Mike had been a star of those high school teams before playing for the University of Wyoming and the Chicago Bears. Not a star in the NFL, but smart enough to invest those earnings well and to retire when his knees threatened to give out.

In his hometown, he was beyond a star—a galaxy all by himself.

"How'd he die?" he asked. "He's not that old . . ."

"He was shot," Dale said.

"*Shot?* Accidentally? Not Keefe. So—No, no way Keefe committed suicide."

"They're not being real clear." Dale's Adam's apple bobbed again at not being able to answer Mike's question. "I just picked up enough to call somebody. They weren't talking about it openly. Shelton told them to keep it zipped on the radio and—"

"Shelton," Mike said in a that-explains-a-lot tone.

And it did.

Not only because Sergeant Wayne Shelton of the Cottonwood County Sheriff's Department would order everyone to keep a lid on chatter—and be obeyed—but also that the sheriff's department had sent their best.

"Murder?" Audrey asked, voicing what popped into all our minds.

"At least suspicious." I turned to Dale. "When did this happen?"

"Someone at the ranch found him dead real early this morning and called 9-1-1. The sheriff's department just left the scene. That's when I picked it up and contacted some people. Not that they told me much. I should have gotten it earlier—"

"Not with Shelton keeping the lid on," I said firmly.

"Why are you still there, Elizabeth?" Mike asked. "Get to the ranch. Find out what's going on. You and Diana."

"And get the story," Audrey added. "You've got time to do a package for the Five. Then, for the Ten—"

"Elizabeth needs to look into this deeper than the live story," Mike said.

"We'll get the color at the ranch. Send Nala to the sheriff's department," I said.

"With Shelton in charge? What will she get?" Audrey answered her own question. "The standup in front to sandwich around your footage from the ranch. Okay."

"I'll drive," Diana said.

We'd get there faster that way. Scarier, but faster.

I held up a hand to delay the breakup of this group and not just to put off going along for the ride with Diana driving to a breaking story. "Wait. I want to know about this ranch—this dude ranch—first."

Mike said, "Only know the general outlines. Started as a working ranch way back. Then some rich family bought it maybe in the 1950s or so. Think they kept it mostly for themselves. But then one of them came out to live permanently and he turned it into a dude ranch. That all happened long before I was born. That owner—Chester Barlow— died and his niece inherited.

"Family's rich. The other Barlows are among the billionaire set over around Jackson. And I suppose Wendy—that's Chester's niece who owns Elk Rock Ranch now—is Cottonwood County's billionaire. Did I miss anything, Diana?"

"That about covers it. I barely remember Chester dying. I tend to think of Wendy Barlow as always owning it."

"Now get going," Mike ordered.

CHAPTER TWO

"Relax," Diana said, looking over at me in the passenger seat.

I really wished she wouldn't do that. At the speeds she attained in this shock-absorber-less torpedo, a second looking at me could cover a couple miles.

This was when I most missed Jennifer working at KWMT-TV.

Her official title was news and production aide, but she was so much more. Including a whiz on the computer, which was why she was in the special program at Northwestern, instead of feeding me more background information on Keefer Dobey and Elk Rock Ranch. While taking my mind off Diana's driving.

"Tell me more about the wedding plans," the driver herself said.

Close your eyes and think of England was supposedly advice from aristocratic English mothers to brides before their first sexual experience.

I turned toward the passenger window so Diana didn't see me close my eyes against her driving and tried to think of my wedding.

"You already know most of it," I said.

She'd heard about it as the major battles had been fought, the division of territories determined, the refugees resettled.

I suppose I shouldn't talk about my upcoming wedding in terms of war, though it felt like campaigns were waged. Not nearly dirty enough, however, to liken them to political campaigns.

Besides, they were waged by people I love. Mostly.

At the outset, I'd lost my attempt at a quickie make-it-legal at the county courthouse event to be followed by a gathering of friends and family, perhaps several such gatherings to keep them low-key and casual.

General Catherine Danniher—aka Mom—won that battle. But I stood firm that the wedding would be here in Wyoming. I was not a blushing child bride to be given in matrimony from my father's home to my husband's. Thank heavens.

Tom and I were two wholes making a greater whole.

Okay, I admit, that doesn't have the romantic ring to it that finding the missing half of your soul or making each other complete does. But it's a heck of a lot more rewarding for the participants.

So, no, I wasn't going back to Illinois to be married from my parents' house. But we were getting married in a church.

Not my idea. Especially doing it twice.

First, in the Catholic church in Cody with a few of the earlier arrivals from my side of the family.

Tom decided on this, saying it was important to honor my family's beliefs.

I don't know—and he won't say—how much Tamantha's approval of the center aisle of the Cody church had to do with this decision. Nor do I know what arrangements she might have come to with her father and/or the priest regarding cartwheels down said aisle. I'm sure not betting against her.

Our wedding that's on the invitations will be at the church Tom and Tamantha attend. Which will be convenient for the out-of-town guests staying in town and the locals, as well as a quick jaunt to the site of the reception—the Sherman Western Frontier Museum.

There are some in TV news who would say my celebrating getting married among historic artifacts is apropos. Though they wouldn't say it to my face.

I like the place. It's convenient, has plenty of space, the parking's good, and the fees help the community.

Three months after we committed to marriage and three months before we will say I-dos, the major pieces were in place. In TV news lingo, the wedding was cued up—in place, ready to be played on-air.

Mostly because Mom or Tamantha started conversation after conversation with the ominous, "I've been thinking about the wedding" and then Tom and I had to act fast to head them off from what we didn't want by finalizing what we did want.

I was beginning to think they did it on purpose.

And sometimes, my husband-to-be—

"I might know most of it, but tell me again anyway," Diana said. "I like hearing about your wedding plans. Or, I should say, I like hearing what your mom and Tamantha have planned."

"And Tom," I mumbled. My eyes popped open and I jerked my head around to face her. "You're interested in wedding plans? Are you—? You and Russ—? Is something—?"

For a professional talker, I was having trouble using my words.

Diana and the new—newish at this point—Cottonwood County sheriff, Russ Conrad, struck sparks off each other from their first meeting.

I was not entranced by the romance of that moment, since he was telling me to stop doing my job insofar as it involved investigating murders. He was fine with me resolving consumers' issues with recurring *Helping Out!* segments. At least I think he was.

Despite little sign that he'd reciprocated, I'd relented somewhat in my opinion of Russ, based on how he treated Diana, interacted with her kids, and made her feel. Which was evident now from added rosiness in her cheeks and a smile that could have fit either Happy or Dopey of the seven dwarfs.

"No." Apparently hearing that her tone qualified for *doth protest too much*, she backed off with a calmer rendition, "No."

"Not yet." I didn't give her any chance to protest that. "I know you two have been using the L-word beyond that time he blurted it out last fall in front of your kids and the increasing coziness is apparent, but if you're at the point of the M-word—"

"How old are you?"

"—you better not be keeping me in the dark."

"You've got a lot on your mind."

"Oh, brother. You're not going to pull the *don't-want-to-distract-from-your-big-day* nonsense, are you? Tom and I are getting married—emphasis on married, as in the beginning of our marriage, not as in emphasis on a wedding extravaganza. If I had my way—"

"I know. You'd fill out a form online and be done with it. Thank heavens for your mom and Tamantha and—especially—Tom, who know it's a big deal and treat it like that."

"Getting back to you and Russ," I said with great dignity.

"We're doing just fine, thank you. And here we are at Elk Rock Ranch. So, Ms. E.M. Danniher, reporter and sleuth, start paying attention."

CHAPTER THREE

THIS WAS A part of the county where I hadn't spent much time.

The western part of Cottonwood County climbed up the eastern slope of a portion of the Rocky Mountains mostly known as the Absaroka Range. *Mostly* because to flatlanders like me, mountain ranges are not neatly segmented like county or state lines. They blur and blend.

Or, they strike out on their own.

Take the Big Horns. They sit well east of here, with a hundred miles of Big Horn Basin stretching between them and the Absarokas, yet the Big Horns are also considered part of the Rockies. Does that make sense? No.

But back to the Absarokas being part of the Rockies, which does make sense, even to this Illinois-bred reporter.

In the southern corner of Cottonwood County, the semi-arid basin reaches farther west than in the rest of the county, with the mountains barely beginning their rising march before you run out of county.

That's where Elk Rock Ranch was located.

From the flatter land, you had a better view of mountains than once you're in them. As the road started climbing, pines obscured more and more of our line of sight. An s-curve-laden dirt road brought us to the classic pole ranch entrance with a top crossbar. A hanging wood sign with wood cutouts announced Elk Rock Ranch.

As we drove in, a familiar vehicle coming out slowed for the driver to raise a hand in greeting and the passenger to wave with a broad grin.

Rubbing it in.

The passenger was Needham Bender, owner and editor of the Sherman *Independence*, the driver was Cagen, his reporter.

They not only got to the story before KWMT-TV, but they were *done* before we arrived.

My consolation was that we'd have the story on-air multiple times before Needham's next edition came out Friday.

Their being here first and our reporting the story first would be parsed in every detail when we next had dinner, most likely cooked by Needham's wife, Thelma.

It required a couple more s-curves on this entry road before the pines retreated and we crossed a wooden bridge over a creek, reminding me of arriving at the home ranch of Tom's Circle B. But instead of a ranch house and multiple working buildings, what we saw ahead here were cabins. Lots of cabins.

Close by, clusters of two or three cabins nestled into the trees and contours of the land, roughly circling a large timber building with a front porch that nearly dwarfed its two stories.

Diana drove to where the road became a dirt loop, connecting the inner grouping of cabins, the big house, a paddock, and, farther back, a large, wooden barn, with other outbuildings nearby, like chicks around a hen.

It all had the air of a well-equipped stage without any actors.

Not a person. Not an animal.

Back past the outermost of the outbuildings, I spotted three cabins that appeared to be the oldest of any I could see. One had yellow crime scene tape around it.

"Back there," I pointed out to Diana.

"Uh-huh. I see the road to get there."

She followed what was less a road than a route lightly passed over by a couple horse-drawn wagons a hundred and fifty years ago. But she did get us close.

The middle cabin had the door in the middle and a window on either side. The other two were mirror images of each other, with the door to one side and the pair of windows on the other. The one with crime scene tape was on the left.

The good news was there was no sign of a current official presence. The Cottonwood County Sheriff's department had been here, done its work, and departed, leaving only the crime scene tape to mark its territory.

The bad news was there was no sign of anyone else, either.

Except—finally—one living creature. A solitary, medium-sized dog, flouting the crime tape by sitting on the porch inside it.

As it took in our vehicle, it slid into a dejected down, chin on paws.

We were not the hoped-for arrival.

I opened the NewsMobile's door slowly, watching the animal's reaction. It didn't move. It didn't look toward us. Its gaze remained focused toward the direction we'd come from.

Also slowly because I was not in any hurry to leave even the NewsMobile's dubious protection from the wind that gave blustery a bad name. The day's bright blue skies were false advertising.

I grew up in Northern Illinois. I know wind. You've heard about Chicago being the Windy City, right? Well, the wind doesn't stop at the city limits. It gets an unencumbered sweep off Lake Michigan, true. But I've come to believe that farther out, it can get up an even better head of steam without all those pesky buildings in its way, especially across the flats of winter-shorn corn fields.

In Cottonwood County, the wind feels like an out-of-control skier, coming down the eastern slope of the Rocky Mountains, picking up speed all the way and bringing along with it the snow-fueled bite of the peaks.

The door of the cabin on the right opened.

That stopped me from wrapping the scarf around my neck and protecting my lower face. Oddly, many people resist being interviewed by a mummy.

A woman came out, settling a cowboy hat into place as she came, shading her face, especially with the sun behind her. She carried extra weight under a pair of overalls that covered a jeans jacket and she moved like she might have arthritis, but wasn't letting it stop her.

"You with the deputies? They didn't say anybody was coming back today." She had a low, rather rusty voice.

Granted, the NewsMobile is not a slick, modern TV news mobile unit, but it does have *KWMT-TV News, Sherman, Wyoming* in bright red and blue letters.

Asking a potential interview subject if they can't read is not the way to win them over. That left stating the obvious as my best option. "We're with KWMT from Sherman, Ms. . . .?"

She picked up the dangling invitation as she walked toward us, calling out, "Brenda Mankin. Needham Bender's already been here."

"Yes. That's for the newspaper, the Sherman *Independence*. We're from the TV. The news. We heard about the death of Keefer Dobey—" I was careful to pronounce it the way Mike had. "And we wanted to talk to people who knew him."

She looked toward the dog, as if it held the answer.

The dog didn't move, didn't change focus.

"I don't know . . . The deputies . . ."

I didn't want her to finish that thought, making it more real, adding an official seal.

"Mike Paycik sent us up to get the story because he thought so highly of Keefe and—Do you know him? Michael Paycik? He played football here, then at UW—" I deliberately used the local shorthand for the University of Wyoming. "—and pro ball with—"

"Of course I know him. Know all his stats from high school, college, and the pros, too. Though the Bears never made full use of his talents the way they should have, always having him blocking for some other gaudy player, when Mike should've been carrying the ball himself."

Not having an immediate opinion on that topic—though I'd bet my dad did—I steered around it. "Yes, well, as I said, he thought highly of Keefe and wants to be sure our viewers know what a fine man he was—you know Mike bought the TV station?" An enthusiastic nodding of the cowboy hat rewarded my decision to skip details of minority ownership by employees and members of the community. "So when he tells us to get a story, we get the story."

Diana made a sound from the other side of the NewsMobile.

Mike would hear all about this. And I'd take ribbing about it.

I could live with that.

Because Diana was getting her equipment out, which meant she thought my approach was working, making it well worth the cost of ribbing.

"We'd like to get closer and film, if that's all right—That's his cabin?"

It's a little sneaky, but effective, asking for the permission, then tagging on the second question, so an answer to one became an answer to both.

The cowboy hat bobbed in a nod. Better yet, she adjusted her trajectory to meet us in front of the crime-scene-taped cabin.

"But the dog . . .?"

"Oh, Suzie Q's as friendly as can be. Couldn't have a dog on the place that's not, not during the season with all the people coming and going and kids and some adults not thinking or asking before they reach out. She was raised to it from a pup. She'll let anybody come up to her, pet her, take her food away, any ol' thing, but she's Keefe's dog, through and through."

The dog's ears flickered at hearing her owner's name, but wasn't fooled into lifting her head.

"She's—" Brenda cleared her throat and started again. "She's waiting for Keefe to come back. That's what she'd do if he ever left without her, which he didn't do often. Almost never if he were doing anything here on the place, but now and then if he went into town, somewhere she couldn't be. And now . . . That's the direction they took him out and she'll set here watching and watching for him to return."

She turned away from us and stomped closer to the crime scene-taped cabin.

At the bottom of the steps, she stretched out a hand to pat the dog, which had the coat of a lab, except for a longer top knot between prick ears. Suzie Q might have looked comical if not for the intelligence in her golden-brown eyes. Now swimming in concern.

Diana had her camera already running and focused when Brenda Mankin turned around toward us, the daylight revealing her face for the first time.

From the way she'd moved, I'd put her age at maybe mid-50s.

Her face had me thinking in terms of centuries.

Saying she had wrinkles doesn't convey the impact. The rippled skin of her face made me think of a Shar Pei made from linen, taken straight from the washer, and left to dry in a crumpled lump.

"I . . . I found him first thing this morning, you know. I called 9-1-1 right away but it's not like they can get here fast. We're all trained in first aid, including cardiac. Have to be. For the guests. Not breathing's one thing. Sometimes you can get them back from that, but even though I tried chest compressions, I knew Keefe was gone . . . Hard not to. He was cold as a witch's—"

She broke off that simile, perhaps in deference to Keefer Dobey's memory.

"That must have been a terrible shock."

"Sure was. He was right as rain last night. In fact, happy as a clam."

She looked up and smiled at us. The sun- and wind- and age- and expression-etched lines shifted into their rightful place—into her rightful face. This was how she'd come to possess those folds. This was how she was meant to look.

"All excited about getting his DNA test back."

My head came up. "DNA test?"

Forensics? Or—?

"For tracing his family. Never knew a lot about that kind of thing—his family history and all—and he's been dying to get it and—" She broke off with a sucked-in breath and a return to the sagging wrinkles at belatedly recognizing her verbal gaffe. "Poor Keefe. Poor Keefe. He was sure these test results were going to tell him he's descended from Oscar Virtanen and that had to give him an inside track on finding the treasure. Though it wasn't like Oscar Virtanen wrote instructions to where he hid what he stole."

"Treasure?" The single word covered my much broader confusion. I figured if I got an answer to that, I might also learn who Oscar Virtanen was and why Keefe wanted to have been descended from him.

But Brenda had another point to make. "Don't get me wrong. It wasn't like Keefe was ever dissatisfied with his lot. I don't want you to think he was one of those people grasping to be something other than he was. That's not true at all." The rustiness in her voice remained. It wasn't from lack of use, it was a permanent feature.

"The opposite. He loved living here year-round. Loved the solitude in the winter and the company in the summer. Loved working alone and loved teaming up with somebody. He was easygoing, that's what he was. Most easygoing person I think I ever did meet. I'm not one to get all worked up like some, but he always was way more that way even than me . . . Mellow. That's the word. Mellow. Sometimes he reminded me of those critters on the zoo shows that look like they're going in slow motion."

"Sloths," Diana and I said simultaneously.

"That's them. Sloths. He moved like that. Not lazy, but not scurrying around, either. Deliberate like. He'd get to where he was going and he'd get the job done, but not with any hurry."

Her face, so naturally disposed to smiling, fell back into the folds of sorrow.

"That's what was so confusing, even before the deputies got here. When I was trying to figure out what happened."

She didn't appear to notice that I hadn't followed her segue from Keefer Dobey moving at sloth speed and her being confused about his death.

Perhaps because she needed more in this moment to say the thoughts in her head than to have them understood.

"There was blood. A lot of blood. Seemed to come from his head. Some of it was there, on the corner of the table by the kitchen, where he ate most times and did a lot of other things, too, because of the windows. Brings in the light. Guess my mind went to maybe he'd fallen, hit his head. You know, tripped over Suzie Q." She frowned fiercely. "But it doesn't figure. I've never known him to do such a thing. Because he moved slow, deliberate, like I said. Not like me. I'm forever turning around and finding Suzie Q or another creature behind me and nearly sending myself ass over teakettle.

"So I guess I was thinking of me. Real sure-footed—both of them, to tell the truth, Keefe and Suzie Q—but it *could* happen. Fact it hadn't before didn't mean it couldn't ever. Get your feet tangled and go down, hit his head, you know, on the corner of the desk. That was certainly what came to my mind, even though that didn't make sense because . . ."

She drifted away for a second, then jerked her head, apparently returning her mind to us.

"Course that was before the deputies said it looked like he'd been shot in the back of his head. Three times, I heard the medical guy tell that deputy named Shelton. Asked me all sorts of questions about what weapons Keefe had, like I kept an inventory of his belongings. And what weapons are around the place—might as well ask me how many sheets and such are around. Inventory's Wendy's area."

Wendy.

The same Wendy that Mike mentioned as the current owner? The county's billionaire?

Seemed likely. How many Wendys could you expect at an off-season dude ranch in one corner of Cottonwood County, Wyoming?

"Besides, I heard one of the deputies, one of them that was collecting evidence, say the blood there on the corner of the table looked to be from Keefe's hand—his hand putting it there, not his hand bleeding. He probably reached up to where he was bleeding from his head—natural reaction—then started to fall, tried to catch himself . . ."

Her gaze went unfocused again.

I wanted her to remember things, but not to drown in the speculative strain of what happened to her friend.

"You said earlier that Keefe getting tangled with Suzie Q was what you thought of first, then you said even though it didn't make sense *because* . . . Because what?"

She blinked twice. "Oh, right. It didn't make sense because Suzie Q wasn't in the cabin. So it never could have been that way, which just goes to show I wasn't thinking right even before they said that about him being shot three times. Keefe must've let her out before. Unless she got out herself somehow after, though I don't see how, when the door was closed when I got there. She's smart, but to close the door after herself . . .?"

"Where was the dog?"

"Circling the cabin. Seeing her out here was what made me come to his cabin in the first place. It was real early, not dawn yet. I got up to use the bathroom, looked out to check around—"

"Why? Did you hear something?"

She nodded, but then contradicted it. "Not that I was aware of. But you're not always tuned into that sort of thing when you've been asleep. That's why I got in the habit of checking. Because sometimes when I get up in the night to use the toilet, it's 'cause something else woke me first." So she agreed with the concept, but ruled it out for this time. "Spotted a lot of bears and such that way. Also guests going for visits to other cabins," she added dryly.

I nodded acknowledgment and patched up my interruption. "So, you got up . . ."

"Used the toilet like I said, then looked out. And there was Suzie Q circling Keefe's cabin."

"Did she bark?"

"No. Not a sound."

I reserved judgment on that. A bark might have been what woke Brenda, without her realizing it.

She went on. "Couldn't be sure right at first, with the other cabin in between, that it was her."

"Does Wendy live there?"

"Hah. Her? No. She's got the main house. Whole thing all to herself this time of year. The center cabin's used for summer, visiting cooks and such. Empty now. But empty or full, it blocks seeing Keefe's cabin easy. And it was dark, so Suzie Q was mostly just a shadow moving. But third or fourth pass, I was sure it was her. Way she moved. Threw on some clothes and got out there."

"Would Keefe put her out during the night?"

"Never. That's how I knew something was real wrong."

She was pushing us to accept the dog being out was enough to raise her alarm, along with all sorts of trailing assumptions and conjectures.

But was that true?

"If she got out shortly before you saw her—"

"No. She'd been out a long time. Her coat was cold as ice and she was shivering."

That matched her description of Keefe's body temperature.

"Couldn't know if that was reaction to knowing something happened to Keefe or the cold or exhaustion from going round and round for however long she did—though she can run beside the horses all day every day, so I doubt it was that kind of exhaustion."

"What's going on here?"

A voice with authority despite being high and light, turned us all toward the figure approaching from the barn.

CHAPTER FOUR

"**THEY'RE HERE ABOUT** Keefe, Wendy." Brenda answered the question without any indication the other woman's authority had an impact on her.

So this was Elk Rock Ranch's owner.

Also Cottonwood County's representative to the billionaire class.

You wouldn't guess the latter from her appearance.

She was short. Not that billionaires have to be tall, but she was really short.

And scrawny.

Not thin, as in you can never be too rich or too thin—in that quintessential twentieth century remark attributed all over the place, including being claimed by Truman Capote. But like a chicken's neck without flesh under its skin.

Yet her face was soft and rounded.

It was like the two women had mismatched heads. Put Wendy's head on Brenda and you had a youthful-looking and youthful-moving senior. Put Brenda's head on Wendy and you had a walking mummy.

Wendy wore jeans, work boots, a jacket with plenty of bulging pockets without masking that scrawniness, and a serviceable cowboy hat.

On second thought, maybe she *was* the perfect template for Cottonwood County's billionaire.

"Hello. Ms. Barlow?" I stripped off a glove and held out that hand. "I'm Elizabeth Margaret Danniher and this is Diana Stendahl. We're—"

I started to answer. Brenda talked over me.

Not the easiest thing to do to a broadcast journalist, but she accomplished it with ease.

"They're doing a story on Keefe. A remembrance. He deserves that and more."

"A remembrance?" Wendy Barlow scoffed without looking at us, much less meeting my offered hand. I gladly put it back in the glove. "Out-of-town vultures wanting to peck away at his death."

"No, ma'am."

Diana's eyelids flickered at my pulling out the *ma'am*, but no one else would have noticed. The other two women reacted more to my emphaticness . . . emphaticism? . . . to my being emphatic.

"We're from KWMT-TV from right here in Cottonwood County and we'd heard so many good things about Keefer Dobey, we came out to do the story as Brenda said. I'm E.M. Danniher and this is Diana Stendahl," I repeated.

"Danniher. I've heard of you. You do those *exposés* about murders."

I don't think she meant *exposés* as a compliment. I twisted it to one for our benefit. "We have done coverage on how murderers have been exposed and brought to justice in our county. I also do the *Helping Out!* feature and—"

"Oh, yeah," Brenda interrupted enthusiastically. "My cousin followed all your tips about holding a garage sale last summer. Because of what you said, she called the deputies about a guy skulking around and they found out he was wanted in Montana."

"That's great. You'll have to give me your cousin's name to see about a follow-up story on that." It would have been nice to have it last summer, but we could dig up a news peg to run it now. Maybe the start of this year's garage sale season.

"I sure will." She scribbled with a stub of a pencil on the back of a paper she pulled from her pocket. "She'd about jump out of her skin to be on TV. Be sure to tell her I was behind this."

"I absolutely will." The paper was the back of a gas station receipt from two years ago, but her handwriting was surprisingly legible.

Wendy was having none of it. "You shouldn't have come out here without calling first. Wasted a trip. We're sure not going to be on TV dressed for work like we are. It's bad for the ranch's image."

"Why shouldn't we be dressed for work," Brenda argued. "This is our work season. No guests to impress—"

"Never will be any more guests if we gross them out—"

"—so we dress for the tasks."

"—by letting them see us like this."

I'd seen Tom come in from some days when gross could apply. This was not it. Granted, neither woman was going to a fashion show, but their appearance would not raise a single eyebrow among our viewers.

"What our viewers want to know are your thoughts about Keefer Dobey," I said.

"Suffice it to say, he's gone to a better place," Wendy said.

Diana murmured what could be taken for agreement. I didn't.

I do not understand that sentiment when someone's been shot in the back of the head. Like the shooter should be thanked for sending the victim to *a better place?*

And even if it *is* better, isn't there a way to get to that better place that doesn't involve bullets in the brain?

I have never argued that point with someone I'm interviewing. It goes against all sorts of journalist guidelines, starting with not wanting to send the interviewee into catatonic silence—whether from stunned recognition of my logic or fury that my comments might edge toward irreverence.

But I think it. Often. And stick to my stance that shot in the head is *not* a good ticket to any place.

Hoping Diana's murmur and my not saying what I was thinking was enough to soften Wendy, I pretended she hadn't previously objected.

"Tell us what he was like."

Neither of them looked at me. Neither answered, either.

I thought Wendy sent Brenda a keep-still look, but the angle was wrong for me to be sure.

Diana had kept her camera running throughout, but without making a big deal of it. I doubted either of the ranch residents was aware she was recording.

We already had enough footage of Brenda to offer the human-reaction angle that would be added to Nala's hard news account of Shelton and the sheriff's department barely acknowledging they'd been to Elk Rock Ranch today, much less that someone had died, and not a hint of the bullets in the back of the head. But we'd gathered hardly anything from an investigation standpoint.

"Give our viewers a sense of the man," I suggested, deliberately using the cliché for its familiarity to put them more at ease.

"Can't imagine there are many of your viewers who didn't know the original."

It wasn't clear to me if Wendy Barlow was saying our viewership was narrow or Keefe's acquaintances were widespread. Possibly some of each.

"Still, they want to be reminded why he was special," I persisted. "And who better to share that than the people who knew him best. He worked here year-round, right? With you both?"

"He and Brenda are both year-round employees," Wendy said.

She didn't say *my* employees, but I think we all got the drift. Brenda certainly did from her sour expression.

"I understand he'd lived here most of his life?" I said neutrally.

Brenda spoke up, clearly not willing to have Wendy take control. "Yeah. Came as a little boy when his mom was hired on as cook and all. They came from back east."

"She worked here year-round? I'd understood most dude ranch employees are summer hires."

"Most. But Ulla—Keefe's mother—kept house for Chester, too. That's Chester Barlow, who brought the dude ranch back to what it started as."

"It didn't start as a dude ranch." Wendy contradicted. "Started as a cattle operation. Went the dude ranch route back in the 1920s. Then my family bought it for a private retreat."

Brenda's mouth twisted at being corrected, but she didn't say anything. I was just happy that correcting the history lured more words from Wendy.

"When Uncle Chester came here to live, the family had stopped coming long before. He remembered it from his childhood, though. He decided to return it to a dude ranch."

"And he brought Ulla in," Brenda said, grabbing back the conversational reins. "She did housekeeping and cooking for him during the offseason, like she'd done for his family, plus helped with other things around the place, too. But during the season, she cooked for the guests. There's a slew of them come summer and they work up quite the appetite with being outside all day, not to mention the summer staff. More than enough to do feeding all those mouths—even with kitchen help.

"When the guests left, it was like we kind of were a family. She'd do big meals for the holidays—Thanksgiving and Christmas and Easter—and it would be Chester and her, and the three of us—Keefe, Wendy, and me—and sometimes friends from town or around the county." She smiled. "She was so used to cooking for the guests, if she tried to cook for just us, we'd have the leftovers frozen for months. So Chester would invite a big group. She worked real hard, right up to the end."

I turned to Wendy Barlow. "You were around when your uncle turned it back into a dude ranch?"

Brenda answered. "She came later. A lot later." Clearly she held that as some sort of advantage over the other woman.

This time, I asked Brenda, "And did you grow up here, too, with Keefer?"

"She was just a neighbor," Wendy Barlow said.

It wasn't something I could ever report, not without multiple sources, but I was satisfied that neither woman would be happy letting the other hold an advantage.

"My folks owned the next place over." Brenda tipped her head to the east. They were good friends with Chester. He stayed with them when he first came here—before I was born. And they helped him upgrade the place. My dad rebuilt the barn, which—"

"Probably why it leaks," Wendy muttered.

"—had fallen to rack and ruin." Brenda either hadn't heard Wendy or was very good at pretending she hadn't. "Worked here a lot of winters, fixing up buildings. Then adding new cabins and such."

She tipped her head toward the cabin surrounded by crime scene tape, then to the one in the middle, and the one she'd come out of.

"When my folks were killed in a crash, I was in high school, working here during the summer as a waitress—youngest one," she said with pride. "Then or since. Chester took me in, said I'd never want for a job or a roof over my head and I never have."

That had an undertone of challenge to it. Had Wendy threatened her continued position here?

Definite undercurrents between these women.

How did Keefer Dobey fit into this apparent rivalry? Or did he?

A "mature" love triangle? A throuple gone wrong? If a romance— of however many angles—existed, I'd discover signposts to it by making a trip to the Sherman Supermarket and listening to head checker Penny Czylinski. Yes, obscure, misleading, frustrating signposts like the ones the Scarecrow gave in the *Wizard of Oz* by pointing in opposite directions simultaneously, but signposts nonetheless.

"But Keefe was the one who'd been here the longest of anybody. He loved this place deeper than anybody, too," Brenda added. "He was never happier than when he'd been out all day and sometimes all night, just on his own with Suzie Q now or any of his earlier dogs. Such peace in the man." Her voice cracked.

Wendy shed no tears, but the delicate skin around her eyes went red.

"And all the guests loved Keefe," Brenda added.

Even with red eyes, Wendy produced a snort. "Unless they were in a hurry. Besides, a lot more guests like the cute college girls and the buff college boys than old farts like Keefe."

"Or us? Is that what you're saying? Because he was younger than either of us. So—"

"Doesn't matter to guests how old we are as long as we do the job."

Brenda jumped on that. "And Keefe always did his job."

Wendy mouthed *Sloooow-leeeee.*

The other woman pretended not to notice. "And you certainly can't argue against me saying the Kenyons think real highly of him."

"So they say."

Before this devolved further, I inserted, "Who are the Kenyons?"

"Robin Kenyon and her father, Randall," Wendy said.

If she hoped a short, direct answer would end the topic, Brenda had other ideas. "Rich folks from back east. He's some big-shot businessman. Robin was a guest here last summer. Came by herself, which not a lot do. And her not much older than most of our staffers, which isn't a group—demographic, as they call it—we get much of. She was a problem from the start. Real snippy and—"

"That is not on the record," Wendy snapped, a hand slicing toward Diana's camera. "Be quiet, Brenda. We don't talk about guests."

"Why not? It all turned out fine—better than fine with how grateful they've been. Thanks to Keefe." She focused on us. "She got hurt up on the trail. Keefe stayed with her while I brought the other guests back and to get help—couldn't use phones up there. And when we got her down and packed off to the hospital, it was like she was a different person. Only found out after that her mother had died the year before. Never said anything. Not until her time with Keefe. So, all thanks to Keefe, like I said. Her father knows it, too. That's why he came here now. Him and Robin, with all that tension between them, trying to—"

"Be quiet." The vehemence of this snap stopped Brenda. Possibly trying to smooth it over, Wendy added, "They don't want to hear all these side-issues."

"That's okay. It's interesting and—"

She cut me off, too.

"You did say this was about Keefer Dobey, didn't you? What his death means. Or was that a lie?"

Fiercely, Brenda said, "It's such a shame it had to happen *now*, when he was so excited."

Unfortunately, while that freed me from responding to Wendy's accusation cloaked in a question, it also closed off any other avenue of discussion.

Wendy's eyes regained their red-rims but didn't overflow as she clicked her tongue in disapproval. "That nonsense."

I had a feeling this referred to the earlier mention of *treasure* and someone I'd never heard of. Not particularly where I wanted to go, but best to take what I could get.

"What was he excited about?"

Wendy rolled her eyes. Brenda answered.

"He was expecting results back on his genealogy test—that DNA—any time now. Years he's been working to put together his family history, tracking down any little scrap. Never seen anybody spend so much time at the library. We don't get the best connection up here, so he'd go to the library and spend hours and hours whenever he could, especially in winter. He's been thinking for a while there might be something in it, but he became certain here the past year or so that he's the descendant of a famous outlaw."

"*Famous*," Wendy scoffed.

"You can't say Butch Cassidy and the Sundance Kid aren't famous," Brenda shot back.

"He was descended from one of them?" I asked.

"Well, no. Doesn't seem so, according to what he was telling me about his research. But that doesn't mean he wasn't descended from somebody famous," Brenda insisted. Then she temporized with, "Famous around here. The Virtanens."

She looked at me expectantly.

I'd avoided exposing my ignorance the previous time she'd mentioned that name. I wasn't getting away with it this time.

Into the pause that followed, Wendy snorted. Brenda's face fell.

Diana looked up from her camera and stepped in to support KWMT-TV's reputation for knowledge of local history. "Of course. The famous outlaws, Oscar and Pearl Virtanen. They were contemporaries of Butch and Sundance."

Brenda beamed on Keefe's behalf. "That's right. They were deeply connected with Cottonwood County."

If *deeply connected with* meant they'd pulled off robberies here, I didn't see the appeal.

"Having a connection to Cottonwood County didn't matter to him," Wendy said. "Could have been Etta Place and the Sundance Kid, could have been Laura Bullion and Ben Kilpatrick he was descended from and he'd have been just as happy. Maybe happier."

I'd heard of the first couple from the multiple family viewings of *Butch Cassidy and the Sundance Kid* mandated by my father as fundamental to his children's upbringings, along with Irish music, and Chicago sports teams.

The second couple meant nothing to me.

At times, ignorance—real or assumed—can be a journalist's secret weapon. Some sources so enjoy teaching that you win them over by letting them teach you. Others can get so involved in showing off what they know that they let far more slip than they intended.

Wendy did not strike me as either of those kinds.

She struck me as the kind who saw ignorance as a weakness that dropped her respect for the other person, giving her the right to dismiss them.

I wasn't going to be dismissed.

I finessed, "But he settled on Oscar and Pearl Virtanen as his more likely ancestors?"

Wendy snorted. She resorted to that derisive dismissal a lot. With a jerk of her head toward me, she said, "She hasn't heard of any of them."

Defending myself that I *did* know about Sundance and Etta Place would display my ignorance of the others. One out of three wasn't bad for a batting average, but not great in these circumstances. I kept my silence.

"Keefe did a lot of research before taking the DNA test, eliminating the others as possibilities," Brenda said. "You see—"

"Nonsense," Wendy interrupted. "It's all complete nonsense. And so is this. You can stay and play to the camera if you want to Brenda, but I intend to get *some* work done today. It'll be hard enough to get ready for the season without Keefe. If we spend all our time talking to deputies and lookie-loos we don't stand a chance."

She turned on her heel.

Nothing to lose at this point. "Wendy, did you hear the dog—Suzie Q—bark last night or this morning?"

"No." She kept going.

I spoke louder. "Did you hear anything else? Or see anything?"

No answer from her, but Brenda shook her head in obliging answer to my questions. "Not anything more than I told you."

If only I hadn't heard that statement frequently from people who were far from telling all.

CHAPTER FIVE

DIANA'S FOOT DIDN'T land as hard on the accelerator on the return trip, but that was only because we were going downhill and gravity satisfied her speed demon.

"Why don't you call Mike and Jennifer. Give them the rundown of what we just heard," she suggested. "Make use of this time."

She was trying to distract me. I bit back the retort that we'd have more time to make use of, if she slowed down, because we'd live longer.

I wasn't entirely sure the NewsMobile's brakes were up to the job of slowing us downhill. *Down mountain* in this case. Might as well impart updates to our colleagues to make sure the knowledge survived . . . even if we didn't.

They each answered quickly and said, yes, they had free time at the moment for consulting via video call.

As we talked, I tried to keep the screen on Diana's profile and occasionally on mine. But with the jolts and swerves of our descent, they likely got their share of blurred Wyoming landscape, too.

Hope it didn't make them homesick. Or motion sick.

"The dog didn't bark in the night—so most likely the killer was someone the dog knew," Mike said. "According to Sherlock Holmes, anyway."

"We don't know that the dog didn't bark," I clarified. "We only know Brenda Mankin and Wendy Barlow said they didn't hear it."

"Brenda did say she almost certainly would have heard Suzie Q if she barked," Diana said.

I *huh'd* acknowledgment that she'd said that, while also conveying that I withheld reliance on her statement.

"The dog could have barked and she didn't hear it. Or the dog might not have barked, because Keefe opened the door for the killer, letting him or her in, while letting the dog out. No reason for the dog to bark then, with Keefe, essentially, vetting the arrival."

"What it comes down to," Diana said, "is we need to supplement Brenda's and Wendy's information on the dog's barking habits before drawing conclusions."

After a beat of agreement, Jennifer spoke up. "Sounds like you're not trusting Brenda, but she said she thought he'd fallen and hit his head and the person who shot him would know that wasn't the case."

I remembered my thought that Brenda needed to express the thoughts in her head more than have them understood, which would fit with her truly being confused. Unless . . . unless she was playing a part quite well.

"Diana and I reported what she said, with no assessment of her veracity."

"Okay," Jennifer said slowly. "If she knew it wasn't true . . . misdirection?"

"Exactly. Thinking that talking about him possibly hitting his head makes us think she didn't know anything about the three shots to the back of his head until overhearing a deputy."

"Sounds like Brenda had a lot to say, lots of throwing in possibilities." Mike looked at me as he added, "You've said guilty people do that to confuse matters."

"True."

Jennifer jumped in with, "You also say people will clam up and it sounds like Wendy did that—along with trying to keep Brenda from saying so much."

"Also true."

Diana proclaimed, "A draw."

"So, that gets us nowhere," Jennifer said.

"We shouldn't expect to get anywhere yet. Far too early. We want to concentrate on not getting too far—"

"No worries there," Jennifer muttered.

"—in any one direction because it might be taking us down the wrong path."

"This also might not be an investigation for us," Diana said.

"Why not?" Mike asked immediately.

"There *are* crimes that we don't investigate," she said dryly. "All the ones the sheriff's department solves just fine without us."

"That sounds like something the sheriff would say."

Jennifer's accurate observation brought a tinge of pink to Diana's cheeks.

She didn't have the easiest time, being loyal to us and being loyal to Russ Conrad. She negotiated that difficult path with amazing calm— even humor—most times.

I started, "And maybe this will be one of those times—"

Mike's surprised, "Why would it be?" sidetracked me from finishing soothing Diana's torn loyalties.

Instead, I said, "Someone shot three times in the head can be a straightforward situation, which is not where we excel."

"We're good at twisty," Jennifer said with relish.

Mike kept to his point. "Yeah, people shot three times in the head after a bar fight might be straightforward. And that's right up the sheriff's department's alley. But a real laidback guy like Keefe, who never harmed anybody in his life, in his own home, away from a lot of people, and with his dog put out of the house?"

Diana cut me a look. What Mike wasn't saying, might not even recognize, was he had an emotional investment in this death investigation.

"It still could be straightforward," I said slowly, "but in case it's not, we should proceed. If we don't, we lose time and information we can never make up."

"Agreed." That came from Diana. Then she added, "As long as we keep in mind that the sheriff's department's not sitting around twiddling its thumbs."

"Yeah, if they did, I wouldn't know I needed to call Aunt Gee." Mike continued with some bitterness, "Even if she is a heck of a lot more close-mouthed since Conrad took over. Okay, Elizabeth, tell us what else you two found out."

Diana immediately slid in an exaggerated, "Of course, Elizabeth will do whatever *you* say, Mike."

She was playing that card now? Right after I'd smoothed the gap between her loyalties? Was that fair?

Mike laughed. "Yeah, right. Since when?"

"Apparently since you became majority owner. She told Brenda Mankin that when you tell us to get a story, we get it, by gum."

"I love it," he crowed. "Maybe the new station motto."

"I did not say *by gum*," I corrected with dignity. "And it worked. Do you want to hear the rest of what Brenda Mankin and Wendy Barlow said or do you want to gloat about how I got them to talk."

Jennifer immediately voted. "Hear the rest."

Mike paused. "Can I save some gloating for later?"

"No."

"Fine. Go ahead and tell us the rest. But, Diana, let's talk later, just the two of us."

She chuckled.

I settled for glowering. In the interest of time, I launched immediately into what else was said, wrapping up with, "From what they both said, Keefe operated in slo-mo. That could justifiably drive an employer crazy. So that's at least a whiff of a motive."

"Seemed to be fine with his co-worker," Diana pointed out.

"Yeah, but the employer's paying for his time and if it took him forever to do anything . . ."

Twin coughs came through the phone.

Diana glanced at me with one eyebrow lifted. "They're saying that's you, Elizabeth. *Your* reaction. Your need for speed in *some* instances." Yes, she said it ironically, obliquely covering my reaction to her speed behind the wheel. "But it wasn't necessarily Wendy Barlow's reaction. And I agree. You saw her eyes, all red-rimmed."

"You heard her *slooooow-leeeee*."

"He'd been working there all his life. Why would he suddenly be too slow now, enough to kill him?" she countered.

"Built up frustration. Couldn't take it anymore."

"Again, I think that's you projecting, Elizabeth. From what we saw out there, both women appeared genuinely saddened." She held up a hand. "Granted, Wendy Barlow was more brusque, but I'm guessing that's her usual style."

I stared at her hand until she returned it to the steering wheel.

"So, what's next, Elizabeth?" Mike asked.

"Depends on who has time for what and when." Thinking things through just ahead of speaking, I said, "I'll leave Diana to handle the story along with Nala, if that's okay—"

"Sure."

"—and stop at the library. Brenda said Keefer spent a lot of time there, checking historical records. I want to find out about this outlaw Keefe thought—or hoped—he was descended from. Then I'll go up to see Mrs. P for what she'll share on Keefer, Elk Rock Ranch, and these two women."

"Not going to get more background before talking to her?" Mike asked.

"No." Though I knew I risked Emmaline Parens finding more teaching moments in our exchange this way—each of which she would use to its fullest. "I can do Internet searches any time, but if I wait too late, I won't get to see Mrs. P today—"

"And this way, after leaving Mrs. P, you can stop by the Circle B for dinner on the way back to town and see Tom and Tamantha, when this otherwise was going to be an evening apart," Diana said.

"Ahh," Mike and Jennifer chorused as if they'd just received a bolt of enlightenment from Buddha himself.

With dignity, I said, "And, you, Diana, are going to plumb your local resources for the views on the setup at Elk Rock Ranch and the *dramatis personae* of the year-round occupants as well as any cracks in the ranch utopia."

She could do a lot of quiet, unofficial asking around that would never make it to a story we put on-air, but provided valuable background.

"So I have my marching orders," Diana grumbled, only half

miffed. "Gossip."

"And send Jennifer and Mike what you shot today."

"Sure."

"I can do some digging," Jennifer said. "Where do you want me to start?"

"Can you with all the work you have for the program? We don't want to exclude you, but—"

"Sure. Besides, I can get the guys to go deeper where need be. They don't mind. Especially since I'm sharing some of the stuff I'm learning."

The guys were fellow computer whizzes Jennifer had formed an online alliance with years ago.

"As long as it doesn't interfere with your school work—"

"And I don't hack. I know, I know."

"What about the guy you're dating?" Mike asked abruptly. "Will he object to you spending time on this?"

Jennifer's eyelids dropped half over her eyes. "We're not really dating."

Why not? almost popped out, but I pulled it back in time.

Jennifer was always a catch in my mind. Now her look had gone sleeker and more relaxed. She looked fitter. Not the kind from the gym, but the kind from life.

She'd spent a lot of time indoors with computers when she lived in Sherman. She still did in Evanston, but some of the computers were farther away. As she told me after a few weeks there, "I live on one end of campus and the program's at the other end. I do a lot of walking."

So if this guy wasn't snatching her up, what was his problem?

Mike didn't back off. "Sure sounded like it."

One of her shoulders moved—half a shrug or a twitch. She said to me, "What do you want first?"

Uh-huh. She could have shouted *I don't want to talk about it* and it wouldn't have been more obvious. What was that about?

I wanted to know—of course I did—but I'd already come to the conclusion not to pursue it before Diana's warning gaze hit the side of my face.

Instead, I said, "A records search for background on Keefer Dobey. The two women—Brenda and Wendy, too."

"What about this Randall Kenyon?" Mike suggested.

"Good. Yes, him, too, please, Jennifer. Business and personal. See how much of a big shot he really is. Anything you can find on the daughter, Robin, too. And about their relationship if possible."

"Got it."

"If you have time." I might have ruined the effect of that caution when I immediately added, "Also see if you can find out where they're staying. It might be Cody."

"If it's not, I bet it's the Wild Horses B&B," Jennifer said.

I wouldn't take that bet. I agreed with her assumption the Kenyons wouldn't go in for the Haber House Hotel—historic, offering its own quirky charm, but not luxury. Their remaining choice in town was the Do Sleep Motel, which prairie dogs wouldn't consider luxury.

"What about me?" Mike asked. "What should I do?"

With him not only in Chicago with a demanding job, but also keeping his hand remotely on the rudder of KWMT, while trying to start a program that might solve a lot of the station's problems long-term, but was tough to staff short-term, his plate threatened to overflow.

"You mean what else should you do in addition to talking to Aunt Gee, getting people hired to fill holes in the staff and to keep Leona from stabbing you the next time she sees you?"

"With her eyes if not a knife," Diana said.

He groaned. "Don't rule out both."

"You could also persuade Diana to finally relinquish this deathtrap laughingly called the NewsMobile—"

"I don't need some state-of-the-art—"

"We're not talking about a mobile production truck—"

Mike jumped in. "Though we really need to replace that ancient truck. I swear it's made out of wood—"

I turned the screen to give him a warning look for getting off topic. "—but a Live truck could combine with new microwave capability—"

Diana came back to her usual refrain. "I'm fine with the NewsMobile."

"You're not. This thing is uncomfortable and—"

"*You're* uncomfortable. I'm fine."

"Only if you don't have any sensation left in your body. Besides, there's no logical reason for refusing to upgrade. So, that's on your list, too, Mike. Get Diana to accept the new, improved NewsMobile you've offered that won't get her and me killed, leaving you with two *more* people to replace."

"Great. Give me the hardest job."

CHAPTER SIX

Entering the Cottonwood County Public Library felt warm and welcoming.

Possibly some of the welcoming came thanks to it feeling warm. Even more than the temperature difference, getting inside its doors represented protection from the wind that had slapped us around up at Elk Rock Ranch.

You might think getting into the NewsMobile for the return trip would have accomplished that. You'd be wrong. By this point, the NewsMobile was the automotive equivalent of Swiss cheese.

My SUV, which I'd transferred to in the KWMT-TV parking lot while Diana went inside to work up what she'd shot for B-roll and background on Keefer Dobey's death for the Five and Ten o'clock news, offered wonderful protection, along with heated seats and steering wheel, which are requirements of civilization in my humble opinion.

The SUV began defrosting me enough that I called my next-door neighbors, Iris and Zeb Undlin, to ask if they'd be willing to feed my dog Shadow tonight.

Yes, was their unsurprising answer even before hearing it was so I could have dinner with Tom and Tamantha.

They'd also let Shadow out and give him treats and love on him. They might take him to their house so he could watch TV with them.

"Anytime," Iris said gaily.

And I knew it was truth for them as well as Shadow.

Once parked at the library, I discovered a downside to the SUV's amenities—they made the slice of wind and cold sharper in contrast before reaching the library's door.

"Hi, Elizabeth." From behind the circulation desk and wearing a bulky blue sweater, librarian Ivy Short smiled, helping shed the chill.

"Hi, Ivy. If you have a few minutes . . ."

She held up an it'll-be-a-second finger. "If you want to wait a little, my break is coming up."

Twist my arm. I wandered from an array of national magazines— yes, they still existed in print—to an announcement of an upcoming tax prep assistance event, to a display on St. Patrick's Day.

Another librarian in a bulky brown sweater took Ivy's spot at the desk. The bulky sweaters were de rigueur because of cold gusts pushing their way inside with each patron.

Ivy led me to the coffee pot in the staff room for cups, then settled us into a study room.

"Good coffee." With newsroom coffee, the emphasis is on caffeine, speed, and availability, and we get all that, but at the cost of taste. "How are you, Ivy?"

She answered for half a cup. Then she tipped her head to one side. "You didn't come here to chat."

"No, I didn't. Though I probably should."

She smiled back at me and waited.

"I'm hoping for background on Keefer Dobey. You know—?"

"Yes. So shocking. Absolutely shocking. If I were asked the last person I would ever think would be shot . . ." She sighed out between her teeth, keeping tears at bay.

"I'm told he spent a great deal of time here lately. I know you won't tell what specifically he checked out—"

"Oh, my, I couldn't possibly remember all the specifics, even if it weren't against the librarian code."

"—but to confirm a general interest, say in Wild West outlaws . . ."

It wasn't much of a leap, having been told he talked about them a lot and spent time at the library.

She looked relieved. She'd hated to deny me information and was happy to confirm what I already knew. "He *was* deeply interested in outlaws from the Wild West era. Particularly those who might have been in this area."

"Wyoming? Or—?"

"Cottonwood County and nearby. This area didn't offer outlaws good targets because most of its development came after their heyday. The famous ones were far more active earlier and around major railroad lines and bigger banks. But they did pass through here frequently on their way to and from, say robbing the railroads across the southern parts of Wyoming and Montana.

"You really should talk to Clara Atwood at the museum. You're friends, right?" Not exactly, though the curator of the Sherman Western Frontier Life Museum and I did have a man in common. My friend, rival, and colleague Wardell Yardley, who was her . . . Hmm. Semi-significant other from two-thirds of the way across the continent and neither wanting to settle down? "Keefe talked about wanting to discuss things he found with her."

"Like what?"

She shook her head gently. "He didn't go into details with me, Elizabeth. He came here frequently, but he stayed focused on what he was doing. He didn't ask for a great deal of help. And whatever he did say was in passing. Very pleasant. Always. He was a sweet man. It's such a shame . . . Especially when he was so excited the last time he came in."

"Excited? About what?" I had a guess, but additional sources are always welcomed.

"He'd had one of those DNA tests—from that company He-lixKin—and he expected to get the results at any moment."

Keefer Dobey certainly hadn't kept taking a DNA test and expecting the results soon a secret.

She raised her palms up. "Truly, that's all I know."

I was far from done fishing for details, though. "Was he interested in specific outlaws?"

"The usual ones around here. The Hole in the Wall Gang, of course, since their hideout was across the Big Horn Basin from here, down in the southern Big Horns. Though most people asking about the Hole in the Wall Gang are interested only in Butch Cassidy and the Sundance Kid."

"But Keefe wasn't? Interested only in Butch Cassidy and the Sundance Kid, I mean."

"He started there, but then he headed in other directions. Less obvious ones." She seemed surprised by that insight.

"Lesser-known outlaws?"

She nodded, apparently still musing over her own words.

"Oscar and Pearl?" I asked. I was on a first-name basis with them because I wasn't a hundred percent sure my memory captured the last name correctly.

"You know about Oscar and Pearl Virtanen? He wanted every scrap we had. But we don't have many scraps. They haven't been of much interest to historians, who are generally the ones who dig up the scraps." Smiling fondly, she added, "They're like archaeologists going after bones. They value every scrap. And then they try to put the scraps together."

She leaned toward me, close enough for me to catch a whiff of coffee on her breath. "To tell the truth, I think some of what they create from the scraps is a real Frankenstein's monster. You know, they can't know which scraps they're missing and the bridges they fabricate to fill in . . ." She shook her head.

Not unlike some journalists building a story. Or, I suppose, investigators.

My turn to muse on an insight.

One of the things I've learned about the murders we'd investigated during my time at KWMT-TV was that the two people most involved—the murderer and the victim—crossed paths somehow.

That might seem obvious.

But it's really very wise.

Honest.

To investigate a murder, you learn about the victims and what brought them to the point where they intersected with the killer. Victimology helps you understand where and how and why the murder happened at that particular moment in the victim's life. Once you stand at that moment, then you can start to see what the cross street that represents the murderer must look like.

It's one of the reasons law enforcement has so much difficulty solving crimes that don't stem from the life of the victim, but only from the path of the murderer. Then, all law enforcement knows is one point in the murderer's path—that crime.

In this case, though, the chances of a random murderer getting to out-of-the way Elk Rock Ranch in Cottonwood County, Wyoming, and into Keefer Dobey's cabin—taking care to put his dog outside—then shooting Keefe *just because*, were way down there with the Super Bowl being held in Sherman next year.

In other words, we were looking for someone who'd had more intersections with Keefer Dobey than the murder.

Along with his life at the ranch, his search into Old West outlaws appeared the most likely point of connection.

"So, no historians have been interested in Oscar and Pearl Virtanen," I recapped, "but was anyone other than Keefer Dobey interested in them?"

She had to be better than that at hiding the flash of awareness in her eyes if she hoped to deny there was someone.

She didn't try to deny it.

She jumped to "I can't—"

I rushed into words to delay the it's-against-the-rules excuse. The problem with privacy protections is that the good people play by the rules, while corporations not only flout those rules, but made so much money off our personal information already that they now threw around their 600-pound-gorilla weight with abandon.

But that was another story. In fact, a 10-part *Helping Out!* series no one wanted to see.

"It's not for a story—even if it were, I'd need two sources for an identity."

"Well, he hasn't made a secret of it . . ." She was talking herself into sharing, which she'd do better without help from me. "I've seen posts on his social media and in open forums about the treasure."

"Treasure?" I probably should have let her go on at her own speed, but the word did keep popping up. "What treasure and was Keefer Dobey interested in it?"

"He was. But not solely searching for the treasure." She was saying the not-yet-named other guy's priorities tipped toward the treasure. "Of course to try to track the treasure, you need to know about Oscar and Pearl. But Keefe was more interested in them as people, with the genealogy possibilities, while Sam's more interested in them as bank robbers."

I could have pounced on the new name. And she could have back-tracked.

Instead, I acted as if she hadn't given me half of what I wanted—the less valuable half, but still half. Keep her talking. That would give her more opportunities to let loose the last name.

I circled back to "What is this treasure?"

"Proceeds from a bank robbery. The money's never been found. And there was enough gold taken that it would be quite substantial today, even if the bills and such are only of historical interest."

Historical interest could translate into value, too.

"It's supposed to be hidden here? In Cottonwood County?"

"No one knows. Oscar robbed a bank down near the railroad line in the southern part of the state. He was supposed to be coming north, to join up with Pearl, but he was shot during the robbery and died enroute.

"But there was no sign of the proceeds from the robbery. The only hint was that he had mud and dirt on him like he'd been digging. Although that came from only one source, an account published decades later in a regional newspaper known for, shall we say, overdramatizing."

"Why decades later?"

"They published the memories of a member of the posse who chased Oscar."

"Do you have a copy of that article?"

"No." Her usually soft mouth went flat with the admission. "There are no copies of it that I have been able to ascertain. Both Keefe and Sam not only asked for it, starting me on extensive searches, but also searched themselves. Sam wanted to know the location of where the posse discovered Oscar's body, while Keefe was interested in a reference to the posse member remembering seeing Pearl and being moved by her grief and dignity.

"But all we have is a single secondary source referring to the article. Everything else cites that secondary source."

A dead end. When you hit those, you tried to pick up another trail. Basically, you just wanted to keep the person talking. "So Keefe signed up for a DNA test and—"

"No. He got it as a gift. You'd think he'd've done one back at the start, but in many ways he was unfamiliar with how things worked, modern things. He didn't even have a laptop computer until this fall. He certainly didn't know about tracking historical facts or trying to connect with a family tree until he started coming here. I don't think a DNA test ever occurred to him until he received it as a gift."

"Who gave him the test?"

"He never said."

The woman in the brown sweater behind the circulation desk gestured to Ivy.

Duty—and library patrons—called.

EXITING THE LIBRARY—without Sam's last name, but with hope that a return visit might secure it—I put my hand in my pocket for my phone, but waited until I was in the SUV to pull it out. No sense giving the Arctic winds the chance to flash-freeze it and my hand.

I had routine messages, plus one from Mike to call him.

He didn't sound urgent, but we'd just talked, which made it slightly concerning.

I obeyed. After all, he was the boss—a sentiment, if I shared it, that would amuse Diana all over again.

"What's up, Mike?"

"I didn't want to burden the others with how bleak the hiring looks."

But he'd burden me.

That was fair, since I'd agreed to consult in turning KWMT into something new and interesting, offering ongoing education for young hires. It's stopped him asking me—whether in the mode of badgering or begging—to take on any or all of the empty positions.

So far.

"I'm running out of ideas of what to try next."

I had a bad feeling that asking me—again—might be included in his remaining ideas of what to try next. I wondered if I could work it into the conversation casually that if he ever did push me into one of those positions, this sort of drop-everything-and-concentrate investigation would be impossible.

Even when he didn't have a fondness for the victim, as he did now, he valued these inquiries, both for their news value and from a strong sense of justice.

As I turned on the SUV for heat, I asked, "What's the latest?"

"I talked to this great woman from Pittsburgh, Octavia Zabel. She's one of the few who hasn't quailed at the idea of a Wyoming winter. In fact, it appeals to her. Problem is, she wants to ski."

"That's—"

"As in ski all winter, every winter. She said she's put so much time into building her career and now she wants the time to ski before she gets too old."

"I don't know if you can talk Leona into anchoring all winter, especially since winter around here is most of the year."

"It's not that bad." His kneejerk response to criticism of the weather. "But . . . yeah, I don't know about Leona, either." He perked up suddenly. "On the other hand, if we get Octavia Zabel in soon, Leona wouldn't have to pick back up until the end of September or so."

"You hear that sound? It's the clunk of a can being kicked down the road."

"I know. But maybe by then . . ." Even his optimism couldn't complete that. "I really don't want to lose Octavia. She's enthusiastic about the idea of bringing along young hires, intrigued by the new challenge, and you should hear the things she says about you."

"I like her already."

"But she's adamant about having the winters to ski. Leaving us only covering part of the year . . ."

"Don't make a decision right now. Think about this a couple days. Try to put it out of your head and then come back to it."

"I like that. It's worked for me before, things like deciding whether to finish out my career with the Bears or try the free agent market. Sorting what I really wanted rather than the dollars and cents type stuff. Worked out well."

"Good. Something else we need to talk about—Diana and replacing the NewsMobile. There's something more going on there for her to be so resistant."

"I wonder if we could afford a mobile production truck—"

"Mike. Concentrate. We have to figure out why Diana doesn't want to replace the NewsMobile."

"You could ask her."

"If she were going to tell me, she already would have. But you *are* the station owner."

He expelled a breath. I waited for a crack about how he was rethinking that move. "I'll see if she'll talk to me. So, did you find anything more related to Keefe?"

Good move, ending one discussion by turning to another.

"Nothing earthshaking."

I pulled out of the library lot, heading for my next destination. By the time I finished telling him about my conversation with Ivy Short, I'd parked near the Sherman Western Frontier Life Museum.

". . . I'll see about figuring out who this Sam is, but for right now, I've just arrived at the history museum to see if Clara's got anything."

"Okay." But he didn't end the call. Even when we both went to silence.

"Something else on your mind, Mike?"

"You heard what she said—they're not really dating?" He meant Jennifer. "That's because the guy's a leech. Just hanging around her for what he can get."

"You mean reflected glory from her brilliance?" I asked hopefully.

"Not entirely," he grumbled.

"You think she's serious about him? Or that he's a danger to—"

"Nah. Nothing like that. I just didn't like the guy. And she knew it and tore into me." He cursed. "Gotta go. Meeting's starting. Talk to you later."

CHAPTER SEVEN

CURATOR **C**LARA **A**TWOOD was not happy to see me.

"I'm really busy, Elizabeth, with all I have to do to get ready for our expanded spring hours and working on the Teague so-called collection to open the first few properties by the end of summer. Even opening it in a limited way to start, it's a herculean task."

In a surprise move orchestrated by Mrs. P last year, Russell Teague's will left his extensive Wyoming property to the museum. It included a jumble of western historical buildings, artifacts, and memorabilia.

"I thought you had funds to hire additional help for that."

"A lot of good that does me. Because I still have to find the right people, then have the time to hire and train them and—"

Mike and I knew how she felt.

"—now with Keefe dead, I don't even have his strong back to move things—God, that was awful. I didn't mean that's the only reason . . . I'm really sorry he's dead. For his sake, not only the museum's. At the same time, it's so crazy busy . . . I really can't chat—"

I cut her off before she could close me off. "It's about Keefer Dobey that I'm here. You know he was murdered? Shot three times in the head. And—"

A grimace scrunched her face. "Awful. Can't believe anybody would do that to Keefe. Completely sweet guy. It's beyond a shame."

"I just want to know if he ever came here and asked—"

"*Ever* came here? He was here *all* the time. Yes, helping moving Teague's things around for us to look at box by box. Incredibly helpful, but also questions, always questions."

I had the oddest feeling she wasn't talking solely about Keefe with that last part. But journalists can't have thin skins about hints that they should go away. Or they'd constantly be turning their backs on sources, on stories.

"Ivy Short at the library said he was interested in outlaws from the Wild West era."

"Obsessed more than interested."

"What about? Specifically. There must have been a particular aspect of Wild West outlawdom he wanted to know about."

Yes, I had what Ivy said and Brenda before that. I wanted Clara's take, untainted by what she thought I already knew.

"Aspect? What do you think with outlaws? Wasn't Sunday School meetings. Robberies," she said impatiently. "He hounded me with questions about robberies."

"Bank robberies or train robberies or another kind? All outlaws? Or a specific group? Or person? A specific time? Or a geographic—?"

"Really, Elizabeth—"

"Clara. If you take a minute to think about it and give me an answer, I'll be gone much more quickly than if I have to drag it out of you word by word."

Give her credit. She recognized the truth of my more-efficient argument.

Her gaze went up and to the left, reaching for the memory. "He wanted to know about outlaws who spent time in or around Cotton-wood County."

That didn't add anything to what Ivy or Brenda said. She needed to do better than that.

"*Specifically,*" she continued with a bit of mockery, so, possibly my reaction showed in my expression. "The Sundance Kid and Ben Kilpatrick. Both part of the loose confederation of outlaws that centered around Butch Cassidy."

This differed from what Ivy said. Though she had mentioned Ben Kilpatrick in association with a woman . . . Laura Bullion. If I had it right without notes. And that Keefe had entertained the possibility of being their descendant at one point. Had he completely jettisoned them in favor of Oscar and Pearl? "Those outlaws, but not Butch Cassidy and the Hole in the Wall Gang?"

"Hmm." Her eyebrows dropped in remembering, then popped up. "Yes. That is rather odd. Most people gravitate to wanting to know about Butch Cassidy—real name Robert Leroy Parker—with Sundance a strong second. To not ask about Cassidy . . ."

Her eyes did that accessing memories slant again.

"In fact, when Keefe started coming in, he was particularly interested in Sundance's and Kilpatrick's relationships with Etta Place and Laura Bullion."

Couples. Potential ancestors, *that* was Keefe's interest.

Clara continued rapidly, "And there was another couple, but they weren't as well known—not then and not now."

"What were their names?"

"Oscar and Pearl—a married couple. Married before they started robbing banks. The last name . . . Virtanen. That's it. He immigrated from Finland and met her here. They were involved in a few robberies, but it was as the authorities were starting to pick off members of the various gangs. Arrested, killed. Butch and Sundance and Etta went to South America in 1901 and—" Her head jerked up and I knew her eyes went to the clock. Uh-oh. "I really don't know more."

"Who around here would? Especially is there anybody else who shared Keefe's interest in Oscar and Pearl Virtanen?"

She clicked her tongue impatiently as she continued to look at the clock. What I had going for me was that her professional inclination was to impart knowledge.

"You mean the treasure legend? Russell Teague was interested—to the extent that he tried to scoop up anything related to it."

"He did that with everything historic around here and beyond. Not to mention he's dead," I objected. "So not only could he not have killed Keefe, but I can't talk to him."

"You asked who shared Keefe's interest and that's who did. There's another guy—Sam McCracken—who's on the hunt for the supposed loot from their last robbery."

Sam McCracken. Ah-ha—a last name.

And one I knew.

An image of a guy with thick dark hair flashed up in my head. He and his family were fairly new to the area. And we'd considered him a suspect in another death.

Interesting.

Someone we'd previously considered capable of murder—things were looking up.

Clara didn't wait for me to fully absorb the name. "But the person you should talk to is Mrs. Parens. At least about the guys," she said.

"Mrs. P is a Wild West outlaw aficionado?" I would have expected her to object on ethical grounds.

"I wouldn't say that. She's helping me with research and organization for several elements in Teague's collection—what a mess. Keefe and I spent a week in December triaging stacks of boxes at Teague Ranch. He's been bringing them to me and Mrs. P, bit by bit. When we finish, he takes them back—labeled and orderly. We will really miss him." Her voice turned astringent. "Russell Teague's records are beyond shoddy. He wasn't a true collector, much less a cataloguer. He just grabbed everything he could."

That matched my opinion of him, though I might have expected Clara to be more forgiving, considering the museum beat him out over disputed ownership of historic gold coins before his death, then inherited his historical holdings thanks to fancy footwork by Mrs. P.

They weren't kidding when they said rival historical experts held grudges, even beyond the grave.

No wonder Wardell Yardley was drawn to her. They both were fierce.

". . . not her favorite area of study," she was saying, "but facts are facts and even Mrs. Parens had to admit that having pieces associated with the best-known outlaws of that era would be a draw for the museum and Teague Ranch. She's tracked down considerable information. At least about the men."

"What do you mean, *at least about the men?*"

"Because she's told me—not that I'm surprised—that it's much harder to track the women associated with them. That's what history often does. But you should ask her directly."

And stop bothering me.

That was implicit, but the fact that she didn't say it made me feel all warm and fuzzy inside.

Not for long.

She spotted the clock again and this time I was booted out for real.

Was Ivy right about Keefe's interest focusing on Oscar and Pearl as people? That meshed with what Brenda said about his belief they could be his ancestors. And that could explain the DNA test.

On the other hand, it could have been meant as a distraction once he had a rival treasure-hunter in Sam McCracken.

Or could it be both? Would being a descendant give him an advantage in the treasure hunt? A secret map left only for the descendant maybe, but how . . .?

Too many questions.

What I needed were answers.

Not from Sam McCracken. Not yet. I needed a lot more background.

Besides, he lived in a part of the county that would take me in the opposite direction from the Circle B.

If I wanted to have dinner with Tom and Tamantha tonight . . .

Yeah, I'd gather more background before I tried Sam McCracken. Later.

CHAPTER EIGHT

I WAS ON my way to see Mrs. P.

Not unannounced.

Even though she didn't drive, one did not presume that Mrs. P was at home and at your beck and call. One did not presume with Mrs. P at all.

So, I called as soon as I left the museum.

She said to come on up . . . or words to that effect.

Up because she lives north of Sherman. I took the highway that paralleled the Absaroka Range, passed the entrance road to Tom's Circle B—*our* ranch—and on to O'Hara Hill, the second-largest town in Cottonwood County.

I can never resist mentioning that because most people looking at the one primary street and a handful of cross-street nubs would not consider it a town at all.

Also *up* because Cottonwood County is popularly divided into the High Side toward the west and the Low Side toward the east, with Sherman in the middle.

I used to half-joke that in the neighborhood where I grew up in Illinois, a waterfall was the flow from a hose left on the curb that dropped onto the street. If Cottonwood County's Low Side suddenly added curbs for some unfathomable reason to its shades of winter dun, rust, and drab, the same would apply.

The High Side rose toward and into the mountains, imparting what counted as lushness around here, but didn't impress someone who'd wiggled childhood toes in the rich, black soil of Northern Illinois.

I left the highway, which continued to and past the Montana border not many miles away, and took a jog west, where O'Hara Hill's single main street ran through a valley.

Did I mention it's small?

On the other hand, it deserves renown for being home to two of the stronger personalities I've encountered in this county or elsewhere—Gisella Decker and Emmaline Parens.

Otherwise known as Mike's Aunt Gee, the sheriff's department senior dispatcher and in charge of the O'Hara Hill substation, and Mrs. P, retired teacher and principal.

You'd think there'd be some sort of disruption to the universe's power system with the two of them living next door to each other. Like the pull of their personalities in tandem could be seen from space.

I demonstrated the impact of those personalities by immediately checking Gee's driveway when I arrived, like a kid scoping out possible penalties for a rules infraction. In this case, not keeping my visits to them scrupulously even.

Empty. Which generally meant she was at work at the substation. She could have run the entire dispatch unit if she'd been willing to move to Sherman. Heck, she probably could have run the state if she'd been willing to move to Cheyenne.

Theoretically no vehicle being visible could mean it was in the garage, but she resorted to that only for major storms. Or it could mean she was shopping or doing other errands, but she almost always took along Mrs. P.

I wondered how the older woman would manage without Gee as transportation.

Then she opened her front door to me and I knew she would manage—somehow.

I caught an angled glimpse through an open doorway down the hall to the room I knew she used as an office. Two columns of file boxes rose, with one box open beside the desk chair. These must be the records Keefe had been delivering to her, then returning in far better order to Teague Ranch.

Mrs. Parens poured me hot tea without asking if I wanted any and offered store-bought shortbread cookies in the front room that combined a classroom and museum library. We sat on hard chairs in the middle of the room.

"You've heard about Keefer Dobey?" I asked.

On the phone I'd merely said I wanted to come talk to her about a Cottonwood County matter.

She rarely gave anything away beyond her carefully chosen words. What scraps did get by could only be picked up in person. No chance on the phone. As for texting, it was the scourge of nuance and implicit meanings. I didn't know if Emmaline Parens texted or not and didn't want to—I had no hope of plumbing her depths via text.

On the other hand, I'd happily texted Tom my plan to stop by the Circle B at dinnertime. He didn't always have connection where ranch work took him and he seldom had free hands for phone or texts, so I didn't wonder when I didn't hear back.

"I have. Any loss of life is felt; however, his death is particularly difficult to fathom because of his nature." She blinked, recognizing in that moment, I thought, the trigger for her next words. "He preferred nature to human company and was acutely attuned to it."

"But not acutely attuned to humans?"

"I believe it would be safe to apply that statement to a large portion of the population, while a substantial percentage of that portion would not consider that the description applied to them."

Mrs. P tapdancing. Interesting.

"Had he been a student of yours?"

"He was not in any of the classes that I taught."

That left plenty of room. He'd been a school-aged kid while she'd taught. She'd surely been aware of him, which meant she'd observed him, which meant she'd learned a lot about him.

All of which she'd keep locked up inside no matter how adroit my questions unless she decided I really, really needed to know.

Her bar and my bar for what I really, really needed to know dwelt in different realms. Hers would top Frans Peak, which I'd recently learned was the highest in the Absaroka Range at about fourteen thousand feet. My bar was somewhere below sea level.

I decided to take it as given that she'd known Keefer Dobey from a young age and push on.

"He was helping the museum by delivering boxes of Teague's hoard for you to sort and put into order, wasn't he?"

"I would not claim to put them in order. Merely to make it more possible for Clara to achieve that goal without starting from a deficit of confusion and dirt. However, in answer to your query about Keefer Dobey's participation, he provided immeasurable help in facilitating the delivery and dispatch of boxes in an orderly manner."

"Did he talk to you while doing this facilitating?"

"It was not achieved in absolute silence." Her primness did not hide a hint of amusement. "In that sense, yes, we did converse."

"About more than the boxes. Perhaps what was in some of them? I'm interested in his interest in outlaws in this area—Wyoming more generally, and Cottonwood County—in the decade either side of the turn of the century from the nineteenth to the twentieth."

She declined her head in acknowledgment of my words, then spoke.

"The history of communication across our state, including, specifically, the history of the Pony Express Company, should be quite familiar to those affected now by the shifts and changes in technology."

I fought back a blink.

Not of confusion. I knew exactly what she was saying. She wasn't going to tell me.

Certainly not right away, maybe never.

I knew better than to point out the Pony Express operated a good forty years earlier than I'd asked about or—worse—to ask what the heck this had to do with what I'd asked. Not if I wanted answers at any point in the near future to what I wanted answers to.

But my eyebrows missed the memo, because one shot up—the traitor—and she spotted it immediately.

"The current generations believe theirs are the only ones who have responded to challenges from radical innovations, when logic dictates that previous generations have been at a minimum equally adept at such measures or we would all be residing in caves to the present time. One of the benefits of studying history is the humility it instills in us at the recognition of what previous generations have accomplished to allow us to progress to where we are now."

I kept my other eyebrow under control, but now my mouth acted up. "Have we progressed so much? Hatreds based on where you're from or how you worship or what you look like?"

She tipped her head at me. With her short stature, she reminded me of a bird. A bird about to peck at me with a very sharp beak.

"You are far too intelligent, Elizabeth, not to recognize that the very fact that you—and others—find such behavior unacceptable represents monumental progress from times past."

The fact that I agreed with her put me at a huge disadvantage.

I sidestepped by asking, "What about the Pony Express?"

Okay, okay. *Not* a sidestep. A full-out giving way to what she clearly wanted to talk about. But only because I knew she meant to talk about what she wanted to talk about before there was any hope of getting to what I wanted to talk about.

However, I didn't surrender completely.

I waved my little flag of knowledge by saying, "Wilson, Wyoming, was named after a Pony Express rider."

No need to admit how recently I'd acquired that particular flag of knowledge.

She lowered, then raised her head in succinct acknowledgement of my factoid.

Then she got down to business, just not the business I was pursuing.

"The Pony Express was not merely a romantic enterprise of young men dashing across the landscape on relays of fast horses—" That sounded fairly appealing to me, though even more appealing to my brothers. I recalled considerable running around our Illinois back yard that was labeled *Pony Express riding.* "—but was, rather, an innovative response to a pressing need."

"To get mail across the country." I hoped filling in gaps might hurry along this process.

"Indeed. It required three to four weeks to send mail overland, a method subject to poor weather conditions as well as attacks from Native Americans, or months by ship from the East Coast, either around the tip of South America or to a point from which it could be conveyed across land, most commonly in Panama, then re-boarded onto a ship, with further dangers of weather and shipwrecks for those methods. By the beginning of the 1860s, with the political tensions pointing toward the Civil War, finding a more rapid method to connect the West Coast with the rest of the country became a vital challenge.

"The Pony Express was created in mere months to begin operation in April 1860, continuing for only eighteen months before announcing cessation of operations two days after the final link of the transcontinental telegraph was connected."

"Telegraph killed it, huh?"

"It could be viewed in current terms as a startup technology that lost out quickly to a more efficient technology."

"Which then happened to the telegraph, too."

"The completion of the transcontinental railroad in 1869 did not eradicate the telegram. However, its new technology and capacity did narrow the telegraph's importance, as we see happen with once-innovative technologies in our times, as well. The telegraph's usefulness was further eroded by the telephone. Though if one considers the need for written confirmation, one could view the fax as more detrimental."

"And now faxes are a niche market. Point taken. But I didn't realize the Pony Express only lasted eighteen months. All the movies, the TV shows, the books ... It seemed like it was an institution. It's certainly embedded in our cultural memory."

"One might attribute that to the fact that the Pony Express filled a need." Her wording indicated she had reservations about joining the *one* who might attribute its cultural prominence to that. "Perhaps it could be said that by securing and accelerating communication between the rest of the country and what is now termed the West Coast, the Pony Express played a vital role in the continuation of the United States spreading from sea to shining sea."

"An east-west split was threatened?"

"The north-south split is undoubtedly more recognized, not the least because it occurred. However, the western region could have split away while the rest of the country was embroiled in the Civil War. That, however, is speculation and not, I believe, why movies are made and books written about the Pony Express.

"Its image captured the popular imagination at the time as well as later. Its prominence in the public's imagination was not a result of happenstance. It was stirred and tended to with great acumen by William Cody, who said he had ridden for the Pony Express, as part of his selling of the West and its history wrapped in romanticism. He did, in fact, deliver messages as a boy for a precursor of the Pony Express. However, his purported heroics with the Pony Express owed far more to his and others' adroit polishing of his exploits than accuracy. Although there were heroics displayed by a number of the riders, in addition to the endurance and skill required of their basic job."

"Buffalo Bill Cody *didn't* ride for the Pony Express, yet he's part of the reason we remember it now?"

She declined her head in acknowledgement of my recap, though it clearly pained her to give him even that credit when he'd perpetuated inaccuracies. I empathized. Accurate is accurate.

I also saw an opening.

"You know, it's sort of about who is remembered and who is forgotten that I wanted to talk to you about." A great segue, if I say so myself. "I was talking to Clara at the museum and she was talking about how little is known about the women connected to the men in the famous outlaw groups of the late 1800s and early 1900s. Why is that?"

From that question, I could see a path to get to Oscar and Pearl Virtanen—especially Pearl—and thus to Keefer Dobey.

Mrs. P took the bait . . . or she was ready to talk about this now anyway.

"Beyond the broad societal bias compounded by the academic bias toward the belief that women did nothing interesting, there were two additional, practical causes for the oversight. The first stemmed partly from the broad societal bias influencing the accounts relayed in newspapers of that period and conveying that only men participated. Indeed, they rarely stated that, as such, because it was assumed it was so, while later information showed women did participate. At times as distractions or to misdirect pursuers, but also as active participants, as detailed to some extent in the case of Laura Bullion."

I should have stuck with my path to Oscar and Pearl, but my unanswered questions about Laura Bullion lured me into the detour like someone waving a chocolate bar under my nose.

"Laura Bullion . . . She was connected with Ben Kilpatrick, right?"

Another newly minted factoid. But Mrs. P didn't need to know that. Especially not if my knowing impressed her.

It did not.

She dismissed it. "She was romantically linked to him, as well as others at various times."

When Mrs. P continued, I realized a faint whiff of distaste I'd picked up from her was not associated with Laura Bullion.

"The Pinkerton National Detective Agency monitored the activities, including the romantic associations, of Laura and other women associated with members of the loosely affiliated gangs of Western outlaws of that period. Much of the material we have now came from the files of the Pinkerton National Detective Agency, as well as contemporary newspaper accounts, with much of *that* also coming from the Pinkertons, in addition to other law enforcement sources."

We were of the same mind here. "Incestuous sources are never good. Echo chambers. Seems like what Person 1 said is being reinforced by a second source—Person 2—when it's really Person 2 repeating what Person 1 said."

Another single nod of acknowledgment. "The result in this case is a narrowed view of those women, as well as limited information on them, with even their names shrouded or lost amid multiple aliases and, I fear, inattention.

"One could say that the agents operated under a handicap in recording the names, especially the nicknames and aliases of those they sought. The outlaws did use a notable number of aliases."

"Goes with being an outlaw," I observed.

"There also was a culture in this region of not asking someone his or her name, not expecting it to be accurate if it was offered, and accepting that any number of people were known as Buckskin or Curly or Kid or for a location, such as Tex or Arkansas or Deadwood.

"However, the Pinkertons also contributed to the profusion and confusion of names. For instance, it is debated whether fellow outlaws called Ben Kilpatrick the Tall Texan or if he was, in fact, exceedingly tall, with prison records indicating he was not. Some surmised he was tall based on a famous photo, not taking into account that he sat on a straight chair between two companions occupying lower chairs. But the Tall Texan was what the Pinkertons called him—in that case likely based on a description from a single witness at one scene—and that sobriquet endured.

"Strict adherence to substantiated fact appears to be disregarded even more frequently concerning the identities of women. As an example, Laura Bullion was not deemed as important to catch as the men, despite evidence she might well have participated directly in holdups, dressed in male attire, as well as monetizing stolen goods, and acquiring necessary supplies for the gang or gangs."

Making Bullion an apt last name, I thought and didn't say. I'd already interrupted too much.

"It is certain she held proceeds from a train robbery when she was arrested shortly after Kilpatrick was in Tennessee. Multiple sources state that Laura's father was incarcerated for bank robbery and that he was responsible for introducing her as a girl to a cowboy named Will Carver. That cowboy married her aunt, who died shortly after."

I was starting to feel Laura Bullion was a new version of the Pony Express. Mrs. P was telling me what she wanted to tell me.

"Will Carver, known as News Carver, became affiliated with several gangs. He might have introduced Laura Bullion into the gangs. After he moved on, she became associated with Ben Kilpatrick.

"It is only by accessing as many sources as possible that a theme arises of Laura Bullion being called variations on Rose, including the Thorny Rose, which was on her gravestone. Some sources say members of the Wild Bunch called her that. Also Della Rose, which resembled the name of the girlfriend of another member, though whether Della was that girlfriend's real name or among the aliases she used is not certain."

Was anything about this certain?

"Another example is the woman most popularly known in current times as Etta Place."

Now, here we entered more familiar territory for me—she'd been the school teacher in *Butch Cassidy and the Sundance Kid*, romantically linked to the Sundance Kid, but out for a bike ride with Butch Cassidy.

With disapproval, Mrs. P said, "There are scant reliable facts to tell us what her real name or occupation might have been. It is worth noting that Place was the last name of the mother of the man who was known as the Sundance Kid and that Place was a name he used among many aliases. Is it not reasonable that she joined him in that practice? One school of thought is that her first name was Ethel or Edith, with Etta either an approximation of the Spanish pronunciation of her name or a mistaken note by the Pinkerton operatives. In other words—Oh, my, is that the time?"

Since she hadn't looked at a clock, watch, or phone, I could only assume she intuited the time.

Or decided she was done for now.

"Mrs. Parens, what about Oscar and Pearl?"

"We must continue this discussion of that particular history another time."

CHAPTER NINE

MRS. P'S EXCEEDINGLY polite bum's rush sent me on my way without delay, which did have one upside.

I'd get to the ranch—the Circle B—where I'd be with Tom and Tamantha, earlier than I expected.

I texted Tom my new ETA. He'd responded to my earlier text while I was with Mrs. P with one word: *Great.*

As I mentioned, my leaving my father's house to go to my husband's house was not a part of the scenario for our upcoming nuptials. Though houses did figure as a bone of contention in some of our conversations over the past months.

Sort of a backward bone of contention. Instead of each of us wanting to spend max time in the house we brought into this coupling, Tom thought we should spend more time in the town house, because it was more convenient for my work and Tamantha's school. I thought the brunt of the bad-weather commuting should not fall on him, so we should spend more time at the ranch.

The topic rose tonight as we prepared dinner, while Tamantha did her homework at a corner of the table. Tom did most of the cooking. I could bake, but otherwise I was a great table-setter.

"Thought we'd stay in town tomorrow night," he said. "Tamantha has a meeting after school, so she could get the bus to the town house."

"And you? You'd have to get up at an outrageous hour to get back here to the ranch to have enough daylight—"

"Never enough daylight this time of year."

"—to do your work."

"If that's your only objection, I see the pluses outweighing the negatives. But if it's something else . . . I hear—" He cut his eyes toward Tamantha. "—you've taken on extra work yourself. Beyond helping Mike with changes at the station."

We hadn't had an opportunity for me to tell him about my day's activities. I wasn't surprised he already knew some.

"Not officially. Not sure there's anything there for . . . us." A tilt of my head away from him and Tamantha indicated my fellow sleuths. "Exploratory for now."

Proving he already knew a lot about it without needing any of my reporting, he said, "Nice guy. Different, and good with that. Sure of who he was."

Mrs. P's discourse on the history of communication across the Wild West had me thinking of these comments as telegraphic. The telegraph's speed might have killed the Pony Express, but its communication style still had impact.

"Dinner's ready," he said to his daughter, which ended even our telegraphic communication over murder or murder victims.

Afterward, Tamantha cleared the table, then pulled out the last of her schoolwork.

While Tom and I put away leftovers, did the dishes, and cleaned the kitchen, I shared some of what Mrs. P told me, figuring tales of Wild West outlaws wouldn't shock Tamantha . . . if she didn't know all about them already. Without mentioning murder, Tom added a few points about Keefer Dobey and confirmed my impressions of Brenda Mankin and Wendy Barlow.

I also found an opportunity to say casually, "If you happen to hear from all your sources in the county, and beyond, that the sheriff's department is about to close an active case with an arrest . . ."

"I'd call you immediately." He looked thoughtful. "Doesn't feel like that's going to happen."

In preparation for the drive to town, I made a pit stop in the master bathroom.

I heard Tom's phone ring, but didn't think anything of it.

His calling habits didn't match a journalist's, but with the number of organizations he was involved in, if not in charge of, he came close.

When I came back into the main area, with the living and dining rooms blended and the kitchen right off them, Tom had his phone propped up on the table, showing a video call—though I couldn't see details of the screen from here. Tamantha sat next to him.

For my first few steps from the hallway into the main living area, I thought Tom and Tamantha must be listening to those on the other end.

I only realized nobody had been talking on the other end, either, when I heard a woman's light voice say, "Oh, is that Elizabeth?"

Tom's parents.

We'd had a few video calls since we'd decided to get married. I'd expected the first one to be awkward. I hadn't expected that they wouldn't get any better.

Tamantha jumped up. "Sit here."

She offered the seat with no less alacrity than a prisoner giving up his turn in the electric chair. She also didn't wait to see if I complied before returning to her previous spot.

I found a smile and took the chair next to Tom.

It was a little spooky how much Tom looked like his father in facial structure, features, and coloring. And infinitely reassuring that you had to look analytically for that resemblance, because the first impression of the two men was not at all alike.

"We're not sure we can get all the way up there for the wedding," his father said.

He made it sound like they'd trek cross-country for months in horse and wagon instead of a few hours' flight or a day-or-two's drive.

"It's not until late June," Tom said.

His father grunted.

As I told Tom later, it was a neutral grunt. Could have been hostile or dismissive and it wasn't. Tom grunted at my comment. A grunt that had a way to climb to reach neutral. I didn't point that out to him.

Now, his mother smiled—genuine, though sandwiched around a sideways look toward her husband at his grunt.

"That's a lovely time in Sherman."

Was that a trace of wistfulness in her voice?

"Exactly why we chose June. Of course, we wanted to avoid the winter months in case of bad weather for people coming from out of town—" Not to mention my husband-to-be and mother ganged up on me to allow months for "proper" planning. "—and spring's so unpredictable with calving season, so late June was the decision."

No one said anything.

I tried again, echoing, "It is a lovely time. The flowers, the birds."

"Unless the grasshoppers hit," Vanessa Burrell said. "There were some years . . ."

Plagues of grasshoppers? I'd seen some around here, but that didn't sound like what she was talking about. "Of course. Unless the grasshoppers hit."

After that topic faded back to silence, his mother said, "How are the wedding plans coming?"

I cravenly pulled in Tamantha to respond there, gesturing her to return to this side of the table. Far more subdued than usual, she updated them succinctly, then excused herself.

With neither Tom nor his father filling in the next gap, I called on my best *this interview is going south but at least I'll live up to the standard of the musicians who played Nearer, My God, To Thee as the Titanic sank* voice and said, "We'll let you know all the details not covered in the invitation—you should get that any day—as soon as we settle them, because of course we very much hope you'll come."

"We'll try very hard to be there."

I had the feeling the hard would come from her husband, the trying from her.

We said good-bye shortly after that.

Another silence developed locally.

"Did you know the musicians on the Titanic, the ones who played music to keep people calm as the ship sank, were mostly in their twenties and early thirties?" I asked.

Tom rolled his eyes toward me. Tamantha's head popped up from her homework.

I kept going. "One was forty, the rest all a lot younger and one was only twenty."

"That's my friend Madison's older sister's favorite old movie. She says she loved Jack, even though he died."

The spray of wrinkles at the corners of Tom's eyes deepened. "Association of ideas—the call, the Titanic?" he said under his breath.

In the same tone I said, "Maybe." Then, aloud, to Tamantha, "Tell Madison her sister should try some of the really old movies about the Titanic. Like *Night to Remember* and another one named *Titanic*. Did you know there was a German propaganda film during World War II about the sinking? It told the story of a lone, brave German officer who saved everyone who survived while everyone else panicked from cowardice."

"*That's* not what happened," Tamantha protested.

"Homework?" Tom asked.

"I'm done. I was working ahead." The girl is remarkably mature and disciplined about some things, but I guessed this incidence of added devotion offered a preferable alternative to her grandparents.

"Good. But it's time for bed now."

She didn't argue, but she didn't head down the hall, either. She eyed me.

"You could stay tonight and take me to school in the morning," she said.

Not a command.

I barely stopped myself from placing my palm on her forehead to know if she was running a fever. Not sure I would have known using that method unless she reached a stove-hot temperature.

At the same time I caught Tom's tightened mouth, but no heightened worry in his eyes.

That translated to no fever, but, rather, a grandparents hangover.

"I can't, kiddo. Shadow's at the town house alone," I fudged, because he might be, although the odds were against it.

"Iris and Zeb could take care of him overnight."

"And they do in an emergency," Tom said. Making it clear this wasn't an emergency.

"He's my dog. Not only is he my responsibility to take care of, I *want* to take care of him."

A furrow tucked between her brows. Not confusion or worry, but a contraction from the wheels behind it whirring so fast. For a flash, I thought I could see her as a woman my age, with a majorly responsible job—possibly keeping the free world rolling along—and that tuck would appear and with it the comfort of knowing all of us in the free world could rest easy.

"Because that's the kind of person you are," she said.

While resisting looking at her father, I felt certain her phrase came from him, and likely in conjunction with the work I did. Journalism and the side-gig with murders.

"That's right. Like your dad, who does so many things to help people around the county."

She didn't say, *Yeah, yeah* impatiently, but she sped past the concept of her father because she had no sliver of doubt in the bedrock of her certainty that he loved her. But I was a newer commodity. And her grandparents reminded her to doubt.

"Me, too? I'm your responsibility and you want to take care of me?"

Okay, not quite ready to keep the free world rolling along on her own. Maybe by fifth grade. Right now, after the awkward strain of the conversation with her grandparents she needed a little reassurance.

"Absolutely."

I braced for the then-do-what-I-want argument, with another round of the neighbors can take care of Shadow and they give him more treats anyway, so he loves it there.

Instead, she said. "Okay. Give Shadow a hug for me."

"Will do." I gushed with relieved enthusiasm.

"Tell him it's my hug," she instructed, not satisfied I took my pledge seriously enough.

"I will."

"See you tomorrow. Good night." She hugged me. I hugged back, a demonstration of my skill which I hoped would allay any concerns that I would not represent her well with Shadow. "Good night,

Daddy."

"I'll be in later."

She hugged him. "You don't have to do that. I'm not a baby."

"I'll be in later."

She sighed, but didn't argue further.

Tom and I kissed good-night by the door for a while. We didn't talk about Keefer.

Tom said, "Be careful" only once. Then I went out to my SUV to drive back to town, offsetting the reluctance to leave them with the pleasure of this bonus evening together.

Charles Dickens nailed it—it was the best of times, it was the worst of times.

DAY TWO

WEDNESDAY

CHAPTER TEN

I STOPPED AT the Sherman Supermarket on the way to the station.

It wasn't precisely on the way and I wouldn't get anything perishable, but my favorite store-bought cookies—Pepperidge Farm Double Dark Chocolate Milano—never went bad before being consumed. Besides, I mostly stopped for unperishable information.

That came from head checker Penny Czylinski.

The information rarely came directly and only when I was in her checkout line, which sometimes required finesse to maximize. The most important factor was having no one behind me, waiting to check out.

On my way to the cookie aisle, I eyed her line—no one behind the person currently being rung up, a woman named Hannah Trusett, a ranch wife and mother of three, who had two heaping carts.

Hoping that would discourage anyone else from getting in Penny's line, I grabbed five packages of cookies and swooped back to checkout.

Penny had completed the first cart.

As excavation of the second cart started, I waited patiently—semipatiently—during her free-ranging soliloquy that touched on sparse resources for rural mental health. Either that or migrating bird populations were down. It was a little hard to tell.

Her customer was a robust woman in her mid-fifties, who clearly had her own system and high standing in Penny's eyes. Because the woman reorganized some of the bags Penny packed and Penny didn't—excuse the pun—send her packing.

I kept a wary eye out for anyone coming up behind me, but one customer went to the line of the young cashier farther down the row and the rest were still in the belly of the store.

Finally, after Hannah Trusett paid a throat-lumping bill, the longed-for words came from Penny.

"Bye now. Well, hi there, Elizabeth. Out to Elk Rock yesterday. Sad—"

"Yes. And any background you can—"

"—business. Poor soul. Special. Always been—"

"Keefer? How?"

"—that way. Spaces between him and people. Open—"

"But he lived with two women for—"

"—spaces best. Saw things there others didn't. Always. She was wise enough to accept, give what needed. Did dance close to the edge, but couldn't know he'd pick up the interest later and—"

The interest? "Keefe's interest in the treasure?"

"—all those years. Sort of a triangle, could say. But—"

"Brenda and Wendy?" I asked a little wildly. "With Keefer?"

"—not what you'd expect. They—"

Not what I'd expect? Well, I couldn't say I exactly *expected* a romantic triangle among Keefer, Brenda, and Wendy, but what else—?

"—already working there when she came from back east."

Ack. I missed something. That's what I got for trying to think, much less speak, while Penny was talking. And now she'd segued to Brenda and Wendy. Had I missed something vital?

"Couple real rocky summers and she told him he was making it worse, but if he'd listened to her, things would have been different—"

"Chester?" I doubted she'd confirm, but it was worth a try to attach proper names, especially with no idea of which *she* was telling him he was making things worse.

"—giving her all sorts of privileges. Then she got the whole thing as his nearest relation. Cut her to the quick."

Left the ranch to Wendy. So that had to be Brenda cut to the quick, didn't it? But how had Keefer felt?

"Might not know it now, but had flaming red hair and temper to match. My, oh my, the—"

A redhead's complexion could have contributed to those wrinkles. Brenda for sure.

"—things she said. A lot of things said. Both sides. Can't unhear those things. Ah—"

"Involving Keefer or—"

"Bye, now, Elizabeth. Well, hi there, Geneva."

The salutations didn't sound nearly as good on this side. Another customer had slid up behind me.

I did not fight the inevitable.

The frustration, however, left me primed for a fight when I walked outside and spotted the compact figure of Sergeant Wayne Shelton standing by the driver's door of my SUV.

Apparently he wasn't in the mood for pleasantries, either, because he said, "Stay out of this, Danniher."

I didn't pretend not to know what he meant. "Not a chance, Shelton."

"*Sergeant* Shelton."

"E.M. Danniher," I countered.

He dropped that pissing match. I'd take that. I hadn't won it, but I hadn't lost, either.

"This is sheriff's department business."

"It's KWMT-TV's business to report on crimes *and* on the activities of the Cottonwood County Sheriff's Department. Not to mention the business—the obligation—of every citizen to further the cause of justice."

"Further it? You obstruct it. You're forever in the way."

"Shall we list the instances when we brought you information to further your investigations or County Attorney Abbott's prosecutions? Not to mention the times we brought you the culprit on a downright platter?"

"You? *You*—"

He clamped his mouth closed. I hadn't said anything but the truth.

We did further the cause of justice. At this moment, however, we—okay, I—might not be furthering the cause of keeping Wayne Shelton's blood pressure out of the stratosphere. I didn't mind elevating it now and then, but not to the point that he blew a gasket. But how to ease up without backing down?

"Never thought I'd miss Thurston Fine," he rumbled.

"Never thought I'd miss Sheriff Widcuff."

That exchange of insults—him saying he'd prefer our former anchor to me, me saying I'd prefer his former boss to him, with neither one of those individuals overly blessed with brains or ethics—put us back on our normal footing. If he blew a gasket now, it would be the result of decades of gasket-pressure-building. Not my doing.

He stepped aside. I got in my SUV and headed for KWMT-TV.

NOTHING LIKE A little sparring to get the blood moving.

After checking in that it worked with Audrey's plans for Nala Choi, I also gave the young reporter the outlines of what Brenda had told me about her cousin's experiences after hearing tips from one of my *Helping Out!* segments.

"Consider it a good news feature, but also see what the guy was wanted for in Montana in case he wasn't just a small fry."

"Potential news story," she murmured as she took notes.

"Exactly. If it was anything big, we should have heard about it when it happened, but . . ."

At the time this story would have happened, a lot of things were falling through the crack known as Thurston Fine, our former anchor. Especially when he turned off the police scanner so as not to disturb his naps. "Be sure to check where in Montana. We broadcast into areas up there."

"Like the follow-up about the Montana deputy's investigating that I did before Christmas."

"Right. We want to keep in touch up there, build loyalty among viewers and contacts among potential sources."

"Got it."

✧ ✧ ✧ ✧

AFTER PRELIMINARY RESEARCH, I took a stab at getting Keefer Dobey's DNA test results from the company HelixKin.

I examined a mental list of paths and started with a cold call, not identifying myself or the station. I told the customer service person that an uncle had received a DNA test as a gift, but he'd lost the results. I didn't muddy the waters with the possibility the results hadn't arrived yet. Let them tell me if that was the case.

She told me to have him log in online with his account number.

Oh, forgetful uncle couldn't remember that, either.

She'd mail him a copy if I gave her his complete name.

Fat lot of good that did me. All Keefe's mail would go to Shelton.

I blithered about him being a snowbird preparing to move north for spring and we'd wait until he'd settled to get back to them, and got off the phone before she noted my number as suspicious.

I debated which tack to try next and decided on media relations.

Some media relations people truly are about being a bridge between their company and the media. They communicate, facilitate, translate.

Too many are human roadblocks. If someone called to tell them they'd won a lottery ticket, they'd spend ten minutes saying it was impossible for the caller to talk to them—even though they were already talking to them.

This time I did identify myself, delivered the sad news that one of their customers had died, with oblique references to foul play, and intimated the death could connect to his recent receipt of the results of his DNA test from them.

"To clear this up and find answers for justice and his family—"

"We cannot give a third party the results. Not even under these circumstances."

I pushed a bit more, but she wasn't yielding.

She wasted both our time by apologizing over and over. That always strikes me as passive-aggressive, meant to manipulate the person being apologized to into saying it was okay.

It wasn't.

She could have spared me that.

As soon as we disconnected, and leaving no time for the woman to put out a talk-to-no-one about Keefer Dobey advisory, I called the VP I'd previously selected from the list of HelixKin executives—making sure there was no mention of a law degree in his background. What *was* in his background was a stint at a company that had imploded from fraud. I'd covered that story.

If he'd been one of the principals, I'd have steered clear. But someone who escaped might just view me in a positive light. Even if he didn't, there was a good chance he was gun-shy about certain topics.

I got past the assistant by using my name and the words *murder investigation*.

He answered quickly, which was promising.

I told him the background—not mentioning his former employer, because why rub it in?

Right off the bat, he tried, "That's not—"

I didn't need or want him to tell me what it wasn't. I could have guessed that from the start, even if the media relations person hadn't droned on about it.

"Your opportunity to establish your company as cooperating with the pursuit of justice—"

"We do. By following the law—"

"—rather than living down to the image of a self-serving, even cold-hearted corporation that—"

"Our lawyers—"

"And lawyering up."

I should have skipped that last line. It probably reminded him of experiences at his former employer.

With him being quiet, I figured the best thing I could do right now was let him work through the benefits and drawbacks.

"As much as we would like to assist in finding justice for our customer—or anyone—we cannot abandon our obligation to preserve the privacy of our customers."

"Your customer is dead." Perhaps not technically true, if Brenda was right that the Kenyons gave it to him. But this wasn't the time to get bogged down in technicalities. "Murdered. And you have the power—"

"I don't." The two flat words closed the door. If you don't learn to recognize closed doors as a journalist, you spend a lot of time hitting your head against them. I have the battle scars to prove it. "I can relay your request and contact information to the appropriate department."

"Please do." It was a 't' to cross that wouldn't get anywhere, but necessary. "I'll let you know when our report runs, detailing your response."

The last line wasn't necessary. But it felt good to deliver it. Who among us is always above petty?

But, having disconnected, my petty faded and the fact remained that I didn't have the information.

Darn.

I could set Jennifer on the trail . . . But how many times had I told her not to hack? And each time because I didn't want her to get in trouble.

Nothing had changed there. Not to mention the other demands on her time now.

I wasn't asking Jennifer to try to crack this information.

But there might be another way . . .

Before I could consider whether this was the time to try to deploy that other way, my phone rang.

It was Audrey, sitting just a few feet away. I looked over. She gestured for me to pick up.

When I did, I realized she'd added me to a call with Mike.

". . . Hartville wrapping up all those isn't fair," he was saying. "They're down in the southeast corner of the state, so of course they've got all those firsts. That's the direction the wagon trains came from and then the railroads and all those other events that spawned town-building and bar-needing."

"Are you still lamenting that?" I asked him.

"Yeah. But then I heard about what you guys were saying yesterday and it got me thinking maybe something in the realm of murder and justice *would* work. Not current, but do we have any claim to fame by way of some of the old-time outlaws?"

"Like Earl Durand?" I'd learned a few months ago about the 1930s manhunt for him after he killed several men.

"Not old enough. We need a classic. Like Butch and Sundance."

"They mostly stayed south of us. The Hole in the Wall is much closer to Casper than us. They robbed trains running across the southern part of the state and I think a couple in Montana—"

"Skipping us," Mike grumbled.

"I bet no one minded back then," I said.

"Not very forward-thinking of them," Mike complained. "Red Lodge not only had part of the Hole in the Wall Gang or the Wild Bunch or whatever name they were going by in their town to rob the bank, but they *foiled* the robbery and returned them to jail after they'd broken out in South Dakota."

"Wait, what's this?" I asked. "Butch and Sundance tried to rob a bank in Red Lodge?"

I'd been in the town just across the Montana border without seeing any mention of that. On the other hand, I'd been intent on meeting Tom's sister, Jean-Marie, who lived there. However, with my parents coming for the wedding this summer and always being on the hunt for interesting side trips to keep them occupied while I was working, my priorities shifted.

"Not Butch. That's probably why things went wrong. He was the planner in those gangs. There was a bank robbery in Belle Fourche, S.D., in 1897 that got less than $100 and was a comedy of errors. Was the Sundance Kid involved? Wasn't he? Some say it was a different person using that name. The records are a mess. Some broke out of jail. Then another group—supposedly with the Sundance Kid, again— showed up in Red Lodge, tried to rob the county bank there, but had to skedaddle before getting any money. The county sheriff chased them a good distance and captured them.

"They got sent back to South Dakota . . . and escaped."

"Wow. That's—"

"Great stuff, impossible to pin down, and no use to us at all," Mike complained. "Because they skipped over us even when they were botching robberies. And that's if it was even Sundance involved."

But it was of use to me. I saw a visit to Red Lodge in my father's near future.

"They probably rode through Cottonwood County," Audrey consoled him. "At least on the way to the robbery. Law enforcement would have taken a different route to return them to South Dakota authorities."

"Even worse. Come look at the spot where Butch—"

"Butch wasn't . . ." Audrey didn't finish reminding him Cassidy was never included in this group.

"—and Sundance's horses' hooves might have touched before they botched a robbery and got sent back to jail. That's not going to get us any hires." In an abrupt change of topic, he asked, "What are you working on, Elizabeth?"

"DNA test scams." It must have been conditioned after mostly hiding what I was really doing from our dear departed news director Les Haeburn—that's *dear* because he was departed. He'd been the furthest from *dear* possible while he was here.

"There's a scam going around about DNA tests?" Audrey asked.

"Yeah," I said.

But she must have picked up something in my tone. "I'm going to get off now and let you two talk."

As soon as she did, Mike said, "I know it's harder with the staff stretched, but we all want you doing investigations when they come up, Elizabeth. And we know they're not going to always pan out—at least I do. You need the freedom to explore and poke around to find the gems. A lot of water flows past when you're panning for gold."

Now I felt really bad.

"I do know that, Mike. I'm sorry. It just came out. Probably partly because there really are DNA test scams that I want to do for *Helping Out!* The scammers approach people on Medicare and say one of the benefits is a DNA test for genetic testing. All they have to do is hand over their Medicare information. And *poof*, the scammers are gone, with their identities."

"Uh-huh. Sounds like a good *Helping Out!* segment." Which we both knew were already abundant. "But what about Keefe?"

"Hey, are you saying you're no more interested in my official beat than Haeburn was?"

He was not going to be guilted into backing down. "Since your official beat now includes exploring stories of potential investigative interest, I'm very interested in it. And if you want to do the DNA-Medicare scam story, that's fine, too. But right now I want to hear about Keefe."

"You will. Promise. When I have something to tell. I'm basically picking up rocks—no, pebbles—and seeing if there's anything under them."

"I can help with that."

"I know you can. But is that the best use of your time, what with owning KWMT, not to mention your job there in Chicago?"

I wondered—worried—if he was pouring more of his money into running KWMT. I hoped not. He needed to take care of his own future. But if he was, he really needed that job in Chicago.

"I don't want to be shut out of the investigations." He made it both plaintive and stubborn.

"You won't be. Diana and I called you yesterday right away, re-member. When—if—there's really something we'll update you."

"Not shutting out Jennifer, either. Because if I didn't make sure of that, she'd have my hide."

"Jennifer, either," I promised.

CHAPTER ELEVEN

WITH MIKE'S ENDORSEMENT, not to mention I needed something to share soon to stem his and Jennifer's paranoia, and on top of my lack of success with securing Keefer Dobey's DNA test results, I decided it was time to get out of the office.

I hadn't fibbed to Ivy Short yesterday. To run a story stating Sam McCracken was a treasure hunter, I'd need two independent sources for that information.

Some might debate if Clara was first or second source, since Ivy gave me only a first name.

But I did not need a first or a second source to go ask the man some questions.

I RECOGNIZED THE white truck parked in front of the impressive timber house with the even more impressive view of buttes and mountains behind it as belonging to Serena McCracken, Sam's wife.

I'd been here before, when Diana, Mike, Jennifer, and I considered Sam McCracken a suspect in an earlier murder. Property belonging to the McCrackens and the murder victim belonged to the same ditch association. As the source of irrigation water, ditches are the lifeblood of Low Side ranches.

Not so much for the McCrackens, who rented out most of their land, as the others.

They were from Colorado, moving up here with their two kids after Sam McCracken reached that level of wealth that no longer required working.

In response to my knock, a woman about my age opened the large front door as a medium-sized white fluff of a dog came skidding to a stop at her side.

"Snowball," I said.

My knowing his name caught the dog in the instant of sucking in air to bark at me. He gave a half-hearted yap—had to use that air and adrenaline somehow—and started waving his tail.

I put down my hand, with the back facing him. He sniffed, then licked.

We were buds.

I scratched behind his left ear.

We were bonded.

I shifted to the woman.

Her slight smile said she'd indulge the dog, but not me.

She had dark hair pulled back in a sleek ponytail from the nape of her neck, which I knew would accommodate a cowboy hat. She wore a t-shirt, jeans, and boots. That could describe the attire of two-thirds of the population of Cottonwood County. She did not shop the same places most of them did.

I calibrated my smile to a few degrees warmer than hers, subtle encouragement to her to match me with the hope that smiling warmly would make her inclined toward me. It was a fine line, though. Too much warmer and I'd come across creepy.

"I remember the name Snowball because it suits him so well. I'm E.M. Danniher from—"

"I remember."

She'd said it neutrally, a big step up from what I sometimes get.

I'd seen Serena McCracken around town, mostly at the supermarket. Which proved we both ate, but didn't give us much common ground beyond that.

"Penny always speaks highly of you," she added.

Penny always spoke—that was certainly true. Whether she spoke highly of me, I withheld judgment.

"Won't you come in?" Serena invited.

Okay, Penny spoke of me at least highly enough to get in the door.

"I hope to talk to your husband—"

"He's not here. Come on in."

I did.

A twinge of something gripped me, but I've done enough interviews to not let unspecified—or specified—twinges interfere.

Besides, I was otherwise occupied with taking in the surroundings.

From the entry hall, with a stairway off to the right that must lead to bedrooms upstairs and recreation downstairs, a small office was visible to the left. Past that, the back of the house opened to two stories. I was vaguely aware of the kitchen at the right side, a massive stone fireplace on the left.

In fact, this space reminded me of a house I'd looked at when I was looking to buy. Including a soaring wall of windows between the kitchen and fireplace. This house's windows showed a spacious deck, then even more spacious vistas of buttes and broken lines of red-tinged earth, including a formation called the Red Sail, for the obvious reason.

Unfortunately, that other house also had a dead body in it at the time I looked at it, which dimmed its appeal considerably.

"You're here about the death of the man from the dude ranch."

As she gestured me to a seat on a leather couch that looked out the windows, Serena McCracken didn't ask, she told.

And reminded me that, while this house didn't have a dead body in it—that I knew of—a dead body *was* the reason I was here.

"I am."

She nodded slowly, taking her seat on a matching leather sofa at right angles to the loveseat so it faced the fireplace. "I only met him once—at the supermarket with Sam one day. He and Sam had an overlapping interest. But he seemed a *nice* man." She paused. "Gentle in many ways, but I could imagine him being fierce in the protection of those he thought needed it."

If she had any inkling her husband was a person of interest—to me and my cohorts, if not law enforcement—this was a really interesting approach. She'd practically painted a scenario requiring adding only a little imagination to envision Keefer Dobey and her husband becoming combative.

Clueless? I didn't think so. Her gray eyes were too intelligent.

Throwing Sam under the bus? Again, I didn't think so. Those gray eyes reflected a brain rolling something around, but it didn't seem to be, *Here, here's my husband on a platter. Cart him off to jail as the prime suspect.*

So, what was going on?

"That overlapping interest . . .?"

I dangled it, wanting to hear how she defined it.

She didn't answer directly.

"Sam was so driven at work. I thought when we moved here he seemed to downshift. But it didn't last." She shook her head slightly, burrowing her fingers into Snowball's fur. "Like after he got rested, he needed someplace to put his—"

I expected *obsession.*

"—passion." Her fingers tightened. The dog turned to look at her. She eased up on her hold. She expelled a breath. "Outlaw treasure."

My impression that she was neither unaware nor tossing her husband to the wolves of suspicion deepened.

Her frame of reference was Sam. All Sam. What was good for Sam. What wasn't.

Outlaw treasure fell into that second category.

The mutual—*overlapping*—interest of her husband and Keefer Dobey.

"How did it start?"

"I have no idea. He started volunteering to take the kids to the library more, but I didn't think much of it when he brought books on local history home. Not at first. Then the online orders started to arrive. From all over. Day after day. Not just books, but also metal detectors—plural—other equipment, all the while consuming books like a starving man."

"What were the books about?" I could make a good guess on what the equipment was for.

She raised one hand in half a shrug, then dropped it so abruptly it slapped her thigh.

"Geology, metal detector operation, history, biographies—"

"Of?"

She gave me a you-already-know look, but obliged anyway. "The Hole in the Wall Gang, the Robbers' Roost Gang, the—No, wait. I have that wrong. The Hole in the Wall was a hideout here in Wyoming, and Robbers' Roost was another hideout in Utah. Then there were multiple names for the gang, which—Oh, hell, I don't know. Sam would be correcting me all over the place. And if I said it involved Butch Cassidy and the Sundance Kid, he'd look superior and say I only remembered those names because of Hollywood and many others among the robbers were more prolific or more dangerous."

Sounded like we should get Sam together with Mrs. P.

"But he sure read enough books about them. All of them."

She gestured past me. To the office beyond the wall behind me? Or farther?

"All the outlaws?"

"*All* of them. And the lawmen. And the chroniclers. And anything else he could get his hands on."

"Did he find books on Oscar Virtanen?"

"I don't know." She sounded weary. "If they'd ever been published anywhere he probably did. He also went down to Laramie and Cheyenne quite a bit. Research, he said. I wondered . . ."

She lifted one shoulder.

She'd wondered if he was having an affair.

Was it better or worse that he truly had gone to those places to bury himself in . . . what? I could guess at letters, deeds, newspapers, and official records from the era. Was there more I wasn't thinking of?

"As if the expensive tools and equipment, especially those damned metal detectors and calibrating them more often than he talks to his family, weren't bad enough." She gusted out a sigh. "I suppose it could be worse. It could be spending all his time at casinos. He's still gambling in a way—and losing—but at least he gets outside. Most of the rest of the time, he spends in his office. Sometimes all night, as he did Monday night. He gets so engrossed he loses all track of time."

Uh-huh. Slipping in his alibi. On the other hand, if she hadn't stayed up all night, she couldn't vouch for his whereabouts.

"Did he connect with Keefer Dobey?"

She looked down at the dog as she petted him. "The man from the dude ranch who died?"

"Yes."

"As I said, they knew each other."

"Did they share information? Cooperate on research? Go out together on searches?"

"Not that I know. He certainly never came here."

I'd count both statements as truthful. And carefully worded.

Time to gracefully withdraw. Until I had more facts to pry harder. And deeper. And preferably with Sam McCracken on hand.

CATCHING A LOOK at the house in the SUV's rear-view mirror shifted the perspective enough to make me not see solely this house, but another one, too.

And explained my earlier twinge.

The McCrackens' home was what Mike's house should look like.

Not the apartment in Evanston just north of Chicago he'd had since his first days playing for the Chicago Bears and that remained his base there now—a one-bedroom in a traditional brick building. Pleasant, small, meeting his basic needs.

But the house on the ranch he'd bought as his rooting here in his home county. Didn't take much imagination or psychological training to see it was his way of getting an approximation of the family ranch his father sold from financial necessity when Mike was younger.

Heck, Mike had nearly said the same himself.

Cottonwood County likely would have continued to claim him as their local hero no matter what, but his buying a *tidy place*, meant he also claimed them and that meant a lot—to him and them.

Even when he'd worked at KWMT-TV as sports anchor, he hadn't had the time or ambition to devote to ranching. Good thing, I suppose, or he wouldn't have had the spare time and energy to push all of us into this murder-solving business. It had required considerable energy at the beginning to push me in this direction.

From the time he bought the ranch, he'd leased out most of his land, as the McCrackens did. Unlike them, he left the big house largely unfurnished and unlived-in.

It had made my heart ache for him when I first saw it. It still did.

I was making my life, my future with Tom. That didn't mean I didn't still love Mike. What I hoped for him was a home like the McCrackens'. Warm and lived in, with a dog and kids and a few horses. And a smart woman looking out for his best interests.

That thought brought me back to why I'd driven to the McCracken place.

Without appearing to, Serena spiked my suspicion's biggest gun— that Sam and Keefer were rivals—and weakened others.

Oh, she hadn't removed my suspicions. They definitely remained. But each had to logically overcome the obstacle she'd placed in front of it.

And where better to find information to achieve that than at Elk Rock Ranch?

CHAPTER TWELVE

I CALLED DIANA and arranged to meet her at Elk Rock Ranch.

The station could always use more footage for tonight's newscasts.

The McCrackens lived east of Sherman, the ranch was southwest of it. Returning to Sherman might have been quicker, would have been more familiar, but it was a day with a blue sky overhead that felt like it pulled your heart up by a string.

Zigzagging my way south and west, I pushed the cover back from the sunroof to get the most of that blue sky . . . without considering opening it. Wyoming. March. Not crazy.

Only one stretch of road had me questioning my sanity, so it was a routine drive.

The NewsMobile sat by the entrance to the ranch.

The sight of it simultaneously reminded me to luxuriate more in my SUV and to wonder at Diana's reluctance to replace it.

"THREE AND A half times as many head of livestock were killed by unknown predators than were killed by wolves," Randall Kenyon proclaimed.

Immediately, I identified him and his daughter, Robin, from photos I'd looked up last night before going to sleep.

They hadn't spotted us, though.

We'd been forced to park on the ranch's main entry road because of the behemoth pickup that must be the Kenyons' rental parked across the entrance to the offshoot we'd have otherwise taken.

How did I know it was the Kenyons' rental? Besides being glossy and tricked out, it hadn't been here when we came yesterday. Pretty good clue.

Robin sat on a bench by the corral fence next to the barn with Brenda sitting on the other end. Wendy stood past her and Randall beside his daughter.

Randall and Wendy were zeroed in on each other and the two on the bench didn't have a good angle to see us approaching, especially with the coverage of that pickup.

"I can show you the statistics from a well-regarded study," he continued loudly and with a hefty dollop of patronization. "People around here are prejudiced. But if you look at the numbers—"

Wendy snorted. "Before you trot out numbers, you should know that *unknown predators* is what they say when they can't a hundred percent say it was a wolf—and only a wolf. A wolf makes the kill, but other predators get after the carcass and that becomes *unknown predators.*"

"Coyotes kill more livestock than wolves," he argued.

His clothes were top quality and new enough to crackle, including the retro red paisley neckerchief that immediately made me think of an outlaw pulling it up over his face to mask his identity.

"Lots more. But nobody's reintroducing coyote packs."

"The reintroduction of wolves in Yellowstone was decades ago—"

"And the monitoring and enforcement gets paid for every year." I had the feeling Wendy had made this argument before.

"Besides," Brenda said, "it's not just Yellowstone. Colorado has a pack that sure doesn't stop at the border. Those wolves kill livestock and they kill dogs—dogs guarding the livestock and pets."

"Coyotes kill dogs, too," Randall Kenyon shot back, not quite as patronizing.

Robin Kenyon had spotted us, was watching us. None of the others picked up on the direction of her attention, though.

Her jeans, boots, shirt, and jacket were the same quality as his— setting them well above the utilitarian rattiness of Wendy's and Brenda's. But hers were broken in. They looked less like a store window outfit and more individual pieces chosen that day.

She had those eyebrows that looked like they were painted on with a fat brush. I'd bet my house she didn't do them herself. Nor the artfully streaked hair pulled back in a low ponytail. She wore her cowboy with considerably more ease than Randall.

"Yeah, but you Easterners don't get as sentimental about coyotes," Brenda said. "Probably because you have problems with them back there, too."

Wendy nodded, united with Brenda on this topic. "People trying to keep livestock alive don't get sentimental about either one—wolves or coyotes."

"Sentiment has nothing to do with—" Randall's vehemence abruptly pivoted toward us. "Who are you? What are you doing?" He interrupted himself a second time and started toward us with the hand out to the camera. "You can't—"

With her camera going, Diana approached him slowly, with me hanging back slightly for the wider angle.

He kept moving his hand, trying to block the shot.

"Hi," I said with cheerful friendliness, then tried to sell it more with, "Brenda, Wendy, it's good to see you again. Randall, Robin, I'm Elizabeth Margaret Danniher and this is Diana Stendahl from—"

"Can see where you're from." After shifting his position, he must have seen the big letters on the side of the NewsMobile. "Go away."

His continued effort to block the camera kept raising the folds of the neckerchief's fabric, reinforcing the impression of an outlaw masking his lower face.

Boy oh boy, did he need media training.

Made great video for us, though, if we decided to use it.

There wasn't much that made someone look shiftier—and thus guiltier—than holding their palm out to the camera. You can start a debate about this in most TV newsrooms, with some holding out that it was the perp walk when an arrestee bent nearly double and pulled a sweater or other piece of clothing over his/her head. I fell into the hand-in-front of the camera as shiftier camp.

Yes, because it was active and the sweater-head shuffle was passive. But more important because of how it looked if it aired—like the person on camera's hand was pushing away the viewer. Like that palm is about to be shoved in the viewer's face.

Not the way to win over sympathizers.

Not the way to win us over, either, but he did not appear concerned with that.

"You can't be here." The dope showed no sign of recognizing he wore the perfect face-blocker on his head—that's how unaccustomed he was to cowboy attire, including his hat. "This is private property."

"Yeah," Wendy said to him. "*My* private property. Not yours."

With the advantage of the property owner viewing me momentarily as a friend as a result of the-enemy-of-my-enemy alchemy, I quickly said, "If you'd answer our questions—"

"No reason I should and no reason to let you film me. If you won't leave, I will. *We* will." He moved toward that vehicle that hadn't been here yesterday, with enough bells and whistles to nearly mask the pickup underneath.

Robin stayed put.

"She said you're doing a piece on Keefe. He was a real good guy. Make sure you say that and—"

Until she spoke, I didn't realize I'd expected at some level that she would whine. She did not. Her voice was neutral, though quick.

"We are. You know him. When did you last talk to him?"

"Yesterday. We came up here and—"

"Robin, be quiet. You have no idea how these things work and—"

"How what works? Keefe's dead. Dead." Her voice broke.

"And that's a shame. But I'm still going to buy this ranch for you and that—"

"Not for me. For yourself."

"—should make you happy, since this place is so almighty important to you. This place that *transformed* you." With the twist of that word, the crack in the façade of his gratitude widened to a chasm. "And you go off with a stranger—won't say a word to me, but you'll talk to him. Tell him everything. Proclaiming me an ogre, telling him—"

"We didn't talk. Not about you. Not about me. Not about anything. That was the *point*. Just to be with him and *not* talk."

"They were like this yesterday, too," Brenda said to the universe. "Keefe tried to square things between the two of them best he could, telling them over and over he appreciated them giving him the DNA test, but he's not—wasn't—the best with people and he—" Her hat tipped toward Randall. "—wouldn't shut up. And she—" Toward Robin now. "—wouldn't talk."

Randall Kenyon was here the day before the shooting. *Interesting.*

"Shut up, Brenda." Wendy's words didn't have much heat this time. Maybe she'd abandoned all hope of quieting Brenda.

Randall had another idea. He backtracked to wrap a hand around his stationary daughter's arm just above the elbow. "C'mon, Robin."

"You gave Keefe a DNA test?"

Neither showed any sign that I'd spoken.

Robin said, "I want to stay."

"No. We're going."

This time he tugged.

She didn't resist a lot beyond grimaces and *RAN-dalls* that made up for the previous lack of whiny. Those *RAN-dalls* were ostensibly on our side, so I can only imagine they sounded worse to him. Along with being called by his first name rather than Dad or Father or Pops—No, he wasn't a Pops type.

He might even be the type to tell his daughter to call him by his first name so he'd seemed younger.

He had her bundled into the passenger seat quickly, went around the back of the vehicle, and got in behind the steering wheel.

Diana, who'd kept shooting, raised a questioning eyebrow at me without removing her focus from getting the shot.

She'd do what she thought best, but I nodded anyway.

Even when the pickup started toward the bridge and the way out, she stepped into the center of the drive, where he couldn't help but see her in his rear-view mirror.

How fast could the guy throw it in reverse and—"Diana . . ."

"No worries," she said. "They're gone."

With the pickup out of sight and her returning toward us, I met her halfway. "Diana . . ." was all I got out.

"Making a point. He nearly touched my camera lens. Nobody but me touches this lens."

Turning back to the others, who'd remained in their spots, I said, "Interesting conversation. But *are* you raising cattle? I thought this was a guest ranch."

"It's not a guest ranch. It's a dude ranch," Wendy said sharply. "Dudes are what we have here. There's nothing pejorative about the word. It means they don't know ranch life and that's why they're here. You don't go seeing a rancher spending his vacation at Elk Rock. We like dudes. We *love* dudes. We need dudes." The last of those statements rang truer than the others. "That's what we call them and that makes us a *dude* ranch."

Okay . . . I'd stepped into some Wyoming vocabulary controversy I hadn't heard of before. I did it less often these days than when I arrived two years ago, but it still happened. And there was no app to translate.

"Dude ranch," I repeated, an acknowledgment that might also be heard as an apology. I'm getting so tactful I'm going to be recruited by the diplomatic service. "So, no cattle? But you have horses for riding for the—" I swallowed *guests* and said, "—dudes. Where are they?"

"Pastured out for the winter."

"You must need a lot of hands come summertime to help, right?"

"Of course."

"Same people year after year?"

"No."

Brenda expanded on Wendy's brief responses. "We've got a steady pipeline of college kids. We try to keep a mix of those who've been here before with a few new ones so we don't have complete turnover when the older ones graduate and we lose them to year-round jobs. That way the experienced kids help train the new ones. We pin down which ones are coming back, then open for new hires. A lot of times the returners or even alums will recommend their friends. We try to have a few kids who aren't part of that—guess you could call it *legacy*— string. Fresh blood." She chuckled. "Because, just like with breeding cattle or horses, sometimes one line will peter out eventually, so you don't want to rely all on one. Need a couple strings runnin'."

Made sense. Even if it was likening hiring college kids to breeding cattle or horses.

"Did Robin work for you?"

"Her?" Wendy scoffed.

Again, leaving Brenda to fill in. "Told you, she was a guest last summer. Not one anyone would've thought would ever be back, not until after her accident and all that happened. Changed a lot."

Wendy *huh'd.* "Yeah, like her even being with her father."

"She did complain a lot about him. You'd've thought she hated him more than anything to listen to her last summer when she was here."

"She *said* she hated him," Wendy said, disparagingly. "Didn't take any thinking at all."

"It's why she took to Keefe so strongly, I suspect. Opposite of her dad."

Wendy clicked her tongue, expressing scorn nearly as strongly as her snorts did. "Anybody here'd be the opposite of him. Don't get a lot of hard-charging CEO types working at a dude ranch. A few come through our staff who will be that later, but not while they're here. And they don't stick around to work all their lives here, like Keefe did." Her voice changed, shifting toward Chamber of Commerce talk. "That's one reason people come to dude ranches—to get away from all that. Whether it's people trying to get away from the boss for a week or two, or even the boss, trying to get away from the pressures of being the boss."

From what we'd seen of her personality, if she'd gone into another business, Wendy could have been a hard-charging CEO type herself.

Apparently I wasn't the only one thinking along those lines.

"Some of 'em never get away from it because they carry it with them," Brenda spoke under her breath, but plenty loud enough to be heard.

Wendy pretended she hadn't heard. "Sure don't want to surround themselves with more of the same while they're here. So we encourage our staff to be firm when it's a matter of safety and what's good for the horses, but not to be tossing around a lot of orders."

"No danger of that with Keefe." Brenda shook her head slightly. "He wasn't slow." She sounded like she'd defended him from that description and I recalled Wendy's mouthed *sloooow-leeeee* from yesterday. "More like he just wasn't interested in what he wasn't interested in, and a lot of that had to do with the practicalities of life."

"What she's not saying is *she* took care of those practicalities for him, right down to keeping him in clean undies."

A flush swept up Brenda's creped throat, into her cheeks, and up her forehead.

Wendy didn't appear to notice and she clearly wasn't praising Brenda for this. "Laundry, shopping, cleaning his cabin, cooking for him more often than not, too."

"Just helping a friend." From stiff and defensive, her voice strengthened. "Besides, all that left him free to do all the things you needed him doing, especially off-season without other hands around to do your bidding."

"Bidding? You mean trying to keep this place going and keeping both of you in jobs?"

"I didn't mean—"

"You've always resented—"

They both broke off and turned to Diana and me as if we'd just intruded on a private dispute, rather than them airing it in front of us.

Brenda recovered first, which surprised me. And reminded me not to underestimate the woman.

"You want to know why that Kenyon man was here today, you ask her." Brenda jerked her chin in the direction of Wendy.

Brenda clearly had something she wanted to share. If I had to reach it via a *Jeopardy*-style pro forma question, no problem.

"Today? Or the day before yesterday? Why did he come to the ranch?" I asked both of them.

"I have no idea," Wendy said promptly.

"Yes, you do," Brenda immediately disputed. "Same reason both days."

I popped out another question in response to her leading statement. "Why was he here the day before Keefe was shot? Did he see Keefer?"

"Keefer? Why would he see him?" Wendy demanded.

"Well, Robin saw Keefe. Though just for a few minutes, after he came in and before Randall stormed off—sort of like today."

"Why'd he storm off then?"

Before Brenda could use her intake of breath on words, Wendy rolled her eyes and said, "I told you then and I'll tell you now, I didn't know he was coming, I didn't know he was going to try to buy my ranch, and I told him no—N-O."

"He wants to buy the ranch?" That was not a deliberate *Jeopardy*-esque question, but surprise coming out.

"Sure as hell does. Said it bold as brass on Monday."

Before Brenda could say more, Wendy broke in. "And you stopped listening and got all emotional when he said it."

"It *is* emotional when someone wants to buy your home out from under you."

"It's *my* home. And he's trying to buy it from *me*."

"See? So you had been talking to him about it. He said he'd been talking to—"

"He hadn't been talking to *me*. He'd been nosing around into what's none of his business. My *personal* affairs." She jerked her head around to us. "He came here—uninvited. Made an offer to buy Elk Rock Ranch—uninvited. I told him no. By the time I could get that word in, Robin had gone off with Keefe. Randall Kenyon wasn't leaving without his daughter, so I left—went into the barn, mucking out stalls. He followed, but only a short way. I wasn't being real careful with where what I threw out of the stall landed. He got the hint. He got out of my sight. No idea what he did after that."

"Did he leave without his daughter? Or—"

"I'm telling you, I have no idea."

"You must have noticed if his vehicle was still here or not?"

"Left about four-thirty," Brenda said.

"See? There you have it," Wendy said, as if I'd never want any more information. Foolish woman.

"Could he have come back? Would you have heard the vehicle?"

They exchanged a look. For all the friction between them, there also was a communication, a connection built from the decades of close contact.

"Didn't hear it," Wendy said.

In a reversal of roles, Brenda snorted. "You wouldn't have heard it if it parked under your window and revved the engine." She turned toward us. "I didn't hear it and I don't sleep like the dead like her. But . . ."

She drew that out.

"But what, Brenda?" That sort of lubricant to keep people's jaws moving was second nature.

"I wouldn't have heard a vehicle if he had an ounce of brains. Because anybody with an ounce of brains would park right as it got to the bridge. Not only wouldn't make the clattering that crossing the bridge raises, but the creek masks the sound of most vehicles before they get to the bridge. And another thing—" She turned a glare on Wendy. "He's not acting like anybody's told him no about buying Elk Rock."

"I can't help how the man acts," Wendy snapped. "I told him it's not for sale. If he won't listen or doesn't understand the word those two letters make, that's his problem—and yours if you take him with more than a grain of salt."

Wendy jerked her hands up.

"Not my problem. Not how he acts. Not what you think. My problem is getting the tack inventory done. And that's what I'm going to do."

With what might be a signature move, she turned on her boot heel as she had yesterday, though this time she headed toward a lean-to structure alongside the barn.

CHAPTER THIRTEEN

I HALF EXPECTED Brenda to complete a similar maneuver—though likely in the opposite direction.

Instead, she said, "Don't let her getting sharp about calling this a guest ranch bother you any. A lot of folks use the terms interchangeably."

"But not Wendy."

"No."

"How does she differentiate?"

"Well, she told you her definition of a dude ranch—that's us. Having people pay to come here and get a flavor of being on a ranch. Not enough to choke them, mind you. But also not having folks loll around on deck chairs being fed strawberries by hand right into their mouths like some of those spa places."

"So, a middle-of-the-road dude ranch."

She smiled and nodded. "Pretty much. Now a guest ranch, to Wendy's thinking is a ranch that has guests come. And guests don't pay because . . . well, they're guests. So, yeah, there are some rich folks with ranches who invite friends and family to spend time, sometimes lots of time, with them. And to Wendy, those are guest ranches."

Some rich folks . . . But not her?

Interesting.

"Is that how other people separate the terms, too?" Best to be sure of the definitions for my Wyoming Speak dictionary.

"Pretty much from what I've heard. In fact, you could say that's how dude ranches came to be. You heard about that?"

"I haven't."

It was an invitation to repair my ignorance and she did.

"Three brothers called Eaton from Pennsylvania bought a ranch in the Dakota Badlands. Loved it so much they were writing letters to their friends back east telling them how wonderful it was, and inviting them to come visit—as guests. One of those letters got in a New York newspaper where a guy named Teddy Roosevelt—" Her mouth quirked in self-deprecating humor. "—read it and he got himself right out there. Loved it so much he bought his own ranch in the area, became friends with the Eatons, then wrote a book about it.

"Trouble was, they were becoming victims of their own success and the view in Western hospitality is that a guest didn't pay. They figured one year that they'd fed 2,200 free meals. Throw in some winters bad enough to cut their livestock count near to the quick, a depression in the mid-1890s, and the spread of railroads dropping cattle prices, and ranchers were hurting. They set out their first guest book and charged ten dollars a week. By 1903, they left the Badlands and bought a place outside Sheridan—Wolf Creek. Been there ever since. Considered the granddaddy of all dude ranches.

"And the thing is, the railroads spreading out that dropped the cattle prices and hurt ranchers that way, also made it possible to bring in more visitors—dudes. Keefe used to say that's the way it was with a lot of things. What looks like all a good thing will turn out to have dark shadows. And what looks like it's all black clouds will have sunlight just behind it.

"But as I said to start, not everybody sees a difference."

"Thank you. Very interesting history." And more succinct than I'd get from Mrs. P. Which was precisely one of those situations she'd just described—faster but less detailed information. "Sounds like Keefe was something of a philosopher."

"If that means he liked to talk your ear off, then he most definitely was not a philosopher." Hard to tell if her chuckle was at her own witticism or fond memory of Keefe. "I sure wouldn't ever accuse him of being the sort Robin talked about." A quick spasm of distaste wrinkled her nose.

"What sort is that?"

"All the new age nonsense. Finding yourself and all that. To Keefe, you were yourself all the time, up or down, sideways or heading straight. Still all yourself, so nothing to find."

"A practical philosopher, then . . . A modern-day Will Rogers."

Her brow wrinkled more strongly than her nose had. "Don't know any Will Rogers. Is he from around here?"

Her question caught me off-guard. "I don't think so, but I don't know." Surely I'd have heard about it by now if he was from Wyoming.

She shifted, as if about to stand, so I quickly said, "Do you think Keefe's approach—his philosophical approach helped him with the situation when Robin Kenyon got hurt last season?"

"Could have, I suppose. Something sure did help that girl. Never seen anything like it."

She wanted to talk about this. I settled back with my most encouraging *tell me* expression.

"She'd been there five days and she still didn't know the names of any of the rest of the guests or the employees. She didn't even know the name of her horse." That, clearly, was the greatest sin.

"I'm taking a group out because the regular wrangler was off. Small group, parents and one kid, low-key. Keefe tagging along. No big deal. Not until Robin comes charging up on us, tries to pass when there's not room—and she wasn't supposed to be on one of our horses at all. She nearly pushed the kid right off the trail, over the edge, but his horse hipped-checked Rio at the same time he stepped back. With her sawing at Rio's mouth, Rio turned around, facing the wrong way, then she just went sideways off him. Could have gone all the way down if there hadn't been a sort of bank of rocks right there.

"I grabbed Rio's reins and Buck's—that was the kid's mount, not that he was going anywhere. He's called Buck because he doesn't. Doesn't do much of anything. Anyway, Keefe got down and got to her, while she's screaming her head off. Not in pain. Angry. Furious. Saying Rio threw her, he was vicious, we had to destroy him, all this rot. Keefe felt her leg—her thigh—and she was screaming about that, too. How dare he touch her. Didn't even stop when he said it was broken. She said—screamed—that she didn't believe him.

"By this time, the kid was crying and the mother was trying to hug her, but their horses didn't cooperate, and the father's shouting at Robin, because her language . . . well, what comes after blue? Because she said things I'd never heard in real life before. I got the horses straightened out. Keefe and I, with some help from the father after Keefe said a couple things to him, got her stretched out fairly comfortable, slit her pant leg where it was already swelling, and splinted it with what we had to hold it some.

"We didn't have any connection at all, not even with our good radios, not even when we sent the father down the trail some to see if that helped. Keefe and I sorted it out that he'd stay with her. I'd go down with the parents and kid, keep trying to reach the ranch. Felt like I was almost on the doorstep before I finally got through, though my brain knows that wasn't true. People at the ranch called for help. And by the time I got back in with the parents and kid, the first search and rescue folks were there."

"Not EMTs?"

"They have that training, too, but for where she was at, no vehicle was going to work. Had to get her out before she could really be treated. I led them back up to make sure they got the right trail. It was closing in on dark before they got her out on one of those single-wheel stretchers."

"How was Robin then? More of the same?"

Her brows crinkled into a jagged, quizzical line. "No. She was quiet. Real quiet. And not like she'd passed out or anything. More like . . . Serene. She was *serene*. Anyway—" She stood.

Before she could say it was time for her to get to work, I said, "It's fascinating to hear about the lifelong associations with Elk Rock Ranch—yours, Keefe's, Wendy's—"

"She never set foot here until years and years later than me."

She'd said that before. It clearly rankled her to not have that acknowledged. But Keefe had been here first. Had that rankled, too?

She started walking. We followed along.

"To know all the history and connections . . ." I left it open-ended.

"Like I said, Chester took me in. Didn't need anything formal like an adoption or such. He was a good man who saw the daughter of his friends needed a place to land and provided it. I've always loved the place. And Keefe was my pal from the start."

She cleared her throat.

"Was he always interested in his family history?"

"I suppose. He felt it sometimes, not knowing who his father was. Used to talk about how sometimes in nature the father's not involved with the kids. But the way he'd say it . . ."

"Ulla—that was his mom. Ulla Dobey. She always said her name meant determination or willpower in Finnish, but Chester would say right back it meant flat-out stubborn. Anyway, she sort of told Keefe—hinted, you could say—that his father was special. I've wondered if that's what started him on, you know, all this history stuff. I never heard her say it, but he told me, more than once. Never told anybody else, I ever heard of."

Her gaze shifted toward the barn and back.

"Was his mother Finnish?" I asked. Had that started Keefe on the path of thinking—hoping—Oscar Virtanen could have been his ancestor?

She lifted a shoulder. "Never heard her say that, or if I did, it didn't sink in. Only that part about what her name meant."

"He seemed to be interested in a treasure associated with his possible ancestors," I said. Though how Ulla saying Keefe's father's family had money meshed with Ulla having Finnish roots and possibly being associated with Virtanen and through him the treasure, I didn't know.

"Did he talk about anyone else looking into Oscar and Pearl Virtanen? Maybe about the treasure."

She frowned. "Some guy from over by Red Sail Rock. He was at Keefe's cabin a time or two. Don't know any more about it. But don't go thinking Keefe was chasing money. He wanted to know who his people were. He didn't care about the money. Besides, he knew he could come to me if he needed money, needed anything." From strong, her voice dipped to near despair. "And now look."

We'd cleared the corner of the barn and Keefe's cabin came into view. The police tape flapping looser after a day of Wyoming wind, the dog at the same spot on the porch.

"The one thing he'd want done would be to look after Suzie Q, but she won't eat, won't move." Brenda shook her head. "Keefe always said that if they weren't outside most of the day she was impossible to live with. Told how when he got the flu one winter, he dragged himself out of bed to make sure she got fed and watered and let out, but by the third day, she was standing on his bed, staring down at him, practically willing him to get up and get them both back to work. And now this . . ."

Another head shake.

"Gotta get her fresh water before I get back to work. See ya."

CHAPTER FOURTEEN

WE TOOK THE long way back to our vehicles by going around the barn.

On the far side, double doors in the lean-to attachment to the barn were open, revealing racks of saddles, harness, bridles, and other horse equipment.

Okay, not the technical name. My riding, which was nonexistent when I arrived in Cottonwood County, had improved under the combined tutelage of Tom and Tamantha sufficiently that I'd graduated from a sweetly sluggish creature named Babe to my Christmas present of Slinger. Also sweet, but not sluggish.

My knowledge of horse paraphernalia still lagged.

Wendy came into view from the left.

She frowned at us. "Oh, it's you."

Impossible to deny that.

"Suppose Brenda's been bending your ear. It's what she's best at. All about how she's lived here so long. Doesn't make her the owner. I am. And she has no right to complain. Her family had a ranch. They sold it."

Remembering Brenda said her parents died in a crash, that seemed harsh. I'd heard a lot of harsh from a lot of people over the years and I was confident I didn't betray any reaction. Diana's face was obscured by the camera and she kept her reactions professionally under wraps. So, perhaps Wendy's conscience prompted the next words.

"Well, people sold it for her after her parents died. And I guess you could say that was understandable because she wasn't that old, not nearly old enough to run a place—if she ever could have been. But that doesn't mean she gets to come to this ranch and think it belongs to her.

"Besides, I earned this place. I worked, I learned, then I ran the place well before it was mine. And in the end, I cared for Uncle Chester. Me. Not some high-priced facility like my brothers put our father, then our mother in. I washed him and changed him and fed him, and put up with—. He was a disgusting old man. And being my uncle, too."

"You mean—"

"No. There was never sex. No." She pulled back from a near-shout. "He groped me. Hands on my bust. Tried it all the time. Trying to feed him or whatever and there those hands would be. All over. Had to slap them away. Wasn't until the last couple days he was too weak to do much about it that it got easier. So, yes, I earned it. This ranch is *mine*."

"What about your brothers? Do they have any part in ownership—"

"No. I said. *It's mine*."

"Do they visit or—?"

"No. They don't ask and I don't invite them. It's too real, too rough for them. They have what they want around Jackson. Pretend they're in the real west by looking out their windows at the mountains while they're lifting their little fingers to drink tea or shove a little ball around an indoor putting green. Never get their hands dirty, never put their backs into it."

With that she turned her back to us, prepared to get her hands dirty. Dirtier.

AS WE DROVE toward Sherman in our separate vehicles, Diana and I agreed we'd stop for lunch on the west side of town.

There we set out a plan for the rest of the afternoon, with messages to Mike and Jennifer for a conversation later. It would have to wrap up in time for me to pick up Tamantha—not after classes ended, but later, because she always had something extra going on.

That left a chunk of time now.

Jennifer sent back a message saying the Kenyons were staying at the B&B. Perfect timing.

A few phone calls set up our fortunate first stop. The second one would be made with no warning.

I won the next battle, so we left the NewsMobile at KWMT's parking lot and Diana got into my SUV.

OUR FIRST STOP was fortunate because our first phone call identified who we needed to talk to and the second informed us where he was right now.

Our quarry was one of the county's few full-time fire district employees. If it weren't for volunteer firefighters, this county would be an ash pit. And he was at the fire department offices, the next door down from the sheriff's department.

We wanted him not because he served the fire department, but because he volunteered for the all-volunteer search and rescue group. He'd led the group that went to Elk Rock Ranch to bring in Robin Kenyon last year.

We were doubly fortunate because he wasn't at the sheriff's department, which oversees the search and rescue group, and thus potentially under Shelton's ever-watchful eyes.

As it was, Diana and I looked around for any sign of Shelton before parking in their shared lot and walking with dispatch past the sheriff's department.

Miller Fernard had an impressive mustache and salt-and-pepper hair. He made me think of my grandfather's expression that someone was as brown and tough as a nut.

We told him we were doing the piece on Keefer Dobey and wanted to include Robin's accident and his response—both true. He immediately agreed, saying Keefe deserved it and the search and rescue group could use the mention and possible donations.

We got plenty of good footage on those topics.

Not until the end, with Diana occupying far more time than usual in putting away her equipment, did I bring the conversation to Robin Kenyon's reaction.

"We were warned going up that she could be a handful. But she was quiet as could be. Although by that time, she had to be in a lot of pain," he said.

"Adrenaline worn off by then," I suggested.

"Yup. Along with a bunch of other chemicals your body pumps out trying to protect you—sending more blood here, less blood there, heightening some nerve-endings, speeding up the brain. Gets a lot of people through that first stretch. Then those chemicals start ebbing away and that's when the fun really starts." His voice went dry. "That's often about the time we show up. Was the case for her, for sure. Even when we resplinted her, she held on. And the trip down was no pool slide, unless your slide's made out of rocks. But she held it together. Pretty impressive, really."

"Did she talk at all?"

"Not much. She did say thank you. And she wanted us to thank Keefe." His brows quirked slightly. "And Suzie Q, Keefe's dog."

✧   ✧   ✧   ✧

A RED DOOR, white trim, and dark gray roof set off the Wild Horses Bed and Breakfast's light gray siding.

We skipped the red front door for the back door, where we knocked lightly. If a guest was in a public area, coming in this way made it easier to catch them unaware . . . if anyone was back here and willing to let us in.

Krista Seger, the owner along with her somewhat-but-how-much-estranged husband, was there in the kitchen and did let us in. Though her feeling of indebtedness to us for previous consideration might be wearing thin, considering her slight eye-roll.

Still, she let us in and murmured, "Front room."

She didn't look up from placing some sort of dough in pans, presumably for the next day's breakfast. Judging by other prepared pans it had lots of cinnamon. I might find a reason to return tomorrow to see if there were leftovers.

Randall Kenyon also didn't look up immediately when we entered the sunroom. His lowered chin tucked under the upper fold of the neckerchief he still wore, reestablishing the masked-outlaw vibe.

Eventually recognizing that ignoring didn't make the new arrivals go away, he looked up.

I smiled warmly. He did not. "I'm not talking to you."

It was presumptuous of Randall Kenyon to assume we'd come to see him. True, but presumptuous.

"We come in peace."

"No camera," Diana added, showing both her hands.

Both of our phones were recording, however. Mine with a tiny mic outside of the coat pocket that held the phone.

"We've heard about your daughter's experience at Elk Rock Ranch last year. We'd like your view on it."

Robin seemed to view it as . . . beneficial. But a parent could easily get hung up on the damage and pain she went through. And *pain and suffering* could trip off the tongue of anyone passably familiar with the civil court system, which I would suspect Randall was.

"Did you have any issue with Keefer or—?"

"Keefer Dobey was the hero. He took care of Robin."

Okay, but he could still hold Keefe accountable for the accident in the first place. Especially if the staccato delivery of those sentiments about Keefe as a hero translated to resentment, anger, or something else negative.

"Did you consider suing?"

"Suing? Hell, no. Gave the guy that DNA test, didn't I? Or Robin did."

"Why?"

"What do you mean, why? Because he wanted to take one. As for me, I wanted to buy the place. *Still* want to buy it, even with Keefe gone. Though I really wish—No use wishing. No Keefer Dobey. That means the loss of a major asset—"

Not the most sentimental way to view a man, especially a murdered man.

"—but I still want Elk Rock Ranch."

"Why?" He did not strike me as someone with youthful cowboy dreams.

"Isn't it obvious? Well maybe it isn't to you." We'd been dissed and dismissed. "For starters, I'd get every friend, neighbor, colleague, and acquaintance back home to send their kids here. And that's without taking it to the next level with investors and professional management. We could make a fortune. And help those kids," he added belatedly.

He had not told that to Wendy or Brenda. He'd have been met with pitchforks if not shotguns.

"What makes you think that could work?"

"Robin. She came back from that place a completely changed person. It was like I sent off a spoiled six-year-old with a platinum credit card and no judgment and got back an adult who could look beyond herself. It was miraculous. Of course I want to buy the place."

"Not such a miracle for Keefe," I said slowly.

"What does that mean?"

I didn't back down from his belligerence, but didn't escalate, either.

"You showed up at the ranch, wanting to buy the place and he was dead that night. Unless that wasn't your first day in Cottonwood County."

An impatient shoulder hitch indicated it was, but it didn't matter— to him.

Half my mind had already taken another tack.

Considering the emotions from Brenda and Wendy—and Keefer, maybe?—it might have made more sense the other way around, that Randall showed up wanting to buy Elk Rock Ranch and *he* was dead a short time later.

Shot by Keefe? That might be a stretch from what we'd heard of him, though he clearly was protective of the place. And by that, I don't mean just the acreage of the ranch, but the wildness around it, its unique nature.

Maybe you feel that way about wherever you grow up if you really connected with the surroundings. I know I felt something chest-expanding when I saw the open fields and rich soil of Illinois. I'd heard others say it of swamps, of coasts, of mountains. Some visceral connection between human and non-human. Maybe that's why they said a baby had to eat a peck of dirt—not only to up the immune system, but to seal that bond with the earth they came from.

So, I could stretch my impression of Keefer Dobey to switch the outcome and include his shooting someone three times in the head to protect what he loved. Barely.

As for Brenda and Wendy?

No stretch required.

But that was all theoretical with Randall Kenyon sitting in front of me, very much alive.

"Coincidences happen," he said.

"Homicide detectives often say there's no such thing as coincidence."

"Bull."

Did he really think that overrode the truism of experienced homicide investigators?

Yeah, he did.

He was wrong, but that's what he thought.

I wondered how much his failure to see reality contributed to his success in business. It could make someone just keep plowing ahead.

On the other side, what did that approach do for—or to—relationships?

"You said you gave Keefe a DNA test because he wanted to take one. Do you know why?"

He looked at me like I was an idiot.

"Didn't matter why. He told Robin all about it while they were up there communing. She got the idea, and we did it. Thought it was the best company, considered investing in it, but HelixKin's taking way longer than they should have. So much for them getting my investment dollars." Abruptly, he shouted, "Hey! Karen, Kathy, Kirsten, whatever your name is."

Krista appeared at the doorway behind us.

"I have a business call. I'm going upstairs. See that I'm not disturbed," he added with a stern look at Krista and a glare for Diana and me.

CHAPTER FIFTEEN

WHEN HE'D CLEARED earshot, I said to Krista, "Which room is Robin in?"

"Oh, no you don't." She moved to the center of the doorway, though we easily could have broken past her. "Not letting you disturb a guest in her room."

Especially not with her contentious father nearby.

I didn't say it. Couldn't really blame her.

Diana and I looked at her without saying anything.

"Okay, okay. I'll go see if she wants to talk to you down here." Away from Randall, which suited us, too. "This *is* about Keefe's death, isn't it?"

"Yes."

Robin came down the stairs behind Krista. Moving slowly, as if reluctant to join us, but her face was intent, interested.

This could go either way. Fast.

"Hi, Robin. We didn't have a chance to officially meet earlier. I'm Elizabeth Margaret Danniher and this is Diana Stendahl. We're from KWMT, the local TV station. We hoped you could give us some background, since you were a guest at Elk Rock Ranch."

She relaxed some. More important, she came into the room and sat across from us.

Was that reaction because my intro moved us away from Keefe's death? Away from Keefe? Away from a time when her father was around?

"Because you were at the ranch as a guest, you can give us some perspectives no one else can."

"Like what?"

Good question. Especially since I didn't want to jump into the meat too soon.

"Like if Wendy is a really sound sleeper."

Her mouth sagged slightly.

"Brenda said Wendy's such a deep sleeper that she'd never hear—" Not the time to bring up gunshots. "—a ruckus at the ranch at night. Say, a dog barking."

"She doesn't have a dog."

"True, but there's Suzie Q."

She relaxed more. "Oh, Suzie Q didn't bark at any of us at Elk Rock. Not the guests, not the workers."

I came at it from a different angle.

"What do you know about Wendy's and Brenda's sleeping habits?"

She snapped her head around toward me. "The two of them—? God, *nothing*. I had no idea."

"You still don't." I could have tried to explain that if I'd meant the two of them together, I'd have said *Wendy and Brenda's*—one possessive apostrophe "s" for the unit. Giving each an apostrophe "s" kept them singular and separate. But I didn't think that grammatical nicety would have made an impression on her. "Sleeping, as in waking up easily."

"Oh. Why didn't you say that," she grumbled. "How should I know?"

"You were here for a week last summer. You had opportunities to observe."

Opportunities, yes. Inclination, probably not. With this a lost cause. I should—

"There was one night," she said abruptly. "Maybe the second night I was there. Some kid started screaming. Guess it was a nightmare, but nobody knew that at the time and everybody came running out of their cabins—you would not believe some of the outfits people had on. Including Keefe in long underwear. Seriously. Long underwear like you'd see someone from *centuries* ago wearing." As she spoke of the night, her intonations seemed to recall her attitudes from that time.

"And Brenda? She was something from a horror movie, with this stuff all over her face. As if anyone couldn't tell her it was way, way late for that. And a pair of men's pajamas, with her feet stuck into her cowboy boots, but not all the way, so she walked like a duck in high heels."

Without moving her feet, she mimicked an awkward, rolling gait, then giggled.

"Anything else?" I asked the question out of an obligation to be thorough. My coolness was for the mean girl/woman she'd been then. The jury was out on now.

"Yeah. What you asked about. Did I notice something? I noticed Wendy didn't come out. Only one who didn't make an appearance, except a honeymoon couple in the farthest cabin. But this kid was in one of those cabins just across from the main house."

So, either Wendy had the steely nerves to not react to a screaming child or she slept like—excuse the expression—the dead, as Brenda reported.

"You said Suzie Q doesn't bark. Not even after you were hurt?"

"No." It didn't have the feel of a complete sentence. "It was mostly quiet up there with Keefe. Except . . . Suzie Q was one of the things he did talk about when he talked now and then.

"He said when he first got her, she barked at everything and everybody. Wendy didn't like that—thought it made the guests feel unwelcomed. She was threatening that he'd have to give up the dog. He said that one day, in desperation, he sat down with the dog and explained the whole situation and what the consequences would be. And he said she stopped barking right then." She smiled, signaling her disbelief in the story.

"Even if she was left alone?"

"She wasn't, as far as I knew. She was at his side whatever he was doing. Whenever I saw him go out on the trail, Suzie Q went with."

"Did that bother the guests?"

"Not that I could ever tell." A bit of defensiveness crept in. Because she hadn't interacted with other guests? "I suppose novice riders might have been nervous," she said with superiority over such riders. "Didn't take long to recognize that the horses accepted Suzie Q and trusted her to stay out of their way. And she did.

"She also . . ." She hesitated. "When we were up there, waiting, after . . . Well, she was . . . sweet. She spent almost the whole time lying alongside me. First one side, then the other. It was nice to have the warmth, but even nicer to have her."

"You were grateful to her—and Keefe. Is that why you and your dad gave him the DNA test?"

"Yeah. Mom used to say that to thank people you gave them what they wanted, not what was easy for you." She ducked her head slightly. "It was easy, but it was what he really wanted."

"He asked you to get him the DNA test?"

"No. He didn't know anything about them, didn't know what they could find out, how it worked. But I knew that's what he needed— wanted. When I messaged him the test was coming . . . he was so excited." With a faint lift of her lips she added, "I was happy for him. I hoped the results would prove that outlaw was his great-great whatever like he wanted. Now it's too late."

She'd approached the edge of real emotion. By her uneasy shifting, that would not make it easy to get more out of her.

I went businesslike. "Had you also given him a computer?"

"Yeah, but he wasn't any good on it at all. That why I moved on to the DNA test."

"Your father said the results were later than expected."

"He knew that?" She hid the surprise in that by saying immediately, "He messaged me about that—Keefe did, about not having the results."

"Why?"

"He wasn't very good at things like that, apps or on the computer or even on the phone. So I checked with the company right before we came out here. They had a record of sending the results and he should have had them. They said they'd send another set to him."

Sure, do it for a Kenyon, when they'd stonewalled me. Though, in fairness, she was asking for a repeat send to the test-taker, rather than the results. Still . . .

"You told your father Keefer Dobey was the architect of your turnaround."

She frowned. "I never said that."

"Not in so many words, but didn't you say how important that time with Keefe up the trail was to you?"

"Sure. And Keefe was nice, especially because he didn't shout at me, telling me how stupid I was or what I'd done wrong. He just kept quiet. *That* was a nice change."

The sharpness of that gave another glimpse into how she'd been as a guest last season. The staff of Elk Rock Ranch had my retroactive sympathies.

Then she sliced a look toward Diana and me, and my sympathies extended to her.

"Your dad?" Diana asked with perfect neutrality.

"Yeah. After Mom died. Before that, he wasn't that interested in me. It was . . . I was so mad at her for leaving me with him. Dying was a release for her. I knew that. Not just from pain . . ." She stared at her hands for three long breaths, jerked her gaze up to us, then back again. "From him. And, yeah, she was under heavy meds, but she said it more than once. She told me she would have divorced him if she wasn't dying."

Robin wasn't asking for sympathy. She had it. And not just on the tough-on-a-girl to lose her mother at that age level.

Still, how much had her mom known what she was saying? Because that was a heck of a burden to put on your daughter.

Damage to the father-daughter relationship didn't seem to be all Randall's doing.

Although the damage to the relationship with his wife might have been, so indirectly, this, too, could have been his fault.

Chicken or egg. We couldn't know.

"So, yeah, it was a nice change to be up there with Keefe not after me about something, everything.

"I don't remember anything particularly wise he said. He'd be quiet for a long stretch, then he'd ask what I saw. And then sometimes rambling, stories about how to do things I never in my life considered doing or about this outlaw and the woman who loved him and how he'd died and she disappeared, all in this low-key mumble that said it was okay if I didn't listen, it was okay if I did.

"It was . . . *different*. I was different. I don't know how to explain it."

She shifted. "Maybe it was the physical pain. Finally feeling in my body the way it felt inside. I was back in sync. Pieces of me together again. From looking up at the tops of the trees and the sky."

We let her be quiet for as long as she wanted.

"The weird thing is, as I got better physically and that pain mostly went away, so did a lot of the other pain. I never expected that. Not all of it went away—either kind of pain. They say I might be able to predict changing weather patterns with my leg for the rest of my life. Just like I still feel sudden jolts or lingering aches of Mom dying. But I can walk and I can ride and I can live."

She said again, "I don't know how to explain it." This time, she added, "But I don't need to."

We'd just encountered her father in her.

AS WE LEFT by the back door, we said thanks to Krista, and I added a question. "Were Randall and Robin here all Monday night?"

She pursed her lips, then a quick headshake.

For a second I thought—

"No way I can know one way or the other. We're in the private quarters and unless a guest calls us, or a fire alarm goes off, we don't have contact until the morning. Privacy for them, privacy for us."

I had to accept that her headshake was that the question didn't apply to her.

CHAPTER SIXTEEN

ON THE OTHER end of the video call, Mike and Jennifer were eating pizza at his Evanston apartment, just north of Chicago.

Diana and I, in the KWMT office officially designated as the news director's, and unofficially Mike's temporarily, were not eating pizza. Being around Tamantha and Tom I'd been conscious of trying to eat healthier meals. Right now, I wished I were in Evanston with the other two, at least for the pizza.

I had started with condensed versions of my trips yesterday to the library, museum, and Mrs. P, as well as today's to the McCracken place.

Diana had put out feelers, but didn't have anything back yet from her sources. Aunt Gee hadn't yet responded to Mike, either.

Jennifer reported on Randall Kenyon's business holdings and financial position.

Mike whistled. "Why's he bothering with a dude ranch in Cottonwood County? He's up there with the Barlows."

"General view was he was a money-making machine until his wife died two years ago," Jennifer said. "Then it's divided about whether he's been distracted because of her death, because of his daughter becoming a problem or both. It's not like he's in trouble—or his businesses—but people talk about if his golden touch is gone."

I caught the group up on my futile pursuit of the DNA test results.

"But would Keefe be that excited if the results hadn't arrived?" Diana asked.

"Pre-excited, maybe?" Jennifer suggested. "Sounds like he tended that way on the topic of Oscar Virtanen."

"What it comes down to is, he could have already received the results or he hadn't—Don't say it, Paycik." He closed his mouth on the obvious rejoinder I'd opened myself up to. "The point is, we follow up on the DNA test."

"If he didn't get the test already, it's pretty much up to law enforcement to pry the results out of the company, right?" Jennifer asked.

"Pretty much. Although we could consider asking Robin and/or her father to see if they have any standing as the purchasers of the test to get the result."

"Could consider," Diana said thoughtfully. "That's not exactly gung-ho, Elizabeth."

"If one of them is involved—or both of them—with his murder that could muddy the waters," Mike said. "I'd think especially if how they got the information became a legally contested issue."

"Exactly," I answered the first part and ignored the ending. "Then, in the other possibility for those test results—that Keefe did receive them—it gets really interesting. Because that means someone took them and—"

"Or he burned them because they weren't what he wanted," Jennifer jumped in to add. "Although it doesn't have to have been burned. He could have thrown them out long enough before he was killed that they've already been recycled or whatever."

"Possible," I conceded. "Though Brenda said—"

"Brenda said?" Jennifer repeated with an undercurrent.

"—he was excited the day before his death, so he wouldn't have had time to dispose of them."

"Having them taken by someone else is a lot better clue to follow than the dump," Mike said.

I couldn't deny the truth of that. "Yeah, we'll leave Shelton and company to pursue that aspect if that's what it comes to. So the question becomes what about those tests would have been worth killing Keefe for?"

"The connection to Oscar Virtanen," Mike said immediately.

"But why? We come back to being proven a descendant of Mr. and

Mrs. Virtanen wouldn't—"

"You're not calling them Pearl and Oscar, like Bonnie and Clyde?" Diana asked.

I'd been showing off—at least to myself—my first grasp on their last names. "They were more formal in the nineteenth century, but if you insist . . . being proven a descendant of Oscar and Pearl wouldn't give him an immediate open sesame to the so-called treasure."

"Some of these people don't care about the money. They're just interested in the history, in the mystique," Mike said.

"The mystique of some old bank robber?" Jennifer asked. "I get wanting the treasure—if there is one—but so what if his great-whatever grandfather was a bank robber?"

"Better than a ditch-digger."

"No it isn't," she said. "Ditch-diggers could be honorable, good, and interesting people."

"Yes, they could." Diana's agreement calmed her down. "But put yourself in Keefe's position. Unlike you, he didn't have any family left. No connections to his father's family we know of and his mother was gone. It would be interesting to be descended from someone who was famous, even if that was mostly infamy."

"Besides, a lot of sources say some of those guys were considered good guys in the day," Mike said. "Like it was said Butch Cassidy said none of his guys were to rob individuals. They robbed companies—the railroads, the banks—not the normal people."

I told them what I'd learned from Mrs. P—the little that connected to this case—and had the distinct feeling it was all old news to them.

We moved on to discussing yesterday's video of Brenda and Wendy. Diana had already sent them today's footage from Elk Rock Ranch and we'd recapped the conversations with the EMT from Robin's accident, then Randall and Robin at the B&B.

"Would you say Brenda didn't like Wendy's comment about her taking care of Keefe?" I asked Diana.

"I would. The interesting question was if she didn't like it simply because it was telling a couple strangers—"

"And our viewership, whatever that might be."

"Yeah, I thought that stung you. But the viewership sees it only if we put it out there and Brenda's reaction was immediate. She never even looked at the camera, so I still wonder if it was having the audience of a couple strangers or if the sting came from something else."

"You think she had other feelings about Keefe?" I asked.

"Possibly. On the other side of that, she was—overall—fairly calm about this death. A few tears, but no wailing or gnashing of teeth."

"The response of a murderer who knows she should be upset, but doesn't really feel any loss?" Mike asked.

"I'll repeat what I just said—possibly. Wendy certainly didn't seem to have anything of that in her reaction."

"No. Wendy's was more practical."

Diana nodded. "And practical could be a problem for her. Keefe did an awful lot around there, knew everything about the place, and kept it ticking over. Even if she finds someone satisfied with living year-round there like he did and likely not being paid a lot, I'd think it would take a long time to train them."

"No motive for her," Mike said. "Either of them, maybe, if his death means a lot more work comes down on Brenda."

I held up a wait-a-second finger. "We don't rely on what either of them says without support. But before we get too tied into being sure this had to have something to do with his life at the dude ranch, I was trying to think of motives for his murder centered around what Keefe did."

Jennifer looked up, frowning. "But that's working on a dude ranch."

"Wider than that. Something he saw or heard that he wasn't supposed to."

"I thought he spent most of his time outdoors," she said.

"I like that," Mike said. "A contract killer took a vacation at a dude ranch and Keefe heard him taking on his next assignment. No, wait, too big a time gap from when the last guests left until Keefe was killed. So, he heard the assignment to kill somebody famous, the hired killer turned it down, but then he reconsidered and he plans to do it sometime in the future now, so he had to come back and kill Keefe before the contract kill, so Keefe didn't react when he heard about the death. Or maybe he got someone else to kill Keefe, because it's a conspiracy that's going to take down the country, take down the whole free world and—"

"You've been binging old *Mission: Impossible* re-runs again, haven't you, Mike?" Diana asked.

"Maybe."

"Don't worry, there'll be another conspiracy threatening the country, the free world, the planet, the universe next week."

"Yeah, I know," he said a bit sheepishly. "But, seriously, what could Keefe have seen or heard during the winter, living on that ranch?"

"I don't know, but we don't rule out the possibility." I argued.

"You said Ivy said he spent a lot of time at the library," Diana said.

"Yeah, that hotbed of crime," Mike muttered before another bite of pizza.

"Something to keep in mind." I recounted my conversation with Serena McCracken.

"Not much there," Mike said.

"Yet," Diana tagged on.

I agreed with both of them. "At the same time, if Keefe wasn't killed for what he did—including seeing, hearing—it seems the alternative is he was killed for who he was. But that seems far-fetched, too."

"Maybe even more far-fetched than Mike's scenario," Diana said. "Mild-mannered. No conflict with anyone. Heck, didn't mix with that many people except the guests during the season, which ended six months ago."

"Something personal," Jennifer proposed. "Like you were talking about—Brenda, maybe from unrequited love."

"But why now and not any time in what sounds to be like the past three decades?"

"Three," I repeated musingly. "He was shot three times. That was interesting. Why three times?"

"They wanted to be sure they sent him to a better place?" Diana said with a glint of mischief.

"Oh, like Brenda said," Jennifer said.

I growled.

I might have been around Shelton too much.

"You should have seen Elizabeth's face when Brenda said that," Diana told the other two. "Mount Vesuvius . . . except it didn't blow. Must give her credit for that."

With great dignity I said, "Getting back to his being shot three times, I was thinking that pointed toward a small caliber gun."

"Yup. A big caliber gun and there wouldn't be much left after three shots." Mike folded a pizza slice and consumed a good third of it in one bite.

"Uh-huh. Thanks for pointing that out," Diana said.

"There might be another aspect to the three shots and wanting to make sure he was dead—an element of not wanting him to suffer." I paused, then added dryly, "Other than killing him, of course. But I mean those small caliber shots can rattle around in the brain and cause a lot of damage that might eventually kill somebody, but they can also hang on a long time, first. Keefe left shot on his living room floor to take who knows how long to die? That could make the shooter add extra shots to end it quickly, as well as definitively."

"Which points to someone he knew," Diana said.

"Unless it was a compassionate hired killer," Mike said.

Jennifer scoffed. "A group known for their compassion."

"Making sure he was dead would also be self-preservation. If he were shot once, then found before he died he might have said who shot him. Killer didn't want to leave a witness," Diana said.

I stuck with the broader question. "Do you see someone hiring a killer to come into Cottonwood County to do away with Keefe?"

"Not all hired killers are the high-priced slick type from movies or even the historical figures like Tom Horn."

Led by Mike, the others turned to me.

"Yes, I've heard of Tom Horn." My indignation was meant to hide that while I had heard the name, I tended to confuse it with Roy Bean.

Or was it Roy Horn and Tom Bean?

My answer didn't stop Mike from explaining.

"He was officially a range detective, but it's pretty much agreed he was hired by cattle barons to kill rustlers." He knew as much Wyoming history as Mrs. P—as long it was about bad guys and wild stories.

"I know, I know. As bad as Judge Roy Bean. Hard to tell which side of the law they were on, right? But a hired killer—"

Mike was not to be dragged away from his topic. "Horn bragged about killing men, then he was caught and hanged for the killing of a boy, though a lot of people think he didn't do that one."

"That's fascinating, but—"

"Horn was played by Steve McQueen," Diana said. "Paul Newman played Roy Bean."

Ah. Now *that* was helpful information.

"Who?" Jennifer barely looked up from typing on her phone.

The rest of us glared at her. Didn't matter if she meant one or both. They were well before my prime movie-watching years started, too, but you owed that history the respect of at least a modicum of knowledge.

However, her film education would await another opportunity.

"The point is, Cottonwood County does not seem like a hotbed for hired killers operating a lucrative business," Diana said.

"Well, a while back, there *was* a story about a guy not far from here who tried to hire somebody to kill his ex-wife to make other charges go away where she was the witness," I said. "He offered the supposed contract killer $1,000 from his Covid stimulus check."

"No." Diana's protest sputtered into a laugh.

"Yes. Doing his part to stimulate the economy. And apparently his accomplice was his step-sister . . . who'd just had his baby."

"Eww." Was the consensus reaction to that detail.

I recovered first. "So a contract—of some sort or another—isn't impossible. But it seems far more likely that the killer was acting on his or her own behalf, is local, and had a connection with Keefe."

"That made the killer both ready to kill Keefe and—possibly—not wanting him to suffer more than necessary to die," Diana said dryly.

"That's the theory," I agreed. "For now."

"Under that theory, Brenda being sad doesn't clear her," Jennifer said. "In fact it would make her more likely. Someone who truly liked him and didn't want him to suffer, so shot him three times to be sure it was over."

"And someone with plenty of time and excuse for having messed around with the scene."

"Maybe somebody who cared about the dog, too," Mike said. "I know, it could have been selfish putting the dog out—not wanting a witness, so to speak. Not wanting to risk the dog reacting in a way that pointed a finger—or paw. But it also could be not wanting to traumatize the dog."

"Traumatize her more," I muttered. "Plus, her being outside exposed her to the cold and predators."

"Yeah, I get that." He started to reach for another pizza piece, then stopped. "You know, Brenda being the killer solves the issue of the dog being put outside in a way. She puts Suzie Q out, kills Keefe, then *finds* Suzie Q outside, which meant finding Keefe, which meant lots of authorities. So Suzie Q wasn't out long, wasn't exposed to the cold or predators."

He got a trio of *hmms* in acknowledgment of his points.

"What are you thinking, Diana?" I asked her.

"Brenda's comment about the center cabin blocking her view of Keefe's cabin . . ."

"Uh-huh," I agreed.

"Uh-huh, what?" Jennifer demanded.

"We both think that indicated Brenda likely kept a closer eye on Keefe's cabin and his activities than she'd acknowledged," Diana explained.

"I wondered why you were accepting everything Brenda said. You suspect her," Jennifer said.

"We didn't say—"

Jennifer talked over Diana's protest. "You talked about Brenda seeing the dog outside like you didn't believe it. And if you don't believe that . . ."

I glanced toward Diana. She rolled a shoulder, saying this was mine to answer. "It's not that I believe or don't believe it, necessarily. It was . . . Brenda presented a view of what happened—that somebody other than Keefe put Suzie Q out of the cabin, most likely the killer— and she wanted us to buy it, too. And the more she tried to direct us that way, the more I wondered why."

Jennifer frowned fiercely enough to make me want to warn her of wrinkles-to-come with a reminder of Brenda. "Like she hadn't seen the dog out at all, but went over there and shot him, then raised the alarm and the dog's a red herring?"

My turn to frown fiercely and I was in far more danger of resem- bling Brenda than she was. "That's an interesting question. Because if she did that—shot Keefe with Suzie Q in the cabin—I wonder how she would have reacted."

"She, the dog. Not she, Brenda," Mike said.

"Exactly. The dog. So maybe that lends credence to Brenda's sce- nario. Pretty clear, she was angling to the theory that the killer put Suzie Q out of the cabin, or had Keefe do it, so the dog wouldn't interfere. And Brenda thought that happened hours earlier—"

"If we buy that the dog's coat was cold," Diana inserted.

"Barring Brenda being the killer, I think we do accept that Suzie Q's coat was cold."

"Which would make the killing hours earlier."

"As cold as it's been lately, it could be minutes," I said and got grimaces in return.

"If Brenda's the killer, all bets are off about Suzie Q being out, much less the temp of her coat," Mike said.

He earned murmurs of agreement.

"It would be good to know the time of death," Jennifer mused. "I might be able to—"

"No hacking," Diana and I said together.

Jennifer huffed and said to Diana, "Well, if you'd just ask the sher- iff . . ."

"Not happening."

We might have all turned toward Mike, because he said, "Fine. I'll ask Aunt Gee—if, when I get her. But no guarantees she'll answer."

"So, if we take what Brenda said as true, we're thinking Suzie Q knows who the killer is. We could set up one of those Perry Mason moments when the dog growls and lunges at the guilty party."

"I'd guess that's what the killer was trying to avoid by having the dog outside."

"If Brenda's telling the truth and isn't the killer herself," Mike slid in.

"Even if she's the killer, she might be telling the truth about the dog," I said. "There's also what she'd said about the Kenyons' pickup and that it couldn't have come across the bridge without her knowing. Which is interesting."

"Why interesting? She could have known that for decades, just from living there," Jennifer said.

"Or she thought it through since Keefe's murder," Mike suggested.

"Also true. Or it could be something she'd considered before that night, making sure there was a way for someone else to be on the property without it being unbelievable that neither she nor Wendy heard anything."

"Wendy already has an excuse because—at least according to Brenda—she's an extremely sound sleeper. Partially confirmed by Robin," Diana said.

Jennifer asked with an edge of disbelief, "You think Brenda would lie to cover for Wendy?"

"No," came from the rest of us.

We all shifted positions, shaking off the certainty of that response. We wanted lots and lots of open possibilities at this stage, not to be closing off avenues of thought or investigation.

"Things to keep in mind," Diana said.

"Another one to consider is Randall Kenyon." I turned to Diana. "Remember Wendy saying he was a hard-charging CEO type? I wonder if that stemmed from her unconscious recognition of conflict there—between Kenyon's world and the world of the dude ranch?"

"Or," Diana countered, "because she has tendencies in that direction, too, and has been irritated by Keefe. Remember the *sloooow-leeeee?*"

Before anyone could respond, she said, "But would irritation, even festering for decades, lead to murder?"

None of us had an answer to that.

Jennifer brought us back to Randall Kenyon. "But why would he kill Keefe, when Keefe helped his daughter. Not just staying with her when she got hurt, but what he said about how she changed. Sounds to me like he was grateful."

I considered that. "You can be grateful for what happened—his daughter changing—but not happy that someone else brought about the change. Especially certain types of people."

Jennifer said. "Jealous. He was jealous his daughter connected that way with Keefe."

I tipped my head, then nodded slowly. "Maybe a particular kind of jealous."

"You might have something there, Jennifer," Mike said. "From your accounts, Elizabeth, he was more crediting the place than the man. And the place is something he could buy—try to buy."

"That's good. Both of you. You're right. If he credited the place, he could try to buy it, control it, reshape it. Then it would be like he was the one who helped his daughter, who would help her even more going forward than she'd been helped initially, because he *improved* everything. He doesn't get that he'd have to break each of those kids' bones and leave them for a few hours in the rough country—"

"With a backwoods counselor who's now dead." Mike pointed out.

"—to have a hope of replicating his daughter's transformation."

"Sounds like he thinks he can buy anything. But he couldn't buy Keefe," Diana said.

I turned to her.

"You're staring, Elizabeth," she said.

"I wonder if he tried."

Maybe Keefe's excitement wasn't about the DNA test. Maybe that was a blind and he was going to get a chunk of Randall's money." It didn't make Mike happy to express that possibility.

"No. He thought he'd get rich because he thought he'd be a celebrity as the descendant of Oscar Virtanen," Jennifer argued.

"How would he make money off that? Being confirmed as a descendant of Butch or Sundance, maybe. But Oscar Virtanen? How many people not from around here even know about him."

They all looked at me.

"Not many." I spoke for all of non-Cottonwood County. I probably could have gone out on a limb and said *None.*

"Or how'd he know that he'd find the treasure," Jennifer said. "One he'd have to divide with Sam McCracken."

"If there is a treasure," I said.

"Keefe believed there was one and that's what counts." Diana had a point. And she added to it. "What would Randall Kenyon *buying* Keefe even consist of?"

"For him to go away so Randall could be the complete hero."

"To expect him to leave his lifelong home and—"

Mike interrupted Jennifer. "Oh, Keefe wasn't from here originally."

"Where was he from?" she asked.

"Somewhere back east, I think," Mike said. "Or maybe the West Coast."

In other words, the huge swath of the country that was not Wyoming.

As he went on, I realized I hadn't covered that part of what Brenda told us, "He came here as a kid. Came with his mother when she was brought in as the ranch's cook. Surprised me, too, because it seemed like he was such a part of the place that he'd been there forever. But he told me once that in order for them to stay year-round, he started learning maintenance really young. All the things the place needed during the season and off-season. Wendy and before her, her uncle, would leave for the winter, but Keefe and his mother stayed year-round. Keefe did most of the maintenance and built some of the new cabins. She kept working until the day she died.

"I have a memory of going to services for her as a kid. Dropping my jaw when I saw this big, strong man crying over his mama. Made an impression. Didn't seem to be any question that he'd stay on there, working at Elk Rock, living in that cabin. Wasn't until more recent that

Wendy started to stay more of the year. Used to be gone all winter in Florida or Arizona, someplace like that. Now it's just a couple months from what I hear."

"More to do around the ranch? Harder to find more help?" Jennifer offered.

"Could be. Though everything I heard said they had no trouble hiring. Even with other places begging for workers, the dude ranches seem to do okay. Of course that's the college kids during the season. Might be different off-season."

I jumped back to something that had snagged my interest. "You said yesterday that her uncle left her the Elk Rock Ranch?"

"Yeah. He'd owned it for years. I don't know more about it than that. Leona would."

Oh, yes, she would.

CHAPTER SEVENTEEN

BUT LEONA WAS prepping for the Five and I didn't dare interrupt her to ask questions.

She wasn't above refusing to answer unless I took her place at the anchor desk and I had another evening with Tom and Tamantha ahead—two in a row on weeknights!

Diana showed up beside my desk, just as I started to turn off my computer. "Something secret?"

"No. Getting ready to leave." I was picking up Tamantha after her after-school activity. Which one was a little hazy—I'm new to this parenting stuff—but I knew the time and place and would not be late.

Besides, she'd tell me as soon as she got in the SUV.

"What were you doing?"

"Looking up Will Rogers. I would have guessed he was born in Texas. Good thing I didn't guess."

"Uh-huh."

"He was born and raised in Oklahoma."

"Okay. Is that significant?"

"Probably was to him," I murmured putting together my belongings. "And to Oklahoma. I also hadn't known Will Rogers was Cherokee."

Like me with Will Rogers, Jennifer had assumed Keefer Dobey was from the place she associated him with. Though her assumption was based on the tendency of younger people to think that how it was when they first noticed was how it had always been.

"Let me reframe that question," Diana said. "Is there a reason I need to know about Will Rogers at this moment, a moment in which I'm trying to get out of here to meet Russ for an early dinner at the Haber House Hotel?"

"Sorry. No, no there isn't a reason. We can both head out and—"

"Not yet." She gestured and I sank back into my chair. "Have you told Tom you want to redecorate the ranch house?"

This was what I'd delayed my departure for? "What are you talking about? I don't want to—"

"All those details about how warm and inviting the McCrackens' house was? The comfort and the style? Granted, you don't have to blend the super high ceilings with human scale at the ranch house the way you say Serena McCracken has done so beautifully."

"Might not have been her. Might have been a decorator," I mumbled.

She examined my face, which turned into my profile as I moved my bag to get out my sunglasses. "So, it's not the ranch house. Then . . . *Oh.*"

She remained silent until I looked at her. Sunglasses can only account for so much time. Putting them on would be chicken. I put them on the top of my head and faced her.

"Mike's house?" she asked.

I nodded.

"Which really means Mike."

I shook my head.

She ignored the denial. "First, you do know that being with Tom doesn't mean you stop caring about Mike."

"Of course not. And Tom would never—"

"No, he wouldn't. It's not Tom I'm talking to. Second," she continued without taking a breath, making it hard for me to break in with another denial, because I not only needed a breath, I needed to think through what she'd said, "you are not responsible for taking care of him."

"He's a friend and—"

"He's my friend, too. We support him and we care about him. We don't fret about his house being a gaping cavern that would make a sworn minimalist start grabbing throw-pillows and tchotchkes by the armful. Maybe we fret—a little—about his life being less decorated with a romantic relationship than we'd like, but we do not take on the job of decorating for him.

"And you—Elizabeth Margaret Danniher—do not blame yourself that you don't love him that way."

"I don't. Not really. I know—"

"He'd have been too nice to you, anyway. Would—"

"Hey. Tom's nice to me."

"—have let you keep at least one emotional foot in the cave you'd completely retreated to when you arrived here. Thing is, Tom was in his own cave. Two of you had to both advance to come together. Mike would have accommodated you by being right outside the cave entrance whenever you felt like coming out. You wouldn't have had to put as much on the line."

I'd have to mull over whether she had a point . . . after I shook off the image of Tom and me being cave-dwellers.

"As much as I appreciate your analysis," I said dryly, "I've got to go get Tamantha."

"Uh-huh. Think about it. But you know I'm right."

With that parting shot, she turned, waving over her shoulder as she walked away.

✦ ✦ ✦ ✦

"PROGRESS?" TOM'S QUESTION meant with Keefe's death.

We stood just outside my back door, watching Tamantha and Shadow play in the fast-fading twilight. I was backed up against his chest with his arms around me, which helped fight the cold.

"Before I tell you about that. We have something else to talk about." I tilted up my head. "Grasshoppers. Your mother said there could be *hordes* of grasshoppers." I untilted my head to keep it from getting stuck.

"She said *unless the grasshoppers hit.*"

"You remember exactly what she said?"

"Yes. Because I saw your expression. Thought you might be thinking hordes of grasshoppers."

"Actually," I said with dignity, "the word in my mind then was plagues of grasshoppers. I *downgraded* to hordes. I knew a couple who got married in a park in Washington, D.C., when cicadas were at their worst. The every-seventeen years kind. Their wedding was outside, in the woods. It was crazy. Needed umbrellas to keep them from dropping on our heads, couldn't hear the vows over the whine. Are we going to have to bat away insects throughout our wedding— weddings—and reception?"

"Not going to be outside much."

"That is not reassuring, Tom. Maybe the grasshopper hordes won't interfere with the wedding itself or the reception, but the cookout at the ranch house for family and—"

"Hold up, Elizabeth. There can be grasshopper infestations, but—"

"*Infestations.* Great."

"—they're not as bad as you're describing, especially not in town. We'll have a better idea come spring—"

With another quick tilt, I shot him a look. March, heading toward April *should* be spring.

He ignored it.

"—when we can check with the USDA."

"The USDA does grasshopper reports?"

"Yeah. They can affect rangeland."

"Sure. Worry about the cows."

He suppressed a grin, saying, "We always do. The outlook's for normal numbers around here."

"They do grasshopper outlooks, too?"

"Sure. Based on the previous year's adult population per square yard. That way they get on potential hotspots early. I know you're mostly joking about the wedding, but grasshoppers can devastate crops and forage. One more thing to stay on top of."

And he had plenty to stay on top of already. I wouldn't be seeing as much of him soon with calving season approaching. He'd also need time to plan with his assistant, Connie Walterston, for the upcoming road construction season.

Summer didn't let up, either. Once I was overruled on a quickie, immediate marriage ceremony, we'd considered a fall wedding so we— he—had more time, but neither of us wanted to wait that long.

The honeymoon would wait for a more convenient time— convenient for the ranch, that was. I was also marrying the Circle B.

I told him what we'd gathered today about Keefe. It felt like a lot of telling for not much progress.

"You always feel that way at the start." Then Tom called, "Time for dinner, Tamantha, Shadow."

He was right.

It was time for dinner. And I did often—*always* was too strong— feel this way at the start of investigating a murder. He was even right that I was mostly kidding about the grasshoppers.

My mother wouldn't be, but we'd deal with it.

As long as we got married, I'd be fine.

A little voice at the back of my head spoke up.

As long as we figured out who'd killed Keefer Dobey, then Tom and I got married, I'd be fine.

DAY THREE

THURSDAY

CHAPTER EIGHTEEN

ONE ISSUE WITH living in the Mountain Time Zone instead of the Eastern was if I wanted to get people before they left for lunch I couldn't dawdle around as long as I liked to in the mornings.

That wasn't nearly as bad a problem as people from the East Coast forgetting it was two hours earlier where I was, but I'd solved that with an app that blocked calls until a civilized hour. Only problems, now, arose from the exceptions.

Specifically my mother, who ignored it was one hour earlier than her Illinois clock.

I needed an app that blocked Mom unless the call involved dire emergencies—*my* definition of dire emergencies. Not hers.

Yes, Mom woke me up to tell me the first RSVP to the wedding had come in. A cousin of my father's called Mom to say the invitation arrived and she planned to come to the wedding with her son and daughter-in-law.

I'd thought they'd be no's for sure. Uh-oh.

"It doesn't count unless she mails it back," I said.

We'd sent RSVP cards to all guests that could be mailed back, with an option to RSVP via the wedding website Jennifer made for us—not an option this woman would take. Jennifer called the site minimalist. I called it something I was really glad she was handling.

Mom said, "I can just tell Jennifer to add her and her kids—" Who were older than me. "—to the website."

"Jennifer's in a rigorous academic program and already doing a lot—"

"It won't take her but a second."

"Mom—"

"What? Aren't you excited? It's really happening, Elizabeth. It's really happening."

It didn't take a distant relative RSVPing to make marrying Tom real. But maybe it did firm up the blurry view of the wedding on the horizon.

"That's great, Mom. And thank you for all you're doing—"

"Stop thanking me. I love it."

"—but I need to get to work."

IT WASN'T THAT simple to wrap up the call with Mom and there was me to get ready and Shadow to care for, but I did get myself to the KWMT-TV newsroom in decent time.

A snowflake, big and sloppy, far more like an Illinois flake than a Wyoming flake, hit my forehead just before I reached the door and slid over my eyebrow onto my cheek.

"It's snowing," I announced to the group standing near Audrey's desk. After all, reporting is my business. "*Snow.* It's supposed to be spring. The snow sure doesn't know it's spring."

"Sure it does," Diana said cheerfully. "It's spring in Wyoming."

Nala chuckled.

She was fitting in here a little too well.

"I was just about to tell the others," Leona said, "I came up with a great idea for Mike for selling Sherman to prospective KWMT hires— we recreate Sally Rand's Nude Ranch. *That* should get some attention."

"Sally Rand?" Nala repeated, obviously not knowing who she was.

"*Nude* ranch?" I repeated. An instantaneous memory of a recent ride on Slinger, the sweet-mannered horse Tom and Tamantha gave me for Christmas, surfaced with the idea of doing it nude superimposed and produced an involuntary, "Ouch, ouch, ouch." It had been bad enough with the effects of cold weather. Take off protective layers and . . . *Ouch, ouch, ouch* didn't do it justice.

"Emphasis on the nude, not the ranch," Leona said dryly. "It was part of a World's Fair in San Francisco."

"San Francisco? Sally Rand was famous for doing her fan dance at the Chicago's World Fair—1933," I added with some pride that I remembered the date. "It celebrated Chicago's centennial. The fair, not the dance."

Diana chuckled.

"And for a bunch of astronauts decades later. You should look that up," I added to Nala's wide eyes.

Leona stayed on topic. "Yeah, I guess. But there was another World's Fair in San Francisco in 1939. And that's the one that had Sally Rand's Nude Ranch—it said Dude, but the first D was crossed off and replaced by an N. The girls were in areas behind glass and the customers moved past . . . or sometimes stopped for a while . . . while different groups of girls did rope tricks or fed baby farm animals or played badminton."

"*Badminton?*" Nala repeated.

"Because one does on a ranch," Diana said dryly.

Audrey sighed. "Might get attention, but not the kind we want."

Leona appeared ready to argue the point. With an eye on the clock, I interrupted "I wanted to ask you, Leona, what you know about Wendy Barlow's uncle, the original owner of the Elk Rock Ranch."

"Not original. Far from original, even if you're just talking about it being a dude ranch. Started as a cattle operation when people were first starting that around here. Another family made it into a dude ranch for quite a while. Barlows were friends of theirs. Came out here for a couple weeks, then bought the place right out from under them."

And now Randall Kenyon was trying to repeat that history.

"Nice friends," Audrey said, "buying the ranch away from them."

"Didn't seem to bother the folks selling all that much. They went off and started another one. New Mexico, I think. They weren't from around here," she added, explaining their odd behavior in choosing to go anywhere else.

"That would have been Chester's father who bought it. A real warm and cuddly type." Her tone said the opposite. "Family came out for the summer for about a decade or so—except the father, who was back East piling up money. Kids got older and that stopped. Seemed like they forgot it. Left a foreman to run the place, which he did just fine with some locals.

"Then, out of the blue, here comes Chester back to take over, turning it back to a dude ranch. What we learned soon enough was he'd mostly broken with his family—or vice versa—after some hijinks back East. Had to be about thirty by then, so he'd had a lot of years of hijinks.

"Guess the other Barlows accused Chester of *playing around* with the ranch, ignoring the *real* work of the corporation. Easy to tell they'd never done any ranch work. Give Chester credit, he did work hard at running the Elk Rock. Expect his family thought he'd come crawling back. Not him. He told them to—well, you get the idea. And the rift continued into the next generation. Except Wendy, who came out here to work one summer she was in college. Apparently, she was something of a rebel, too, and the family thought a summer of hard work would cure her, though not prepared to hand her over to just anybody to administer her discipline. So they sent her to Elk Rock for a summer under her uncle. And she never left."

"How'd that go over with the Barlows?"

"Major, major tizzy. Her father was the big muckety-muck in the family business by that time and he restructured the trust or something or other so she'd only get an equal share if she came back into the fold. She blew raspberries at him and his trust. Not that she was cut off entirely. Still was part of her grandfather's trust, though most of that rolled into the next generation—except Chester, of course. Still, Wendy probably got more each month than Cottonwood County's version of big earners make in a year or so. But nowhere near what her brothers got when their father died. And keep getting.

"Still, she's made a go of the ranch with enough left over for winters away. And, as far as I hear and see, she's happy with that."

"She's not part of the social scene in the county?"

"Not the core group, that's for sure. More connected with the businesses around that are useful to her for running the ranch or entertaining the dudes. Oh, she'll donate now and then. But seeing her at any of the events meant to be fun or going to be seen and see others? Not the past ten, twelve years, I'd say."

"I heard she was Cottonwood County's representative in the billionaire set."

"Could be from the trust along with the land value of Elk Rock. But like the rest of them? No way. Pretty sure the current chairman of the board's her brother. For sure her father was. And other brothers are in the stratosphere, too—power and money. But she parted ways from the family ages ago."

Leona's turn to check the time.

"I gotta go," she said. "I'm invited to a planning lunch for a charity event and I'm going home first to get ready like a normal person, despite this wretched job. Don't worry, Audrey, I'll be back in plenty of time to prep for the Five. Might not be totally sober, but I'll be here."

She was kidding about that last part. Pretty sure she was.

I CALLED MY longtime friend Matt Lester in Philadelphia.

We'd gone to grad school together. He and his wife Bonnie and my now-ex Wes and I had all been close.

They not only stuck with me during the divorce, but took me in after the worst of Wes' skulduggery.

I'd talked with both Matt and Bonnie a few weeks ago. A lot of that conversation revolved around family, friends, and the unrelenting buyouts and layoffs of journalists by newspapers. So far, Matt was still standing.

Now, after a brief catch-up, he said, "So what can I do for you?"

I told him.

"Want me to research? Or off the top of my head."

"Start with off the top of your head."

"The Barlows are more Connecticut than Pennsylvania, but one branch migrated down here in the early twentieth century and immediately built a mansion in Gladwyne—still occupied by Barlows. Because of them, we keep an eye on the activities of the Connecticut crowd, too."

"Ever hear of Chester Barlow? He's been dead for decades, but he owned a ranch out here that his niece, Wendy, now owns and runs."

"Oh, yeah, Chester is famous. Outsiders might view him as a rebel or renegade, but to the Barlows, he was Benedict Arnold. It was quite a story at the time. His father basically cut him out of the trust, gave him a lump sum, which presumably he used to buy this ranch you're talking about, and the other Barlows washed their hands of him.

"Of the Connecticut branch, his older brother and their sister never had kids—probably too busy piling up cash. His younger brother had three boys and a girl—"

"Wendy."

"Right. Who was considered cut from the same cloth as Chester. In other words, the black sheep of her generation. Though from what I'm hearing, this generation is overachieving in the black sheep department. A couple have been in jail—and one wasn't even for white collar crime. How the mighty have fallen. I mean, fraud, insider trading, that's not *really* criminal, that's just playing the game hard. At least in their circles.

"Anyway, back to Wendy. She was given pretty much the same treatment as Chester. Not quite as severe from what I understand. Little contact with the rest of the family, but that seems to be more apathy than a never-darken-my-door-again decree. And the word is she does get a subsistence level income from the trust. You know, enough for her to live on like a regular person, but not like a Barlow."

"Any idea how much?"

"Dollar amount? No. The Barlows are strictly Don't Tell. Anything. Ever. That'll have to do for now, Elizabeth. I've got a lunch."

See? I knew it.

CHAPTER NINETEEN

With the East Coast out to lunch, I decided to head to the McCrackens' unannounced to see if I found Sam this time.

Apparently, my SUV had other plans, turning west—toward the center of Sherman—when I pulled out of the KWMT parking lot.

Might as well see where it—and my subconscious?—led.

Turned out to be behind the Cottonwood County Courthouse. In other words, the sheriff's department.

My subconscious might have been tuned into something because Sergeant Shelton and Deputy Richard Alvaro came out the back door of the building and headed toward a marked truck as I parked between it and them.

I loved it when my subconscious set it up so I could return the favor to Shelton of skulking in a parking lot.

I stepped in front of them.

Shelton considered going around me, then decided not to after a look at my face.

"Any progress on the Keefer Dobey murder?" I asked.

"No comment," Shelton said without heat.

"Close to making an arrest? Should we hold a spot in tonight's newscasts for breaking news?"

"No comment."

"Did you know he'd had a DNA test?"

Richard's eyes flickered, Shelton's did not. He truly was a tough nut.

But I had my answer.

And that was worth more than keeping the information to myself would have been.

First, because it told me the sheriff's department hadn't known Keefe had a recent DNA test. Which meant the DNA results had not been in Keefe's cabin.

The sheriff's department almost certainly hadn't questioned Brenda and Wendy in a way that got them talking enough to mention that Keefe was excited about the DNA test results and his hope—expectation—that they would show he was descended from Oscar Virtanen.

But they would not have missed the test results during their search. And if it had arrived since Keefe's death, they'd know about it that way.

Second, knowing about the test's existence would set Shelton in pursuit. And he had law enforcement tools to pry the information out of the lawyers' chronically constricted fingers.

After a long enough pause to make it clear Shelton hadn't employed his previous answer, making it clear this was different, I said, "Don't strain your voice—I know, no comment."

Still nothing. But they also didn't move past me.

"Not a paternity test," I said, shaking the ball in front of their eyes to be sure I had their full attention.

Richard blinked, presumably at the concept of Keefe being the subject of a paternity test, indicating their victimology assessments were similar to ours.

Shelton didn't.

"It was to look into his relations." I used that word rather than ancestry, because Shelton would be much less interested in dead people he couldn't get his hands on than live ones subject to a satisfying arrest.

Neither blinked. I liked to think that was because they were awed at our knowing this information.

"Robin Kenyon bought the test for him as a thank you. Well, officially, I suppose it was her father's money and he certainly knew about it." Tossing the ball, I added, "It was done by the HelixKin company.

Keefe told several people he thought he'd have the results by now."

Go, fetch.

Problem was, Shelton was about as good a retriever as Shadow. Did just fine on chasing what I threw, but lousy at bringing it back to me.

On the other hand, once they chased it down using the clout of the judicial system, we'd gather some of its results by their next moves.

SERENA AND SNOWBALL answered the door together again.

Instead of inviting me in, she left the dog inside—to his chagrin—snagged a jacket and pulled it on as she gestured me to go back down the stairs.

"Sam's out in his office—what used to be the workshop. I'll take you out there."

Sam McCracken's workshop/office was a steep-roofed shed beside the barn.

Serena opened the door then gestured for me to enter, but did not follow. "Sam, Elizabeth Margaret Danniher of KWMT-TV is here to see you."

She closed the door behind me.

I barely noticed.

I don't think Sam noticed at all.

My inattention stemmed from the sight before me.

I now understood Serena's gesture when she'd touched on Sam's book-ordering. The fruits of his clicking finger stretched from floor to ceiling and wall to wall around three-quarters of the shed. The fourth wall held a desk with five computer screens along its length, with Sam McCracken on a wheeled chair that moved from screen to screen a lot based on marks on the floor.

Clerestory windows brought natural light in without interrupting the bookcases.

Sam's inattention to his wife's departure stemmed from the sight of me.

"What do you want?"

Not the most welcoming of greetings, but better than get the h—
out of here.

"When I was here before you'd just gotten four horses for you and
your family."

He answered the implicit question with, "Riding the horses is nice,
but not something you can do all day, every day." His gaze went in the
direction of the house though a wall of books—and what they
represented—blocked his view. "At least I can't. Tried running some
cattle, but decided that wasn't for me, either."

"Looks like you have another—" I rejected the terms *hobby, rabbit
hole, craze, obsession.* "—pastime now."

He lifted one shoulder as his focus slid to the bulletin board behind the closest computer monitors. It held printouts, photos, replica
wanted posters, maps—lots of maps. "This is interesting. Fascinating."

Interesting, even fascinating, maybe. But his expression did not say
fun.

When we'd met, I'd thought he wouldn't be mistaken for a rancher
despite being comfortable in the attire, because his skin didn't reflect
years outside in every weather. Now his face looked downright pale.

Of course, ranchers aren't as tanned in March as in August, either,
but this was more than winter limiting exposure to the sun. This was
pallor born of choosing inside over outside, day after day after day.

He hadn't invited me to sit, but I did anyway—on a stool that put
me half a foot lower than his commander-of-the-kingdom desk chair.

It was my only choice. This was not a place set up for McCracken
to entertain visitors.

"You've heard that Keefer Dobey was murdered?"

I was sure Serena would have relayed that even if he cocooned
himself from other sources of news.

"Yeah."

"He lived such a quiet life. Seemed the only thing that took him
out into the wider world was his pursuit of Oscar Virtanen."

He took a different approach to the topic.

Still staring at the bulletin board, he said, "Treasure hunting, for
wont of a better name for it, has become trendy. You know anything

about it?"

"I know about all the people who went after the treasure chest Forrest Fenn buried in the Rocky Mountains then wrote the poem with riddles to solve for finding it," I said carefully.

What journalist didn't after the stories about extremists among the seekers—five died while searching, others threatened Fenn and his family, untold vacation hours and budgets were devoted to it.

And some haven't stopped—even though the bronze chest was found in 2020. The location hadn't been revealed and people who'd spent years looking for the location are willing to spend more years searching for where it *was*.

Especially since Fenn didn't reveal where it was found before he died and the finder says he never will.

And then some believe it still *hasn't* been found, so they're still looking.

"Those people," he said with disgust. "That whole thing was a Disney event."

Tell that to the families of the five who died.

"The real pursuit isn't Disney. It takes intellect. It takes research. It takes imagination. It takes all of them together and more or you get nowhere.

"If you simply do basic research, you are treading over the same ground others have trampled before you. That's what I discovered with the Butch Cassidy treasures. People crossing and re-crossing the same territory. Utah, Wyoming, Montana, Colorado, Nevada—that's a lot of territory but they've still trampled all over it."

"What makes you think Butch Cassidy buried treasure in the first place?"

"What do you mean?"

"If he had money from a previous robbery buried somewhere and he needed money, why not go there and dig it up, instead of leaving the money from a previous robbery buried and robbing another train or bank or whatever and increasing his chances of getting caught?"

For a second he stared at me like I had two heads and the best he could do was try not to look at either one. Then he blinked, sat up, and he was another man. Much more like the one I'd met previously. "That's it exactly! It's far more likely they spent what they stole—high living, all the horses they needed for getaways—and they couldn't steal all of them, keeping their remote hideaways operating, probably bribing ranchers if not lawmen. And then they had to steal again. Or they had something else that made it worthwhile robbing again. *That's* why I'm searching for Oscar's treasure."

I wasn't going to call the man a liar to his face, but it sure seemed like he'd only just recognized that angle. I suspect his transfer from Butch Cassidy to Oscar Virtanen stemmed from a realization of all those other people before and beside him on the search.

"Had you worked with other searchers?"

"No."

CHAPTER TWENTY

"NOT **K**EEFER**?"**

He examined my face for how much I knew, then looked away. "We talked a little, that's all."

"With his local knowledge, he must have been helpful," I suggested mildly.

"He'd done some research, sure. But he hadn't employed a detailed, organized approach. He seemed to think that if he just sat among the information long enough everything would be revealed to him. That might be okay for yoga—" Clearly not a fan. "—or letting woodland creatures come up to him, but to find new information about historic figures who weren't well known in their day and haven't been researched since, you have to be aggressive. Go after every lead. Pursue every possibility." He looked up at me. "You know about that."

"Yes, I do. I can imagine that might cause conflict with someone like Keefer Dobey. Including over access to resources."

He frowned. "We weren't rivals, if that's what you're thinking. He did things his way. I did things my way. We had a few things in common, but we didn't share a lot—we were interested in different things."

"For example?"

I deliberately left that a choose-your-topic question. He could answer about the few things they had in common or their different interests.

"I am focused on the treasure."

"You said treasure—singular. Aren't there several?"

"More than several. You can get lost forever in chasing this tidbit or that if you don't keep laser focused. That's why I've narrowed focus. It's natural to start with the better-known robberies, because there's more material. You train yourself on *how* to research before you advance to the lesser-known events."

The way he said it, combined with a glance around the bookcases, told me he'd given Serena the same explanation. Possibly when more deliveries arrived.

"So I started with a lot of material on Butch Cassidy and the Sundance Kid. Although, actually, they didn't team up until late. Elzy Lay was Cassidy's closest friend in the gang for a decade. Only when Elzy was arrested in 1899 did Cassidy team up with Sundance. At first, I thought that tracing some of the other members of the gang—ones not as well-known now—would be the key. But the more I read, the more I thought most of the others were far less likely to have stashed their shares of robberies. They were arrested spending the money or found with a lot of it on them and, in general, didn't show the sort of forethought and organization Cassidy did.

"You know it's accepted by many that he planned the successful robberies, even ones he might not have participated in. He set up the system of fresh horses waiting along the escape routes, so they could outpace the posses. Outpace and outsmart. He didn't need to resort to violence." He chuckled. "Except against vaults, of course. But he said he never killed anyone."

"But would he have left his share from bank robberies here when they went to South America in—when was that?"

He answered the questions in reverse order "Early 1901. Maybe." Defensiveness tinged that. "If he thought he'd come back someday and might need a stake, it would make sense. Or even if he just couldn't get to where he'd hidden proceeds from one or more robberies because of the heat on him or on the location."

"Possible," I conceded.

"Probable," he pushed. "The upshot, though, is that a lot of people concentrated on Butch Cassidy, along with a sprinkling of his confederates. Better known and more documentation. Recognizing that, I struck out on a different path."

I cut through his caginess. "Oscar and Pearl Virtanen."

"That's not for publication," he said urgently.

First, KWMT-TV didn't publish. Second, most of our viewers probably already knew at least the outlines of the story. Third, they didn't seem to care. Fourth, if a rare individual did care, they would have almost certainly gone to the county library early in their research—in other words when the online info on Oscar and Pearl ran out—and thus have encountered Sam and Keefer.

Just as they encountered each other.

I tamped down all that realistic irritation bubbling up in me and gave him the super spy secret handshake he craved.

"It's off the record unless it has a direct bearing on Keefer Dobey's death." Before he could require a blood oath, I pushed on. "So, you and Keefer Dobey shared an interest in Oscar and Pearl."

"We did, but with different slants. And then we realized that a certain aspect could serve each of our slants."

"Which was?"

I didn't waste time or energy on these questions because I'd realized he *wanted* to tell me this. He wanted a listener for each step, half-step, quarter-step, and toes-inching-forward bit of progress he'd made.

I guessed he'd worn out Serena as such a listener quite a while ago.

"We were both interested in the women."

Okay, that did spark my interest. Not that I needed to express it. Just listening passively worked for him.

"Of course it was obvious for Keefe, since he was looking for family ties—he wanted to know if any of the women associated with outlaws had babies or could have had babies that would have led to him a few generations later, across the blankness of his paternal line. He started tracking the better documented women before recognizing better documentation made it less likely the women had babies no one knew about."

I wasn't so sure. Not only because the Pinkertons fell down on the job when it came to the women, but also because women had had babies *unofficially* back into the stretches of history as a result of any number of circumstances, with no documentation tracking the event. Whether the baby stayed in the family as the child of a sister, cousin, or parent, for example, or was given up for adoption.

"So he, too, came around to thinking a less documented couple could be more fruitful. My pursuit, however, wasn't as easy."

Hadn't he just said Keefe's wasn't easy because his paternal line was a blank? What was harder than a blank?

He'd paused and I dutifully asked, "How was it not as easy?" Apparently passive only went so far.

"Nobody had thought of this before. That tracing the women was the answer—could be the answer," he amended with obligatory caution he didn't really believe. "All the other researchers traced the moves and timelines of the men involved in the robberies. But the women weren't given as much attention."

Wanting more from him, I didn't mention that Emmaline Parens was way ahead of him—not only in recognizing that fact but in pointing it out to me.

"But the women being the key to finding the treasure makes so much sense. Not only because that angle hasn't been pursued before, but also because of the men wanting to take care of their wives—or girlfriends or whatever they called them—and families if they had them, but also because some of the women bought supplies for them, sold stolen goods. For sure Laura—"

"Bullion. I know."

Not the best interviewing technique. I usually favored letting people talk on and on to get me to where I wanted to be, because especially in these early encounters I didn't always know where I wanted to be. But Sam had been denied an interested audience long enough—had denied himself one with his secrecy, had worn out Serena's spousal support, and had diverged on this matter from Keefe—that his explanation would include every supporting fact he knew.

"Oh. You do know about her." He rallied from that disappointment. "Then you know I'm right."

"It does make sense."

That seemed to satisfy him.

And the satisfaction seemed to be enough to let him remember my reason for being here.

"Keefer and I might have started as rivals, looking for some of the same information, but we realized we weren't really and we cooperated. Because his finding out more about his parentage didn't derail my search for the treasure and vice versa."

"Are you sure there is a treasure?"

"Yes. The last bank robbery Oscar Virtanen pulled, they never found what he stole."

"And Keefer wasn't interested?"

"Not in that part of it. Ask those people where he lived, they'll tell you."

Except they—at least Brenda—referred to the treasure. So where did that get us?

One thing we'd learned about this man in that other investigation was he could hold a grudge.

My Irish ancestors approved—if they hadn't held grudges, they wouldn't have kept rebelling against the English until finally reclaiming their independence after 800 years. (That's a lot of grudge.)

My journalistic instincts said a significantly shorter grudge could be a motive for murder. Perhaps over coveted research?

"And we shared," he continued. "He told me he came across this reference to an article written about some guy who'd been in the posse that chased Oscar—"

Ah, the article Ivy mentioned. "He found the article?"

He shook his head. "References only, including paraphrasing this posse member reminiscing decades later and it mentioned the guy feeling really sorry for the young widow—Pearl. And it indicated she might have been pregnant. Didn't come right out and say it, but Keefe was still real excited about that.

"Another time, he found a letter that he shared with me. Somebody from here wrote to her brother in school back east about the robbery and the manhunt for Oscar and the rumor that he'd buried the proceeds from the robbery somewhere on his route, which went through part of their ranch. And the brother wrote back saying he bet he knew where it was. And he described the place in detail. And when he got back, they'd go search for it. That didn't have anything directly about Oscar and Pearl, but from the dates and geography, it sure seemed like Oscar's last robbery."

"Did they?"

"Did who what?"

"Did the brother and sister search for the treasure?"

His expression went grim. "No. He died. A fever."

"So, it might be where he—"

"No." Grimmer now. "I figured out where he meant and checked. It had been dug up all over that area. Who knows how many people he wrote to or she told. But it had been worked over years ago."

"Maybe someone found it and never told anyone."

He cut me a you're-crazy-lady look. Clearly the concept of not telling anyone about such a find didn't factor into his thinking.

"No. I checked and the family's fortunes didn't suddenly change."

Ah, so the reason I was crazy was for not realizing he'd already thought of that and checked.

That made me feel oddly better about Sam McCracken as I wrapped up this conversation—keeping open the door to plenty more, as well as making the point that if he had something to add to call any time.

He was back into his computer before I reached the shed door.

Too bad he offered no proof of this cooperation with Keefer Dobey he claimed beyond his say-so. Opposed to that, we had the impressions of Ivy Short at the library and Clara Atwood at the museum. . . . and possibly Serena McCracken at home?

Though I wasn't sure of that last one.

CHAPTER TWENTY-ONE

OUT OF SIGHT of the McCrackens, I pulled over where anyone coming behind me would see my SUV from a good distance.

Sure was easier when I could call Jennifer and ask her to search in real time, rather than lining up behind her school work and—possibly?—a boyfriend.

Didn't mean I was helpless.

The forums and discussion groups for treasure-seekers—of all kinds—posed a rabbit hole the size of the Grand Canyon.

I sidestepped around it carefully and found, instead, a piece on what kind of people became treasure-hunters. Only one piece—always want two independent sources—but interesting, nonetheless.

Three-quarters who identified themselves as treasure-hunters were male. They liked risk and challenge. The reward—beyond any treasure—was a sense of striving, leading to mastery. They competed, not against themselves, but the other treasure-seekers.

I sat staring out the windshield for a while, considering that.

Then I called Mrs. P.

"SO THE WOMEN'S names as we know them today came from Pinkerton?" I asked as a recap to get us going again.

We were back in her front room, on those hard chairs, with Emmaline Parens as serene as ever and me pretending to serenity.

"In part, yes. There is a school of thought that the woman companion of the outlaw popularly nicknamed Sundance Kid, who was, in fact, Harry Alonzo Longabaugh and—"

"Longbaugh? The Sundance Kid was a Longbaugh? Like James, the lawyer in Sherman?"

He wasn't the only lawyer in the county, but he was by far the best. His family had been lawyers here for generations.

"The outlaw's last name is Longabaugh, with an 'a' after the 'Long' in a number of public records. Although it does appear as Longbaugh without the 'a' at times, including on historical markers."

She'd chosen to discuss the least interesting aspect of this.

"Uh-huh. Typos happen, even on historical markers, but is James related to the Sundance Kid?"

I couldn't see how that fit in with Keefe's murder, but it would tickle my dad. And, I had to admit, I found it intriguing.

"I am not aware of the complete branches of James' family tree, only being familiar with those of that name who have resided in and served our county for three generations. I can assure you, none of the Longbaughs I have known have ever been on the wrong side of the law."

Well, that was disappointing, but not the end of my speculations.

Perhaps reading my reaction, she added, "You would need to make your inquiry to James for any further information on that topic."

She compressed her lips in a way that said the matter was closed. She had firm rules about indulging in gossip. And a very strict definition of what qualified as gossip. I wanted to protest the ruling: *C'mon, it's not gossip when it's about someone who's been dead for more than a century.*

On the other hand, did I want to use up any chance of earning a gossip exemption on a topic that wouldn't further our investigation? No.

"You were saying something about the woman companion of Sundance or Longabaugh, whose name might have been Etta Place. Or might not have been anything like that."

"Yes. There is the school of thought that the woman associated with him and commonly referred to as Etta Place was named Ethel, with Etta an approximation of her name's pronunciation by the locals from the period when they, along with the man known as Butch Cassidy, lived and ranched in South America. In short, there was not great care taken to get the correct names of the women. In addition, as I earlier indicated, when a male outlaw died, interest in his female associate or companion evaporated. One might have expected better of the Pinkertons, since the agency was far-thinking in using women and minorities as agents when that was unheard of. Not, I fear, from a concept of right or fairness, but because they could pass unnoticed more readily than their male counterparts. A premise they then proved by their own conduct."

Another woman, say, Wendy Barlow, might have snorted to punctuate that. She sniffed. Delicately.

"Altogether, this lack of attention to the women meant that a number of them disappeared into the mists, whether permanently or for an extended period of time. It is widely accepted that the woman known as Etta Place was in San Francisco in 1907, having returned there accompanied by Harry Longabaugh some time earlier, before he returned to South America, where he reportedly met his death in 1908. At a later date, a woman whose description matched that of Etta Place approached a consulate official, trying to obtain a death certificate for Harry Longabaugh."

"That's interesting. Why would she want a death certificate? If it happened today, you'd think for an insurance claim, but somehow I doubt the Sundance Kid had life insurance. Settling an estate? There'd have to be a will. Another stretch for Sundance. Or they'd been legally married and she wanted to remarry. Has there been any evidence they were married?"

"Not that I have encountered in my reading. The other motives you enumerated also have no support in the limited factual record."

"Limited? The factual record is a string. A skinny string with frayed ends."

She did not pause to sympathize. "Another woman associated with an outlaw of that period did have success in obtaining a death certificate and with that documentation was able to sell land in the southeastern corner of Cottonwood County. It is largely the area now known as Elk Rock Ranch. It was once owned by Oscar Virtanen."

CHAPTER TWENTY-TWO

"**WAIT A MINUTE,** let me get this straight. The outlaw Oscar Virtanen owned land in Cottonwood County. He robbed a bank in southern Wyoming—not his first stickup—and was shot in the process. He started north, presumably to meet up with his wife, Pearl, who was somewhere—we don't know quite where—but possibly in the vicinity of Cottonwood County, which would make sense since they owned land here."

I took a breath, she waited patiently. Possibly trying to model ideal behavior to me.

"The posse caught up with him, finding none of the proceeds of the robbery but—at least according to one secondary source—with evidence that he'd been digging. He then died of his wounds. His wife—who might or might not have been pregnant at the time— obtained a death certificate for him and then sold the property. Do I have that all right?"

"I believe so, with the caveat that the official record confirms only parts of it."

Big surprise.

"And that property eventually became the Elk Rock Ranch, where Keefer Dobey lived most of his life, recently becoming fascinated with whether he might be descended from Oscar and Pearl Virtanen."

No response.

That was not going to fly. "He must have asked you, Mrs. Parens."

"He did ask me questions, however, as I've said, the official rec- ord—"

"Did that satisfy him?"

"No." Her sadness softened me.

"What did he tell you, Mrs. Parens? If it helps to find his killer . . ."

Were rules on gossip more important?

I didn't speak those words. We both understood them.

"As I stated, he largely asked me questions, while I could not supply the answers. He told me he had first explored the possibility of Harry Longabaugh and Etta Place or Ben Kilpatrick and Laura Bullion being his ancestors, however, he transferred his attention to Oscar and Pearl Virtanen. He expressed frustration with the dearth of information."

"Did he say who else he'd talked to about this?"

"He told me what he'd learned from Ivy Short at the library and Clara Atwood at the museum. He also expressed frustration with the lack of interest in his endeavors shown by Brenda and Wendy, particularly when he learned of Pearl obtaining the death certificate and selling the property."

"How did he learn that? Did you tell him?"

"I did not."

But there'd be the faintest flicker of her eyes toward her office. "Russell Teague's vacuum cleaner approach to historical information picked it up," I concluded.

"Anything in those papers is the property of the Sherman Western Frontier Life Museum and use or dissemination of the information in them as well as the papers themselves is entirely the purview of the museum."

If she'd found the material, she'd never have shared it with him, not without getting Clara's okay. And if Clara okayed it, why not tell me? "He found the information himself."

She looked unhappy.

"He wasn't just delivering and returning boxes, he was dipping into them."

Even more unhappy.

"I expressed myself quite firmly on the topic to Keefer. I told him if he did not cease that practice, I would inform Clara Atwood and his services would no longer be used. He appeared genuinely confused over why anyone would be upset about his looking at the materials. He said it would become accessible to the public in the due course of time, so why shouldn't he see it now, especially if it assisted him in determining his lineage."

"Did he mention Robin Kenyon or her father, Randall Kenyon?"

"That is the young woman who was injured at the end of last season?"

"Yes."

"He did mention them, briefly. Primarily in expressing gratitude for their obtaining a DNA test for him to take to explore his lineage. That conversation occurred on his previous stop to return to the museum those boxes I had processed and to bring me ones not yet assessed. The last time we spoke, the day before he was found dead, I am sorry to say that we did not talk beyond the necessities. I thought at the time that he needed more time to absorb and adjust to what I had said previously." Her eyebrows dropped in a microfrown. "In light of his death, of someone murdering him, I do now consider the possibility that he was being what one might term *cagey*."

Emmaline Parens was fretting that her words prevented Keefe from telling her more and that in so doing she had somehow contributed to not preventing his murder.

Nothing I said to her would help with that. Finding out the murderer might. Maybe. Or it might confirm her fears.

Either way, it would be the truth and we both valued that.

But she was leaving something out. Brenda and Wendy weren't interested. Ivy and Clara helped him. Who else . . .?

"Sam McCracken," I said.

She didn't blink.

Like she was working hard to not blink.

"He told Sam McCracken about the land, the death certificate, and the sale."

"Keefer did not mention a name, however, he did convey that someone was going to help him with further inquiries because the proceeds from Oscar Virtanen's last robbery might be on the property he once owned."

Had to be Sam McCracken.

Time for a reset.

With all she'd said and hadn't said swirling in a question soup in my head, I pulled out one thing to say. "So, an outlaw ranched in Cottonwood County."

"Those who pursued outlaw ways were quite fluid in their other employments," she said with a return to her usual manner. "Many, if not most, worked as cowboys or ranch hands at times. It is often reported that Butch Cassidy's first name came from a period occupied as a butcher southwest of here. He adopted Cassidy as his last name from a wrangler and rustler who served as what some term as a mentor in his early career as an outlaw. In addition, some historians hold that Butch Cassidy owned a ranch in the Wind River area."

"Did he?"

Delicately she hoisted a shoulder. "If so, it was not a financial success. I have heard the opinion expressed that the endeavor was to mask other occupations."

"The Wild West's version of money laundering?"

Her opposite shoulder rose this time. "Further, the Virtanens' endeavors on their land did not qualify as ranching, even by the standards of that period, which had dwindled drastically compared to the open range era."

She didn't insult me by asking if I knew what the open range era was. I knew it was when ranchers ran huge herds on public land. And I knew it ended, but when and how that intersected with the period of outlaws . . .?

I needn't have tiptoed around my ignorance.

She could sniff out ignorance like a truffle being hunted down by a—I know, you're thinking *pig*, but, no—dog.

Several breeds of dogs have been trained to hunt truffles. They have advantages over pigs, starting with easier transport than a 400-pound pig and a better record with the *Drop It* command.

"The open range was the heyday of the cowboy as he is popularly envisioned now, including the cattle drives that brought herds into this region," she said. "Beginning with the devastating winter of 1886-1887, with blizzard after blizzard and temperatures believed to have reached negative 60 degrees, killing hundreds of thousands of cattle, the large-scale ranchers experienced pressures squeezing from multiple directions. More population, especially homesteaders, as well as the burgeoning mining industry in Wyoming, brought competition for the range lands, as well as a swing in political power. As the open range shrank, more and more cowboys no longer had jobs."

"They turned to crime because they were unemployed?"

"That is a recognizable correlation, whether it is causation is not proven. A majority of those involved with the well-known gangs had worked as cowboys and continued to off and on during their outlaw period." She tipped her head. "You might also recognize that the outlaw gangs were not largely populated by store clerks."

"Okay, but getting back to Oscar Virtanen. He wasn't an out of work cowboy. He owned land here. Who was this guy? I haven't heard about him, much less her." But I hadn't grown up around here. Now, Lincoln was another matter. I could trace his footsteps from Kentucky to Indiana to all over Illinois and into history. Oscar Virtanen was no Lincoln. "Are they well-known around here? The Butch and Sundance of Cottonwood County."

She pursed her lips. "Those two individuals were not as well-known here as they are now until that film came out some time ago. It did not adhere to even what facts are known, starting with the fact that Elzy Lay could be more accurately portrayed as Cassidy's most frequent partner in committing crimes and the group of outlaws known as the Hole in the Wall Gang was a very loosely tied association of individuals, rather than a gang."

That matched what Sam McCracken said.

But I couldn't resist defending the movie, "It was written for entertainment value, rather than education."

She sniffed. "It could have achieved more of the latter without sacrificing the former."

"If you were writing the Oscar and Pearl Virtanen story, being historically accurate, of course, what would it say?"

A glint came into her eyes. She rose, went directly to a section of her extensive bookcases, chose a book without hesitation and handed it to me on her return.

Picking that book out was more of an accomplishment than it had first seemed, since it did not have the title on the spine. I saw why when I looked at the cover. "Myth and Reality concerning those designated as outlaws in the Wild West, 1889-1912."

The spine wasn't nearly thick enough to hold that title. The cover barely had room for that and the name of the author, Esther Rama-larga.

"This looks quite old," I commented.

"It is the dissertation written by a colleague of mine, a mentor, really. A remarkable woman, who acquired her PhD well beyond an age when most people do, much less women of that period. It is, to my knowledge, the only work on Oscar Virtanen and Pearl Virtanen. You may borrow it."

Less *may* and more *shall*.

I thanked her suitably. "Can you give me a preview?"

"They were a newly married couple when they arrived in the southwestern corner of the state. They are believed to have gone to work on the Bassett ranch there. The Bassetts were an interesting family from the contemporary accounts. It was a changing time in Wyoming, including the cattle industry. There occurred a great deal of conflict between smaller, newer operations such as the Bassetts' and the large operations trying mightily to hold onto their position and privilege from the open range era by all means at their disposal, including violence. The Johnson County War is well-known as a major range war—"

If not *the* range war.

"—with large cattle companies bringing in hired guns against small ranchers and farmers, accusing them, with little to no evidence, of rustling. There might well have been rustling and other depredations, however some of these cattlemen did not wait for the justice system to sort out matters, but lynched those they had accused."

"But the Johnson County War happened on the other side of the

Big Horn Mountains, while Oscar and Pearl Virtanen were here, right?"

"Similar, if not quite so spectacular conflicts occurred in many areas. However, I know you most desire to know about the Virtanens." She mildly disapproved of my narrowing my knowledge-gathering in such a way, but she would humor me. "When they first came to this region, they were not in the vicinity of what is our county now. They were in the southwestern part of the state, where Wyoming, Colorado, and Utah come together. There are conflicting reports of whether they worked for or were neighbors of the Bassetts, who were quite well known in the area, not the least because they had two lovely daughters.

"The Bassetts, whether by design or accident, established connections and friendships with those now known as outlaws, including, notably, Butch Cassidy. Those associations, the frequent visits of such persons, and the making known of the consequences that would occur if human-wrought misfortune befell the Bassetts accorded them a large measure of protection from the large cattle companies in the area who might otherwise have tried to eradicate the Bassetts' ranch.

"There are accounts that the two Bassett daughters, Ann and Josie, had strong connections with a number of the outlaws," she said delicately of what sounded like more partner switching among outlaws and a limited group of women—presumably ones trusted to keep outlaw secrets. "How many of those accounts stem from their own later tales is not known. There have even been assertions that Ann, specifically, and Etta Place were one and the same, despite confirmable historic dates contradicting that."

She drew in a breath.

Fearing a recitation of all historic dates and how they conflicted, I shifted in my chair.

Giving no sign that she'd been thwarted other than a blink of her eyes, she continued, "From a few letters Pearl Virtanen wrote home to her family that have survived and are quoted in full in the dissertation—" She tipped her head toward the book I held. "—we know that her husband and she were given shooting lessons by the Bassetts and unnamed visitors, and that each member of the couple showed an aptitude that drew favorable comment from their instructors. Though neither, apparently, proved as expert at riding horses.

"The next event in their lives, though speculative rather than confirmed, was the robbery of a bank in a town a day's ride west of the Bassetts' ranch. Newspaper accounts disagreed on whether the robbers were two men or a man and a boy. It was later associated with the Virtanens, based on witnesses who came forward. Each identified Oscar, while one claimed that Pearl Virtanen was the other perpetrator. By that time the Virtanens had left that area.

"A second robbery attributed to them, well to the east, involved holding up a bank in a railroad town just before it closed, tying up the two employees remaining in the bank, then boarding the train about to depart town. They paid for their tickets to a distant stop, but at some point left their seats, heading toward the baggage compartment. When the robbery was recognized later that night and news telegraphed ahead, they were no longer on the train. Nor did a couple matching their descriptions arrive at any of the stops the train had made. The speculation is that they had changed their appearances, stepped off the train at one of the stops, and disappeared into the town, where they had a prearranged means of departure."

"Echoing Butch Cassidy's planning."

She nodded. "Very shortly after that, the deed for the land here was issued. From the dates, it is possible that proceeds from that bank robbery could have been applied to that purchase, while not providing firm proof.

"The following year, however, Oscar Virtanen was wounded when he and two other men robbed a bank in the southern part of the state. The others escaped south, bolstering the belief that Pearl was not involved, for if she had been, she would have gone north with Oscar, when all reports agreed he was alone. In addition, there were reports that she was in Red Lodge. The posse that headed south lost those robbers, but the one that went north had greater success tracking Oscar. When he was found, he was quite near here."

"And was muddy, as if he'd been digging," I said.

"That was the report," she confirmed. "He died of his injuries by the next night. It is unclear if Pearl saw him before his death. Not long after, she appeared and demanded a death certificate, stating her identity. Perhaps startled by her audacity or perhaps knowing they had insufficient evidence to hold her, they issued the certificate and let her go. The following week, she transferred the deed to the land that became Elk Rock Ranch."

"She packed up and left? Returned to the Bassetts? Went to work for someone else? Joined another gang? Went back east?"

She raised her palms up in a familiar, but unusual for her, gesture of not knowing.

"There is no further record of her that has been found." She pointed to the book in my lap. "The diligent efforts to find further evidence of her are detailed in the dissertation. I cannot imagine efforts to trace the woman known as Etta Place have been any less diligent, while having the advantage of certainly being more numerous."

"But nothing?" Her nod confirmed my words. "So those two—Pearl Virtanen and the woman known as Etta Place—disappeared permanently, but you said some other women disappeared for an extended period. That means they were found later?"

"I was referring to Laura Bullion, whose whereabouts and activities were not known for a span of approximately six years before she arrived in Memphis, Tennessee, where she spent decades until her death. However, it is time to go next door to assist Gisella."

"Gee's house? I still have questions—"

"As you will continue to have," she said serenely, in contrast to how I felt about unanswered questions. "Gisella has been cooking for several needy families, and I promised I would help her pack the meals. You can assist."

"Mrs. Parens—"

"Are you aware that Gisella was a protégé of Ulla Dobey, the long-time cook at the Elk Rock Ranch and Keefer's mother?"

CHAPTER TWENTY-THREE

GISELLA'S STALWART FORM commanded her immaculate kitchen with ease.

It was hard to believe how clean it was, considering the array of food waiting to be wrapped up and divided into boxes. She had to clean each speck as it appeared.

Amazing.

She put Mrs. P and me to work immediately. I was in charge of the plastic wrap.

I have never plastic wrapped better in my life. I don't know if it was because I and the plastic wrap container were cowed into submission, but there was only one slight hint of twisting wrap and none of the blobbing tangles I too often encountered. Without them, it was actually rather relaxing.

As was talking with Gee. No drawing impressions and opinions out of her with a pair of pliers.

Get her started and let 'er rip.

"With the three of them up there at Elk Rock Ranch for long, long stretches . . . Some would say they're surprised there hasn't been a death before now. And this time of year most likely to bring it on. You've got all the build-up from going through the worst of winter—though nobody could say Keefe got cabin fever, because he was out in any kind of weather. Still it wears on most people and maybe even him a little, and there's still a good long stretch to go, especially before the guests come and add a sort of cushion between them, if you know what I mean."

"Are you saying . . . There was a romantic triangle?"

She stared at me a beat then burst out laughing. "No. No way."

It wasn't *that* far-fetched. "Wendy made a comment that Brenda resented her."

With a grin lingering on her mouth, her eyes went thoughtful. "I suppose she did. But not over Keefe."

No credit to me for asking the next question. "Over what then?"

"I suppose you could call it sibling rivalry for Chester's attention and affection. Like Keefe, Brenda was basically brought up at Elk Rock. Had the run of the place. And a lot of Chester's attention."

"Keefe didn't have his attention?"

"No. Oh, I'm sure Chester was fond enough of him, but Keefe wasn't ever a talker. He'd sit and stare off and you felt like you weren't in the same hemisphere as far as he was concerned. He'd watch the birds, watch the horses, watch the cattle, watch the critters. Sit there so still and silent, even wildlife would get back to acting normal, walking past him, paying him no mind. That row next, Elizabeth, so Emmaline can finish those boxes."

I swear she didn't even breathe before continuing, "Saw it myself when he was real young and I went up in the mountains with him for a report for school. I was a senior in high school and he was little—third grade, maybe even younger. But he said he'd guide me and he did." Her focus softened into memories. "Amazing."

Hearing her own word seemed to pull her out of her reverie.

"And that was with me there. Probably fidgeting. Surely not smelling like a mountain creature, which he did more often than not if someone wasn't on him about it. Later on, one of the guests got him to wear one of those cameras they use to film stunts and such. Only this one showed him barely doing anything—walking and sitting. But then, if you watched long enough, things started to happen around him. Like he'd been a stone dropped into a pond, setting off ripples, but after a while the pond settles back into normal, like the stone wasn't ever there.

"The guy—the guest—put it up online, along with footage of Keefe he took. Might still be there somewhere. Pretty boring to start *and* for stretches even after the ripples smooth out." She blinked, not focusing on me. "Don't suppose Keefe would ever have said it was boring. Not to him. He was one-of-a-kind."

"You knew him through his mother?"

Gee looked at Mrs. P immediately, simple recognition of my source, with no shred of blame or censure.

"Yes. That's how I ended up going out with him in the woods that time—I was talking about the project while I helped Ulla in the kitchen and he piped right up that he'd take me out."

"How often were you in the Elk Rock kitchen?"

"As often as I could be. Even when I wasn't working there."

"You worked there?"

"Sure. They'd hire from away for wranglers and servers and such. Those college kids flow through like water. Ulla said that was fine for cleanup. But she didn't want to retrain a new crew every summer. She liked to hire local help for prep, cooking. When she found someone good, she took them under her wing."

Mrs. P spoke up smoothly, "She took only you and Scott Hoole under her wing in all her years of cooking at the Elk Rock Ranch, Gisella, because you are and always have been extremely talented in the kitchen."

"Amen," I agreed with a wave of the plastic wrap box to the bounty before us.

Gee turned rosy with pleasure. "Ulla was the true talent. Gave me some of her recipes, too. You've had some of them, Elizabeth. Though I had to cut the ingredients way down from what she wrote down for me."

Maybe she'd cut them some, but nobody who'd eaten at Gee's house would say the portions had been cut *way down*.

"What was Ulla like?"

"Oh, she kept them all in line. Chester, Wendy, Brenda. Wasn't until after she was gone and with Chester not as strong as he'd been that Wendy and Brenda's sparring graduated to a power struggle—not one Brenda can ever win, considering Wendy owns Elk Rock. Doesn't stop her from trying."

"What started it?"

"Wendy coming here. You did know she wasn't from here to start?"

I nodded.

"Well, when her family back east decided she was the black sheep of that lot of them, they sent her out here to be with her black sheep uncle."

I nodded again.

"Two of them were a pair all right, those Black Sheep Barlows. A lot alike and it drove them both crazy. But, for all Chester talked about his family being as worthless as people as they were worth a lot in money, his blood tie to her held him tight from the minute she arrived.

"Thing was, before Wendy came, Brenda was his favorite. And in a way she stayed that. If Wendy hadn't been a relation . . . but she was. So that set them sparking against each other from the start. Add in that Wendy came in here from the east, ignorant of ranch ways, which gave Brenda a leg up, but glamorous, and that gave Wendy a leg up.

"One summer, in particular, there was a staffer who came in and they both set their caps for him. You'd never get either of them to admit she wasn't the first to like him and the other went after him just to spite her, but from what I heard, it was a dead heat. And the thing was, he wasn't interested in either one of them."

"A third girl?"

"Nope. Keefe. That's who'd caught his eye. Though nothing came of *that*. Don't think Keefe was even aware of it, but I heard his mother telling other people—forgetting I was there visiting, because I didn't work there anymore—that she worried at first when she saw which way the wind was blowing with Simon. The girls, though—Wendy and Brenda—were so locked in their battle, they never even noticed. Some of the other summer guys were miffed at the two best-looking girls both going for Simon and, because he wasn't interested, it never cut either one of them loose that summer. Feel kinda sorry for Simon in retrospect. He never came back, even though Chester said he was a top-notch wrangler. My, we were all so young then."

"Where was Keefe in all this?"

"Oblivious," Gee said. "Not interested."

"I concur with the latter, but not the former." Further proof Mrs. P had known Keefer Dobey earlier in his life. "As for that sibling rivalry between Wendy and Brenda, it did attract a good deal of attention from Ulla and Chester, particularly with Ulla enforcing the peace. But do not misread that into believing Keefer was excluded. He not only had his relationship with nature, indeed, his relationships with each element of nature, he also had human relationships. He was Ulla and Chester's much-loved boy."

Gee cast a sharp look at her neighbor. For only half agreeing with her on Keefe's reaction? For putting in her opinion at all? . . .

"Okay, get those last three wrapped, Elizabeth, and we can finish this up," Gee said.

. . . Or for holding up her production line.

I wrapped and we finished, and then I began to load the boxes into Gee's vehicle while they cleaned up what only could have been microscopic crumbs.

After my last trip, they came out. Gee pointed a finger at me. "You know who you should talk to is Scott Hoole."

"Scott Hoole?" Why did that name sound familiar?

"Yeah. They've been friends since Keefe first moved here."

Friends here? In Cottonwood County? That didn't seem right. Because the familiarity of the name didn't strike me as associated with here or wider Wyoming. Something from longer ago. From—. "Wait. Scott Hoole, the *chef?*"

"Uh-huh."

"Scott Hoole, the celebrity chef?"

"I guess." Gee was not impressed by celebrity.

"He lives here?"

"No. Over in Cooke City, now that he's retired. I've got his number here somewhere. I'll send it to you. Anyway, he'll remember a lot more about all that ancient history, because he was working there at the ranch at the time."

"Thank you." I looked at Mrs. P. She did not meet my gaze as she got in the passenger side. "I do still have other questions—"

"Another time, maybe," Gee said. "Time to make our rounds."

I left. But not with my usual sense after encountering these two that all was right and orderly in the universe. I felt oddly jangly and unsettled and I didn't know why.

I CALLED JENNIFER as I headed south out of O'Hara Hill, described the video of Keefe that Gee mentioned and asked Jennifer if she could track it down.

"Sure. Easy."

"Without—"

"For Pete's sake, Elizabeth, I know—without hacking." She sounded sharper and more tired than usual.

"Yes, and without interfering with your work for the program. That comes first."

"As if I don't know—. Fine. Yes. Without interfering with the program. I'm not an idiot, you know."

"I do know that."

"Then please tell Mike. It's like he suddenly decided he's a hundred years old and I'm a baby. He's not my father. He's not *anything* to tell me who I should or shouldn't see. It's none of his business. I'll see whoever I want to and I don't care what Mike or anyone else says."

"Understandable." I said that after swallowing a whole bunch of words about heeding those older and more experienced.

I knew Jennifer's parents hadn't yet been to Evanston to visit her, so they hadn't met this guy Mike didn't like. So, who was *anyone else . . .?*

Ah.

"Have any of the guys been to see you in Evanston?" I asked, as if changing the subject with the reference to her long-time online pals.

"Just for a couple days."

"That was nice of them."

"No, it wasn't. They were here for some job, consulting for a company downtown. They just came up to campus to pick my brain and take credit for it."

Whoa. That didn't sound like Jennifer at all.

Where did this come from?

Yup, I jumped immediately to this guy she was seeing being the origin. And that it was part of an effort to isolate her from her long-time friends, even family. Classic moves from the controlling boyfriend's handbook.

Another one was to drop hint after hint that her friends and family didn't trust her judgment. I wasn't getting anywhere near something that would trigger that defense.

"You'd have seen right through that if they ever tried before. Did they?" I asked, as if it had just struck me.

"No," she acknowledged, which told me she wasn't totally under this guy's influence—if that's what was happening.

"Huh." I bit my tongue to keep from saying more. Suggesting the boyfriend was defensive or jealous or anything else would put her back up.

She needed to consider those things herself.

And, really, as I said to Diana after recounting the conversation when I called her as soon as Jennifer and I ended our call, it might not be anything other than me being overly sensitive to what she said because Mike didn't approve.

"Huh," Diana said.

"What does that mean?"

"Nothing in particular," she lied.

I recognized a Diana stonewall when it was erected in front of me.

"Okay, you're not going to tell me what you're really thinking, I know that. But promise me one thing."

"Depends on what it is." Sometimes she's a little too wise for my good.

"Don't tell Russ whatever it is you're thinking about this topic that you're not telling me now until after you've told me."

She thought a moment. "Deal."

CHAPTER TWENTY-FOUR

I COULDN'T RESIST stopping by the Circle B to see if Tom happened to be around.

He was. In the barn, preparing a dose of antibiotic for Tamantha's horse, Roxanne. As he said he didn't like the look of a cut on her leg.

"I want to interview this person Gee describes as Keefe's best friend. He lives in Cooke City, Montana. I thought I'd drive up there and—. Why not?" I asked in response to Tom's shaking head.

He stopped shaking his head, but I knew it wasn't because he withdrew his objection.

"I'd check the weather, of course," I said, "but I looked at the map in my SUV and Cooke City's just north of Yellowstone, barely into Montana and not that far west of Red Lodge."

"Uh-huh."

"So that's not that far away. Doesn't look like it would be much farther than Red Lodge."

That's where Tom's sister lived and they visited back and forth regularly, including taking Tamantha up for visits. We'd stayed there a couple nights to celebrate New Year's.

"You've got a few mountains in the way to reach Cooke City," Tom said dryly.

"But Jean-Marie was talking at New Year's about seeing her good friend who lives in Cooke City."

He nodded. "They do get together regularly . . . during the summer."

I eyed him with suspicion rising in my heart. "Why only in summer?”

“It’s not Red Lodge,” he said quickly, apparently divining the direction of my suspicion. “Not really. But what connects the two towns most directly is the Beartooth Highway and that closes in the winter. Snows pretty much every month of the year on that road,” he added thoughtfully.

I might have grimaced, because Tom said consolingly, “It’s not all Beartooth. The Chief Joseph Highway gets most of the way to Cooke City.”

“Most of the way.” Suspicion had gone to certainty.

“They don’t try to clear all of Colter Pass, so you can’t actually drive it, although snowmobiles usually get through. Snow coaches, too.”

“Snow coaches?”

“Don’t think of public transportation,” Tom said. “People who don’t want to face the cold on a snowmobile get tours in Yellowstone in them. Big windows. And they sit up high, with some serious tires.”

Dragging him back to the point, I said, “Cooke City is cut off for the winter?”

“Not usually. Highway 212 through the park’s kept open pretty much, even when all the other roads are closed to anything but snowmobiles and the snow coaches. So they can go across the northern part of the park to reach Gardiner, Montana, and go north from there.”

“But Jean-Marie and her friend don’t do that?”

“It’s a long way around. It’s two-and-a-half, three hours in summer. Figure you’d be pushing five hours with good weather and no *events* in winter. Add those in and no telling. To get there, you’d have to first drive to Red Lodge, then make that round-about trip.”

Every time I thought I had the Wyomingness of Wyoming figured out, it revealed a new layer.

Though in fairness, this time was more the Montananess of Montana.

His phone rang.

“Will you check that?” He held up his hands, indicating the impracticality of picking up the phone.

Though we both know he would have if he'd been alone, in case it was Tamantha.

"Sure." It was no hardship sliding my hand into his pocket for the phone. "It's your parents."

Our eyes met for a moment.

I accepted the call. "Hi, it's Elizabeth. Tom's here, too, but he, um, has his hands full. I'll put you on speaker."

"Oh, Elizabeth. I'm glad you're there." That was his mother, alone. No hint of his father in view. Plus a further hint that he wasn't there in her lighter than normal voice. What a sad commentary that was.

"Hi, Mom," he called.

"He's, uh, doctoring a horse, but I can get closer so you can hear him." I kept my back to his doings.

"I just heard about Keefe Dobey and was so shocked. Do they know anything more? Have they arrested anybody?"

Tom didn't answer, so I said, "Not yet. It seems to be a mystery to them."

Us, too, but I didn't say that.

"Of course it is. Can't imagine why anyone in this world would want to harm that sweet man. And poor Wendy Barlow—she's had enough hard knocks, and now this."

"Hard knocks?"

"Mm-hmm. She had to sell her lovely home down here and rent a much smaller place. It was either sell this one or the ranch and everyone knew she'd never sell Elk Rock Ranch. And all because her brothers resented how the uncle left her the ranch in his will and they tightened the purse strings on her income that comes from the family business, while they get plenty."

They all worked for the family business, as I knew from Matt Lester in Philadelphia, so they might be justified in that.

"You must be good friends with Wendy Barlow," I said mildly.

"I wouldn't say that." She looked slightly puzzled, then it cleared. "It was after a lunch we'd happened to attend together. I suppose I was a connection to home amid all those other strangers. We sat next to each other and . . . well, she did have a number of glasses of wine. She didn't even seem to remember telling me the next time we saw each other, because she pretended she was still living in the same place, when I knew she wasn't."

She shot a quick look over her shoulder, as if checking for her husband, but he wasn't there.

"Thomas always liked Keefe. Said he was restful. Didn't talk your ear off.

"But that sad topic wasn't why I called. We received the wedding invitation today and it's beautiful. We're so touched the way you included us and your parents in the information for the reception."

That had been one of the surprisingly easy decisions.

Invitations for first-time weddings usually included the parents, especially if they footed the bill. Since this was a second marriage for each of us and we were paying, the wedding invitation came from us. On the invitation for the reception, we'd included language about joining our families . . . and named Tamantha, my parents, and his parents.

"*We?* Speak for yourself, Mom," Tom said loud enough for her to hear.

A wince flickered across her face. "We—I . . . I appreciate you keeping us updated on the wedding preparations, Elizabeth. I do so hope to come."

"Then come," Tom said. "I'll get you a plane ticket. If he doesn't want to come—"

"Oh, it's not that, Tommy. Truly. It just brings up . . ." She looked into the screen at me, asking me to understand. "He was so proud of Tommy's basketball."

To my mind, that translated as Thomas living vicariously through Tom's success.

Perhaps that silent judgment showed in my face, because she added with the pleading for understanding now in her voice. "It was hard for him when Tommy left college."

Hard for him? What about Tom?

He'd given up his scholarship when Tamantha's mother said she was pregnant. They got married. And then she wasn't pregnant, a situation clouded in doubt for years before he knew for sure that she'd lied about ever being pregnant. By that time, Tamantha had come along.

Their divorce followed. But their daughter tied them together in uncomfortable ways. Until his ex's death.

Tom grunted. "He should have been happy I left school. Meant he had me to work on the ranch, while he built up the road construction business." Tom kept both of them going now, though in a reversal from his father's priorities, the ranch was more important to him. "And what's this about my basketball being important to him? Never said so when I was playing. Work he wanted done always came first. No basketball game or practice excused the chores. Schoolwork, either."

"You have to understand. His own father was the same way. So was mine. It's why Thomas . . ."

When she didn't say more, Tom moved over to be onscreen. Gently, he said, "We're glad you like the invitation, Mom. And we mean it about getting you a ticket."

"I know, Tommy. But I still hope . . ."

"I know you do, Mom."

She swallowed. "Yes, well, I better let you two kids get on with your day. Thank you again."

Amid the good-byes, I heard her words again.

His own father was the same way. It's why he . . .

Never loved the ranch?

Never wanted to visit?

Never showed his son affection?

All those were guesses. Tom rarely talked about his parents or his upbringing. I knew it was a wound, but it seemed to be one he'd found a way to not only live with, but not allow to impinge on his life now.

"Want to put it back in my pocket?" Tom asked, tipping his head to the now blank-screened phone.

"You bet."

When I'd finished, taking longer than necessary, which had both of us grinning, I stepped back and said, "You deliberately set out to be a different kind of father."

He turned back to his work, saying lightly, "Who wouldn't?"

"Your father. Most people. The vast majority replicate what drove them nuts in their own parents because it's what they know—all they know. It takes a very strong person to strike out in another direction. As you have. You do know you're an amazing father."

He half grinned, but his eyes were serious. "Got an amazing kid."

"No argument there."

"Are you marrying me for my parenting skills?" Now the grin reached his eyes.

"They don't hurt your resume any." Neither did certain other skills he employed. *We* employed.

Though not at the moment. So I used another of my skills and said, "Something I've wondered about . . . you're not using junior."

"I'm not a junior."

"Thomas Burrell—" I pointed at his chest. Then switched to point toward his phone. "—Thomas Burrell. Doesn't that get confusing? Documents and stuff, if no other way."

"He's Thomas Yoder Burrell."

And the man before me was Thomas David Burrell. "Ah."

I could ask about the different middle names. It was unlikely to open the topic of the trouble between father and son.

But I had a thought.

That question to a different person might just open the topic of the trouble between father and son.

For now I left it with that comprehending *Ah.*

"You do know your mother's homesick for Cottonwood County?" I asked him.

"She's not coming back as long as he's alive."

Startled, I said, "You don't think there's any chance they'll come to the wedding?"

"Back here permanent, I meant."

He turned off that conversational road. "So, that could explain what you heard about Wendy spending less time away the past few winters."

I let him make that turn . . . for now. We were not done with the topic of his parents for good. "It could. Also an attitude I picked up from Wendy about her brothers."

"I see that look in your eyes. Go on, Elizabeth, get out of here now. Go get more answers to those questions I see piling up."

CHAPTER TWENTY-FIVE

AS I CONTINUED toward Sherman, I tried to put concern about Tom and his father aside and stick to the murder investigation.

I replayed the conversations with Mrs. P and Gee in my head. It felt like trying to put pieces of confetti back together into a whole when the scraps originally came from dozens, maybe hundreds of different sheets.

Needham Bender emerged from the courthouse and started in the direction of the *Sherman Independence* as I drove up.

I pulled alongside him, lowered the passenger window, and said, "Want a ride?"

"Hey, Elizabeth. I probably should walk—according to Thelma, I'm about a negative thousand steps a day. But for the pleasure of your company, I'll risk my wife's ire."

"Brave man."

He chuckled as he got in.

"Something big at the courthouse?" I asked.

"Wouldn't tell you if there was."

"Fair enough."

"I like that youngster you folks have hired—Nala Choi."

"So do we."

"More coming?"

"Hiring is going slow. Excruciatingly slow."

"Young folks don't want to come out here? Where's their spirit of adventure?"

"It's not the younger would-be hires. We have a good crop of submissions there. It's the established TV news folks that are hard to line up."

"Don't want to come to the country's smallest market, huh?"

"Surprisingly, that's not the obstacle. Some of them sounded downright eager to try a place where there's no place but up. And they like the idea of coaching the rookies, especially with less of a news load on their plate. The issue is they're entrenched. Sometimes in the job— needing more time for a better retirement or up for a promotion or addicted to the pace. And even if it's not the job, it's the spouse's job, kids' school, aging parents nearby. One guy even said he didn't want to leave his cardiologist. Even though I pointed out he might not *need* a cardiologist if he eased up on the stress, cigars, and drinking."

"That's the way to recruit, Elizabeth," he said dryly.

"He wasn't coming anyway." I sighed. "Mike thinks we need an attraction. Something that makes Cottonwood County famous, alluring."

I recounted our brainstorming along those lines.

He didn't join in with more outrageous ideas the way I thought he would. Instead, he seemed to grow more serious. But when I finished, he said, "I might have an idea." So perhaps I misjudged him.

"What? Happy to take anything back to Mike."

"What about a newspaper person."

It took a second to shift from an idea to promote the county to an answer to our hiring situation. "A newspaper person? To run a TV newsroom?"

"Sure. The news is the news. They'd need someone to cover them on what's peculiar to TV news—and I do mean *peculiar*—as well as tech stuff. At least to start. But reporting, news sense, working a beat or the phones, all the core requirements they'd be great at."

When I found myself wondering if my Philadelphia buddy Matt Lester might have any leads on individuals, I knew Needham's suggestion might work.

"Here's the other thing." His voice sounded heavy. "There's a good number who need jobs. It's not good times for newspapers. Buyouts when they're lucky, layoffs otherwise, and bankruptcies affecting retirement plans all too often. I've had people reaching out for leads on jobs—including joining our minuscule staff here. People who should be running this place."

"Nobody could run the *Independence* the way you do."

"Thanks. But I mean it. At least half of them could teach me a thing or two."

"That's really interesting, Needham. Let me talk to Mike. We would need to fill the broadcast knowledge gaps for someone with a newspaper background . . ."

Although, with KWMT being so far from the cutting-edge of technology that it was like a distant contrail in the Wyoming sky, that was never going to be our selling point. Grounding in the fundamentals and the opportunities to do a lot of flavors of work fast were the big selling points we pitched to young hires.

"Do you ever think we're fighting a losing battle, Needham? Seems like half the people don't want news, but only confirmation of what they already think, and the other half puts their faith in crowd-sourcing."

He grunted. "Crowd-sourcing news isn't news. It's also not new. It's been around forever. It's otherwise known as gossip."

I snorted in appreciation and agreement.

"A long tradition from the original tabloids to what now gets churned around as celebrity news—with huge, disbelieving quotes around that use of the word. In the early days of this country, the newspapers were not many steps above that. They were frequently the voices of parties or factions, without a thought to being factual, much less fair, and balanced. What was new—for most of journalism—in the twentieth century was an emphasis on those qualities. The outlets that didn't achieve it were dismissed as rags."

"So, we're returning to the bad old days?" I asked as I pulled up in front of the *Independence* building, whose century-plus old brick façade demonstrated a good aspect of the old days.

"We aren't. Some might, including those consuming the euphemistically titled crowd-sourced news, but we're still aiming for those goals of factual, fair, and balanced." He exited the SUV, then leaned back in.

"You and me and a lot of others, Elizabeth. Still doing it right. Battle's not over."

BACKTRACKING SLIGHTLY, I came around to the museum's rear entrance.

My goal of catching Clara without being announced—and thus cutting her time to build resistance to talking to me—failed, because she was there, doing something in the open back of the museum's van. It was as well-aged as the NewsMobile, which was more appropriate for a history museum than a news station, but not as durable.

She groaned when she saw me.

So did the other woman standing on the ground beside the open van doors. Vicky Upton worked in the museum's gift shop and baked delicious brownies sold there. She also held a grudge against me about a murder investigation focusing on her family.

Some people are overly sensitive.

Although we had reached an entry-level of détente over another inquiry a few months ago.

"Elizabeth, I really don't have time," Clara said immediately. "I need to get all these boxes inside and Vicky's leaving me—"

"I already made ten trips and I told you I had to leave—"

"We're nowhere near done and—"

"I'll carry boxes."

My words stopped them both.

Vicky swung around and put the box she held into my hands. "Great. I'm going, Clara. It's way past when I said I'd stay."

"Don't go inside empty-handed," Clara ordered as she pushed boxes from deeper inside the van toward the doors. "Take a box on your way."

Vicky took the box out of my hands. "Fine. I'm going."

As she left, I said to Clara, "I'll carry boxes if you'll talk while we work."

Clara's eyes narrowed. She jumped down from the back of the van and put a box in my hands. Then she stacked a second on top, watching me with narrowed eyes. When I didn't object or drop the boxes, she said, "Deal."

I DISCOVERED ANOTHER reason my sometimes cohort Wardell Yardley could be drawn to Clara Atwood.

The woman had endurance. I was huffing and puffing but she kept talking as we went in the museum with one set of boxes and came out with another. Trip after trip.

At the start, I let her ramble over the general top of Wild West outlaws—it was a tactic to relax her. Not just because I was trying to get a rhythm along with catching my breath.

"You know," she said as we headed back toward the van, "for all the talk—and movies—about Butch Cassidy robbing banks and trains, he was never imprisoned for that."

"Really?" The boxes heading this direction tended to be lighter, presumably because extraneous material was removed, so my huffing wasn't as obvious as the inbound trip. "I thought I'd seen a photo of him from prison. Square-faced guy giving nothing away."

"One of the two most-frequently used photos of him. The other is the one called the Fort Worth Five—Sundance and Butch sitting on either side with Ben Kilpatrick in the middle and John Carter and Kid Curry—Harvey Logan, officially—standing behind them. Curry was the one law enforcement really wanted. He killed around a dozen men, most of them lawmen."

"But Butch Cassidy never killed anyone?" Sam McCracken had said that.

"Well," she drew that out. "He and Sundance were said to have *claimed* they never did. But, if the shootout in Bolivia was their final act, then witnesses who saw the bodies identified as Butch and Sundance said Sundance had a number of wounds, with one to his forehead. While Butch, next to him, had one in his temple—the inference being that, with no means of escape, Butch shot his badly injured partner, then himself. If that's true, he did kill someone—Sundance."

"*If that's true?* You believe they got away?" Don't think I was mocking her. From the first time I saw the movie as a kid, I've been in the *They got away* camp.

With those boxes in the van, I took two more. So did she.

"Belief is immaterial. And the evidence is inconclusive, starting with comparing photographs of them from better days to ones taken of the dead gunmen in San Vicente, Bolivia."

"They have photos of their dead bodies?"

"So some sources said. I've never seen them. Not authenticated ones."

"Non-authenticated? There's a black market in photos of corpses?"

"Used to be the done thing. There's a photo of Ben Kilpatrick's dead body being held upright by the guys who objected to him trying to rob their train and killed him with the proverbial blunt instrument to the head."

"And people talk about the violence now."

"They've done forensic DNA tests on some bodies in the San Vicente cemetery where Butch and Sundance were said to have been buried in an unmarked grave. At least one set of remains that was supposed to be Butch was proven absolutely to have not been. And no other tests have definitively linked bodies there to Butch or Sundance. But who's to say one of the many other bodies buried there isn't one of them? Bodies weren't interred with a lot of organization," she said dryly. "They'd have to test every body to be able to say they weren't there."

I put my boxes on the growing stack in the storage room and sucked in air.

"Maybe they did make it out. And maybe the reason Etta disappeared from the records is that Sundance—and presumably Butch— made it out of Bolivia. Maybe she went to join them wherever they were, whether back in the United States or somewhere else."

I liked that idea.

Clara didn't look impressed, however, as she pointed to the next boxes to go. "You're not the only one thinking that. There's a theory that a rancher in Utah was really the Sundance Kid. But, again, DNA said no. Only the proponents of that theory are saying maybe someone else's DNA got mixed up with the rancher's because the cemetery flooded. Or maybe Sundance was adopted by the Longabaughs and that's why a distant relative's DNA didn't match. Yeah," she said in response to my raised eyebrows, "they're grasping at DNA straws."

Couldn't argue with her there. "Let's go back to you saying Cassidy was never imprisoned."

"I didn't say that. I said he was never imprisoned for robbing a bank or a train. He was, in fact, in the Wyoming prison in Laramie after being found guilty of larceny of a horse, which he claimed he bought. Some historians say he might have bought the horse, but from a rustler friend. And some say he might have been an equal partner in the rustling. He was found guilty and sentenced to two years in prison. That's when it got really interesting."

"*That's* when it got interesting?"

"Uh-huh. He hadn't done a whole lot at that point. Oh, yeah, the judge who sentenced him said he also thought Butch had been guilty on a charge of rustling he'd been acquitted of the year before, but nothing like what he did later. And apparently he impressed a lot of people. The judge who sentenced him wrote to the governor asking that his sentence be commuted, saying he thought Butch could become a leader of men—"

I *huh'd*.

"For good," she clarified. "And the governor did it. Butch got out after eighteen months. There was a legend Butch told the governor he'd leave Wyoming alone. A promise he didn't keep.

"He organized robberies in Idaho and Utah, then, three and a half years after the pardon, came the job on the Union Pacific in Wilcox, Wyoming. The next month, Butch's best friend, Elzy Lay was arrested. That could be seen as the start of the disintegration of the gang, especially with several dying in shootouts with lawmen. Butch might have seen what was ahead, because Butch tried to reach out for amnesty. Accounts differ of whether the authorities ever seriously considered it."

Somehow she had to be picking lighter boxes than I had.

She had plenty of breath to say, "Probably also didn't help that some of his known associates pulled off other robberies and Kid Curry killed a number of lawmen around the same time. Maybe Butch saw it wasn't going to happen. He and Sundance and others robbed a Union Pacific train near Tipton, Wyoming, in August 1900 and amnesty was off the table.

"In December 1900 came the other photograph you've probably seen—him with Sundance and others in the 'Fort Worth Five' the Pinkertons got ahold of and used for wanted photos. By February the next year, he and Sundance and Etta Place left for South America. And you know what happened—or didn't happen—there.

"A couple sidenotes. The governor who pardoned Cassidy in 1896, was not reelected in 1898. In fact, he wasn't even nominated by his party to run again."

"Because he pardoned Butch Cassidy?"

She rolled a shoulder. "Probably didn't help, but with him not winning his party's nomination, you've got to suspect more general politics at play. The other sidenote has to do with Elzy Lay."

"Butch's friend, sentenced to life for murder," I remembered.

"Right. In New Mexico. He became a trustee, even accompanying the warden on a trip. While they were gone, inmates took the warden's wife and daughter hostage. Lay was credited with persuading the inmates to let them go and was pardoned in 1906. As far as anyone can tell, he never committed another crime. Had a family. Lived in Wyoming, then moved to California, where he died in 1934."

"Is any of that history in these boxes?"

"Heaven only knows. Teague—blast his disorderly hide—sure didn't know. Or care."

"What about history closer to home, like Oscar and Pearl Virtanen?"

"Ah-hah. That's what you're after. To find out what—if anything—about them Keefe found in the boxes he looked in. Yes, Mrs. Parens told me about that. Of course she did—and that was before he was murdered." Her head jerked up as she deposited her boxes in the storeroom. "You don't think he was killed over something in the boxes—?"

"Can't know until we know what—if anything—he found. That's why I want to look through—"

"No."

"—or have you look through them immediately."

"No. There is a method to this and I will not jeopardize the work for the museum on a longshot." She hefted two more boxes and walked out.

I had to scurry to get my two and catch up with her at the outside door. "Murder. Justice," I huffed. "You couldn't move them up in the rotation?"

"No. But I'll tell you what," she said as we reached the van still holding a dozen boxes to move inside, with an equal number to come out. "You help me to the end and I'll let you know when I do get to those boxes."

"Deal."

I'd keep working on her to get to them sooner.

CHAPTER TWENTY-SIX

I BRUSHED MYSELF off as I got out of the SUV, but I still looked like I'd been doing hard labor in a dusty attic.

Ivy was occupied, so I sat at one of the computer terminals, looking up names of the outlaws we'd encountered. I'd done this at home and at KWMT, too, but the library had different resources.

Not much at all on the Virtanens, as Ivy had said. I segued to Laura Bullion and Ben Kilpatrick, confirming much of what I'd already seen. Also confirming an impression.

"Are you waiting for me, Elizabeth?"

"Yes, and thank you." I turned toward her as she sat in the empty spot beside me.

She smiled in protest. "I haven't done anything."

"Oh, yes, you did. You saved me from looking up Butch, Sundance, and Etta, again, and getting a headache."

"A headache?"

"A thousand contradictory stories, often stated flatly as fact."

She laughed, then covered her mouth in an instinctive reversion to the old *Hush* days of libraries. "I *know*. And they don't cite their sources or specify dates, so it's hard—impossible—to tell *when* they're contradicting each other or what's already been proven untrue."

She shook her head in commiseration, which I appreciated.

I wondered if Keefe and Sam had felt the same frustration. Or if they, like some of the writers of the online articles, picked a particular version of the story and went with it, not acknowledging pesky contradictions.

"Ivy, I know the person who shared Keefe's interests, especially in the Virtanens is Sam McCracken. Did they talk about going to Elk Rock Ranch?"

"Keefe mentioned Sam coming to his place a few times. In fact, he said Sam was coming—"

Her eyes widened.

On video I'd have made her say it herself. Now, I spared her. "Just before Keefe was killed."

"Yes," she said in a small voice. "But that doesn't mean—"

"Did you observe them together? In conversation, sharing notes—"

"They did share notes," she said eagerly, as if that proved murder was impossible between them. "And they'd sit together sometimes, so if I'd find something—anything—I'd bring it to both of them. That was a relief, because they often asked for the same material and it was awkward giving it to one first, though I always based it on who asked first and—"

Before she wound herself into an unbreakable knot, I jumped in with, "I wonder why they became so fascinated?" I already had a good idea for each, so I broadened it. "Why people are drawn to . . . well, thieves?"

I understood the allure of the Butch and Sundance characters from the movie. But that was a movie, not who the men had been in real life. After all they did steal things and I've never gotten the draw of thieves. Okay, Cary Grant in *It Takes a Thief*. But, c'mon, Cary Grant. Besides, he was reformed.

Even as a kid, I was not entranced with Robin Hood the way my brothers were. Stealing from the rich, giving to the poor was a stop-gap measure. You needed a more systemic solution. Granted, those take longer, and a free press is vital, which they didn't have in the Middle Ages. But, still, not my favorite movies.

Ivy tipped her head, considering my question seriously.

"It's seen as a period when the Wild in the Wild West was fading away and people—especially men—can get nostalgic about that. The idea that men were free to roam the west and not be connected to the markers of civilization, like churches and schools and such. In fact, they robbed two symbols of the taming of the west—banks and railroads."

I suspected that had more to do with the fact that that's where the money was, but I wouldn't argue.

"In this area, the turn from the nineteenth to the twentieth century was viewed as a far more major shift than moving from the twentieth to the twenty-first was for us. Those outlaws started operating a few years before and most of them were dead by the end of the first decade of the new century.

"So, yes, some nostalgia. Seeing it as a more romantic period. For example, did you know the Wanted poster on Butch Cassidy for one of his robberies referred to him as a Highwayman? So did Wanted posters for Oscar Virtanen."

Okay, that was kind of cool.

"Highwaymen." She rolled the word around on her tongue "So much more appealing than bank robbers. One certainly wouldn't call the Al Capones and John Dillingers of the 1930s *highwaymen.* Far too dashing and romantic for them. Then, the emphasis was on how many people they'd killed—think of Bonnie and Clyde. But with Butch Cassidy's gang it was—" She paused. "It was mostly the amount of money they stole, which was considerable."

"You're thinking of Kid Curry as the exception, because he did kill around a dozen people."

"Yes, as a matter of fact I was. If you're interested, I can show you copies of those Wanted posters."

I was and she did.

The photo of Butch Cassidy was from his time in prison. The one for Oscar Virtanen had no photo, but instead a sketch. He could have been just about any young man of that era with regular features and no distinguishing marks. I thought I saw some indication of Butch Cassidy's personality in his photo, but there was none of Oscar's in the sketch.

"And here's a reward poster for Laura Bullion."

She was called away after that and I left, thinking about the posters.

Sure, *highwayman* was romantic—if you weren't on the opposite end of the holdup. But I was also struck that the reward for Laura Bullion was one-tenth of that offered on Butch and one-fifth of that offered on Oscar.

But no reward for Pearl.

That sent my thoughts down another trail.

Pearl was in on the two earlier robberies with him.

Why did she not accompany him on the last one?

Could she have been pregnant?

Sam said the secondary source about that now-lost article commented on the posse member's deep sympathy for the widow. Why such sympathy for a dead outlaw's wife? But if that young wife was also pregnant . . .

Speculation. Total speculation.

But as long as I was speculating, it also occurred to me that with the planning that had gone into the second robbery, with getting out of town on a train, then laying a false trail that they were going farther than they did, and getting clean away, perhaps there was other planning.

Like where to hide the loot if a posse was hot on his trail?

He'd gone north, toward where Pearl was, where their property was. Also toward a pre-designated spot?

So, if he did bury the proceeds, she would have known where it was. Were these men chasing something that—if it existed in the first place—most likely was removed by his accomplice, his wife not long after it was buried?

Would it matter to Keefe?

I got the idea that he wanted the connection, not the fortune. At least he wanted the connection more.

But Sam McCracken?

How would he react if someone pulled the treasure hunt rug out from under him?

I thought of what I'd read about the searchers for Forrest Fenn's treasure. A few went off the deep end—during the search and after it was declared over.

If Keefe told Sam he was the proven descendant of Oscar Virtanen . . .

Sam wouldn't care. Unless it affected finding the treasure.

It wasn't like Keefe would inherit the money even if he had been proven to be Oscar's descendant, since it was stolen.

So, was there anything that could have pushed Sam over the edge?

CHAPTER TWENTY-SEVEN

I **PUT THAT** question to the group during a video call, back in the KWMT news director's office, eating takeout dinner from Hamburger Heaven with Diana after the Five.

Before the broadcast, I'd called James Longbaugh's office for an appointment. To my surprise, he had one available for the next morning.

Three of tonight's top stories had Diana's video from today's assignments. I edited a couple pieces for Leona, so I wasn't a total waste of newsroom space.

"Keefe taunted him," Jennifer said. She was in her apartment in Evanston.

"He doesn't sound like the taunting kind. No—" I held up an objecting finger to my own objection. "Ideas first. Then we'll consider them. So, Keefe taunted him."

"Keefe told him there was no treasure," Diana offered. "Though how he would come to that conclusion, I have no idea."

"Keefe told him he had an inside track on the treasure because he'd been proved as a descendant. The only descendant as far as we know." From an office at the TV station in downtown Chicago, Mike added, "That's assuming he had the DNA test results."

Skipping over that last part, I said, "Oscar and Pearl were married young, so that cuts the chances for kids beforehand. No word of their having any kids before they went into bank robbing. That lasted about two years. Then Oscar's killed."

"So how did Keefer think he was descended from them? There

had to be a kid in there somewhere for that to happen," Mike said.

We were all quiet for a moment, except for faint chewing.

"It's interesting," Diana said slowly, "that Pearl was his accomplice except for the last one."

I tried not to grin. I'd bet she was on the same track I'd followed earlier.

"What are you thinking, Diana?" Mike asked.

"That she might not have ridden with him on that job because she physically couldn't, having just had or being about to have a baby. I know, I know, there's no proof."

"I labeled it speculation when I wondered the same thing today. But that's what we're doing right now—letting our minds run wild with speculation, hoping we land on something."

Diana said, "A baby on the way or just born could be *why* Oscar pulled another job without waiting for her to participate. He wanted a bigger nest egg with another mouth to feed."

"Maybe there's no treasure at all. Maybe the bank people lied about how much he stole and they took the money."

That foray into deep skepticism by Jennifer caused a silence I covered by saying, "Boy, I wish I'd thought of that to tell Sam McCracken."

"You'd have made the poor man's head explode," Diana said.

"I know. That's why I wish it."

"What have you got against him?" Diana's voice went thoughtful and dry. "Other than he's wasting time he could be spending with his wife and kids. I did hear from several people that's caused tension between him and Serena. The word 'obsessed' kept coming up."

"There's a flaw with that," Mike said.

"A big flaw—he's making stupid choices." Was she thinking about her husband, who'd lost the opportunity to ever again spend time with his wife and kids in a fatal ranch accident years ago?

"Huh? Oh. No, not that. Jennifer's idea about the bank people saying Oscar stole more than he did and them keeping the difference," Mike said. "They couldn't have known he'd die from his wounds."

"If he got away, that worked, too," Jennifer argued.

"But if he got caught—as he was—he could have exposed their lie."

"If the authorities believed him." She clearly didn't think they would. "Why would they take the word of a bank robber over employees."

"If he had the money with him to *show* them the amount—"

"They'd say the other guys who went south took the money. Or he hid most of it—which is what they said after he died."

"But—"

"Whoa, you two," I protested. "That's all stuff that concerns Sam McCracken. Not us. Because it didn't concern Keefe."

"You're right," Jennifer said coolly. "We focus on Keefe. And Ivy said Keefe said Sam was going to his cabin, so that's opportunity."

"If he actually went." Mike spoke low enough that Jennifer didn't respond.

I said quickly, "It is. But the more I think about Sam McCracken as a suspect, the less enthusiastic I am. Yes, we considered him in that other case. But his motive then would have been to protect his wife and kids. That could stir a lot more people to murder than the possibility of finding out about lesser-known outlaws who might or might not have buried loot somewhere."

"Does he have an alibi?" Jennifer asked.

"Shaky, if any," I said. "Didn't try to pin down Serena until we know the time of death."

"And we don't have time of death with Aunt Gee stonewalling me," Mike grumbled. "But McCracken's passionate about these outlaws and treasure. If he thought he was getting close, then Keefe blocked him . . ."

I couldn't argue with the reasoning.

Besides, he covered all the bases.

"You're right. He stays on the list."

"Are we confident about focusing on Oscar and Pearl to the exclusion of the other women?" Mike asked.

"Let's consider that. Etta Place—or whatever her real name was— disappeared after 1907. On at least two of her reported return trips to the United States from South America, she and Sundance went to medical facilities. There's the possibility she was ill, which could have led to an early death."

"Or she was pregnant," Jennifer said.

"No reports of a child, were there?" Diana asked.

"None that I know of. As for Laura Bullion, she disappeared shortly after Ben Kilpatrick was killed in 1912 trying to rob a train, barely a year after getting out of prison. Nothing's heard from Laura for years. She resurfaced in Memphis in 1918, claiming to be a war widow from World War I."

"Well, she could have been with that kind of gap," Mike said.

"I suppose. But her war widow story wasn't given much credence."

"When you say disappeared, you mean . . . what?" Diana asked.

I considered. "In essence, it means the Pinkerton agency stopped paying attention because they were after the men. Although they really should have kept track of Laura Bullion, since evidence points to her dressing as a man and participating in robberies. But maybe they figured they'd gotten the money back, so forget her."

"They got the money back? Not from all the robberies," Diana said.

"No. But most of the money from the Great Northern Railway near Wagner, Montana, on July 3, 1901. Ben Kilpatrick, Kid Curry, and a third man got away with tens of thousands of dollars in unsigned bank notes."

"Kid who? Not Sundance?" Jennifer asked.

"No. Mrs. P said newspapers of the day frequently attributed actions to one or the other erroneously, but this was definitely Kid Curry. Not only had Sundance, Etta, and Butch left for South America earlier in the year, but Kid Curry's girlfriend was arrested for passing notes. He got away, temporarily.

"St. Louis police arrested Ben Kilpatrick and found a hotel room key in his pocket. When they got to the hotel, they found Laura Bullion checking out. She had unsigned banknotes from the robbery in her luggage. Laura got out of prison in 1905. Kilpatrick got out in 1911 and was killed the next year trying to rob another train. From 1912 until around 1918, when she surfaced in Memphis, there's little or no information on Laura. She remained in Memphis until her death in the 1960s. Apparently late in life she didn't keep her identity secret."

"What happened to the other robbers?" Jennifer asked.

"Curry was caught in 1902, imprisoned, escaped, then shot himself after being caught stealing horses. The third robber was killed in a drunken shootout with law enforcement, possibly a self-inflicted wound."

"Not a lot of longevity," Mike said.

"It was that kind of occupation. And the women slid away into the mists."

"You want me to find out where the women went?" Jennifer asked.

"I appreciate your offering, but I won't do that to you. That's a majorly dangerous rabbit hole. Etta Place has baffled researchers for a century-plus. Theories all over the place, from dying, to becoming a prostitute, to marrying a fight promoter, to being shot in a domestic dispute, to becoming a schoolteacher. In South America or here. Living only a couple years longer or surviving into the 1960s. And each researcher's positive he or she is absolutely right. Similar story with Laura Bullion's blank of five years before she settled in Memphis."

Abruptly, Jennifer said, "Did you know the first guy Laura Bullion paired up with had been married to her aunt? I read up on her during a break today."

"He dumped the aunt for the niece?" Diana asked.

"No. The aunt died from fever a year into the marriage. He connected with Laura later. Then they split the blanket and—"

I interrupted, "Split the blanket?"

"Pretty self-explanatory for ending a relationship. Handy when it's not officially a divorce," Diana said. "Also torn the blanket."

I'd have to remember those.

"*Anyway,*" Jennifer said with impatient emphasis, "she hooked up with that guy, then Ben Kilpatrick, then that guy again before she went back to Kilpatrick. When she disappeared after Kilpatrick died, maybe she went back to the first guy—"

"He'd already died—killed by law enforcement who suspected him of a murder he hadn't committed in 1901."

"So, still a blank in Laura's history," Diana said.

Nodding, I moved on. "And Pearl Virtanen's after Oscar died."

"I'll get the guys on it. Start with the census."

I had a momentary vision of Jennifer's guys encountering these women and their outlaw significant others in the timelessness of the cyber world. I'd pay to be a spectator if that meeting took place outside my imagination.

"Doesn't have to be from right after Oscar Virtanen's death, either," Jennifer said. "Later censuses could show her with a kid of the right age."

"Good point," I said. "I'll let you know if there are any pointers in the dissertation Mrs. P gave me. But it did rather give away the ending up front by saying what happened to Pearl was not known."

Diana tipped her head. "We don't want to eliminate other possibilities, just because Keefe zeroed in on the Virtanens. Laura Bullion being *disappeared* for those years after Ben died, could fit with a woman having a baby, staying a few years, then leaving it to be raised in a more stable situation."

"Or the kid could die."

Diana and I stared at Mike. Jennifer huffed in disapproval at his grim outlook.

He stuck to his guns. "Well, it could. High infant mortality rate's a historic fact."

"I was thinking," I said, leaving that topic behind, "knowing the historical truth one way or another might not affect this investigation, because it wouldn't change what Keefe *believed* was true."

"But," Diana said, "how could it have led to his murder? Unless . . . unless there's some special information about the location of the treasure being held for someone who proves descent from Oscar and Pearl?"

"We haven't heard anything about something like that," Mike said. "Along with the fact that if someone somewhere held the secret location of this treasure for an Oscar Virtanen descendant, why wasn't it collected by earlier generations? Keefe's parent or grandparent, say, assuming he's related. Or—"

Jennifer jumped in. "Previous generations didn't know or couldn't prove the connection in pre-DNA days."

"Or," Mike repeated emphatically, "why didn't whoever's been holding this secret of the location for more than a century—and presumably passing it down to younger folks, because it sure isn't one person from the early 1900s to now—take it?"

"Honesty," Diana said.

"Afraid of Oscar Virtanen's ghost," Jennifer offered.

Mike shook his head. "Buried treasure—it's such a long shot."

"You're getting stodgy," Jennifer tossed at him. "Before you would have loved the idea of buried treasure."

"Before what?" he snapped.

"Before you got that big job in Chicago, and got all stodgy."

Diana and I looked at each other. We'd both thought they were getting along better recently. But this felt even sharper than they used to be. Especially Mike.

"You're in Chicago, too. Or close enough, so—"

Diana cut across the squabbling with the ruthlessness of a mother of teenagers. "We're off topic. Back to this inquiry about why a man's dead."

I might have let it run a little longer to see if it revealed anything interesting. You could say that made me a better journalist, while Diana qualified as the better friend.

But I cooperated. "Mike, you said something early on about Keefer Dobey that's stuck in my head—that he's never harmed anybody. But Randall Kenyon could feel Keefe harmed him."

"By helping his daughter when she was hurt? Hard to say how much Keefe had to do with her transformation, but he sure as heck was there and just for that, her father should be down-on-his-knees grateful." Mike's vehemence also spoke of his regard for Keefe.

"That's what he's saying," Jennifer pointed out. "Over and over— how grateful he is. And how that's what made him want to buy the place."

"That and running the financials," Diana said dryly.

Was there something in the fact that the two of us who'd met him in person didn't trust Randall Kenyon?

"He could be grateful for Keefe's role in Robin's epiphany and still feel harmed by him," I persisted. "Jealous that Keefe was, at least partially, the instrument of that. Resentful that she still seems—or seemed—to turn to him."

"That would *really* suck if Keefe was killed by an egotistical father with his nose out of joint."

Mike hadn't yet reached the stage of grief when he realized logically that no one cause of death was going to suck less than another.

"He's not a man accustomed to not being able to direct things the way he wants them to go," I said.

"I wonder if that's some of why his wife's death hit so hard—and why it hit Robin so hard, too, because she does seem to be like him."

"Good point, Diana. Robin is definitely his daughter, under her layer of recent kumbaya-ness. Of course there's real pain and grief for each of them, but I think the other is part of it, too. Not only that his wife, her mother died, but that they haven't been able to bend the grief to their wills. They have to live through it, like everybody else."

"That's the part that bugs them—*like everybody else.*"

I nodded at Jennifer's words.

But would a sense of helplessness against his own feelings have been enough to make Randall Kenyon kill Keefer Dobey?

Plus, I didn't see it applying that way to Robin.

"One more thing," Jennifer said. "I found the video of Keefe. The one by the guest."

CHAPTER TWENTY-EIGHT

SHE SHARED HER screen so we could watch it together, with our faces thumbnailed down the side.

I wasn't sure how it helped us, but it was fascinating. In a slo-mo sort of way.

Wendy had a point with her *Sloooow-leeeee*.

Also, I saw what Penny meant about spaces between Keefer and other people. There was a detachment about him. Not cold. Not superior. Simply . . . disconnected.

I also remembered Sam McCracken's comment about Keefe *letting woodland creatures come up to him.*

Because Sam saw this video?

If he had, it wasn't by accident.

It took even Jennifer and her crew an effort to find it. As a non-whiz, Sam would have had to really dig.

But what stuck in my head, even after we wrapped up and I got back to work recasting a story for the Ten, was a litany.

Etta Place disappeared. Laura Bullion disappeared. Pearl disappeared.

Yes, women did die or disappear, especially in that era.

Yes, the Pinkertons did not follow up on the women once the man they were connected to died. So maybe that bit of short-sighted sexism was a benefit.

That allowed the women to disappear.

Did it allow them—any of them—to go on to full lives.

And possibly have children.

✧　✧　✧　✧

HAVING ALREADY EXCHANGED good-night messages with Tom, I was in bed, reading the dissertation by Mrs. P's friend/mentor, when Mike called.

The dissertation was slow going, being academic and written in an earlier, more formal style. Yet a hint of wry humor came through to me now and then. Or was that my imagination or wishful thinking?

"I'm still wrestling with whether to hire Octavia Zabel," he said without preamble.

"Half an anchor in hand is worth one in the bush," I said.

"Worth even more than none in the bush." From that gloomy response, he bounced back immediately. "You're right. I'm hiring her. Gets us at least a little farther along."

"I was talking with Needham . . ."

I shared his idea about how we might benefit from the journalistic experience being jettisoned by newspapers.

He was quiet for a long moment, then said, "Our people already know how to put together a newscast. With an experienced anchor— or two—we'd cover more of the broadcast angles. A news director from a newspaper background could offer valuable journalistic experience . . . We'd still be sort of piecemeal, instead of the usual newsroom structure I'd hoped for."

"When has KWMT ever been usual? You're spoiled from being there in Chicago. Cast your mind back to working under the Haeburn-Fine regime," I said, invoking the dread names of our former news director and anchor.

"Yeah. I get that. I was hoping to offer really top-notch folks for the mentoring, what you dubbed post-grad training."

"So, we build more slowly. We take our piecemeal gains and we keep building on them. The reputation comes a bit more gradually. We'll still get there."

"It would mean a crash course in visual reporting for a newspaper hire."

"Maybe not as much as it would have before having an online

presence required newspapers to offer multimedia, too."

"Good point."

"We already thought we'd be teaching the young hires more about good video, with Diana as our secret weapon. We just expand the lessons to the news director."

"I hate to take her off assignments."

"Then don't. Send new hires out with her. Have them shoot the B-roll. Let her talk through what she's doing as she's doing it. Most of them are multimedia types anyway. Let them do the reporting while also honing their visual skills with her."

"Hmm. Are you going to talk to her?"

"We both will. Together."

He seemed satisfied as we said good-night, but not chipper.

Me, either, as I returned to the dissertation.

DAY FOUR

FRIDAY

CHAPTER TWENTY-NINE

I HADN'T INTENDED to be early for my appointment with James Longbaugh because I'm not a fan of waiting.

But I ran out of time for another stop at the Sherman Supermarket beforehand. I had no specific goal for a trip through Penny's lane, leaving my motivation low.

So, there I was in the tiny waiting area of the hundred-year-old converted house down a side street near the courthouse that had served Longbaugh lawyers for generations. The desk at the far end of the narrow room—positioned so its occupant could stretch out a leg and trip anyone who tried to rush James in his private office at the back—occupied by a young woman who did not appear like a leg-stretcher-tripper type.

Just then I heard—we both heard, judging by her lifted head—a raised male voice from the conference room on the other side of the wall from this waiting area.

It wasn't James Longbaugh's.

It was Randall Kenyon's.

I didn't catch the first spate of words, but heard what sounded like, *will not be denied by small-town and small-minded hack* before another lost patch of eloquence, then . . . *even in this backwater, I will make this deal happen. It's in the bag.*

I heard movement in the room, then the door swung open.

James stood at the door, holding it open as a not-so-subtle hint.

"You might get it done, Mr. Kenyon, but not with my representation. If there is a negotiation, I will be on the opposite side of the table." He was too smart a lawyer to put in words what his tone conveyed. That he'd do his best to make the other man pay with lots of dollars. "But I will be more surprised than I have been in most of my professional life if it comes to a negotiation. Good day."

"I'm not done. I'm—"

"You are. Elizabeth, if you'll come to my office." He looked at the assistant. "Please call the sheriff's department."

It was nice to have that last part aimed at Randall, not me.

James gestured me ahead of him down the short hallway toward the back. I would have strongly preferred to bring up the rear to see how Kenyon reacted. I had to be satisfied with looking back as I walked, trying to see around James.

Still, I heard Kenyon tromp out.

James pivoted to go to the front door and lock it behind him. He told the assistant. "If anyone tries to come in or knocks, call for me. Don't open the door."

"Do you still want me to call the sheriff's department?"

"Not unless he comes back."

In his office, he gestured me to a chair in front of the big old desk and took the one behind it.

"Randall Kenyon was here to . . .?" I invited.

He declined with, "Discuss a business matter."

I'd gotten that much on my own.

"And what are you here for today, Elizabeth?"

"I want to know about the setup at Elk Rock Ranch, especially how Chester Barlow set it up for the current generation."

Actually, I wanted to know everything and anything he knew. But saying that wouldn't get James to spill.

He considered for a moment. "I'll tell you what's a matter of record—which you could find on your own—but I'll save you the time."

"That's fair. I understand Chester treated Keefe and Brenda like they were part of the family, but never made that official?"

"Chester helped raise both of them, true. Keefe was a grown man when his mother died. As for Brenda in the early days after her parents' deaths, that, of course, was not something I dealt with, though my father did. Brenda has been and is this firm's client. Chester was not. He considered law a do-it-yourself project. But, no, there was nothing official in Chester's care for them."

"So neither Brenda nor Keefe had any claim on Elk Rock when he died?"

"None legally. And Chester made no provisions for anyone."

"No will?"

"Chester wasn't a man who accepted that he'd ever die." The way James said that made me think he'd encountered a few of those. "Closest living relatives were his niece and nephews."

"Wendy Barlow's brothers hold a share in the ranch?" I'd been told they didn't, but I wanted his take on the ownership.

"No. They wanted nothing to do with it. Nor did they require the money it would have brought at sale. Each signed over his rights of inheritance for that property to Wendy Barlow. She is the sole owner. That's all public record."

He cleared his throat.

"Off the record, I will say to you, Elizabeth, that they seemed to consider it a good bargain to keep her here, distant from the rest of the family. Well, not all that distant since at least two of them have bought places near Jackson. But separated."

Yeah. Cottonwood County definitely was separate from Jackson, even if not very distant.

I considered him.

After that daring foray into *off the record*, he'd returned firmly behind the line, perhaps even farther back from it than usual.

Sometimes, a new angle can open up a source.

"I recently heard that your last name has been spelled Longabaugh with an 'a' in the middle at times and that your ancestors came from Pennsylvania. And that the Sundance Kid's real last name is mostly spelled Longabaugh, but sometimes Longbaugh without the 'a' in the middle and he came from Pennsylvania. Spill, James. Are you related?"

His mouth compressed. Not in anger, but to contain a grin. "I can neither confirm nor deny a connection."

"Oh, come on, James—"

"Truly, Elizabeth. I don't know. On one side, you can say it's not that common a name. In addition, as you said, my grandfather's people came from Pennsylvania originally, as did Sundance's. Some old family papers do show the spelling with the 'a' in the middle. On the other side, no family papers or census records confirm a connection."

"So you did check into it."

"Sure, wouldn't you?"

"Absolutely. Did you ever talk with Keefer Dobey about his research into his family?"

His expression took another giant leap back from the off-the-record line.

"He mentioned his interest in the topic casually."

"Did he bring up specific names?"

"He mentioned Butch Cassidy and the Sundance Kid."

That was like reporting Keefer Dobey used the word *the* in a sentence.

"Anyone else? Less well-known, perhaps?"

"Elzy Lay. However, his life and family after he got out of prison is quite well documented."

"Uh-huh. Okay, I'll quit fencing—" In the hope he would, too. "—and say I know he was hopeful that he could track his lineage to Oscar and Pearl Virtanen."

"Did he have success doing that?"

"You're asking *me*?" I let my full disbelief at the reversal show.

"Yes," he said.

Narrowing my eyes, I asked, "Did Keefer Dobey come to you for information or help or advice about his possible connection to Oscar and Pearl Virtanen?"

"He did not."

"Have you or your firm at any time represented or held any material concerning Oscar and Pearl Virtanen or their estate or holdings?"

I'd surprised him, at least a little. And he took a moment. I suspected considering each aspect of what I'd asked.

"No."

Darn.

I considered him again. I respected his legal acumen. I deplored his—in my opinion—excessive discretion on matters not strictly legal.

I tried again. "There's something you're not telling me, James."

Deadpan, he said, "There's a lot I'm not telling you. That's my job."

CHAPTER THIRTY

I RELAYED WORD for word the little I'd heard to Diana. She was the only one I could reach and she was on her way to an assignment.

"What do you make of that, Elizabeth? I mean the scene with Randall Kenyon. The rest of it's pretty straightforward."

I considered for half a beat.

"Randall Kenyon had been trying to persuade James Longbaugh to represent him—to make the sale of Elk Rock Ranch from Wendy to Randall happen.

"James declined.

"Randall used the well-tested method of winning over people by calling them insulting names.

"Somehow James withstood those blandishments and kicked the man out of his office."

"Makes sense," Diana said.

"Doesn't get us any further."

"No, it doesn't."

SCOTT HOOLE WAS home when I called from the station.

That wasn't a huge surprise.

More snow fell in the mountains overnight. In Sherman we got slush. When they said the eastern pass to Cooke City was closed for the winter, they meant until summer. Spring—even Wyoming spring— didn't count.

But Scott Hoole not only didn't seem affected by being snowed in, he didn't even mention it.

When I identified myself he responded, "Gee said you'd call."

I did not rush out my appreciation for his food or which of the restaurants he'd been associated with was my favorite.

Not that I was above that.

But, first, I was calling about the killing of his long-time friend.

Second, common sense said that a man who'd retired to Cooke City, Montana, was not longing to relive his giddy celebrity days.

So, I warmed up Scott Hoole with questions about how he started working for Elk Rock Ranch and if that was how he and Keefe became friends.

"No, we were already friends. Some of the kids at school thought he was weird. I liked him. He wasn't much interested in being my friend back, but I wore him down." He chuckled. A nice sound. Low and warm, like melted chocolate. . . . which made me think of one of his signature desserts that—

"As for working at Elk Rock, they didn't hire too many locals— most kids who had wrangling skills worked on their family's place, not for somebody else. But I was from town." He chuckled. "And Keefe's friend. His mom knew me and she ruled the kitchen.

"Started as kitchen assistant. Worked my way up. Gave me a taste for cooking, so to speak. Learned more from Ulla Dobey than all of culinary school. I kept getting better and better jobs, farther and farther away. But everyplace I went, one of my conditions was I had three weeks of vacation during the summer. I'd go back every year, cook for Elk Rock, see my family and friends . . . Though there aren't many of those left. My family's all gone or moved and now Keefe . . ."

He cleared his throat.

Then he asked, "How's Brenda doing? I need to call her."

"She's a very strong woman. But she also seems quite sad."

"She is strong. Yeah, I need to call her. What about Suzie Q?"

"Brenda has her."

"That won't do. She has a good heart, but she's not active enough. And if Suzie Q's left to her own devices . . . She might be okay in the summers, but too many predators come too close around the home ranch in winter."

He'd warmed up nicely, but I still eased into meatier questions—was it only because I was interviewing a chef or because I was hungry that I was thinking in food metaphors?

"Were you already working at the ranch when Wendy came?"

"That would have been my second year. Just a kid."

I wasn't going to let him extend a ten-foot pole between him and what I wanted to know about.

"But smart enough to pick up on the changes and the rivalry between Brenda and Wendy."

Still trying to back away from it, he said, "Didn't get all the nuances."

"But enough to recognize tension."

He gave into my statement. "Hard to miss. And Ulla would get talking and forget I was there." He chuckled again. This one ever so lightly flavored by rue. "Got an education sometimes. Not only about those two going after Simon—have you heard about that?"

"Yes."

"Ulla got talking about his interest in Keefe. But it wasn't like that. Simon wasn't like that. He was fascinated by Keefe. Called him a savant—I remember looking up the word after he used it—and not an *idiot* savant."

That word rang with recalled anger, so someone *had* used the phrase about Keefe.

"I was with them a lot of the time and there just wasn't any of that. Not to mention Keefe would have told me. He *did* tell me. Years later when he declined the advances of an older man, then after he and a woman guest . . . He said it wasn't *unpleasant*, but he didn't see what the fuss was about. That was Keefe. He certainly was not sexual with Simon.

"A while back, the ranch put together a sort of yearbook of folks who'd worked there over the years and what they were doing. Simon did real well back east in wealth management. Well enough he had his own wealth to manage. Saw him a time or two when I was chef for a restaurant in Boston. He's a nice man."

"Were there other men Wendy and Brenda wrangled over?"

He appeared struck by that question. "Hadn't thought about that, but, no. Not head-to-head, so to speak. Looking back, I don't expect either was celibate, but maybe their tastes diverged. Or they worked out a way to stay out of each other's way—you know what I mean?"

I did.

Without ever saying a word, a pair of women could agree to not let head-to-head competition happen. Out of friendship, sure. But I'd also seen it happen without a friendship at stake. More like a wise preservation of emotional resources.

I suppose the same with men.

I flashed back for a second to when Tom and Mike each expressed his attraction to me. In that case, they hadn't agreed—implicitly or otherwise—to not pursue the attraction, instead, letting time and events show how things would turn out, while treating each other with respect and friendship. Entirely mature. Sometimes it drove me nuts.

But we were well past that. Since Tom and I were to the stage of saying—

"I do." I quickly added, "Know what you mean."

I thought of Jennifer's comment about unrequited love.

"You said Keefe wasn't really interested in . . . relationships. But what about other people caring for him that way?"

"People care about him, sure. Feel responsible for him in a way. Brenda for sure. Wendy, too, in a way. Like she inherited him, along with the ranch, and whatever anyone might say about the rough edge of her tongue, she loves that ranch. Or even me, even though I haven't—hadn't—seen him as much as I should have, especially since I moved here."

I thought I'd lost him. Either to contemplation of the drive from Cooke City to here I'd heard about or—more likely—to regrets for not seeing his friend.

So his next words startled me slightly. "But someone wanting a romantic relationship with Keefe? I don't see it. I know there's been talk about Brenda and him. But I don't see it. I truly don't. Not now, not ever.

"Now, with Wendy it was different. Early on, there wasn't that element of childhood friendship in her feelings toward Keefe that there always was with Brenda. I could see her entertaining, uh, interest in Keefe. But when she got the ranch, it was like she put all her feelings into the ranch. Saw Keefe as an asset to the ranch, not a potential paramour any longer.

"And, in fairness, over the years, I do think a kind of friendship grew—among all of them. As much with Keefe as you could be friends."

"I've heard you called his best friend."

"I might be. I loved the guy, for sure. But there was something in him ... You know how we—people—look at wildlife? Interested, respectful mostly when we see them. But we're not going out and living with them. We're not building relationships with them. We don't open ourselves to them. Well, that's how Keefe was with people."

I considered that. "And he was more like people are with each other with wildlife."

He chortled. "Except for the passions—sexual and otherwise. But, yeah, I think more of his inner life or whatever you want to call it connected to wildlife, nature, outdoors—and his dogs—than with people."

"When did you last talk to Keefe?"

"Last weekend, a couple days before he was murdered. I called— he never called me or anybody."

"What did you talk about?"

"He was waiting for the results on the DNA test he'd taken. And he was excited about something else, but he said he couldn't tell anybody anything until he had those DNA results. He said the young woman who'd gotten it for him, the one who got hurt last year—Sorry, don't remember her name. Anyway, she was getting on the company because the results were taking longer than they should have. Then he said she and her father were coming to Sherman, though he was vague on exactly when."

The something else had to be what he'd found in the museum box. But what was it?

"Did he talk about a fellow researcher, someone else interested in Oscar and Pearl Virtanen?"

"Yeah, yeah. An Irish last name. They were planning a trip to check locations on the ranch where this guy thought there might be something buried. But Keefe indicated this whatever that he was excited about that he wasn't telling anybody would make that unnecessary."

"In what way unnecessary? Like he knew the precise location? Or—?"

"Sorry. Really. You had to know Keefe. It was stunning he talked as much about it as he did. I can't give you any more on that."

As we wrapped up, I edged toward a celebrity-related question.

"Do you mind me asking why you decided to retire to Cooke City?"

He chuckled. "My earlier comment about Suzie Q not being safe at Elk Rock in winter because of predators circling closer made you think of this place, huh? It's not that bad. Not all winter. I spend a few weeks on a beach somewhere to break it up. In fact, when I first retired, I thought I'd be on one beach or another permanently. But I discovered a real drawback.

"No, give me Cooke City. In a way, its location keeps the predators from circling in too close to me. Weather's just bad enough that when someone calls and wants me to work a couple weeks in their restaurant because they're in a desperate situation, I can always say, *Sorry, I'm snowed in—yes, even in May or October*—and they'll believe it. It's the only way to protect being retired."

I joined in with his deep chuckle.

CHAPTER THIRTY-ONE

"**Now what are** you looking at? You've practically got your nose pressed to the screen."

Diana's voice came from over my shoulder, so she could see what I was looking at.

I backed up, but only because I'd completed my closeup inspection and now wanted an overall perspective.

"Diana, do you think these two photographs are of the same man?"

She looked at me before looking closely at the screen. "Why?"

"Some people claim this was Sundance in his later life. The nose is different—"

"It is, though the photo quality is so bad . . . No. Not the same man. Look at the ears. Ears can get bigger as someone ages, but the shape of the earlobe and the way it's connected to the head—No. Not the same."

"Good eye, Diana." I flicked to another pairing. "What about these two? I say the older man's eyes weren't as deep-set as the younger man's and—"

"Aka Butch as the younger man," she murmured, leaning in to look at the photos. "You're right about that and it generally goes the other direction—eyes getting more deep-set, not less. Plus, the ears again. No. Why are you studying these? Do they have something to do with Keefe's death?"

She would have to ask that.

"I could say yes, because theories about men who lived into the

1930s being Butch and Sundance could tangentially add credibility to the possibility of Pearl Virtanen having a baby who turned out to be Keefe's ancestor."

"Tangentially," she repeated.

"Yeah, that's a weak spot."

"And wouldn't those theories about these men being Butch and Sundance have to be credible to add credibility to anything else?"

"And that's an even weaker spot."

"You know, when you used to play Freecell it was easier to see when your brain downshifted. Sorry to have interrupted your meditation."

I grimaced, not expressing my fear that meditation was all we could do until the DNA results came in.

And that was assuming we got to see the results.

Even if we did, where would that get us?

If Keefe was descended from Oscar and Pearl and there was another descendant who was rival for a possibly mythical treasure who learned about Keefe's quest and decided to stop him . . .

It was straw-grasping time.

Silently, I waved good-bye as Diana left the newsroom on assignment.

I turned back to the screen.

My noodling around led me to looking up a world's fair in San Francisco—not that I doubted Leona, but going for a second source is engrained too deeply to ignore. It celebrated the completions of the Golden Gate and Bay bridges earlier in the 1930s. And, sure enough, Sally Rand's Nude Ranch was a popular feature on the midway.

Why did I not see that happening in Sherman?

An image of a promotional postcard showed a lineup of women in cowboy boots, decorative belts, kerchiefs, and cowboy hats, with the suggestion that they wore nothing else. Suggestion because they were lined up behind a fence, with the horizontal boards covering strategic elements of their anatomy.

Boy, the idea of a splinter from that board . . .

But the more interesting question was how and why Leona knew so much about Sally Rand.

I asked her that as she came in just before lunch to start another double dose of anchor tours.

She didn't blink or hesitate. "My grandmother was one of the girls in Sally Rand's Nude Ranch. Look hard enough and you can find postcards of her bare behind. She always pointed out that she was not one of those whose breasts showed.

"Suppose that's where some of my rebelliousness came from. Hippie types and free love didn't seem all that different with Sally Rand's Nude Ranch in the family genes."

"You were a free love hippie? I didn't know that."

A look of more than her usual cunning came into her face. "And you won't know more as long as I have to work as anchor. Get me out of this job for good and I'll tell all."

I HAD LUNCH with Connie Walterston at the Haber House Hotel dining room, probably the best food in town. Although I heard from good sources that the Wild Horses B&B had great breakfasts. Not a competition I'd ever judge, what with it happening in the morning.

Some people call skipping breakfast intermittent fasting. Some call it sleeping as late as possible.

I'd set up this lunch after the video call with Tom's parents.

Connie works for Tom. She now essentially runs Burrell Roads, the highway construction business his father started. Pieces I'd picked up indicated Tom's father devoted more of his time and attention to that business than ranching. Tom flipped the priorities when his parents retired and left the state.

But no one—related or otherwise—could say he'd abandoned Burrell Roads, by putting it in Connie's capable hands.

Lunch was mostly to catch up about her three sons, and how they were successfully rotating schooling and running their family ranch, along with her questions about wedding plans.

All to set the groundwork.

Because this was not the place to ask my other questions. Far too easy to be overheard. But it provided a nice background for what I planned next with Connie.

The text I received brought our pleasant lunch to a close.

Dale, the news aide, reported that the Cottonwood County Sheriff's Department had removed the crime scene tape from Keefer Dobey's cabin and Diana was waiting for me at the station to go to Elk Rock Ranch.

CHAPTER THIRTY-TWO

I**NSIDE, IT TOOK** a moment for our eyes to adjust, with not a lot of natural light coming from small front windows tucked under the porch's overhang.

A rock fireplace dominated, with a worn leather sofa in front of it. On either side of the fireplace, a door led to a small bedroom.

The one on the right appeared to have been Keefer's, with men's clothes hung on a metal tube between two walls, a single bed—made—and two open cabinets with shelves holding folded men's underwear, t-shirts, and socks.

The second bedroom must have been his mother's at one time, from the floral wallpaper frieze that had darkened with age. Instead of a bed, it held a desk stacked with folders and books except for an open space directly in front of the old, wooden rollable chair.

"Computer?" Diana asked from over my shoulder. "Think the sheriff's department took it?"

"Probably and probably. Ivy Short did mention a laptop. And it makes sense for the kind of research he was doing. Trying to do."

"Uh-huh. A lot of dead trees research, too," she said.

In addition to the desk, shelving cabinets like the ones holding clothes in his bedroom held more folders. Books crammed a large bookshelf that leaned slightly to one side.

"Shelton must not have thought the answer to Keefe's death was in these papers," Diana said. "I sure hope he was right."

I grunted agreement. Going through these materials wouldn't be as arduous as going through Sam McCracken's, but close. Keefe had fewer books and denser paper files.

Coming back to the main area, we passed a table for two under a triple window on the back wall that looked to the woods, with a misty peak in the distance. It was the primary source of natural light. One corner of the table showed a stain that could have been blood.

More of the stain showed on the wooden floor nearby.

With the window at our backs we could see the living area better. Not that there was much more to see. Except an unframed painting propped on the mantel. It was pleasant, but clearly the work of an amateur.

Diana looked from the painting to out the window. "Same view."

The cabin was scrupulously neat, but not clean. The home of a man who wore his dirty boots inside, but didn't kick them off in the middle of the floor.

Shelton's minions apparently respected the neatness by not tossing the place with the abandon I've seen some law enforcement do.

Just beyond the table was the kitchen area. A door across from it stood open, showing a bathroom that might have started as rustic in the fifties and now was just old.

Beside the kitchen sink, set under a small window I'd need to bend down to look out, two coffee mugs sat out by an old-fashioned coffeemaker. No French press for Keefer Dobey. But clearly a heavy coffee drinker, since the worn surfaces said this was the most used area of the kitchen.

For a second that surprised me, since he'd shared this cabin with his mother the cook. But she'd died a long time ago, and before that, as Brenda indicated, the brunt of her cooking was done in the cookhouse.

I opened the cabinet above the coffeemaker. On the left, another half-dozen mugs whose dust coverings declared they hadn't been moved in years.

On the right, were glasses. The few in front shone clean in the light from the window—two water tumblers, two juice glasses that could stand in as highball glasses, two champagne flutes, which did add a surprising element to Keefer Dobey. Behind and above them showed groupings of those varieties, plus white and red wine glasses—all shrouded in fine dust—completing a thorough set.

I moved on, opening another cabinet door.

"Looking for something?" Diana asked.

The cabinet had dishes reflecting similar usage—regulars at the front kept clean, specialist dishes high and wide, dusted with disuse.

"No. Thinking."

A narrow cabinet next to the stove held spices, oils, and salt. The salt and oil on the bottom shelf were well-used. A double-tiered lazy Susan held small jars and tins of spices, many with the now familiar dusty film. I gave the lazy Susan a half-hearted spin, watching the names of unused spices go by.

"Because it looks like you're snooping," Diana said with mild amusement.

"You're easily misled."

"Any blinding insights?"

"He had a lot of nutmeg. Must be a big fan of egg nog, though you'd think he'd have used some of this up over the holidays."

"He doesn't strike me as a big holiday entertainer. Not to mention, you can use nutmeg in a lot of other things. Pasta sauces, potatoes—especially scalloped or au gratin, meatballs, and meat sauces, and I know people who put it in chili and tacos."

"Nutmeg? In chili and tacos?"

"Yup. I ask again, any blinding insights from your thinking, which is definitely not snooping?"

"Not blinding and not much of an insight. He'd narrowed his life to the essentials. But either he alternated his glassware or he did entertain a second person now and then."

"Brenda?"

"I'd say Brenda was a coffee mug visitor." I tipped my head toward that collection. "Or maybe single malt drinker. I just don't see Keefer and Brenda sitting here, drinking champagne."

Diana's eyebrows came up. She went to the glassware cabinet, opened it, and studied it for a long moment. "Water, juice—or, as you say, single malt—and champagne. Sam McCracken? Celebrating progress?"

"Most likely answer. Doesn't sound like Brenda and Randall's visit Monday would have had anyone breaking out champagne."

By the outside door I paused and looked back. It was dark enough to think in terms of a cave, with the true opening to it those three windows by the little table—windows looking toward the outdoors.

From all we'd heard, it reflected the man's priorities.

Coming from the direction of her cabin, Brenda transferred her frown from the NewsMobile, which Diana insisted on for her equipment, to Diana and me as we crossed the porch of Keefe's cabin.

We didn't let it prevent us from each reaching down to pat Suzie Q, in her same spot. She didn't acknowledge our touches. She seemed thinner to me.

"What are you doing here?" Brenda called out.

"No police tape anymore," I said.

That wouldn't have satisfied Wendy. Nor would my next foray have distracted her. But they worked with Brenda.

"I understand Chester was a difficult patient during his last illness."

I'd been wanting to broach this to Brenda since Wendy's comments Wednesday about Chester's groping.

To my surprise, she chuckled. "He was, right up to the end. Not that I was there at the last, because Wendy wouldn't hear of that. Oh, no. I was good enough to help in the last three, four weeks before the end, but not at the very end. No chance to say good-bye."

"It must have been difficult."

"It was. It had seemed like he'd be around forever, you know? I guess because he always had been. That last spring, I remember seeing him one day and thinking it wasn't even Chester Barlow. I suppose I'd been blind to the changes and this one day they just stepped up and slapped me in the face. And there he was, a sick old man. And lonely after Ulla died. I saw that, looking back. Wendy sure wasn't any comfort to him. Barely even company. Always wanted to be out doing the fun things with the guests, none of the work. All she'd do was complain about how he didn't understand her, how old-fashioned he was. Mocked how he ran this place—well, all I can say is it was doing fine under him. Can't say that under Wendy Miss High and Mighty Barlow."

That seemed harsh, since it seemed to have run well under Wendy for a lot of years.

Though there was that account from Tom's mom about Wendy selling her second home in Arizona. And the ranch showed no signs of new or lush or expensive additions.

On the other hand, it didn't show signs of disrepair or ignored maintenance, either.

Of course, if Keefe did all that work as part of his normal duties . . .

"Were you aware of Chester Barlow, uh, expecting things from Wendy? Physically."

She stared at me a moment, then snorted in disgusted amusement. "Is that what she said? Is that her excuse? That he owed the place to her because of what he put her through? I got an earful of that whining all those years ago and I'll tell you what I told her then. It was bull. Through and through. He never—you know. Not like real sex, not even if you get all shifty with your definitions like Bill Clinton. So what if he wanted a little cuddle now and then. You'd do that for any other breathing human, as sick as he was toward the end. And especially one who'd done so much for me. *And* her. Difference is, she thought she deserved every bit of good he or anybody else ever did for her. Not a grateful bone in her body.

"Not a generous one, either. She wouldn't let either one of us—Keefe or me—see him in those last couple days. She *said* he didn't want to see us, didn't want us to see him so low down. Didn't sound like Chester to me—he never thought he was low down, no matter what. Though I suppose when people get near the end like that, they can change. So maybe he didn't want us to see him, maybe he didn't want to see anybody, just like he got so cold she had a fire going in July. He'd always been a warm one, not needing so much as a sweater when others were shivering. But what with my parents dying young in an accident and no other family to speak of, I don't know how those things go at the end of a life."

She brightened suddenly.

"And then there was no will and Wendy had to be *grateful* to her brothers for not selling off the place, but letting her keep it all herself. She hated that. Even better, with being owner, she had to do a whole lot more than she used to. Turned her right around. You might not believe it now, but she was a real flitty thing. Having to work soured her on just about everything. Well, she was already soured on me, but sure soured her on Keefe. She'd been sweet on him to then."

She colored slightly. "I've done things for him these last years, things a friend would do. But she used to . . . Well, it was a long time ago and he didn't hardly notice, much less do anything about it. And it ended when she became the owner. Couldn't just be Miss La-di-da Hostess. She had to buckle down and really work."

Brenda's wrinkles conformed to her wide smile, though it wasn't nearly as pleasant as usual.

❖ ❖ ❖ ❖

I PICKED UP Tamantha after her organizing meeting for the science fair.

Our next stop would be to pick up her friend Madison for a sleepover at the ranch.

Tom and I would have a sleepover, too. I figured the more fun the girls had, the less we would have.

I brought the dissertation to go through again and keep my mind off our missing fun.

My first read had confirmed most of what I already knew.

There was a part at the end that described a legend that Oscar buried gold and bank notes from a robbery. Some said the burial site was in Cottonwood County.

Of course, the author pointed out, that was mostly people from Cottonwood County.

Mrs. P's mentor seemed to dismiss the legend.

Voices coming nearby warned me of Tamantha's arrival. I placed the book on the passenger seat as she climbed in the back seat and buckled up. She was tall enough now to no longer need a booster seat.

"How was school today?"

"Pretty routine," said the fourth-grader verging on forty. "But the science fair should be good. I might do something about visual effects in old movies."

After she told me about that, she asked, "What's the book on the front seat?"

"Mrs. P gave it to me to read."

"Homework," she said wisely. "You'll have a quiz."

"Yup."

DAY FIVE
SATURDAY

CHAPTER THIRTY-THREE

"WILL YOU GET me the white pepper?" Tom asked.

"Why white pepper?"

"Madison worries when she sees dark specks in her scrambled eggs that it's bugs. Tamantha tried to talk her out of it, talking about when I make bacon then use the same pan to make the eggs how there're bits of bacon in the eggs and they're a different color and it's delicious—"

"It is."

His breakfasts were actually worth getting up for. Even ones that came after a night of giggle-interrupted sleep.

"Madison was having none of it. So I bought white pepper. She thinks it's salt and is happy."

"You're a good man, Tom Burrell." I turned back to the cabinet. His spices sat on a plastic gizmo shaped like bleachers, so each row stood higher than the one in front, making them all visible . . . in contrast to the hodgepodge in the town house. I wondered if that drove Tom nuts. It drove me nuts sometimes and I wasn't nearly as neat as he was.

I spotted the white pepper, snagged it, and handed it to him over his shoulder, then reached for the cabinet door to close it.

I should get one of these bleacher things or a lazy Susan like Keefe had.

The memory of his lazy Susan of spices turning—well, lazily— flashed into my mental vision. The names of the spices on the tins and bottles going past slowly, then stopping.

"Nutmeg," I said aloud.

"You've never said you like nutmeg on eggs," Tom said from a distance. "Don't think it will work for Madison, different color, still too bug-like. Happy to try it another time."

"No. Not on eggs. Though according to Diana, you can use it in practically anything."

He turned, spatula in hand. "Like what?"

"Chili and tacos—that's what really got me. But she also said potatoes, meat dishes, and . . ." I scoured my memory. "Sauces. Like creamy ones for pasta."

"Interesting."

"Okay, Chef Tom, but that wasn't the point. I was thinking nutmeg being in Keefe's kitchen cabinet."

"It's not salt and pepper, but it's not so exotic I can't imagine him having it. Sort of thing you buy and keep forever. Ulla could have bought it, for that matter."

"He had four tins of nutmeg. I could see an ordinary person having two—you're not sure you have it for a specific recipe so you grab it to avoid another trip to the supermarket. But he had four."

"Four nutmegs?" Tom repeated.

"And at least two were new." I squinted into my memory. "Or newish."

He turned back to the eggs. "I take it we're going to Keefe's place after breakfast."

I'd come back to the present enough to hear the faint grin in his voice, envision the deepening of the lines around his eyes.

"Darn right we are. Or I am—"

"Not alone. Not where somebody was murdered."

We'd talk about that later. "—right after we eat those delicious eggs and all the pounds of bacon you made and deliver the girls to Madison's parents."

TWO OF THE containers from Keefe's kitchen cabinet held only nutmeg. Both of the newer ones. That was either smart of him—the new tins were certainly the ones that seemed more likely hiding places to me and the ones I checked first—or he had nothing hidden here.

Tom picked up one of the older, worn tins. "Hmm."

"Hmm, what?"

He held the tin up to the light from the window. "Looks like . . ."

He poked at the tin.

"Looks like what?" He was driving me nuts.

He didn't answer. Instead, he took out his pocket knife, deliberately and delicately pressed the tip along the raised rim all around the bottom of the tin.

"Tom—"

"Be patient."

Before I could protest that patient was already in my rear-view mirror, the bottom of the tin dropped into his palm.

"There's something in the tin. Your fingers will fit better—"

He didn't need to finish the invitation. While he held the small tin by its sides, I slid a finger in, caught a fold of plastic wrap with my nail and drew it down until I could secure it with my thumb. A shower of nutmeg dust fell. Keefe must have covered this with nutmeg so that from the top it looked like another spice tin.

Tom pulled off a length of paper towel with one hand, then set the tin and its separated bottom on it. I set what I'd pulled out onto another section.

I peered at it. "Looks like paper wrapped in plastic wrap."

I opened a drawer and took out two forks.

"And thoroughly dusted with nutmeg. Elizabeth—what are you doing?"

"Opening the plastic wrap."

"If you disturb fingerprints—"

"Shelton will have my head on a pike. That's why I'm using the forks. Besides, my fingerprints are already on it from finding it."

"Wayne's not going to see it that way," he said dryly.

I was aware of him watching over my shoulder as I tried to manipulate the clingy plastic wrap with the tines of the fork. It was like trying to use chopsticks with boxing gloves. I kept at it, seeking a spot with just a tiny gap of space to get the tip of the tine into.

"Hey, Shelton and his minions had their chance. It was sitting here all the time. The first time they searched and the second—after he knew about the DNA test. He can't complain about us finding it after he had two chances."

"Yes, he can. And will. This isn't a game, where you get a turn after—"

The cabin door opened around the corner, followed by the sound of a dog padding in.

"Tom Burrell, is that you?" Brenda Mankin called.

Of course she knew his truck.

I scrambled to wrap our find in the paper towel, securing the two pieces of the tin at the same time. Whatever prying progress I'd made was lost, but they were out of sight and Tom had the other tins restored to the lazy Susan and the cabinet door closed before Brenda came around the corner.

She stopped short.

"Oh, it is you." That was directed at me.

"Hey, Brenda," he said easily.

"Hey, Tom." Her gaze stuck to me. "What are you doing here again? You were just here yesterday."

Sliding our find into my coat pocket brought my hand in contact with my phone and now I pulled it out—leaving the rest in the depths. "My editor insisted I get interior shots of Keefe's home for the piece. Lets people identify with him. We've got the kitchen, but I'd like to take shots of the fireplace area. It's too bad there's no fire."

"I thought Diana did that yesterday."

"I *know*," I said with emphasis, as if she'd not only pinpointed the issue, but empathized with me over the poor judgment of the mythical editor in sending me to get visuals. "But with the crime scene tape just coming down and other assignments and deadlines coming up and—" I flapped one hand at the totality of all the circumstances conspiring to bring me to this moment in this place.

I moved past her, focusing my phone's camera on the fireplace and tapping as I headed into the bedroom-turned-office. "I want to get the bookcase, too."

On its top shelf, in front of yet another stack of folders, it held a photo taken in front of the kitchen building with Wendy's uncle and Keefe's mother standing with Brenda, Wendy, Keefe in front of them. Brenda and Wendy were in their early twenties. Keefe was a mid-teenager. It was unframed, but appeared to be bonded to a stiff cardboard that held it upright.

I took several pictures of that from various angles.

Brenda trailed in behind me. Tom remained by the fireplace. I doubt he could have fit in this room with us comfortably.

My actions drew Brenda's attention to the photo, as I'd hoped. Even better, it seemed to draw her closer and closer. I took several more shots of her looking at the photo—never touching it—without her showing awareness of having her picture taken.

I tracked Tom moving around near the fireplace, and thought I heard clicks of his phone camera, too. It was really sweet of him to add to the cover story, though it didn't make sense that he'd take photos for my mythical editor.

Several more photos, with me moving around the small space as if I could outdo Diana with a few clicks on my phone.

Although a couple shots of Suzie Q, lying on the hearthrug, head on paws, staring dolefully straight ahead might capture the essence of the mood. If the technology kept it in focus, because I sure didn't.

"That should cover it," I said brightly.

Brenda blinked and turned from her extended consideration of that decades old photo.

"Okay," she said. "Let's go."

I'd hoped for another moment in the kitchen without an audience, but she made it clear she wasn't leaving first.

"Keefe would be rolling over in his grave—if they'd let us put him in his grave. All these people in and out of his cabin. Not you, Tom. I'm sure he'd be okay with you. But not that Randall Kenyon."

That hurt, being lumped with Randall.

"Don't care if Robin did give Keefe the computer and the DNA test. And I don't care what Wendy says about how she's told Randall no when he talks about buying Elk Rock. That man sure seems to think he's welcomed here any time he wants, anywhere he wants, acting all high and mighty and sweeping out and saying he was buying the place, when he was already acting like he owned it. C'mon out of here," she said to Suzie Q.

Brenda was past militant with evicting the dog.

Suzie Q whined without raising her head.

"Fine, stay here, then. But I don't have the time to come checking on you every two minutes." She followed us out and closed the door firmly.

Without a farewell, she went toward her cabin. But she watched until we drove away in Tom's truck.

"Poor Suzie Q," I said, feeling the lump safely in my pocket from the outside. I wasn't going to risk taking it out until we were where I could look it over carefully.

"Brenda will see to physical needs, no matter what she says, but Suzie Q was so much Keefe's dog, it's going to be tough for her. Here—" Steering one-handed on a road that would have taken both my hands—and possibly both feet on the brake—he pulled out a wad of paper towel from a pocket. "This might cheer you up."

He opened his fingers and the paper towel unfurled enough to show what it covered.

Tom had pocketed the other old tin that we hadn't had a chance to check yet.

I grinned at him.

"There's more," he mumbled, going one-handed into another pocket. Another paper towel covered a folded up sheet of paper. Even when the paper towel fell back, there was nothing on the paper to see. But this was the back of the paper and there certainly could be something on the other side. "It was behind the painting. We have to take all this to the sheriff's department."

"We will. As soon as we've had a chance to look at it in good light at the house. And take photos."

He groaned. "Wayne's going to have my head on a pike, too." But the wrinkles at the corners of his eyes gave him away.

"Hurry up," Mike said.

"Be quiet. Or next time, we won't call you until it's all over."

"Next time?" Tom repeated bemusedly.

"You don't think there'll be a next time she finds documents hidden in nutmeg tins or you find something hidden behind a painting?" Diana asked. She'd dropped her Saturday chores to join us at my house.

"I'm afraid to think."

"Shh." I ordered them all.

Jennifer was the only one not harassing me as I used the fork trick again to tackle the paper Tom found first. It wasn't as tightly crumpled as the two from the nutmeg tins. It also wasn't wrapped in plastic, so I tried that first.

She was otherwise occupied with copies of the pictures Tom and I took today.

We would turn those in to Shelton. He'd huff and puff about deleting them from our phones.

If he wanted to get really picky, he could get tech types to track the copies we sent to Jennifer. But they'd never find what she did with them next.

Neither would I, for that matter. But I didn't need to as long as Jennifer could retrieve them.

I had the paper flat enough now, with the edges held down by knives, that we could all read it. Diana held my tablet over it for Jennifer and Mike.

It was a printout. Including the *Keefer* at the top and the name at the end.

In between, it said:

You can't just say it's over after all these years and expect me to accept it.
I won't stand for it.

Wendy

Mike whistled.

"That's motive," Jennifer said.

"Could be."

Mike jumped on my words. "Only could be?"

Diana filled in my lack of answer. "How did you find it, Tom?"

"When Elizabeth and Brenda went into Keefe's office, I stopped by the fireplace. Looked over and saw something white."

"Behind the frame?" Jennifer asked.

"No frame," Diana and I said together.

We all looked at Tom.

"Sticking out past the edge of the painting. Reached behind it and the paper was tucked into the corner of the stretcher."

Diana and I looked at each other. She said, "I didn't see it, but it was dim in there. I'll check the footage."

"Send it to me," Jennifer ordered. "I have a way better program than KWMT does to enhance for low light."

"Good," I said, as Diana began that process. "And ditto on not seeing it, but not *not* seeing it either."

"Probably just the angle from where I stood," Tom said modestly.

"What about what was in the nutmeg tin?" Mike asked, trying to peer through the screen.

"Starting now."

I moved down the countertop to where we'd set one of the plastic-wrapped wads from the nutmeg tin. This was tighter and dirtier.

"How'd he get something in there?" Mike asked.

Tom said, "It's neatly cut around the bottom. Fits back together very snug. Like some can openers can do with cans. But I'd say this was done by hand. Had to be cut in exactly the right spot. There's a light glue, but that didn't do the main job of holding it together . . ."

I was aware of the others commenting on that and other topics, but all my concentration was on the wad in front of me. The plastic wrap raised the degree of difficulty considerably.

As it slowly revealed the paper, I muttered, "Looks like a journal or diary . . ."

At last, we had this one flattened—sort of—and held by more

knives.

It wasn't nearly as easy to read as the printout, with the handwriting loopy and small. Diana used her phone camera to zoom in and add more light.

Jennifer typed in what we found as we deciphered it.

"Okay, here's what I have," she said as I sat up, arching my back against being scrunched over the sheet.

"It starts with the boring stuff about a recipe for scalloped potatoes—"

"With nutmeg," Diana inserted.

"—then it says, *I probably told my boy too much today, with hints about his paternal line. That decision was made long ago for many reasons and with careful consideration for his well-being. It is a good decision. I know he is curious, but he doesn't need that to be happy. And my boy being happy is what matters most.*"

"This could refer to what Brenda said Keefe told her about what his mom said," Mike recapped. "You think he found it after she died? Maybe searching for any hint of his father's ancestors."

"And this was all he got," Jennifer said. "That's sad."

"I was remembering something Penny said and I thought it was about Keefe's mom, that she danced close to the edge and couldn't know he'd get so interested. I wonder if that's what this entry's about."

"Sounds a little like she's arguing with herself," Diana said.

All that was true. So was something else.

"One more wad to unwad." I moved down the counter to the last piece we'd found.

CHAPTER THIRTY-FOUR

THIS WAS HARDER than the printout, easier than the journal. It hadn't been wadded up as long as the journal, but it had plastic wrap over it.

"What is it?" Jennifer asked as I placed a second knife on a freed edge and the non-blank side began to be revealed.

"It looks like an old newspaper article," Mike said. "A clipping. But it's shrunk to fit on the page and it's really hard to read from here."

"Not easy from here, either." Diana used her phone camera again.

When she turned on the flashlight to supplement the light, a spattering of words in sub-heads caught my eye.

"May I use that?"

I didn't really wait for a yes, but was looking through the lens in a second.

I returned the phone to her and sat back, coming up against the welcomed support of Tom's chest as he leaned over my shoulder to look.

"I think—I think this is a copy of the original newspaper article with the posse member who'd chased Oscar Virtanen."

WE COULDN'T READ every word, but all agreed that, based on what we could see, I was right.

Diana took pictures and video of it, zooming in methodically and sending it all to Jennifer to see what miracles she could perform.

"This has got to be what he found in the museum boxes," Mike recapped.

"I'd bet on it," I said. "This could make Clara Atwood rearrange her priorities."

"You're going to show it to her?" Tom sounded surprised.

"Not yet. Jennifer, have you got all those files from Diana?"

"Got 'em. Will you take all three of these to Shelton?" Jennifer asked.

"We will," Tom stated.

"Absolutely," I agreed.

Jennifer frowned. "I'll see what I can do with this, but if you scanned it in, high res, that would be better and the original would be even better than that. You could make a copy for Shelton and send me—"

"Original's going to Shelton," Tom said. "And we're not taking time to scan it in ourselves."

"Why? You said the sheriff's department released the scene, so it's their own darn fault . . ." Jennifer's words faded out as she appeared to lean forward to peer at me. "You're trying not to smile, Elizabeth."

I tried harder.

"Oh. It's *because* they released the scene and you want to rub it in that they missed it."

"Elizabeth won't be turning these things over to the sheriff's department," Tom said. "I will."

He pretended not to hear my mutter of "Spoilsport."

"And we better get to the sheriff's department now."

"Not yet," Jennifer said. "Send me pictures of the letter and nutmeg tins before you take them. Just in case."

As Tom and I pulled up in front of the sheriff's department, I got the all-clear message from Jennifer. All files were secured. So at least Shelton couldn't get angry that we'd sat outside his office instead of coming in right away to hand over the evidence.

✧ ✧ ✧ ✧

TOM CALLED A neighbor to meet Tamantha at the ranch when she returned from Madison's house, then left for a slate of committee meetings. Jennifer basically said not to bother her while she and the guys worked their magic. Mike went to work his real job—being sports anchor tonight for his Chicago station.

Diana stuck around.

"Want to play Freecell?" she asked me when I came in after Tom dropped me off, possibly looking dissatisfied.

Which consisted of waiting. For Jennifer or Shelton. Whoever came first.

I was pulling for Jennifer, since I wouldn't learn anything from Shelton.

"Want to talk about it?"

"What is there to talk about?" I kicked my shoes off and curled up into one of the upholstered chairs. "Shelton has his suspect and no doubt an arrest to follow soon. All the history we found—even if Keefe's proven to be descended from Oscar and Pearl—has nothing to do with it."

"No knowledge is wasted."

I grimaced. "Thank you, Mrs. P Junior. Anyway, it's done. Over."

"I'd be more inclined to believe that if I couldn't see your face. Something's bothering you."

I tipped my head back so I couldn't see her seeing my face. "Not a thing. It's all over."

I might have fallen asleep as a result of last night's sleepover.

When I sat up, my neck was sore, but the light in the room hadn't changed.

Diana was looking at her phone and smiling.

The smile faded when she transferred her attention to me. "What?"

"Something Brenda said. Well, she's said a lot, but there's something tugging at the back of my mind."

Diana tipped her head. "About Randall trying to buy the place?"

"Mmm." I figured that sounded more encouraging than *I have no idea*. But whatever it was in my memory had enough muscle behind it to keep tugging.

Trying to help, Diana said, "Wendy kept saying she'd told him no."

"Mm-hmm."

"And it was his problem—and Brenda's—if they couldn't under-stand the word *No*."

"Uh-huh. But that's Wendy talking. I'm almost certain it was some-thing Brenda said." Almost.

"Okay. Brenda said the bit about Randall and Robin leaving at four-thirty. Then—"

"No—"

"Hold on, let me keep going. Then about whether he could have come back in that truck. How Wendy wouldn't have heard him no matter what, and how he'd have made it so Brenda didn't hear him if he was smart."

"No. Not that."

"Let me think. She went back to when Randall was there. Some-thing about him acting like he owned the place and Wendy—"

"Wait. That's it . . ." But it wasn't quite right. "*Maybe* that's it." I uncurled my legs. "That *is* it. Except it was today. To Tom and me. That Randall came sweeping in and—No. *Not* sweeping *in*. She said he was sweeping *out*."

"Out of where?" Diana asked.

"*Exactly.*"

She frowned. "I suppose that makes sense to you, but she might have just misspoken."

"She definitely said *out, sweeping out*. That's why it kept tugging at me. She said he acted like he already owned the place. She could have meant it as hyperbole or something specific. And then she said he swept out. So your question *Out of where?* is the key. But you could be right that she misspoke. We'll just have to ask her and—What are you doing?"

"We're going back up to the ranch, aren't we? I'm calling my kids to take something out of the freezer and defrost it, because I won't be home in time to do that myself."

CHAPTER THIRTY-FIVE

BRENDA LOOKED LIKE she'd aged a decade. I wouldn't have thought that possible with all the wrinkles, but it was the spaces between the wrinkles. The downturn of her mouth, the pinch of her eyebrows, the confusion in her eyes.

"Did you hear what's happened?" she demanded before we were all the way out of my SUV.

I was grateful for its four-wheel drive as we'd found snow as we climbed. More than grateful that we weren't trying to get to Cooke City and beyond grateful Diana wasn't driving the NewsMobile.

From the lightning look we exchanged, both Diana and I thought she might mean Wendy being taken in for questioning by the sheriff's department. But I didn't want to put words in her mouth.

"What's happened?"

"They took Wendy. Asked her a bunch of questions here, then took her. They're crazy. They've got it all wrong. They asked me a lot of questions again, too. What they're thinking—that is just wrong. That's not Keefer. Hell, that's not Wendy, either. They got it wrong. And I told them so. I said, right to his face, *You got it wrong, Wayne Shelton.*"

Tempted as I was to hear more about how she'd told Shelton he got it wrong and how he'd reacted, I moved on.

"Brenda, can you list exactly who's been in Keefer's cabin since you found him?"

"*Exactly?* With all the people coming and going, going and coming? It's like the end of the week when one set of guests leaves and another set arrives, only this is worse because it's every day and no tellin' when somebody'll turn up." Belatedly, she added, "And what does that have to do with them taking Wendy?"

I felt safe ignoring that last part. "You talked about Randall Kenyon being here and acting like he already owned the ranch."

"He was and that's just how he acted."

"Was he inside the cabin since the crime tape came down?"

"Him and everybody else. Came right after you two left yesterday. *And* he was back today, standing there watching, him and Robin, while the sheriff's department dragged Wendy in. I'm telling you, they got it wrong—"

Before she could go another round of that refrain, I hurried on. "You said he came sweeping out—"

"He did. All high and mighty and—"

"No. Wait. Go back. Which day?"

"Yesterday," she said, impatient. "Just told you. After you two left."

"Tell us exactly what you saw."

"Him coming out of Keefe's cabin, like I said—that's exactly what I saw. I asked him what he thought he was doing and he got all high-handed about seeing what he was getting for his money and I told him—"

Her voice faded into the background as Diana and I looked at each other.

"We could wait until we see what Jennifer has from what you and I shot," she said. "That would support us saying there was no paper sticking out from behind the painting yesterday."

"But she's not doing that until after enhancing the copy of the newspaper interview. Even if we told her now to rush it . . ."

"And you don't want to wait."

We have to go to the sheriff's department.

As the thought formed, I said it aloud.

There was no forming-a-thought gap before Brenda said, "Go the sheriff's department? Not a chance. I'm staying here. Somebody's got to stay here."

Following the direction of her gaze to Suzie Q lying on the porch, I was already hitting speed dial on my phone.

"We'll take care of her."

I swore to myself when I heard the voice answer on the other end.

Ferrante. He was the embodiment of the word *no* in human form. I don't know how he and his wife—a very nice woman—ever had kids considering his hundred percent turn-down ratio.

I could have clicked off. But never let it be said I didn't cross every 't', dot every 'i', as well as ram my head into every brick wall.

"It is vital that I talk to Sergeant Shelton immediately. Vital for him and—"

"He is not available."

"He will not thank you for—"

"He is not available. I'll tell him you called." Click.

That result was so predictable, I was already onto the next step.

First, I texted Richard Alvaro's number, figuring he'd more likely check that, even if he wasn't inclined to answer a phone.

URGENT. Going to call you. ANSWER.

I did and he did.

"Elizabeth, I'm busy."

"I know. I have to talk to Shelton immediately."

"No way. He's doing an interview—"

"I know. Wendy Barlow. And I know you have more evidence to process now. But there's something he has to listen to, something Brenda Mankin has to say."

From behind me, she said, "I'm not saying anything to him. He's got it wrong. Besides, Suzie Q—"

I tried to wave her to silence.

He might have said more, but I heard the no-way-on-earth in a single word, "Elizabeth—"

"I swear to you, Richard. He wants to hear this. Well, not *want* to. But he needs to."

My brain was catching up with the what-could-happen sequence that got me to the unshakeable conclusion that we *had* to get to the sheriff's department.

They arrested Wendy.

Then Brenda's observations put a different angle on the provenance of that note.

With the Barlow connections behind her, Wendy brought the Cottonwood County Sheriff's Department to its knees.

Sheriff Russ Conrad was tossed out.

Diana was miserable. Or she went with him, wherever that was.

And if Shelton went? I might not even be happy with that outcome, if only because it could get worse. This county had had worse. Lots worse. Shelton was a pain in the ass, but he did his job. We could get somebody who didn't.

"I'll tell him you called when he's done and what you said—"

"No. That won't cut it. We're coming there."

I ended the call.

"I told you—" Brenda started.

"I know. You won't leave Suzie Q alone. She's coming, too."

ON THE DRIVE to town, with Brenda and Suzie Q in the back, Diana and I talked it over, right after calling Jennifer and asking her to check any shots of the painting on the mantel as fast as possible.

Brenda agreed to go after a promise that she could tell Shelton he got it wrong and that he'd listen. Suzie Q was picked up and carried.

Storming the sheriff's department office would play to their strengths. Including lockable doors, Ferrante at the front desk, and weapons. Lots and lots of weapons.

I was pretty sure Shelton wouldn't shoot me—very sure he wouldn't shoot Diana. But I preferred better odds than that with weapons involved.

"I could call Russ," Diana said. "If I ask him to order Shelton to listen so he doesn't take the investigation in the wrong direction—"

I was shaking my head before she stopped. "No. Thank you for offering and some other time we might take you up on playing that ace in our pocket, but I think . . . Yeah, I'll call Tom."

Fortunately, he answered. Even more fortunately, he was on his way to his next committee meeting. And that meant he was passing through Sherman right now.

No, I don't know which of the forty-seven committees he was on it was for. And didn't care. Unless it was the Committee to Keep the World From Blowing Up Tonight.

Even then I might have pushed him to delay the meeting a few hours.

I told him what I wanted from him in straightforward terms. As for why . . .

"I can't tell you details, Tom." I wasn't sure how much Brenda could hear from the back seat, but enough. Maybe she'd piece it together on her own, but I had to be able to say I hadn't done it for her. "I can say that it will be a whole lot better for Shelton, the sheriff's department, and the case if he does this."

"I'll try."

From Thomas David Burrell, that was a pledge to the death. If it could be done, he'd do it.

The trouble was Shelton.

We went to my house to wait.

Shadow greeted us at the door, happy to see Diana and me, though clearly noting the irregularity of me coming in the front door.

He watched Brenda with the reserved neutrality he employed with most strangers.

His reaction to Suzie Q was also reserved, yet intensely curious, especially since I carried her in. He looked up at me with a world of questions in his eyes.

"This is Suzie Q. She's visiting for a little while. She's had a tough time lately."

I had the feeling I didn't need to add that last part.

I put her down not far into the room.

Neither dog's tail wagged. Neither made any attempt to sniff the other. That would have concerned me more with other dogs. Shadow stood back and regarded her. She stayed where I'd put her. Not moving. Not looking around. Not caring.

Jennifer called with answers, which I messaged to Tom.

While Diana made coffee and put cookies on a plate—I'd worry later about how she knew where what I considered my backup super-secret stash of Pepperidge Farm Double Dark Chocolate Milano cookies was kept—I lit the already laid fire in the fireplace.

I called Suzie Q. She didn't budge.

I put a spare leash on her, then drew her close to the fireplace, and ordered her to sit. Before I could add the next command, she slid into a down. Shadow gave me a questioning look. I tipped a shoulder in a faint shrug.

He came over to the fireplace and laid down parallel to her but not touching. After a half dozen breaths, he shifted onto his hip, putting his back to her now, but touching her side. She didn't move away.

We three women were each on our second cookie when Suzie Q stretched her head out on her paws and expelled a sorrowful breath.

"She's accepted that he's not coming back," Brenda said quietly.

"A lot more grief to go through, but she has accepted it," Diana agreed.

I was focused on Shadow.

He'd heard a vehicle outside.

CHAPTER THIRTY-SIX

TOM MODESTLY GESTURED Shelton and Richard in ahead of him when, by all rights, he should have entered to a hail of rose petals and trumpets for his achievement in getting them here.

If he'd come in first, he might also have buffered those of us inside from the waves of fury pulsing from Shelton. To say Shelton was thunderous would be likening a tsunami to bathtub splash-over.

"What the—"

He couldn't get more words out. Possibly because the only ones that came to his tongue were curse words and he rarely indulged.

Still, Shadow rose and put himself between the two men in uniform and Suzie Q.

That drew Tom's attention to the dog. He raised one eyebrow at me.

I responded *later* with a look.

"Sergeant Shelton, you know Brenda Mankin. She observed something that you need to hear about immediately. Brenda—?"

"Wait," Richard Alvaro said. "I want you to be aware I'm recording this, Ms. Mankin."

"No skin off my nose."

Shelton grunted.

Brenda didn't need any further urging.

In almost the same words as she'd told us, she related how Randall Kenyon came out of Keefer Dobey's cabin yesterday after Diana and I had left.

"Diana's photos before, mine after," Tom said quietly. The man was a diplomat not mentioning me. Diana's showed no sign of the paper visible behind the painting in Tom's photos.

That earned a laser glare. But Shelton didn't waste much time on it, because he grasped the possibility immediately.

Richard wasn't far behind, judging by the way he jerked his head from Brenda to Shelton to check if he got the implication.

"How long?" Shelton rasped at her.

". . . with no cause or right to—How long? What kind of fool question—"

She'd kept on with her tale, so it took a moment for the interruption to halt her.

I parted my lips to straighten out the miscommunication, but Diana put a hand on my arm. She was right. Better to stay out of the line of fire. Besides, she also handed me a cookie.

"—is that? I knew right off when I saw him. That's the stupidest—"

"How long was he in there?" Shelton's dentist was going to make a fortune off this case judging by how he was grinding his teeth.

"I don't know. I—"

"So he could have just been standing at the door and you only thought he was coming out."

The red of anger suffused Brenda's wrinkles. "No. I haven't lost my mind or my eyesight, Wayne Shelton. I came out of my cabin and started across toward Keefe's with a bowl of food for Suzie Q. Not that she ever eats it, but I've been trying since the day I found him. And that's what I was doing—taking the bowl I'd filled up in my kitchen over to where she was on the porch.

"First thing I saw was the back end of that rental truck Randall Kenyon's got peeking out from behind the barn. Like it was parked so nobody in the main house could see it. I got closer to Keefe's cabin, the door opened and there was Randall Kenyon himself looking out. Thought he was going to bolt back inside for a second and I bet he did, too. Then he decided to try to bluff it out. Before I can get out much more than *What the hell—?*, he jumps in with *Did you see 'em?* Course I say, *See who?* And he starts in with all this bull about seeing someone inside the cabin and that's why he went in and he thinks they went out the back before he could spot them good enough to ID—"

And there we had Randall Kenyon's line of defense for denying he planted the letter implicating Wendy Barlow. But if he printed it out at the B&B . . .

Shelton's jaw bulged out in another likely tooth-on-tooth assault.

"—but he said I must've seen them, because they ran across the back toward my cabin. Which was bull of the first order, because I looked later on and we'd had that snow and footprints would have shown back there. But if what he saw weren't critters no bigger'n a possum, he was lying just the way I knew he was."

"What did he say to that?" I asked.

I got warning looks from Tom, Diana, and Richard, but Shelton didn't blink. Even better, Brenda answered. "Didn't give me time to check. When I said I hadn't seen anything, he switched like a leaf caught in the wind and said maybe he'd been mistaken, maybe it had just been shadow and light playing tricks on him and he had to get going and—poof!—he was gone."

"Did you see anything he did in the cabin?" Shelton asked.

"I would've said if I had, wouldn't I? I told you what I saw, what I said, what he said, what he did."

I could think of a number of questions, but Shelton appeared to have slipped into a reverie, which did not abate the warning looks sent my way from Tom and Diana.

Richard shifted his weight. Without looking around at the young deputy, Shelton lowered his chin.

I wouldn't have taken it as more than a twitch in the back of his neck, because Shelton rarely nodded at me. But Richard being his protégé created a different context.

Richard asked, "Can anything help you narrow down the amount of time he could have been in there?"

Not only was it a good question, but his wording indicated he accepted her account. That and the general effect the pleasant young man had on people softened Brenda's tone.

"As a matter of fact there is. I'd taken water over to Suzie Q first. Can't say if he was there or not, but his truck wasn't where I saw it minutes later. I took the food dish she hadn't touched from the previous day back to my cabin, emptied it into the garbage, washed out the bowl, then had to attend to some private matters." Pink crept up the wrinkles of her neck, but she set her chin pugnaciously and said, "The toilet. I had to use the toilet. When I came out, the dish was about air-dried. I finished it off with a towel and put more food in. So, I'd say ten minutes anyhow. Could've been fifteen."

Plenty of time for Randall to stash the letter behind the picture frame.

Shelton was beginning to let himself believe it was possible Randall Kenyon had planted the letter.

It wasn't like the clouds cleared from his brow, but he could probably imagine a time when they might.

His people hadn't missed both the nutmeg tins and the letter. Sure, they'd still missed the nutmeg tins.

And he knew I'd never forget that. Worse for him, *he'd* never forget it.

I found that comforting. You know, in case I got amnesia.

This shift in Shelton didn't show in expression or posture. But he said, "We need you to come to the sheriff's department to make an official statement."

That meant he was ducks-in-a-rowing before he tackled Randall Kenyon.

"That can wait until tomorrow, can't it?" Tom half-asked, half-stated.

Shelton grunted.

"If one of your people would drop Wendy off here, we'll see that they both get back to the ranch tonight. Take the next step tomorrow," Tom said.

Another grunt.

Shelton turned to leave.

I scrambled up to get to the door just after he'd exited.

"Good to see you, Sergeant. Good night, Sergeant. Sleep well, Sergeant."

Richard rolled his eyes at me as he passed me in the doorway and I could feel Tom and Diana doing the same behind me.

But it was worthwhile.

Shelton growled.

Some people count their treasure in land or gold or stock or bitcoin. I hoarded a stash of remembered Shelton growls.

DIANA LEFT FOR her delayed family dinner.

With the external warmth of the fire and—in the case of Brenda, the internal warmth of a small whiskey Tom poured and she chugged—Brenda and Suzie Q dozed.

Tom and I held hands and our silence, sipping our drinks, watching the flames and the dogs.

Richard was back with Wendy in under half an hour. He escorted her to the door—his knock stirring the dozers—but didn't come in with her.

Wendy looked even smaller. Shrunken almost. Her thinness no longer making me think of wiry, but fragility.

"How was it?" Brenda asked, as I escorted Wendy to the easy chair beside her.

I'm not sure even she would have asked that if she hadn't been dozing and possibly feeling the effects of that whiskey.

"How do you *think* it was?" Instead of Wendy's usual snap, that came out querulous.

Tom handed her a whiskey. She cupped her hands around it as if the glass gave off warmth before taking a small sip.

"Never want to be in a situation like that again. Can't be," she added in a vehement murmur. "Won't be."

"You should have called James Longbaugh." Brenda eyed the glass Wendy sipped from again, then glanced at her own sitting empty on the coffee table.

I was glad Tom didn't take the hint. I didn't want her falling asleep for the night in my living room.

"Like anyone around here would be any good." That reflection of her remaining Eastern snobbery was said with more of Wendy's usual snap. At least between that and the whiskey her color was better.

"What did they ask?" I asked.

"Nothing that made sense." She sipped the whiskey. "All sorts of things about if Keefe and I had a relationship. A *relationship.* Like we were lovers or something, had been for decades, then he broke up with me—and that's supposed to be why I killed him?"

Her voice rose with the last part. She took another sip.

"What made them think *that?*" Brenda sounded astonished.

I wondered which part she referred to—the relationship, the breakup, or the killing—but apparently Wendy had no issue parsing that. "They had something they said I'd written and given to Keefe. Never did. In my whole life, never did."

"Why would you? If you had something to say to him, he was right there and you said it. Like any normal person."

Wendy expelled a sigh. "Who knows what those idiots are thinking. I just want to go home now."

"I'll take you." Tom stood. To me he said, "I'll call."

He'd be going back to the ranch, relieving the neighbor watching Tamantha, and preparing for an early start to a long day of work.

Wendy drank off the rest of the whiskey. Brenda gave her glass another look, then stood, too.

I accompanied them.

At the door, Tom kissed me on the forehead.

"What about—?" he tipped his head toward Suzie Q lying by the fire.

Wendy said, "If she comes back to the ranch, she'll mourn herself to death." Her stark words were true and not devoid of sympathy.

Wouldn't have mattered what she or Brenda said, though. Suzie Q was not going back there.

Neither of them looked at Suzie Q and she never lifted her head at their departure.

✧ ✧ ✧ ✧

I SAT ON the floor by the fireplace, offering Suzie Q food from my hand.

Her nose twitched slightly but she didn't move.

I looked at Shadow. He was looking at the food. It was his.

"Sorry, buddy."

I offered the food to him.

He accepted happily.

Suzie Q raised her head. Careful not to crow, do a happy dance, or otherwise upset the equilibrium, I took two more portions from the dog food dish by my knee, one in each hand. I held out the Shadow hand slightly before I opened my fingers from around the Suzie Q hand.

She looked over at him as he ate his.

Still watching him, she took a piece of food from my hand and swallowed it. Her next mouthful took it all.

She hadn't eaten for days and if she wolfed this down, I was afraid it would come right back up.

Altogether, I'd probably given her about a sixth of Shadow's daily intake. He'd had about the same. All extra for him, but he wasn't complaining.

"WHAT ARE YOU doing?" Tom's warm voice made up for the cold of the phone near my ear.

"I have the dogs out for last call."

Even here in town, stars glittered so sharply against the depthless dark of the sky that I found myself holding my breath, waiting for it to shatter like a frozen pond.

"How's Suzie Q doing?"

"She's better, I think. No. For sure. She's definitely better. She's eating a little. She followed Shadow outside just fine."

"But . . ." he prodded.

"But she's so *sad.*"

"Uh-huh."

Two syllables that said that was to be expected, that the grieving process took time, that perhaps it was even harder on an animal who could not apply the band-aid of justice for the dead to the wound of loss.

"She has that routine with the fence . . ."

He knew what I meant. He'd seen it the first time we'd let her outside while we waited for Richard bringing Wendy.

Suzie Q stood and stared at the fence for the longest time. After she did her business, she walked along it, circling one way, then the other, while Shadow sniffed and explored all over the yard.

Again this time, she made her circuits and stared at the fence like it was as unexpected and unwelcomed as an alien spaceship, but she couldn't work herself up to really care.

I sighed. "I hope she'll get past this."

"She might not. She's no puppy," he said. "And she's used to a certain kind of life. Can be hard on an animal adding that kind of change to what she's already gone through with Keefe being gone."

That kind of change meant my little house in town and its fence.

We'd agreed that trying her at the ranch house was a non-starter. Tom wasn't there enough to watch her, while having Zeb and Iris next door here as backup was a godsend. Not to mention Shadow.

"Not going to solve it tonight," Tom said. "Get some sleep."

We said our good-nights.

Not a lot later, as I was drifting toward sleep, I heard his voice in my head, as I often did.

Not going to solve it tonight . . . Did he mean only Suzie Q's situation?

He was right, whether he did or not.

DAY SIX

SUNDAY

CHAPTER THIRTY-SEVEN

"YOU GOT ANOTHER dog?" my neighbor Zeb Undlin called over from his driveway.

Before I could answer—it was morning and I wasn't fast with an answer—he directed another call in the opposite direction. "Iris. Come see, Elizabeth has another dog."

"That's Keefer's Suzie Q," Iris declared.

So, I sat on the kitchen floor feeding Suzie Q breakfast, with Shadow impatient but cooperative with his portion being doled out slowly to keep her eating, while explaining the dog situation to the Undlins.

They agreed with Tom.

That was mildly irksome, but after seeing Suzie Q repeat her fence routine like a prisoner of war allowed only a tiny portion of space and sky, I was inclined to agree, too.

On the other hand, she wouldn't starve, thanks to having Shadow around.

The Undlins more than compensated for agreeing with Tom by volunteering to feed Suzie Q—and Shadow—small portions several times during the day any time I was away from the house.

"We'll have to get her a dog bed," Zeb said.

"I don't think she's used to a dog bed." Though I wouldn't go out on a limb to say she hadn't slept on Keefe's bed.

"It's only fair," Zeb said firmly.

"Fair? How—"

Iris interrupted me. "Didn't we tell you? We got Shadow a bed."

"He has a bed." In fact he had one on each level of the town house and another at the ranch house, though, I strongly suspect he spent more time on Tamantha's bed than his own when they slept in the same house. I steadfastly didn't look.

"Not at our house, he didn't. And that floor can get hard and cold on the bones. He's not an old fella yet, but he's not a young chicken, either."

"That's right," Iris said in full support. "So we got him one that fits right by where we watch TV. Gives him a good view, too."

"He likes to watch the birds," Zeb told me. "I can tell you which shows are his favorites."

I was really falling down on this paw-parent stuff. I watched what I liked on TV without considering Shadow's viewing preferences. He had seemed to enjoy the Andy Hardy movies we watched with Tamantha. I liked the spirit and the music. Tamantha viewed them as historic artifacts.

✧ ✧ ✧ ✧

TOM AND TAMANTHA picked me up to attend Mass at the Catholic church in Cody.

I don't remember how this worked its way onto our schedule. I know there was talk about familiarizing Tamantha—or was it Tom?—with the church's practices. I just know it wasn't my talk or my idea.

I didn't fight it, either.

So we sat in a pew about a third of the way back that Tamantha picked.

"This is your church?" She looked at the statues, the details of the altar, then zeroed in on the Stations of the Cross around the perimeter.

I would have let the question slide by, except I suspected the alternative would be her demanding a detailed explanation of the ardors depicted. "This is the Catholic church that also serves Cottonwood County," I said carefully. "What you'd call my home church—where my family still attends—is in Illinois."

"Does it look like this?"

"It's bigger. Fairly modern. It was built during one of the intermittent modernizing Kumbaya periods."

"What does that mean?"

"It means that aesthetically—how it looks and how I react to how it looks . . . well, I prefer historic churches. There's one in Ireland that—"

A woman in the second row turned and gave me a look that made me think she either was a nun—hard to tell these days with habits gone freelance—or a shaming lay person.

Either way, I lowered my voice. "I'll tell you later."

After Mass, with Tom joining in on the kneeling, but not the signs of the cross, Tamantha doing both, and me revealing my rust, we were out in the parking lot when Tamantha gave her verdict.

"I like it," she said firmly. "I'm glad the first wedding's going to be here."

"Is that because you have persuaded the priest to let you do cartwheels down the aisle?" I'd seen how he'd greeted her just now as parishioners filed past—like an old friend, when they'd only met once, when we made arrangements after the first of the year.

Of course, Tamantha is unforgettable.

She grinned.

"Just one cartwheel. But I mean today—the Mass. I like it."

Tom gave nothing away by expression or sound, but his slight stillness did convey a reaction.

"Why do you like it, Tamantha?" I asked.

"The singing sounds better." She dashed ahead to get to the truck, ready for a promised waffle breakfast in Cody.

I dug an elbow into Tom's side. "Relax. It's acoustics, not conversion."

The lines around his eyes deepened and the stillness dissipated.

✧　✧　✧　✧

WE STOPPED AT Elk Rock Ranch on the way back, since it was practically on the way.

Tamantha opted to stay in the truck, reading. The absence of animals in sight probably tipped the scales for her.

Wendy and Brenda were just getting out of a truck.

"Just back from town?" I asked cheerfully.

"Waste of time," Wendy grumbled. "Couldn't even pick up supplies with everything closed for Sunday morning."

Brenda grunted. "Everything closed except the sheriff's department. Did that formal statement they wanted. That was a waste of time, too. Told them the same thing as yesterday. That young Richard Alvaro said he was recording it, so don't know what they needed from me saying it again, anyway."

She clearly wasn't wise in the ways of law enforcement—or journalists—wanting things on the record. At the same time on the lookout for any discrepancies between Version One and Version Two.

Apparently, Brenda hadn't had any such discrepancies, because it sounded like an efficient trip to the sheriff's department.

The vulnerability of the previous day was gone. Both women had returned to their impregnable selves. At least outwardly.

Wendy said, "I got paperwork to do. You never trouble yourself with it and—"

"Why should I? I'm not the high-and-mighty owner."

"—if it doesn't get done, we close up faster than a cardboard suitcase and we'll all be out of a home."

"Keefe's already out of a home. Out of a life, too, and—"

Brenda broke off and we all turned at the sound of a vehicle clattering over the bridge like someone sweeping a hand over piano keys.

Randall Kenyon's rental truck careened up the drive toward us, bouncing from one side to the other as it hit end-of-winter ruts and gullies.

Why was Randall available to arrive at Elk Rock in this or any other fashion?

I'd expected Shelton to have all those ducks lined up by now and be grilling Randall on the planting of the letter that pointed suspicion toward Wendy. Plus, using the planting of the letter as leverage on possible murder charges.

The motive still needed work, although—

"That girl," Brenda clucked. "Rides a horse the same way."

"Not any of my horses," Wendy said. "Never letting her on another Elk Rock animal."

Robin Kenyon driving the truck.

Ah, that made more sense.

The truck skidded to a halt in the middle of the drive. The door flung open and Robin stumbled out.

Before anyone could react to try to catch her, she righted herself.

Okay, before Tom or I could react, because neither of the older women showed any sign of moving to her aid.

With tears tracing her cheeks, Robin shouted at us, "You have to do something. You have to stop them."

Stop who from doing what?

The question was right there, begging to be asked. No one asked it. Probably not surprising in the case of Brenda and Wendy. But me, professional question asker?

Sometimes it's important to not ask questions. Asking can make you a participant, when you can learn different things by remaining an observer.

I felt Tom's look on the side of my face. He, too, remained silent.

Not getting an answer, Robin repeated, louder, "You have to do something. Right *now*."

Wendy clacked her tongue and said with her usual snap, "What are you talking about?"

"My father. They have my father at the sheriff's office. They came to the B&B and they took him away in one of those marked cars—"

Probably an SUV or truck—but I wasn't participating, so no throwing in corrections.

"—and they didn't say a lot, but the little that short guy said—I know what they're thinking. But he didn't. He *couldn't* have killed Keefe. I know he didn't."

Not the same words as Brenda's *They got it wrong*, but with as much conviction.

It didn't carry the same weight.

Nobody could imagine Brenda making up a story to clear Wendy. They weren't exactly enemies—or if they were, the enmity had aged so long that its sharp edges were worn off, leaving habit—but they weren't sisters of the heart, either.

And, yes, Robin and Randall had issues, but everybody could imagine her lying to clear her one remaining parent.

"How do you know he didn't?" Wendy asked.

Robin gaped at her, so shocked that her tears stopped.

With the silence continuing, Wendy made a get-away gesture with her hand toward the young woman. Instead of waiting to see if it would be obeyed, Wendy spun around and walked toward the main house.

Robin came back to animation with a gasp that let loose a new gush of tears and words. "She's awful. Just awful. What a horrible, horrible thing to say to me."

"Well, she does have a point," Brenda said judiciously. "Your father tried to frame her. Unless you saw who killed Keefe or did it yourself—"

"*Me?*"

"—you can't say for sure your father didn't. Nobody can say that about anybody else. 'Less they did it themselves or saw it. That's all I'm saying. The logic of it."

"My father didn't kill him. I *know* he didn't."

Brenda said, "Look at the bright side. If they arrest him and keep him in jail, you've still got a nice enough place to stay at the Wild Horses B&B, with us not open yet for the season."

Robin's focus stuck on an earlier word. "Arrest . . .? *Arrest?*"

"A nice place to stay and plenty of money for food. You'll be fine."

With Brenda's bracing personality threatening to knock over Robin, I slid in, "Perhaps you should call your father's lawyer. Get him to get in touch with someone local, just in case."

"In case what?" Robin demanded with flared eyes and nostrils.

Brenda gave me an exasperated look as if I'd been the untactful one. "Never mind that," she told Robin. "Come with me. I need another pair of hands anyway to reposition a stall door while I fix the hinges."

With the promise of that take-your-mind-off-your-father-being-suspected-of-murder treat, Brenda reached for Robin's arm.

Robin yanked away. "Hold a door? *Hold a door?* I'm not—"

She half ran back to the truck and roared away.

Brenda shrugged and turned toward the barn.

Tom made a *what next* sound.

I checked the time. "Town, so I can get to the station."

I was anchoring the Five today while Leona covered a charity event. She'd be back in time to do the Ten—which would no doubt lead with her charity event no matter what hard news tried to push to the front. But my taking the Five gave her time to prep for the event and, possibly, get a little more rest.

As Tom drove us toward Sherman, I thought about Robin. I felt sympathy for her. At the same time, there was one thing I found interesting.

When Brenda explained her logic to Robin about how no one who hadn't been a witness or the killer him-or-herself could be certain that someone else wasn't the killer, I'd immediately heard in my head the expected, natural, automatic response from Robin:

Why would my father kill Keefer Dobey? He had no reason to kill Keefer Dobey.

She hadn't said that.

CHAPTER THIRTY-EIGHT

I **HATED THIS** waiting.

Preparing the Five for me to anchor and the Ten for Leona didn't offer much distraction.

It was a slow news day. I gladly apportioned more time to Sports, with college basketball at its hottest, and tried not to grimace over a wire piece on happy daffodils across swaths of the country.

Nala Choi and I prepped two pieces, one for each broadcast, with background on Keefer Dobey's murder that could be topped with the breaking news of an arrest . . . if that happened.

It didn't.

Which brought me back to waiting.

And thinking.

If Randall Kenyon killed Keefer Dobey, the biggest question was answered.

That was a black and white question.

My questions were better suited to answers with lots of gray in them, maybe some paisley or plaid.

Yes, there remained the question of why. But that might require therapy, rather than an interview—law enforcement or journalistic.

Also questions surrounding his heavy-handed attempt to throw suspicion on Wendy Barlow.

Not that heavy-handed surprised me terribly in connection to Randall. He was the bull accustomed to getting what he wanted by threatening to enter the china shop.

I did a little reading on his history of buying out companies.

Then I placed a phone call.

The first one went to voice mail and I told Wardell Yardley to call me back, nothing urgent. He was a stretch anyway. Business was not his area of expertise—though he'd never admit that.

Matt Lester answered at home.

"Hey, Elizabeth, the whole family's here, so I—"

"Of course, of course. You go. Give my love to everyone—"

"Wait. Tell me what you called for."

"More of your thoughts, this time on Randall Kenyon."

"He's involved in the mess out there that connects with the Barlows?"

"Maybe. If it's confirmed, I'll give you a heads-up."

"Thanks. What do you want to know?"

"The business world's take on him."

He was silent a moment, putting together his thoughts.

"Generally admiring. Divided on how smart he is, including whether he was smart enough or lucky enough to hire really smart people. Want to start those shark types drooling, ask about Randall Kenyon's staff. Despite many efforts, only a few have been poached, because he's definitely smart enough to pay them so much they don't look elsewhere."

"Is he known for being impulsive? Making rash moves?"

"No. Good timing's one of the things he's credited with, even by those who think the staff carries him. I'll send you a link to a profile a friend did a couple years ago. That was before Kenyon's wife died and there has been talk that's deeply rattled him, but it will give you a good grounding. Anything else?"

"Depends on your time."

He chuckled. "I'm getting out of potato-peeling duty. Go ahead."

I POSED THE question of whether he knew any recently unemployed newspaper editors who might serve the needs of KWMT.

He laughed without humor and rattled off names.

"Wait. Stop. What about those who might be willing to move to

Sherman, Wyoming."

"That narrows the list."

"And can make the transition to TV news."

He snorted. "They could all do that. Whether they're willing to . . .?"

He gave me three names and said he had more in mind, but wanted to check. Then he reported for potato-peeling duty.

MATT UNDERSOLD RANDALL Kenyon's reputation for timing in the business world according to the profile.

He rushed things. He stumbled around like Godzilla in his death throes. Because he was unsure of his daughter.

The man with the perfect timing for business deals rushed himself right into a mess.

But did that mess include murder?

JENNIFER SENT MESSAGES asking for a group call ASAP.

We had to slot it in between Mike's broadcasts and after the Five.

I was home, had let out and fed both dogs, and had fifteen minutes to spare when attachments started coming in from Jennifer.

It took a while to sort them, then decide printing out would help with comprehension.

When the call came in, I had the eight-by-ten sheets spread out on the counter, some of them sideways because it wasn't big enough.

"*Jennifer! You did it!*" I'd like to think I said it, but it probably qualified as a squeal.

"I only got to look at a couple, but, is this what I think it is?" Mike asked.

"It is," Diana said firmly. "Amazing."

Jennifer tried not to grin.

She had blown up the individual photos we'd taken of the newspaper article Keefe found and enhanced it so we could read two-thirds of the words.

"It's got to be the article that secondary source cited, don't you think?" she asked. "The one with the guy who'd been in the posse chasing Oscar Virtanen years before."

"Definitely," Diana said. "And in case you didn't see it, Mike, among the reasons the old guy said he felt so sorry for the mourning widow, even though she'd been reputed to be involved in robberies, was because she was *heavy with child*."

"You guys were right," he said. "That's why Oscar did the robbery solo. She was too pregnant to join him. And probably his motive—to grab enough money to get far away, settle down, and have their family."

"And," I said, "the guy being interviewed said he heard later that she had the baby. If so, that makes Keefe being Oscar and Pearl's descendant possible, since they actually had a descendant."

"My question is why she didn't remain where she was in Montana? Because it says she started traveling south before the robbery, much less hearing Oscar was shot and being chased," Diana said. "Had they prearranged a meeting place?"

"Which could indicate they'd also prearranged a drop spot for the loot if necessary," Mike said. "And if this guy's right, she could have had the baby, waited a bit, then collected the money never to be heard from again."

"That never to be heard from again agrees with the dissertation by Mrs. P's mentor, though no mention of a baby, drop spot, or retrieval of the loot."

"This makes it less likely the treasure's out there waiting to be picked up," Mike noted. "You two going to tell Sam McCracken?"

I looked at Diana on the screen. "Feels like we're all on hold, pending whether Randall's charged with murder or not. Once that's settled . . ."

"I say we tell him. After we know about Randall," Diana said.

"That's the thing about this article," Jennifer said. "Even if it's one-hundred-percent accurate, it doesn't advance us on the murder, does it."

The answer to her non-question was *No.*

We fought back from that downer realization to celebrate her achievement in making this find mostly readable to the extent it deserved before wrapping up.

DAY SEVEN
MONDAY

CHAPTER THIRTY-NINE

EVERY MEMBER OF the news staff who was in the building, crammed into the news Director's office for a video call with Mike.

Leona being among the attendees at an earlier time than she'd usually report was the first hint she knew what was coming. The second was that, while she wasn't beaming smiles at anybody, her level of hate had dropped.

But not gone.

That became clear when, after Mike announced hiring Octavia Zabel for an anchor spot, Leona said, "But only when the skiing's not good."

That required more explanation from Mike, to which he added, "And we're looking for at least one more anchor to complement Octavia's schedule."

"Any advance on a news director? GM?" Walt asked.

"Not that I can share now, but we're exploring ideas. And if anyone has recommendations . . ."

That got a laugh, which built when Walt said, "Sure. Leona."

She whacked him, Mike groaned, the rest laughed.

Before the meeting broke up, Mike said, "Diana and Elizabeth, will you two please stick around a bit."

We did, as the rest of them filed out amid congratulations to Leona.

With the two of us left and the door closed, Mike immediately asked, "Diana, why don't you want to replace the NewsMobile?"

The rat.

I'd told him he had to ask her, but I'd intended that to be between them. With her knowing my feelings on the topic, it might make her defensive.

"I don't need something big and shiny."

"Not what I asked," he said mildly. "Why don't you want to replace it?"

She gusted out exasperation, but hard to tell if it was at us or herself, especially when she looked away.

"The station sinks a lot of money into a new microwave truck and you're going to want to get the most out of it. If that's my station vehicle, then I'm going to be out on breaking news whenever it happens. With the age the kids are I want to be home more for them—"

Also, I suspected, for our sheriff, Russ Conrad. But I can keep my mouth shut when it's called for.

"—whenever I can. They'll be off to college soon—Jess really soon—and we won't have this time again. So, no, I don't want the big, new truck with all the tech, because I don't want the work-hour strings that come with it."

"Make it clear you aren't using it after your shift. As long as it's available for someone else to use—"

"You know that's not how it works. Jenks has come around a lot, but techy he is not. It will take forever to train him or the others on the newest tech—"

Mike interrupted us by laughing. Loud.

"You think we're buying something with the newest tech? State of the art? Really?" He went off again. Apparently catching a closer look at our expressions, he restrained himself with a few more gulping guffaws. "Sorry. You were stalling because of that? No need, because there's no way we'd make that sort of outlay for a single piece of equipment. Especially one that could get hit by a semi or go off the road or run into a cow or deer or moose."

I'd noticed Mike expressing concerns befitting an insurance agent more often since becoming majority owner of KWMT.

"Well, what are you planning to get?" Diana asked.

"Something used with better tech than we have now, which means, basically, anything since World War II. But now that I know how you feel, maybe I'll look at just getting you a vanilla van—because the NewsMobile is an embarrassment to have our name on—"

"Hey!"

"It is," I said, loyally supporting the station majority owner, as well as reporting factually.

"—and save for a more recent live van. Probably could get a satellite truck used at a better discount with them not being used as much, but—"

"Not satellite," Diana said emphatically. "But what about two used live vans?"

Ah-hah. Not having the only one wouldn't make her feel obligated to be on hand for every story, but she'd still have one.

"*Two?* That's getting expensive—"

"Not that bad." She now was fully into lobbying for this. The employee no longer refusing an upgrade from the owner, but instead asking for more. The world was no longer spinning backward. "Maybe get them a little older than you'd planned. Or one of them, anyway."

"Good idea to have a backup," I stuck in.

She picked up on that. "Right. If one breaks down—because, you are talking used and how many live trucks get driven by little old ladies going to church—"

Certainly not the ones she drove.

"—we'd still have the capability we needed."

Mike ran a hand through his hair.

Have I mentioned he had great hair. He should do that now and then on-air. His female viewership in Chicago would expand beyond true sports fans.

"I'll look at the numbers and see what's available—no promises."

"Of course not," she said with understanding. Perhaps she understood his position. She certainly understood she was almost certain to get what she wanted. And I agreed that would serve KWMT-TV well.

✧ ✧ ✧ ✧

NOT EVEN AN hour later, Audrey rolled her eyes at me and said, "Don't you have a murder to solve or something?"

I parted my lips, but that was as far as I got.

"Your prowling around here is driving everyone nuts." I glanced around and received several confirming nods. "And, no, you cannot ask Dale to do a little work for you. I need him. And everybody else on staff."

Surely that didn't include Diana.

I called her after I'd left the building. Hoping for inspiration, I asked her to meet me at the entrance to Elk Rock Ranch when she finished her next assignment.

"I had a feeling you weren't satisfied with Randall Kenyon," she said.

"Not yet, anyway."

She'd keep me posted on her progress.

After a quick stop at home—where I was a distraction from the well-oiled feeding-Suzie Q machine that was Iris and Zeb Undlin, and included plenty of side-treats to Shadow so he didn't feel left out—I left.

But I had a stop to make on the way.

✧ ✧ ✧ ✧

MAKE THAT TWO stops.

The first one came when I recognized Gee's vehicle parked by the museum's rear entrance.

Possible she was there without Mrs. P, but unlikely.

The back door wasn't locked. Shoddy security for a museum. How could they expect people not to walk in?

"Not again," Clara Atwood said. She and Audrey could have been eye-rolling twins.

"You'll be glad I came."

As I started telling her about the nutmeg tin with the copy of an old newspaper article—but not about the other finds in Keefe's cabin—Mrs. P and Gee came into sight down the hallway.

Under the power of those two women, Clara gestured us all into her office. They took chairs, I sat on a spare desk, continuing my account.

". . . and we know all that from the amazing job Jennifer Lawton did with enhancing it."

"It you damaged the original—"

"It was photos of the copy Keefe made. The original's lurking somewhere in your boxes. If something happens to it while it waits for your priorities, that's not on us."

"I want those enhanced images."

"I'll send you Jennifer's contact info so you can thank her appropriately while asking her for that favor."

She breathed out through her nose. "I have to talk to someone up front. You can stay here as long as you want," she said to the other two women.

"She's thrilled," Gee said once Clara was gone.

"She should be. Jennifer did amazing work. And Keefe found it amid all those boxes. She should be grateful."

"She is," Gee said. "In her way. But you didn't come here for that."

"No. I saw you were here and . . . I'm trying to sort out if there were long-standing jealousies or—Well, we know there were between Brenda and Wendy. Not only from when they were younger over at least one specific guy, but tension over Chester, too. And I wondered if there was something with Keefe . . ."

Gee turned to the older woman, putting the ball firmly in her court.

Mrs. P didn't hit it back.

I tried again. "I mean, two women and a man. Especially when they were young—not that I'm saying people past their first flush of youth can't be passionate—" Only when the words were out did I realize they could be applied to these women. I'd meant Tom and me. But come to think of it . . .

I backtracked to pick up my thread.

"So maybe the triangle still jabbed with its three sharp points or maybe time smoothed out aspects of it, but resentment remained."

This time Mrs. P accepted the opening to speak. "An alternative explanation could be that such feelings never existed or dissipated with the recognition, whether conscious or not, of the futility of them."

When she stopped—after a much shorter statement than her usual—I said neutrally, "Futility of the feelings . . ."

"You referred to a triangle, Elizabeth, with three sharp points and contemplated the possibility that time smoothed them. However, that is based on there having been three points at the start. It is difficult to have a triangle with two points, while the third . . ."

She looked at me steadily, waiting for the student to reach the correct conclusion on her own.

"Was *never* a point." Making Randall's fake note even more inept. I thought about Scott Hoole saying Keefe substituted wildlife and nature for human relationships. "Keefe wasn't gay . . ."

"No, he was not. It is likely that he could be considered as qualifying as what is now termed asexual. Scholars are only now studying it, with varying stances on whether it is a sexual orientation, as well as what percentage of the population to which that term applies, whether self-identified or otherwise. In addition, there is research and writings viewing a spectrum under that umbrella. Such interest in clarity is, perhaps, new, while it is highly unlikely this variation in human sexuality is new."

Figured she'd talk of this with ease. It was educational.

"You believe Keefer Dobey was asexual." She ever so slightly tipped her head. "Okay, you don't like *believe*. You—" She would like *conjecture* even less. "—have formed the hypothesis that he was asexual."

"My observations, limited and uneducated in this matter, do not rise to the level of a hypothesis."

"But, if he were asexual, how would that lead to his murder?" I saw her objection brewing and spoke quickly. "Or contribute to the complex interactions that might have led to his murder?"

She shook her head. I had not headed off her objection. "I would suggest that you consider the contrary. That if he was not one of those three sharp points that you described as forming a triangle that it is another shape or another cause you are looking for."

I could just barely stretch to believing that Keefe being asexual might have been a factor back when Wendy and Brenda were younger and wrangled over men. Each could have misread the situation and suspected his lack of interest stemmed from his being interested in the other.

But now? After decades of knowing the man?

I'd hoped for more clarity from this conversation, not fewer motives.

Which was interesting, because wasn't I waiting for Randall Kenyon to be charged?

I was so lost in that thought I missed what Mrs. P said and had to ask her to repeat it.

"I asked if you have enjoyed reading the dissertation I lent you."

"Enjoyed? I wouldn't say that. Your friend Ethel—"

"Esther."

"Sorry. Esther had some details I hadn't seen elsewhere about Oscar's and Pearl's early lives, as well as their early married lives and the beginning of their outlaw career, including what could be seen as her justifications for their actions. But Esther Ramalarga is short on details of what happened to Pearl after Oscar's death and, especially, now that we know she was pregnant, that seems . . . well, I'd say slipshod. But there's this odd undercurrent that she's in on a joke that nobody else is."

Neither reacted.

In fact, the complete lack of reaction became a kind of reaction.

I heard myself repeating, "That Esther Ramalarga's in on a joke . . . *Esther Ramalarga.*"

Esther. Ethel. Etta . . .

I caught a look from Gee.

"What?" I asked her.

"Do you know what the Spanish phrase *rama larga* means in English?"

"Gisella—"

I spoke over Mrs. P's protest. "Large something."

"Long branch."

"Long branch?" I repeated.

Gee clicked her tongue at my slowness. "Branch as in—"

"*Bough*," I practically shouted. "B-O-u-g-h, as nearly *b-A-u-g-h.*"

Gee compressed her mouth, not prepared to answer, but satisfied with stirring my questions.

"Esther Ramalarga of Sherman, Wyoming—a schoolteacher, no less—and your mentor, Mrs. Parens. *Was* she really Etta Place, the significant other of Harry Longabaugh and previously a resident of Argentina and Bolivia?"

"I have always heard she spoke excellent Spanish," Gee said.

"There is no proof whatsoever of such a connection." Mrs. P sent Gee a disapproving look. "It is speculation at best."

"But what did she say about it—Esther?"

"I never asked."

CHAPTER FORTY

HOW DO YOU respond to that?

Not *ask?*

Emmaline Parens appeared unperturbed by my astonishment, at the same time displaying impatience with my continued questions. I also displayed impatience—but with her lack of answers.

Gee broke the impasse, saying they were leaving to pursue errands.

"I'm not done with this," I warned.

"You will find nothing that satisfies your desire for facts," Mrs. P warned back.

ESTHER RAMALARGA.

Etta Place.

The dissertation writer knew details about Oscar and Pearl's exploits yet no clue to Pearl's whereabouts or mention of a baby. Protecting someone also associated with the gang whose outlaw love died?

And Emmaline Parens didn't ask.

If I hadn't had this other stop to make, I would have taken the time to let my head explode.

But I still had my original stop to make.

I went west out of Sherman, passing the turnoff Diana used to go southwest toward Elk Rock Ranch.

Between Diana's turnoff and where I would turn south on the highway, sat a substantial construction trailer with a sign that said

Burrell Roads, with Connie Walterston's pickup out front.

This marked the southern edge of Circle B land. Sometimes I thought Tom would like to kick it off the ranch completely.

Safe to say, Burrell Roads was not the enterprise of his heart.

Connie opened the trailer door and called, "Elizabeth, what are you doing here?"

"Thought I'd stop by for a bit, if that's okay."

"Sure. Can do most things from home, but I wanted to get a few things straightened out here in anticipation of the season." She tipped her head consideringly as I passed her in the doorway. "I told you I planned to do that today when we had lunch, didn't I."

"Did you?" I asked lightly.

"Uh-huh. So I wouldn't believe it if you told me you're here to tell me all about the wedding dress you keep side-stepping talking about."

She'd caught me off-guard—focused on what I wanted to ask, not what questions might come from her—but I thought I masked it well while taking a seat on the visitor side of the desk that looked neat even with her organizing piles on it.

"You don't have a dress yet, do you, Elizabeth."

I hadn't masked it. "I'll find something."

"*Something.*" She wrang out every available drop of disdain in her pronunciation of the word. "It's your wedding. You want more than *something.* Does your mother know? Tamantha?"

"Good heavens, no. Please don't—"

"I won't. I have something else in mind."

"Connie—"

She gave me a stop sign hand. "I won't tell your mother or Tamantha. That's all I'll promise. In the meantime, you didn't come here to confess you haven't found your wedding dress yet—have you even looked? Never mind. It doesn't matter, since you haven't found the right one."

I had looked in my closet, but I didn't think that answer would satisfy her, so I jumped on the sliver of an opening she'd given me.

"You're right that I came about something else. I'm curious about Tom's parents. His father, really. They're saying they *hope* to get here for the wedding." Connie sighed audibly. "I think she wants to, wants to very much."

"He's a good man," she said immediately. "Not necessarily an easy man, but a good one."

That could also be said of his son, but I couldn't imagine how many armies would be needed to keep Tom from his daughter's wedding . . . in the far, far distant future, of course.

"You worked with him when he ran Burrell Roads?"

"Yes. Basically an assistant—secretary, according to T.Y. Then I stopped for a while because of the ranch and the boys and before we knew about Brian's health." That was her husband, who'd had a degenerative disease before his death a year and a half ago. "When I knew I had to go back to work because we needed the income and insurance so desperately, T.Y. and Nina had retired. Tom hired me on the spot, gave me a raise and a free hand. I'll never stop being grateful—to both of them, in different ways."

"They do seem quite different. Look, I know it might feel awkward, my asking questions—" Though considering she'd been among the most vocal urging me toward Tom . . .

"I understand. You don't know T.Y. at all and I know Tom holds things in." She met my eyes for an extra beat. "Holds hurts in."

Then she stalled.

Good questioning techniques don't help only with news stories and murder investigations, so I gave her breathing room, while keeping us focused on the topic.

"You call him T.Y., but I've only heard Nina call him Thomas."

"Most people do—call him Thomas, I mean. He was Thomas, Tom was Tom. Since his parents left, Tom gets Thomas used a lot more with business, legal dealings—" An eye flicker reminded us both that one *dealing* had been charges by the former sheriff against Thomas David Burrell. "—and such, but to most people he's still Tom.

"I started calling Thomas T.Y. when I got to know him and realized . . ." I saw her shoulders drop the instant she decided to tell me. "He liked T.Y. because it distinguished him from his own father as well as Thomas David—no, that's not exactly right. It wasn't really

Tom. It was Nina's father, that's where the David comes from.

"With his own father and his father-in-law, T.Y. couldn't do anything right. If it turned out good, it would have turned out better if only he'd listened to them." She clicked her tongue. "Strong men who'd have been even stronger if they'd been a little softer . . . if that makes sense."

"It does."

"And in some ways, T.Y. was no better," she said tartly. "He took out his problems with the previous generation on his son, like Tom was responsible for his grandfathers—and I told him that."

"You did?" No questioning technique behind that, I blurted it.

"I did. Not that it did any good. And I said he was hurting his wife at the same time." She half grinned. "I was pregnant and the hormones were running rampant."

"What did he say?"

"Not a thing. His ears got real red and I thought he might erupt, but he just got that real calm, controlled, impenetrable way Tom does, too, and he walked out that door. Miracle he didn't fire me on the spot."

No, a Burrell wouldn't fire a pregnant woman for speaking her mind. But he would walk away, aiming to regain the mastery over himself he required. Maybe there were more similarities between son and father than their facial structure.

CHAPTER FORTY-ONE

I'D THOUGHT THAT first day that the Elk Rock Ranch cabins and barn and other buildings and fences formed a stage with no actors on it.

As we pulled in today, after I picked up Diana from where she'd parked the NewsMobile, the play appeared to be in progress. Though which act was impossible to tell.

Wendy moved back and forth, back and forth inside the two open doors to the tack room.

From just outside, Randall, again in a version of Western wear, mirrored Wendy's movements, like a predator trying to adopt its prey's coloring.

A truck I'd seen before was parked off the entry road near the front of the barn. I detoured to look in the front passenger window as Diana and I walked past. Books were on the back seat, a file box in the footwell. One glance at the book titles and I said to her, "Sam McCracken."

He was not in sight—off stage for now, but Serena sat on the steps of the unoccupied middle cabin, her head down as if contemplating her hands clasped between her knees. Brenda was not around.

That left Robin, leaning against the fence opposite the tack room, watching her father, looking torn between relief and unhappiness.

"Go away," Randall shouted at us. "We're talking business."

"No, we're not," Wendy said emphatically.

Leaving them to sort that out, I tipped my head toward Robin and Diana and I went to her.

"You must be feeling a lot better than yesterday," I said.

"Yeah."

"Why aren't you and your dad out celebrating his release?"

And why *was* he released?

She had her shoulders hunched under her jacket, maybe against the chill wind, maybe not. "That deputy guy said not to leave town."

"You weren't going to anyway, were you? Not right away."

"I suppose." With her fear for her father under control, she was much less forthcoming.

"What's all that about?" Diana asked her, sliding her eyes toward the duo at the tack room entry.

"I dunno."

"Don't you?" I asked mildly. "You said your dad could offer Wendy a lot of money, but what would she do with it if she didn't have the ranch."

Wary but unsure where the danger stemmed from, she acknowledged slowly, "I guess I said that."

"But you know what she'd do with a lot of money if she had the ranch?"

She relaxed. "Sure. She'd pay bills, get rid of debt, fix up things she's put off."

I tried to imagine Wendy Barlow confiding those details to Robin Kenyon. Especially last summer when everyone—including Robin— agreed she had not endeared herself to anyone at Elk Rock Ranch. "How do you know?"

"My father told me."

My brain jammed even worse trying to imagine Wendy sharing such information with Randall Kenyon. "How did he know?"

"He started researching after he got the idea to buy the ranch."

"When was that?"

"Last fall."

"When you gave Keefe the computer, followed by the DNA test." An example of Randall's timing in angling for an ally?

Did Robin participate knowingly?

She ducked her head. "To thank him. It . . . What happened when

I was here changed my life. Not just getting hurt. But . . . Do you know what happened. I mean what led up to it?"

"I heard some."

She smiled. At least that's the best term I can think of. It had a foundation of a saint's patient lifting of lips for the foibles of a sinner, combined with a self-directed grimace of that sinner.

"I bet you did. About me running Rio and staying out late and slipping the wranglers. That's when they said I had to leave. I couldn't believe it. I was so angry. And it was only after Wendy said I'd have to go on the next van to the airport that I realized I *liked* it here. I didn't *want* to leave."

As she spoke, her voice sped up. On those last words, I heard an echo of petulant entitlement. As if she were not simply remembering events, but reliving them as the person she'd been.

"I was supposed to stay in my cabin until someone drove me to the airport the next day. I slipped out and started up the trail on Rio. Alone. Breaking rules again.

"And I was crying. A lot. So I didn't hear the group ahead of me. Not until there was no avoiding them. Keefe was at the back. He spotted me, but didn't say anything. It was all Brenda, shouting how horrible I'd been to Rio and I shouldn't be allowed on another horse the rest of my life, with those other people staring at me. I tried to get past them, to get off by myself. I . . . ."

We waited a long time for her to continue.

"Rio didn't throw me. I lost my balance and fell. Onto rocks. Broke a bone in my leg. Bad break. Hit them just wrong . . . Or maybe just right."

"Must have hurt like hell," Diana said.

"Not really. Not then. In fact, I didn't believe them that it was broken. Tried to get up. I couldn't. I couldn't move my leg. I couldn't do anything. I don't think I passed out, but when they splinted my leg, it was like . . . like I went calm sort of. I could hear all the voices deciding what to do, but from very far away, and talking about someone else.

"Then they were all gone and it was Keefe and me. He put a jacket under my head, got it so a roll supported my neck and it felt like all the muscles in my neck just . . . let go. Like I'd been holding my head up forever, but in that moment I didn't have to.

"And then he asked me what I saw." She'd said that at the B&B, but not with her guard down as it was now. "I opened my eyes and looked up and there were the tops of the trees way, way up, with the sky beyond them and I felt like I floated right up to them. Swaying.

"We talked some. Not a lot. I know I told him about Mom dying and he said, 'That's tough.' Just like that. Nothing more. But it was like that's all he needed to say, all he could say. It *was* tough. Still is. But it's . . . bearable, I guess. Lying there, drifting up to where the tops of the trees met the sky, it was bearable. For the first time."

She seemed prepared to stop there. I wasn't.

"You must have been in a lot of pain."

"Oh, hell, yes." This smile was wry, but grim. "After a while, absolutely. Like an electric shock of throbbing heat. Wave after wave. Couple of times I thought I'd pass out. Maybe I did. I never asked Keefe. I'd come to or the waves would ease back, and he'd be there. Sitting beside me. He'd ask again what I saw. I'd look back up to the trees and the sky and then I'd float up to them and we'd talk. I don't remember all of it. I know he said how to fell a tree. Another time about a truck engine he'd fixed. And then he'd talk about how he might be the descendant of a famous outlaw from the Wild West. I didn't follow most of it. It didn't matter. It was the sound of his voice. Then he'd ask me again, what did I see . . ."

She shifted against the fence at her back, pulling the lapels of her jacket to overlap.

"Keefe gave Wendy some wildflowers for me when she came to the hospital in Cody, and said he'd come see me his next day off. But by then Dad was there and arranged to take me home, even though I wanted to stay. It wasn't until we were home that Dad and I talked. Really talked. And I told him about Elk Rock. I wrote to Keefe. Nothing deep, just a thank you, and to tell him I was coming back for all of the next season, if Wendy would have me.

"Dad said there was no *if* about it. The more we talked, the more he got excited about buying Elk Rock. Said he'd have me run it—with help, of course. Experienced help. I thought—I expected—that would include Keefe. I know he wasn't a manager or anything, but he knew the place like nobody else. I'll still love it here, but I'll feel his absence, like I feel Mom's absence at home."

She seemed to re-set herself, choosing to set aside those sorrows.

"You know, he's not that bad. My dad. I guess he was pretty lost after Mom died, too. After I got hurt, when Keefe and I were out there, just the two of us, waiting for the help, I started crying. I told him it was from the pain, but it wasn't. I mean, it did hurt, but it was from wanting my mom. It made no sense, because even if she hadn't died, she wouldn't have been with me. She'd've been home with Dad. But I think even being able to say out loud, *I want my mom*, and knowing she was somewhere in the world would have helped.

"I don't know if I said something or Keefe just knew, but he started talking about him and his mother. How he'd never known his father and how lost he'd felt when he was little, even though he loved his mother a lot. Then they moved here and he started learning about the outdoors.

"He said he realized he'd been hard on his mom, had held back from her, like it was her fault his dad wasn't around. But being here let him see his mom for what she was and not what she wasn't—which was his dad.

"And I got thinking about how I used to love my dad when I was little and wondering if he'd really changed or if I'd been punishing him for not being my mom."

She drew a breath.

I could have asked a question—let's be honest, I could have asked dozens of questions—but sometimes the best thing you can do is wait.

"I'm not saying he's perfect. He still wants to be in charge and everything, but lying up there, I decided to do my best to love him again. I sort of forgot about that." She looked at us. I saw surprise. "And he's been trying, too."

"Like trying to buy this ranch?"

"That's even more reason why my father never would have killed

Keefe and I told that sergeant that over and over. Keefe had nothing to do with negotiating the sale of the ranch."

"And everything to do with your emotions," Diana said quietly.

I wish she'd had the camera running to catch the widening of Robin's eyes, but there are things the camera's not meant to catch. Or maybe they don't happen when the camera's there.

"You think highly of Keefe." I didn't need her agreement to keep going. "However much a role he played when you were hurt last year, he was there, with you at an important moment in your life. If only by being there, he helped you through it. That could make a father frustrated about not connecting with his daughter feel . . . jealous."

"Jealous?"

We'd caught her attention.

Not the way I might have expected. Unlike yesterday's fear and anger, this was tentative, delicate even. "You think he'd do that? For me?"

She seemed to have forgotten the act Randall would have committed as a result was murdering a man. Not only an innocent man, but one who helped her.

Inner mean girl self-centeredness sure didn't loosen its grip easily.

CHAPTER FORTY-TWO

WENDY HAD GONE deeper into the tack shed, leaving Randall still pacing in front of its open doors, but with no one to shoot words at.

"I understand you looked into the ranch's finances after Robin got home," I said without preamble.

"After I got her home and she was on the road to recovery," he corrected. He looked toward his daughter. "Is that what you were talking about?"

"But you did look into the ranch's finances?"

"Of course. Due diligence. Wouldn't make an offer without looking closely at all aspects of a business. Though it's harder with these little mom and pop places—or just mom in this case. Corporations' required information gives you a place to start. Never the whole story, or the whole truth, but a start. But these little places and all their privacy . . ." His mouth twisted as if with something sour.

"Uh-huh," I said with false sympathy. "Private companies, private property."

He came as close to saying, "Bah," as I could imagine him getting. "Nothing's really private. Some measures just make it harder and longer and more costly to find out what I need."

"You know that Wendy's uncle left her the ranch?"

"Not directly, he didn't." He said it casually, not showing off. "Left it and the rest of his estate—which wasn't much—to her and her siblings. Thought that would be my way in—they're businessmen. I could deal with the Barlow brothers."

His inference being that Wendy was emotional and unreasonable and female in not wanting to sell to him. While he was supremely rational and businesslike and male in relentlessly chasing the acquisition of the place where his daughter turned a corner in her life.

Was he so out of touch with himself, his reactions, his emotions that he didn't recognize why he wanted Elk Rock Ranch?

. . . Maybe.

Did that make him potentially irrational, even dangerous?

. . . Maybe.

The door to Keefe's cabin opened.

SAM MCCRACKEN CAME out of Keefe's cabin with a file box.

"You're letting him take things?" Randall demanded of Wendy.

"Saves me throwing it out."

"It belongs to the ranch. If there *is* a treasure—"

She cursed, but he'd already turned away, heading toward the cabin.

"Dad," Robin called.

He stopped halfway, staring at Sam.

At the same time Serena stood. "Sam. Please. Just leave it."

He didn't, but he altered his path toward her.

Diana and I walked toward the McCrackens.

". . . said to go ahead and she's the owner," he said.

"I don't care. It's—" She broke off, seeing us approach.

This didn't feel like a time for subtle.

"Did Keefe tell you your trip into a specific area of the ranch wasn't going to happen?" I asked Sam, deliberately poking.

"What? No. Of course it was going to happen. We were mapping it out the last time I was here. That's why I need this. We were closer than ever to the treasure."

Serena emitted a sound. "We don't need treasure. We—"

"It's not need. It's the chase. It's figuring it out when many others tried and failed."

"Devoting all your time and attention to beating strangers at treasure-hunting. But, Sam, you already won. *We* won. We have the kids and the time to spend with them we always wanted in a place we're coming to love. We *have* the treasure."

She didn't have him. Not in the kind of turnaround on a dime she might want. But I hoped she saw that she had a crack. A definitive fissure in his obsession.

Did it come too late for Keefer Dobey?

Sam McCracken wouldn't be the first driven by an obsession to do something terrible, only to have that act return their senses. Too late.

"Please," Serena said. "Please leave me to talk to my husband."

To see if she could persuade him here and now to leave the box, the treasure hunt behind.

Diana and I started toward the tack room door.

I turned back just before I would have been out of earshot.

"Sam, did you and Keefe have champagne at his cabin?"

He frowned. Then it lifted. "Once. Middle of February. I brought some after Ivy first found the secondary source referring to that interview of the posse member. Keefe liked it. I said I'd bring more when he got the DNA results. And I'd bring a case if we ever found the treasure."

WE STOPPED IN an open space, not too close to anyone else.

I was aware of Diana beside me. Of Randall Kenyon, now over by his daughter against the fence, while keeping an eye on Sam. Of the McCrackens talking in low voices, while Sam kept an eye on Keefe's cabin.

Brenda was nowhere in sight. Wendy continued her sorting, clearing the front saddle rack. Back and forth, back and forth.

I scuffed at the dirt under my foot.

I was thinking about grasshoppers. How they could be under the ground, giving no indication anything was there, but when the timing was right, they rise. Outbreak, infestation, hordes, plague.

I was thinking of Mrs. P and her stance that I needed to understand the history—including how Pony Express routes set the pattern for the railroads, which set the pattern for railroad robberies during the outlaws' heyday. To know what came before to understand what was now.

I thought of the video of Keefe sitting in the woods—no, not of him. Of what he saw. Because we were seeing the scene through his eyes in a way. He wasn't perfectly still—maybe that would have been more suspicious to the wildlife around him. But his movements were slow and infrequent. They almost seemed to keep time with the movement of the tree branches.

I thought about Robin, her leg, her life broken, spoiled and bratty and devastated and lonely, staring up to tree tops meeting overhead with the blue sky beyond. And how Keefer Dobey's stillness and quiet, along with Suzie Q's comforting presence could lure someone like her out of her hiding place.

I thought about people whose endings aren't truly known—Pearl Virtanen, Etta Place or whatever her real name was, along with Sundance and Butch. Also Jacques La Ramée. Or Laura Bullion, who disappeared for years, then showed up, claiming to be a widow of a World War I soldier.

People who were lost. People who were found . . .

People who didn't want to be found . . .

People others didn't want found . . .

But where did that get me?

The DNA test results cued up to reveal the past.

Someone who didn't want DNA to find Keefe as the descendant of Oscar and Pearl?

Was the treasure truly worth that much?

Or was the finding of it, more than the financial gain, what mattered?

I thought about Brenda saying *sweeping out* and that sticking in my head, which led to realizing Randall hid the fake note.

There was something else . . . Something Mrs. P said.

Not about Esther Ramalarga or Pearl Virtanen.

Something tickling at the back of my brain. Something I was missing.

And I could swear, somehow, I could hear my own voice saying . . .

But that was to Robin. While what Mrs. P said—

Oh.

I had it.

And it shifted everything.

But was I making too much of it?

Making too much of something Mrs. P said?

No way.

Mrs. P said it and she meant it. And that meant . . . I'd been looking at this all wrong. We all had.

CHAPTER FORTY-THREE

THE FIRST RACK visible in the tack room held only one saddle. Wendy disappeared for a second, then brought another to the rack and rested it there. Considering its stirrup hung by a ribbon of leather, I guessed she was gathering the saddles that needed fixing.

"Wendy, we need to talk."

"I'm busy." She didn't stop her methodical movements, back and forth, back and forth. A third saddle. A fourth.

"It was the DNA test, wasn't it, Wendy?" I kept my voice calm and reasonable, careful not to lead with an accusation. "Keefe was getting the test results back and you couldn't have that. Did you intercept results once already? But how many times could that work? How many sets could you destroy?"

Wendy went for another saddle—and reappeared immediately with a shotgun pointed at us. It must have been behind the door.

I heard Diana's quick intake of breath beside me.

I'd rushed it. Too far, too fast.

She'd been close to the edge, pushed there by her own knowledge and Randall's fake note.

"Get your hands out of your pockets," Wendy ordered.

I'd unlocked my phone, but didn't persist.

She gestured for us to back up slightly. Afraid we'd rush her? Or not wanting blood and . . . *evidence* . . . all over herself?

The Kenyons and McCrackens were silent behind us. They had to know the shotgun could reach them, too. Though she couldn't get everybody before somebody could rush her.

Small comfort with Diana and me in the front row.

"Should have used this on him instead of that peashooter. But even Brenda would have woken up. She's always trying to make out *I'm* the deaf one, but she's worse."

I thought I heard footsteps. Right or wrong, the best thing I could do now was stall.

"Did you see the DNA results?"

"The DNA results, the DNA results. I am so tired of hearing about those damned things. If the results were just about those stupid outlaws he was always going on about, everything would have been fine," she snapped. "My uncle said—but I thought maybe he was wrong or Ulla lied to him. But those results said it was true. Showed him right there with the other Barlows."

"You destroyed the first set of results. Like you burned your uncle's will. Did he leave the ranch to all three of you or just you and Keefe?"

She blinked at that, but didn't say anything.

"What the hell are you doing, Wendy?" Brenda demanded from my right.

"Get back in the barn," Wendy ordered.

Brenda kept coming.

"Go call the sheriff," I shouted at her.

She didn't stop and she didn't pull out a phone.

"I'll shoot you, Brenda."

Wendy swung the gun in that direction.

We couldn't possibly reach cover before she could swing it back. But Diana and I must have had the same idea for taking advantage of the distraction, because each of us had a hand in a pocket, hitting buttons on our unseen phones.

"Yeah?" Brenda mocked. "You could've done that anytime these past decades. What's it going to get you? What's any of this going to get you? Somebody'll get away. And that'll be the end."

"It's my ranch. I can—"

"You can't. It's the end."

The gun wobbled in Wendy's hold. I didn't consider that much of an improvement.

Brenda said, "Drop it."

Wendy didn't.

She gave a strangled shout and ran to one of the ranch trucks.

Before getting in, she turned back to us and swung the shotgun around like a kid with a hose, as if to hold us all at bay. None had gotten any closer.

In fact, Diana and I moved of one accord toward the tack room doors. Randall tugged Robin to behind him. Sam, Serena, and Brenda stood rooted where they were.

The truck rumbled to life and headed out.

"Shouldn't we—?" Sam started.

"Go after her? No," I said. "Call the sheriff's department? Yes."

Diana held up her phone, indicating she was fulfilling that duty.

I went to Brenda. "Are you okay?"

"Why shouldn't I be?"

"You said the sheriff's department got it wrong for arresting Wendy for killing Keefe, but I'm afraid—"

"They did. Not wrong that she *could* kill him or *did* kill him, but that she did it over some supposed romance they had."

"You . . . you thought she could have killed him? You thought that all along?"

"Sure."

The truck rattled over the bridge, then slowed.

It was too far away to see if Wendy Barlow turned back to look at the ranch she loved enough to kill for.

The truck lurched forward under a heavy foot on the accelerator.

CHAPTER FORTY-FOUR

"I DON'T DISBELIEVE it," Diana said. "After all, I saw it. I just don't understand why. And I'd really like to, considering the woman held a shotgun on us."

Our debrief with Mike and Jennifer had to wait until Shelton was done with us.

No big surprise he let Diana go first.

No big surprise, either, that Tom showed up at the sheriff's department, making sure I was okay and following me home to make sure all over again, before kissing me thoroughly, saying we'd talk about this more, then going home to his daughter.

I didn't mind the showing up and the kissing, accepted the going home to his daughter as part of the package of our relationship, but the future talking wasn't my favorite.

"What started it," I said, "was remembering Mrs. P's apostrophes. And that reminded me of talking to Robin Kenyon about them."

"Well, that explains everything," Diana said.

We couldn't get all of us together until after Mike's last broadcast. He'd traded his on-air wardrobe for a t-shirt and probably jeans. The rest of us were in t-shirts, too. I was in bed after a long shower, with Shadow and Suzie Q on nearby beds.

It was a remote pajama party.

"It does explain everything," I agreed. "Instead of saying Ulla's and Chester's, Mrs. P said Ulla and Chester's. *He was Ulla and Chester's much-loved boy.*"

None of the others jumped up and shouted *Eureka!*

I wrote it out on a piece of paper, then held it up so all could see.

Another couple of non-*Eureka!* beats, then Jennifer said, "Oh. . . . Oh."

"You've got it Jennifer?" Diana asked.

"It's that rule Mrs. P talked about. I don't remember what she called it, but I thought of it as fighting over custody or joint custody—that's not what it was called, but my friend's parents were getting divorced and she had to talk to a judge about stuff like that, so that's what I connected it to."

"Makes sense. Now, can you explain it to these other two, who must have been sleeping when Mrs. P taught them that lesson."

"When each person gets his or her own apostrophe, it's like individual custody, but—"

"Mrs. P didn't talk about custody," Mike objected. "Take it out of custody."

"Fine," Jennifer said with irritation nibbling the edges of her voice. "Say you're talking about . . . about a new van for the station. If you say Diana's and Elizabeth's, then they each get one. But if you say Diana and Elizabeth's, then it's joint and they're sharing one."

"Heaven forbid sharing a news ride with Elizabeth," Diana muttered. "Everything would be over by the time we got to the assignments."

"But that wasn't about vans or custody—" Mike broke off with a whistle.

He'd gotten it. So had Diana.

Having caught up after her timeout for a crack about having to share a ride with me, she said, "*He was Ulla and Chester's much-loved boy,* meant the two of them. Together. When you explained it to Robin, you were saying Wendy and Brenda were *not* a couple, but Mrs. P was saying Ulla and Chester *were*. But—"

"Don't rush it. So, the apostrophes got me thinking of them as couple. A unit. Joint." I nodded acknowledgment to Jennifer. "And that got me thinking maybe they really *had* been a couple. I did wonder if I should give it any credence."

"Not because Mrs. P isn't an entirely reliable source, but whether she said what I thought she said—"

"With Mrs. P's enunciation, you heard it, all right."

"That was the conclusion I came to. In fairness," I said meekly, "I did immediately dismiss the possibility that Mrs. P hadn't meant the grammatical distinction."

"Oh, yeah, she meant it. She wouldn't have gotten her apostrophes wrong. Not ever," Jennifer said.

"So I started thinking what if they had been a couple. And I remembered Ulla had worked for the Barlows before he brought her and Keefe to work and live at the ranch, which started me thinking about the *hijinks* he might have committed that led to his break from the family. Getting the help pregnant might have been one thing to the Barlows, but wanting a role in the child's life?"

"But he didn't marry her, acknowledge Keefe," Jennifer protested.

"No, he didn't. Maybe he couldn't make that big of a leap from the Barlows. Who knows—maybe Ulla didn't want marriage. Maybe she wanted to protect him from any possibility of Barlow interference. Anyway, wondering if Keefe could have been Chester's son put a whole new light on the DNA results."

"You think that's why he took the test? He suspected?"

"We can't know for sure, but I'd guess no. I'd guess he truly took the test hoping to find he was descended from Oscar and Pearl. But the results would have shown that he had relatives and that almost certainly would have led to connecting the dots to his parentage. If Keefe didn't have the knowledge to do that, Robin Kenyon did."

"But Chester didn't leave him anything in his will." Jennifer was not liking how Keefe was treated.

"Officially, he didn't leave anybody anything. Wendy talked like Chester left the ranch to her, but that wasn't ever true. James Longbaugh said everything went to Chester's closest relatives—*known* relatives—which included Wendy, but also her brothers. They, basically, gave her the ranch. Continuing the previous generations' washing of hands when it came to anything Chester related."

"So, if Keefer Dobey proved by DNA that he was Chester's son he could have claimed a share of the ranch," Mike declared.

I raised my shoulders. "*Maybe's* the best we can do. For sure, he'd have to establish paternity first. And the fact that the estate was distributed decades ago . . . It would go through the courts and that makes it hard to predict."

"But Wendy could have thought it meant that," Mike said.

"Oh, yes. She could have. Especially because I've got to wonder if she didn't orchestrate the way inheriting the ranch went."

I reminded them of what Brenda said about when Chester died.

"A fire in July," Mike mused.

"Intriguing, isn't it?" I asked.

Jennifer sat up. "You think there *was* a will?"

"I don't suppose we'll ever know for sure unless Wendy Barlow decides to tell and why would she? It would just make her guilty of more. It might have been a risk—what if her brothers didn't turn the ranch over to her? Although the Barlow attitude made that a good gamble. But if there was a will that didn't leave her the ranch or divided it among her, Keefer, and Brenda, then what did she have to lose?

"Plus, if she didn't know or suspect Keefe was Chester's son, why would she care if he had a DNA test? She *had* to know. Otherwise the DNA test would have represented only Keefe's fantasy of being descended from Oscar and Pearl, as it did to everyone else As for a will, it didn't absolutely have to exist. Chester might have told her Keefe was his son—"

"He might have told her, true, but burning a will explains a fire in July," Mike said, "Also why she kept the other two—Keefe and Brenda—away from him at the end, according to Brenda."

"Chester telling her then that Keefe was his son also explains why she suddenly stopped being sweet on him, as Brenda said," Diana said. "He was her cousin, as well as her rival for the ranch."

"I can guess which bothered her more." Jennifer's insight to the woman was impressive, especially since she'd never met Wendy in person. "Oh. What if Chester left *everything* to Keefe? That whole give-it-all-to-the-guy nonsense. That would explain everything she did, too. Even her being kind of bitter. Can't really blame her, either."

"Except for the part where she shot Keefe three times."

EPILOGUE

BEFORE SHELTON COULD make the arrest, Wendy Barlow was gone.

It was not a happy time at the Cottonwood County Sheriff's Department.

Think the deepest, darkest cloud blotting out the spring sun. In the case of Shelton, whose cloud was deeper and darker than all the rest, a cloud quite close to the ground, too.

Think multiple bears, each with a huge thorn in its paw, taking it out on humanity. Especially the portion of humanity known as the local media. Despite several representatives of said media being the reason the sheriff's department even knew there was an arrest they wanted to make.

I wondered how Diana was faring with Russ. When I raised one eyebrow in a sympathetic *How's it going?* query, she shook her head in a clear, *Don't ask.*

The Cottonwood County Sheriff's Department received the official report from the HelixKin test.

It was nice to have the official confirmation.

Keefe was Wendy's uncle's son.

More than official confirmation, though, it was about gloating that we'd gotten there before them and without needing no stinkin' confirmation from no stinkin' corporation.

But gloating very, very subtly.

One of the best things about dealing with Sergeant Wayne Shelton was he picked up on the subtleties.

Then word came that Wendy Barlow, a member of the wealthy

Barlow family of Connecticut, had been reported dead outside Jackson.

"When they bother to say somebody's wealthy around there, you know they're loaded," muttered Leona.

The local Jackson media said she'd been visiting her oldest brother, who owned a "cabin" there—those Jackson-area cabins are equivalent to the Newport, Rhode Island, "cottages" of the Gilded Age.

Interesting that after the things Wendy said about her brothers, she ran to one of them.

Maybe she had nowhere else to go. Maybe she didn't know what she intended to do, she just ran. But I also remembered her reaction after being questioned at the sheriff's department and her vehemence that she would never be in a situation like that again.

So maybe she did know what she intended to do, but didn't want to do it at Elk Rock Ranch.

The account that came to us was she went for a hike and when she didn't return at the expected time, the family and staff mounted a search. The next day, her body was found off the trail, as if she might have fallen.

Only then did they call authorities.

The Shelton cloud turned into a volcanic eruption.

I happened to meander over to the sheriff's department after that report came in—covering the distance from KWMT at Diana-like speeds.

So I was there to hear eruptions of steaming lava from behind closed doors that barely tamped the volume.

In this mode, Shelton was not above questioning the ethics and intelligence of his fellow law enforcement professionals.

That's how I learned Wendy had a bullet hole in the head. A contact wound. But law enforcement for that small, billionaire-dense enclave was not pursuing an investigation. They were satisfied with the fell-while-hiking explanation, which let the family avoid the pesky matter of her being accused of murder in Cottonwood County.

Russ Conrad, as sheriff, and Jarvis Abbott, as county attorney, took it up with their counterparts. No one expected any change in the case's status.

It wasn't justice. The perpetrator deciding on her punishment is not justice.

It *was* an ending.

But not one we liked for a special on the investigation.

WE WERE STILL discussing special or no special when I took another trip to the McCrackens'.

He had been riding with his kids and wife. They were all smiling. The kids volunteered to take care of his horse, so he could talk to me. They were in the stage of horse fandom where even cleaning out stalls seemed exotic, much less unsaddling and rubbing down their mounts.

"Was Keefe descended from the Virtanens?" he asked first.

I considered it a good sign that he didn't ask about the treasure first.

I explained that unless someone did or paid for a whole lot of family tree research, that would remain unknown, but that it didn't seem any more likely that Keefe was than he was.

The few things Ulla said that Keefe had interpreted as possibly connecting him to the Virtanens had been about Chester and the Barlows.

I shared the material from the dissertation saying no one knew Pearl's whereabouts—without any of my speculation about its author's origins. That left for last the news about the original newspaper interview with the Oscar Virtanen posse member and what it said.

I left Sam to voice the conclusions.

"If Oscar and Pearl had a prearranged drop spot, she got the money and left with their baby. I'd thought Elk Rock Ranch made sense as a burial site because it was their land, but that also makes it more likely she knew where he'd put it. If they didn't have a prearranged drop spot, it's back to being anywhere between where the robbery took place and where they captured him."

"Unless someone found it in the past century."

He winced, but I thought that was from habit. "Guess I'll have to wait until the museum lets people look at the original article."

"It could be a while."

He looked toward his office, jam-packed with all that treasure research, all those clues, then over toward the barn, where the voices of his family could be heard as they tended to the horses.

"That's okay."

WE HAD ALL that material on Pearl and Oscar, on Butch Cassidy and friends.

In coverage of Keefer Dobey's murder, we ended up mentioning it only in connection with what sparked the gift of a DNA test.

Much of the rest would never make it on-air. The vast majority of our listeners already knew a lot of it—it was news to me, not them.

But Nala and I did put together an in-house piece on the history of Wild West outlaws as it connected to Cottonwood County, which really narrowed the scope. It was for the newcomers who'd be coming to KWMT-TV from all over, starting with Octavia Zabel of Pittsburgh.

Hard to tell who was more excited about that impending arrival— Mike or Leona.

Nala was also doing a three-part piece for on-air about Oscar and Pearl Virtanen to run on the anniversaries of their major robberies, with their connections to this area highlighted in between.

As for Keefe's murder, we did not do a special on the investigation. Instead, we went back to our purported project and ran a shorter piece on Keefer Dobey, a character formed by and representative of Cottonwood County.

Nala got some great memories of him from former seasonal workers and long-time dude ranch guests. Longer versions aired on the station's website.

Robin taped one of those and held off her tears until the very end, which made it even stronger.

CLARA FOUND THE original of the article from Keefe's nutmeg tin in one of the boxes still at Teague's property. A box not yet scheduled to be assessed by her or Mrs. Parens.

Clearly, Keefe had searched well beyond the boxes he moved.

I told her to give Shelton a copy, as an "i" for him to dot. Better it came from her than me or my cohorts. More eruptions couldn't be good for him.

I also took another run at Mrs. Parens.

With the two of us in Clara's museum office before they had a work session, I asked bluntly, "Do you think Esther Ramalarga was Etta Place—"

Her lips parted and I quickly amended my question.

"Do you think she was the woman the Pinkerton wanted posters called Etta Place?"

She paused. Long enough for me to accept she wasn't going to answer and consider what to ask next.

"I do not know."

My surprise must have shown, because she said more strongly, "I do not know," though my surprise was for her answering at all.

"Even had I asked her, how could I or anyone know for a certainty the full truth? As it was, I did not ask her. I knew her as an excellent teacher who was wise and kind to me at the time I most needed wisdom and kindness. When she died, a letter instructed me and her legal representative—"

"One of the Longbaughs?"

She declined her head in a slow nod. "—to send her remains to a family in Pennsylvania. She wrote that they knew her wishes."

We looked at each other a long moment before I said, slowly, "The Sundance Kid's family—Harry Longabaugh's family—came from Pennsylvania."

Another slow nod.

"But I suppose a lot of people did." Including James Longbaugh's ancestors.

"Indeed."

✧ ✧ ✧ ✧

"**. . . SO MRS.** P doesn't know," I told Tom that evening. "Not if Etta Place survived, not if her friend and mentor was really Etta Place. How's that for a twist? There's something Mrs. P doesn't know."

"But you think she did survive, even if she didn't end up in Cottonwood County."

He took my silence as an answer. Smart man.

"Any evidence?" he asked.

"Great. Mr. Believe-in-Everybody wants evidence? For starters, there's no confirmation they're buried in Bolivia. Friends and family of Butch said he visited in the 1920s or 30s. And I find it interesting that Etta disappeared from the record."

"Could've died."

"Or not," I shot back. "There's also the fact that Esther Ramalarga wrote her dissertation on Oscar and Pearl Virtanen, with information and detail that can't be confirmed by records still in existence now."

"Things do get lost over time."

"And that she said so clearly that there was no evidence of what happened to Pearl. Along with no mention of a baby. Feels like complete misdirection."

"You do know, even if you're right about Etta living out her days in Cottonwood County, even if Pearl and her baby rode off into the sunset, even if those friends and family were right about Butch visiting them back then or Sundance became a rancher, they all were long dead before we were born."

"That's not the point. They would have had long, full lives—that's the point. You know how you feel when you walk through an old cemetery, see the stone for someone who died in their seventies or eighties compared to how you feel if you see one for a child?"

"Can't remember last time I walked through a cemetery, old or otherwise. But I'm looking forward to you walking down the aisle to me."

I grimaced at him.

He kissed me.

Unexpectedly, he said, "I know you're not enthusiastic about the wedding. You going along has me looking forward even more to marrying you, Elizabeth Margaret Danniher."

"Considering your first wife was ready to have you convicted of murder, that's not a high bar for me."

He chuckled. "Beyond that . . ." His eyes went a bit unfocused a moment, then he came back to me. "First time I'm marrying for love."

This time, I kissed him.

"When's dinner?" Tamantha called from her room.

WITH TOM'S ARM around me, I leaned into him as we sat on the sofa, watching the dogs sleeping side by side in front of the fireplace again, even though there was no fire in it this time.

It was cold enough.

There just hadn't been time with getting dinner, listening to Tamantha's rehearsal for the talk she was giving in class the next day, then getting her to bed.

We'd be following before long, but this was a nice breather.

Except it recalled an unresolved situation.

"Maybe she could adjust." I used the pronoun to not disturb the canine sleepers, certain Tom's thoughts were on the same track.

It only worked halfway. Shadow's ears twitched around to us.

Tom said, "She's a ranch dog—a dude ranch dog, granted, but she wouldn't be happy in town."

"You have a ranch."

Yeah, we'd agreed it wouldn't work, but with the dogs lying together by the hearth . . .

I felt Tom's grin, then sat up to see it. "*We* have a ranch. But I spend more time in town than would work for her. Wouldn't feel right leaving her on her own at the ranch when I'm here."

I dropped my head on his shoulder, acknowledging the validity of his position.

Then I popped back up.

"What?" he asked.

"I just remembered something Penny said."

"Penny at the supermarket?"

"Is there any other?"

He appeared struck by the point. "Can't think of one. Certainly not one comparable. What did she say?"

"Something about people I talked to when Deputy Redus went missing."

I PULLED INTO the open area of the Johnsons' property—called a ranchette around here because the modest acreage was less than the size of a county back east.

I'd opted not to let Tom or any of the other volunteers come with me, to avoid putting undo pressure on the Johnsons.

I had not, however, come alone.

After following the protocol of beeping my horn to let humans and animals know of an arrival, I got out. No animal greeted me, but I was aware of movement inside the small, tidy house.

Suzie Q gave me a miffed look when I hooked the leash on her, but I ignored that. No way was I risking her running off and ruining this meeting.

"E.M. Danniher," Roger Johnson Senior greeted me—far more friendly than the first time I'd come here. This time the bib overalls on his portly frame were topped with a jacket. It was, after all, spring in Wyoming.

"Please, call me Elizabeth."

"Elizabeth," he conceded with a slight smile. The smile was mostly for Suzie Q at my side. "What can we do for you?"

His wife, Myrna, appeared at the door behind him. "We can start by inviting her in, Roger."

That was a decided turnaround from my first visit, too, when she'd run me off. Politely, but unmistakably.

"Thank you. And is it okay for Suzie Q—?"

"Of course," she said warmly, though I caught the sheen of unshed tears in her eyes as they led me to a comfortable room at the back.

They gestured me to a loveseat, while they each occupied one of the chairs paired in front of the fireplace and with the best view of the TV.

I didn't beat around the bush. "I know you lost your family dog recently. I'm very sorry to hear that." A memory of that black and beige dog waiting for the son who never returned lumped my throat.

It might have shown. Myrna muttered a thanks. Roger Senior cleared his throat—not in preparation to speak.

"This is Suzie Q," I said.

She lifted her head at her name and looked from me to each of them.

"I thought your dog was named Shadow," Myrna said.

It still surprised me what people around here knew about me—and everyone else. I suppose knowing my dog's name, though, wasn't unexpected. Especially not since he'd appeared in a couple of the specials we'd done for KWMT-TV.

"He is. Suzie Q belonged to Keefer Dobey. She's been left alone in the world. She could maybe stay at the dude ranch, if the new owner agreed." I made that sound doubtful. "But even if she did, she wouldn't have anyone to look after her."

Or for her to look after.

I saw they understood that part, too, when they exchanged a look.

And she'd keep looking for someone who never came.

I didn't intend to bring that parallel to their attention.

"I hoped you might find it in your hearts to open your home to her."

I let her leash drop.

With exquisite timing, Suzie Q walked across the space to the spot where the front corners of their two chairs nearly met. She looked at each of them.

Myrna's hand trembled as she reached out to pet Suzie Q's head.

The dog licked her hand, turned partly around, sat on Myrna's feet, then rested her head on Roger Senior's knee.

Deal sealed.

WENDY HAD GONE to one of her brothers, but the ranch didn't.

She had a will from several years ago, which left equal shares of the ranch to Brenda Mankin and Keefer Dobey. Since he predeceased Wendy, everything went to Brenda.

Considering the financial issues Wendy had faced, what with needing to sell her second place in Arizona and otherwise tightening her belt—by Barlow standards—that might not sound like the best deal for Brenda.

Speculation rose quickly that she would sell to Randall Kenyon.

Consternation rose even faster.

The tenor of the mildest comments was it was nice he wanted this for his daughter and maybe she really liked it here in Cottonwood County but, surely, he'd be a better fit in Jackson. The more astringent comments . . . Well, I hoped those didn't reach Randall.

Not out of concern for his tender feelings, but because he seemed the type to stick it out whether he wanted to or not, whether Robin wanted him to or not, just because he'd faced opposition.

But then Penny told me something surprising—okay, told might be misleading. She didn't come right out and say it, and her references to *her* and *she* could have connected as readily to the Queen of Sheba as to Brenda. But I'm pretty sure she meant Brenda Mankin.

Driving toward the ranch to check that out, I had a call from Scott Hoole in Cooke City.

He wanted to know more about how and why his friend died.

At the end, he sighed deeply.

"If Wendy had been better at reading people, she wouldn't have killed him, because she would have recognized Keefe never would have done anything to change Elk Rock Ranch. He could have inherited the entire thing and he would have left her not only in charge, but as owner."

"I've heard a rumor that the changes at Elk Rock might not be as extreme as some worried. I'm headed that way now."

He chuckled. "Don't let me hold you up."

✧ ✧ ✧ ✧

"IT'S ALL MINE," was how Brenda greeted me, her grin even bigger than the wrinkles.

Randall and Robin stood nearby. Her words to me had interrupted something he was saying, fast and vehement.

I nodded to them, smiled back at her. "I heard the will left it to you, but will her family—?"

"Got in touch with that brother of hers who's running Wendy's estate and doesn't sound like there'll be any problems over the ranch." Her grin turned sly. "Don't know if he just wants to be rid of it, if he can't believe land outside of Jackson's worth anything, or if he's afraid I'll go after more of Wendy's estate, but he's not disputin' a thing. It's all mine."

"It's expensive to run a ranch," Randall said, "especially a dude ranch, and to upgrade—"

She blew out her lips at the idea of upgrading.

It didn't stop him. "You have no idea—"

"Only lived here most of my life."

"Wendy handled the finances," he shot back.

"There *are* a lot of expenses," I said to Brenda. "Have you talked to other ranchers? Maybe Tom—"

"Finally, someone talking sense," Randall butted in. "I'll get this place for you yet, Robin, it's—"

"You won't," Brenda stuck in.

But Randall's attention was on his daughter. Well, much of it. The rest was for himself.

"—not over. I'm not done."

A gracious response might have reassured him he hadn't failed her—because that's what he was really saying.

But maybe Robin knew gracious wouldn't work. "I don't want it. Not to own. I just want to come here. I don't have to own it to come." She looked to Brenda. "Can I come sometimes?"

"Sure, if you pay your way and behave yourself, not like last time." Brenda wasn't done. "And you need lessons on a couple horses in the corral before you're allowed to take any on the trail. First time you break the rules, you're out of the saddle. Can't risk any of the horses getting a neck broke because of you."

"That . . . That . . ." Randall sputtered.

Robin meekly said, "Okay." Leaving her father off-balance as she turned to him. "See, Dad. We can enjoy things without buying them. Without *owning* them."

Her father's reaction split down the middle between stunned pleasure that she'd called him Dad and stunned disbelief at her disavowing the perfection of owning.

The fact that the latter was only half of his reaction left me with a spurt of optimism that father and daughter might find each other, at least on some level.

"Last year, after I got hurt, and we were up there waiting, Keefe said we none of us owned any of this." She turned back to us. "I wouldn't go that far."

Relief that his daughter hadn't gone completely mad suffused Randall Kenyon's face.

"See, it's all working out great," Brenda said to me. She tipped her head. "Considering paying cash for supplies. Never did like how Wendy ran up debt each year."

"*Cash?*"

"I told you, Keefe knew he could come to me if he needed money."

She had told me that. I just hadn't thought she'd meant ranch-running money. More like going to McDonald's money.

"How . . .?" That much was out before considerations of privacy and nosiness reared up.

"Told you that, too. When my parents died, sold our place. There was an insurance policy, too. The Longbaughs—first his father and now James—took care of that. They put the money in a trust and had some financial people invest it. Nothing too risky. They showed me how if you let it be for long enough, it can grow and grow. Never needed any of it, with living and working here. So—" She lifted a shoulder. "—it grew and grew.

"James says he's got it set up to support me fine even if the ranch goes belly-up and I'm in one of those homes. I figure if the ranch is gone, it wouldn't matter to me where I am. Besides, that wouldn't be such a bad life. Sort of like being a guest here. Other people setting your schedule for activities and meals and such, but no worries, either."

"But with that much money, why did you stay here? Taking orders from Wendy when you could have gone anywhere?"

"She had Elk Rock Ranch. I couldn't leave here."

I'd thought at one point, that there'd been no love among the three solitary people living here year-round. But there had been.

Great loves.

Keefe's and Brenda's for the land, for the ranch. Wendy's, too. Though hers had twisted her.

"Have you to thank for one thing," Brenda said to me.

I expected it to be bringing the murderer of her friend to account.

"You talking about Scott Hoole made me give him a call. He's going to move from Cooke City to here on the ranch and get us special chefs to come. Maybe some classes with these real good cooks. That kind of thing. Plus, he's got experience hiring people, so he and James are going to find somebody to run the business side—do all that work, so I can do the fun stuff with keeping up with the animals and such."

Yeah, no work involved with that at all.

THE WEDDING PREP is almost completely cued up after Connie told Diana I didn't have a wedding dress yet.

Diana recruited Tom's sister, Jean-Marie, and Tamantha. If you think I had a choice about the shopping trip the next week, you've never met any of these females. We picked up Jean-Marie in Red Lodge, then drove on to Billings.

Jean-Marie strategized our trip, and she and Diana approached each store by dividing to conquer.

The dress was in the fourth store.

Until that point, I'd felt nearly extraneous. A mannequin to try on dress after dress.

I put that one on and we were done.

It's long-sleeved Mikado silk—the wedding's in June, but this *is* Wyoming—with a U back. One of those dresses people call deceptively simple.

I do love it.

I also loved that seeing me in it made Diana tear up, Jean-Marie grin and clasp a palm to her chest, and Tamantha's eyes widen and her mouth pop open as she said, "Wow."

I hoped the reaction would run in the family.

We'll find out in late June.

THERE'S A MEMORIAL service for Keefe planned for early June, after Elk Rock Ranch opens its season, with dedication of a bench and plaque to him on the property. It's going to be out on one of the more distant trails, where someone could sit alone and quiet, stare up to the sky and learn a few things.

The End

Author's note

Oscar and Pearl Virtanen, as well as their robberies, are entirely fictional, as is Esther Ramalarga.

When James Longbaugh entered the world of Cottonwood County as Tom's lawyer in **Sign Off**, I had no idea Longabaugh was the real last name of the Sundance Kid. When I realized the near-connection of the names while writing **Cue Up**, there was maniacal laughter and dancing around the room.

Sometimes the fictional gods give us gifts.

As for the history of Sundance, Butch Cassidy, and the better-known Wild West outlaws named in the book, it's as big a mess as Mrs. P and Elizabeth describe. Contradictions, far-flung theories, maybes stated as certainties, and a scarcity of confirmed facts abound.

The aliases alone are name spaghetti, compounded by multiple people using similar names or borrowing each other's, plus the Pinkertons and thus the newspapers of the day messing up the names. As noted, the Sundance Kid and Kid Curry (whose real name was Logan), were often identified interchangeably. That's just one example.

The Pinkertons did drop the ball on the women to a great extent. Yet they remain the most accepted source of information on all the personalities.

I've tried very hard to state as fact only what is known or generally accepted as fact, including dates and places of robberies (though who participated is often not agreed on), deaths, travel, and imprisonments. According to multiple sources citing documents, Elzy Lay was convicted of murder and was pardoned for persuading fellow prisoners to release the warden's wife and daughter. Laura Bullion's time in Memphis from 1918 to her death in the 1960s also is documented in census and other records.

I am extremely grateful to the following people for welcoming a cold caller with lots of questions about dude (or is it guest?) ranches in Wyoming:

> **—Natasha Melendez, administrative director of the Wyoming Dude Ranchers' Association**
> **—Tara Matushinec of the 7D Ranch, Cody, Wyoming**
> **—Kristin of Eatons' Ranch, Wolf, Wyoming**

They were particularly helpful with background when most people don't see the ranches—the off-season. Their love for the ranches and what they do came through so clearly. As did their generosity in answering my questions.

Happy Reading!
Patricia

Enjoy **Cue Up?** (Hope so)

Elizabeth and friends ask if you'll help spread the word about them and the Caught Dead in Wyoming series. You have the power to do that in two quick ways:

Recommend the book and the series to your friends and/or the whole wide world on social media. Shouting from rooftops is particularly appreciated.

Review the book. Take a few minutes to write an honest review and it can make a huge difference. As you likely know, it's the single best way for your fellow readers to find books they'll enjoy, too.

To me—as an author and a reader—the goal is always to find a good author-reader match. By sharing your reading experience through recommendations and reviews, you become a vital matchmaker. ☺

The Caught Dead in Wyoming series

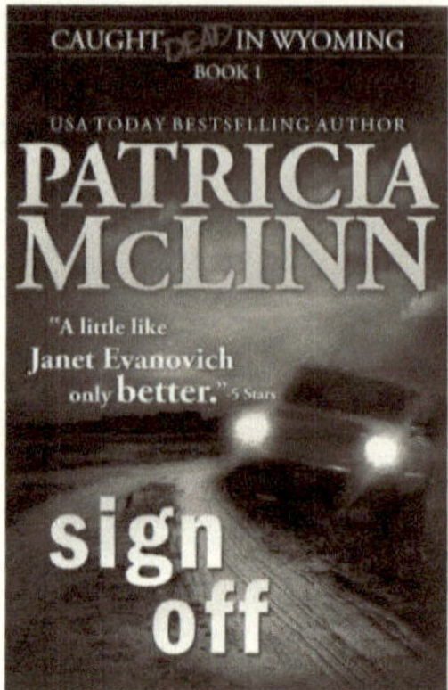

SIGN OFF

Divorce a husband, disrupt a career … grapple with a murder.

LEFT HANGING

Trampled by bulls — an accident? Elizabeth, Mike and friends dig into
the world of rodeo.

SHOOT FIRST

Elizabeth and friends delve into old Wyoming treasures and secrets to save lives.

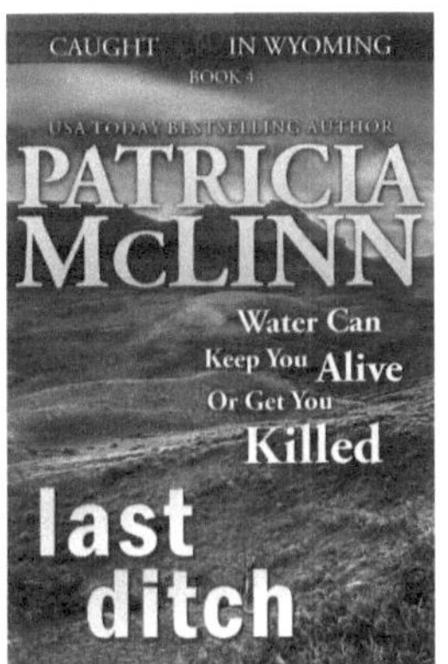

LAST DITCH

Elizabeth and Mike search after a man in a wheelchair goes missing in dangerous, desolate country.

LOOK LIVE

Elizabeth and friends take on a misleading murder with help — and
hindrance — from intriguing out-of-towners.

BACK STORY

Murder never dies, but comes back to threaten Elizabeth and her team
of investigators.

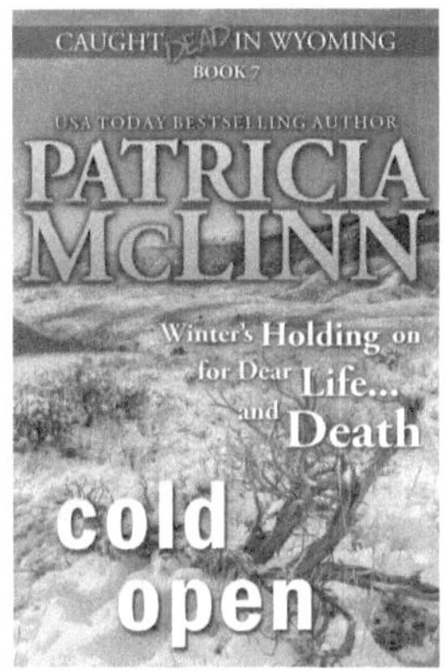

COLD OPEN

Elizabeth's search for a place of her own becomes an open house for murder.

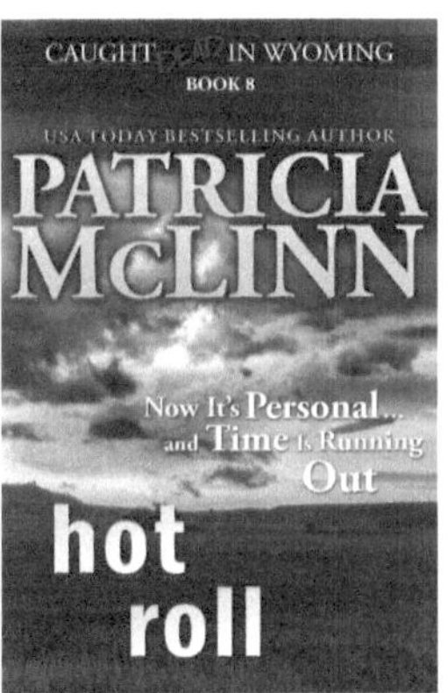

HOT ROLL

One of their own becomes a target — and time is running out.

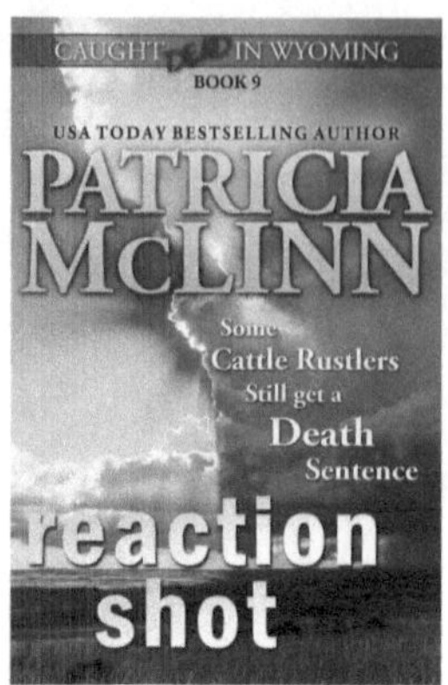

REACTION SHOT

Sometimes cattle rustlers still get a death sentence.

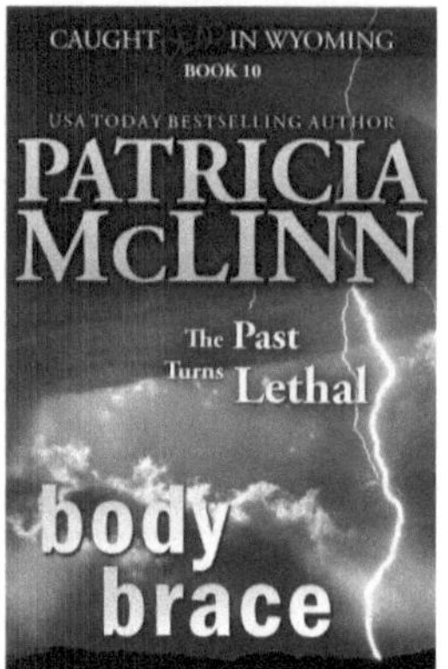

BODY BRACE

Everything can change, but murder still comes calling.

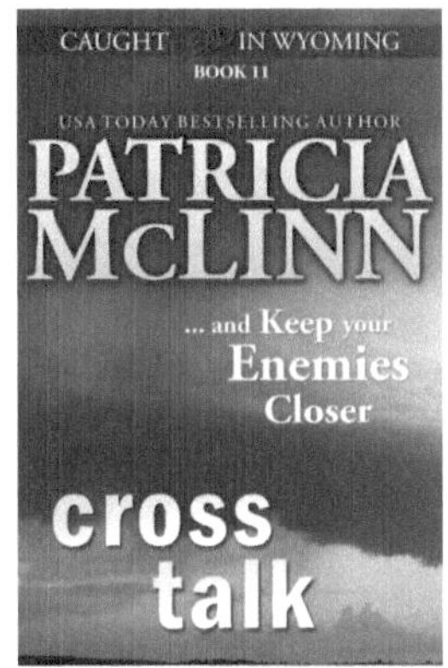

CROSS TALK

Prime suspect: The most annoying man in Sherman.

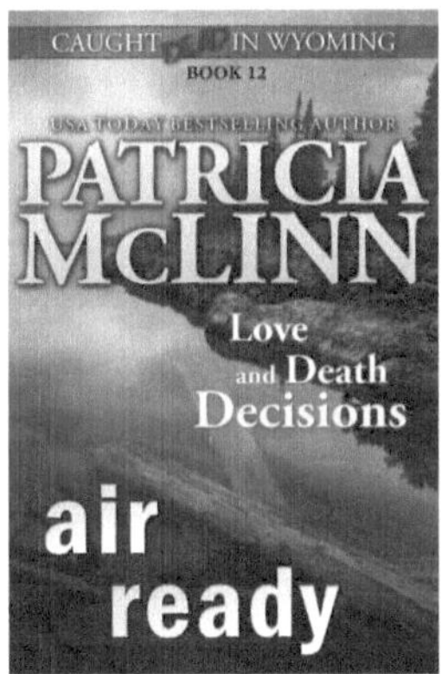

AIR READY

Love and death decisions.

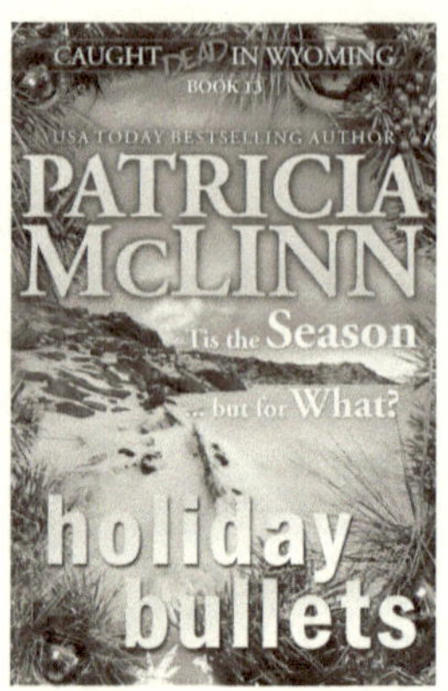

HOLIDAY BULLETS

A mystery with Elizabeth's name on it.

CUE UP

On the trail of murder.

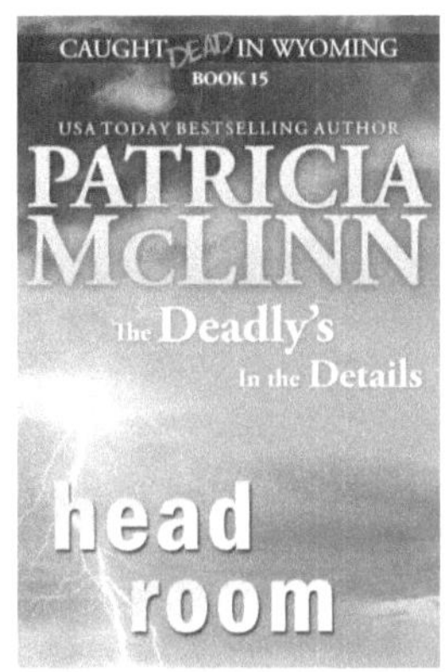

HEAD ROOM

The deadly's in the details.

More mystery by Patricia McLinn

Secret Sleuth series

DEATH ON THE DIVERSION

Final resting place? Deck chair.

DEATH ON TORRID AVENUE

A new love (canine), an ex-cop and a dog park discovery.

DEATH ON BEGUILING WAY

No zen in sight as Sheila untangles a yoga instructor's murder.

DEATH ON COVERT CIRCLE

A supermarket CEO meets his expiration date.

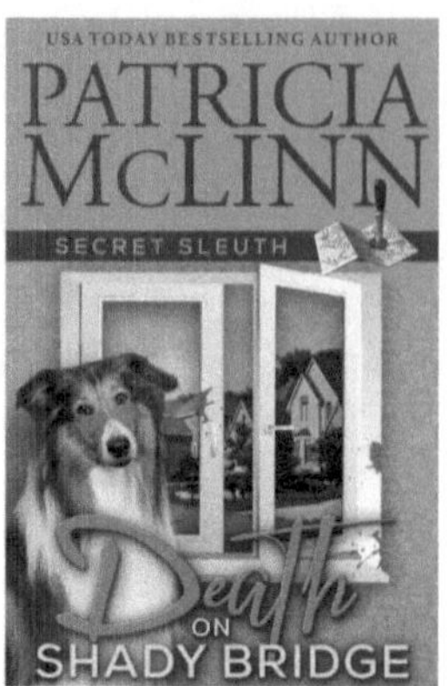

DEATH ON SHADY BRIDGE

A homicide cold case heats up.

DEATH ON CARRION LANE

More murder is brewing in Haines Tavern.

DEATH ON ZIGZAG TRAIL

A spooky legend twists grave matters.

DEATH ON PUZZLE PLACE

Season's greetings: Whodunit?

DEATH ON RIDDLE ROAD

The Innocence Trilogy

PROOF OF INNOCENCE

She's a prosecutor chasing demons. He's wrestling them.
Will they find proof of innocence?

PRICE OF INNOCENCE

To solve this murder Detective Belichek will risk everything — his
friendships, his reputation, his career, his heart … and his life.

PREMISE OF INNOCENCE

The last woman Detective Landis is prepared to see is the one he must
save.

Explore a complete list of all Patricia's books

www.patriciamclinn.com/patricias-books

Or get a printable booklist

www.patriciamclinn.com/patricias-books/printable-booklist

Patricia's Bookstore (buy online directly from Patricia)

shop.patriciamclinn.com

About the Author

Patricia McLinn is the USA Today bestselling author of more than 60 published novels cited by readers and reviewers for their wit and vivid characterization. Her books include mysteries, romantic suspense, contemporary romance, historical romance, and women's fiction. They have topped bestseller lists and won numerous awards.

She has spoken about writing from London to Melbourne, Australia, to Washington, D.C., including being a guest speaker at the Smithsonian Institution.

McLinn spent more than 20 years as an editor at The Washington Post after stints as a sports writer (Rockford, Ill.) and assistant sports editor (Charlotte, N.C.). She received BA and MSJ degrees from Northwestern University.

Now living in northern Kentucky, McLinn loves to hear from readers through her website and social media.

Website: patriciamclinn.com

Facebook: facebook.com/PatriciaMcLinn

Pinterest: pinterest.com/patriciamclinn

Instagram: instagram.com/patriciamclinnauthor

9 781954 478978